Peter Sheridan was introduced to the world of theatre by
his father when he was sixteen years old. So began a life of
acting, writing and directing. His first book, *44: A Dublin
Memoir*, recounts the story of his baptism into drama. It
was published to great acclaim in 1999 and was nominated
for the *Irish Times* Non-fiction Literature Prize. He
followed this with *Forty-Seven Roses*, a hymn to his
mother's courage in keeping the family together through
difficult circumstances. He has four grown-up children;
Rossa, Fiachra, Doireann and Nuala, and lives in Dublin
with his wife Sheila. He writes in a shed at the end of the
garden where he is sometimes joined by two Labrador
dogs, Juno and Ruby.

Praise for Peter Sheridan

'Sheridan can add his name to that list of Irish writers in whose hands the English language plays like a harp: endlessly yet effortlessly lyrical' – *Kirkus*

'Sheridan's prose style is Chekhov by way of Monty Python and Rabelais ... hilarious' – *The New Yorker*

'You'd need a bag of adjectives to do justice to Peter Sheridan's (writing) ... sharp, ragged, jazzy, hilarious and often painful' – **Frank McCourt**

'Marvellously funny and loving stuff' – *Time Out*

'Sheridan's crackling prose and details about Dublin life recall the fiction of Roddy Doyle' – *Publishers Weekly*

'Extraordinarily upbeat ... the writing is sharp and witty'
– *Literary Review*

'Warm, witty, humane and, above all, authentic ...
I laughed, I cried, I marvelled at the skills of the author'
– **Deirdre Purcell**

'Remarkably honest, involving and compassionate'
– *The Scotsman*

Peter Sheridan

Big Fat Love

Tivoli

an imprint of Gill & Macmillan Ltd
Hume Avenue
Park West
Dublin 12
and associated companies throughout the world

www.gillmacmillan.ie

© Peter Sheridan 2003

"OH, WHAT A BEAUTIFUL MORNIN' "
Words by Oscar Hammerstein II and music by Richard Rodgers
© 1943, Williamson Music International, USA
Reproduced by permission of EMI Music Publishing Ltd,
London WC2H 0QY.

Excerpt from 'The Concrete And The Clay' (Moeller/Parker)
reproduced by kind permission of Apollo Music Ltd

07171 3668 X

Print origination by Type IT, Dublin
Printed by ColourBooks Ltd, Dublin

*The paper used in this book is made from the wood pulp of managed
forests. For every tree felled, at least one is planted, thereby renewing
natural resources.*

A catalogue record is available for this book from the British Library.

1 3 5 4 2

In memory of
Laura O'Dwyer
1989–2002

1

Philo took the knocker in her hand and lifted it up. It was heavy, a wrought-iron circle stiff with age. She didn't want to knock too loudly. It was very quiet beyond the mahogany doors that faced her. She could feel the solitude of the convent like it was a presence. The nuns would be in bed or at prayer. It was five past ten and that was late for nuns.

She held on to the knocker and wondered how much force to give it. Too little and they wouldn't hear it, too much and they'd jump out of their holy skins. In the end, she took her chance and simply let it go. It moved about a quarter of an inch before it jammed – stuck its chin out and defied gravity. She hadn't come this far to be thwarted by a lousy knocker. She leaned her hand on the stiff metal and brought it crashing down. Only the terminally deaf could escape its call.

She stood back and waited for the door to open. Nothing happened. There wasn't a sound or movement. Perhaps they thought it was a gun going off, or the backfiring engine of a stolen car. Such things were nightly occurrences in the North Wall. Philo took hold of the knocker and banged the bejasus out of it, ten or twelve good slaps of iron. By the time she was finished, the knocker moved like it had been given a dose of lubricating oil.

Philo heard approaching footsteps, urgent on the hard floor. A flap in the door moved back and a country voice spoke out to the darkness.

1

—We don't give alms at night, the voice said. Call back tomorrow.

—No, wait. I don't want alms. I've nowhere to stay, I'm homeless, Philo said.

There was a silence. Philo looked at the face in the square opening and thought she was looking at a painting. She could see two red cheeks and dark, bushy eyebrows, with a pale nose in the middle like a mountain.

The young nun looked back at Philo and thought she resembled a Viking. Her shoulders were square and her head seemed attached to her body in a peculiar manner. Then Sister Rosaleen realised this woman had no neck.

Philo knew her looks could intimidate. It was one of the reasons she kept a curl in her hair. She was five foot six and weighed over two hundred and forty pounds. Her face was round and surprisingly feminine for a woman so big. Philo, with her name rhyming with pillow, described herself to the world as pleasantly plump. The world didn't always respond in kind, so, in order to deal with it, she adopted a humorous persona whenever she could.

—I feel like Julie Andrews in *The Sound of Music*, Philo said. I've nowhere else to go.

Sister Rosaleen looked her up and down. She couldn't see any similarities to Julie Andrews. Julie Andrews was the real world, and this felt like a cartoon.

Philo bent down and picked up her suitcase. She held it up so the nun could see.

—I'm just back from England. God pointed me here.

Sister Rosaleen was taken off guard by the mention of God. The flap closed, and she disappeared for a moment before one of the doors opened and she asked Philo to step inside. Philo made no move because she knew she wouldn't fit through. She held her ground and waited for the Holy Spirit to bring knowledge to the nun's thick skull. After a few awkward moments, Sister Rosaleen pushed back the bolts

2

and opened the other door. Philo took a deep breath and stepped in out of the world, hoping that she would never have to face it again.

Sister Rosaleen showed Philo to the parlour. The smell of polish was all about. Every surface in the room was gleaming, and everywhere she looked she could see images of herself reflected back. They made her bigger than she already was. She did her best to ignore them but it was impossible. She looked down at the leg of the table and saw three fat women, one on top of the other.

Sister Rosaleen returned. She'd spoken to the Reverend Mother. They had a unit in the convent for families in distress and, fortunately for Philo, it was vacant. Sister Rosaleen brought her up the stairs and showed her to a bedroom.

—We'll see you in the morning, she said, and closed the door behind her.

Philo sat on the bed and couldn't quite believe where she was. For years she'd wanted to escape into a convent and become a nun. Anything to get away from Tommo and the prison she called home. The hardest part was leaving the children, of course. The pain of that was overwhelming. She'd been gone seven days and it was getting harder by the minute. Every time she slept, they were crying out for her in her dreams. Every time she awoke, she realised the tears were hers.

She looked at the simple cross that hung on the wall above her bed. God was good, she thought. For the first time in her life she identified with him – the pain etched on his face, his body broken and bruised. He'd suffered, just like she was suffering. It was the first time she'd made that connection, and it made her sad and happy at the same time. She hated men, but maybe that was about to change. She knelt down and put her head in her hands.

—My Daddy, who art in heaven, hallowed be Thy name – she started, and stopped because of the tears. But as she knelt by her bed, spluttering out her version of the Lord's Prayer, Philo was at peace, for the first time in a long while. She prayed they would let her stay in the convent. She prayed for a long time.

Then she lay on the bed in her clothes and stared at the ceiling. She knew she wouldn't sleep. She slept during the day, for the most part – an hour in the morning after her breakfast, half an hour to three-quarters in the afternoon after her dinner, and if she was lucky an hour in the evening after tea. Because she slept during the day, the nights were long and painful. By way of diversion, she busied herself through the hours of darkness with tasks normally carried out in daylight. She washed, prepared food, took baths, cut her nails, hung wallpaper and made lists of all her bills. Most of all, she ate. Food was her password to sleep. She never slept without eating, and once food was put into her mouth and swallowed, she always did her best to take a nap.

At six o'clock in the morning, Philo heard the first stirrings of life. A distant door opened and closed, followed by the patter of stockinged feet – a quiet noise, if there was such a thing. Within minutes there was much to-ing and fro-ing, all of it respectful. No one spoke. Perhaps they were all too busy listening out for God's voice. When it seemed appropriate, Philo left her room and followed the moving habits. They took her to the oratory, where they filed in for Mass. She knelt at the back, keeping several rows of empty pews between her and the female congregation.

The celebrant was a small man with silver hair and a face dominated by thick black glasses. He reminded Philo of Buddy Holly; from the neck up he was the spit of the bespectacled singer. At the consecration, he stuffed the host into his mouth and chewed on it like he was eating a packet of crisps. It looked vulgar and cannibalistic. On reflection, Philo had to admit to herself that it was a form of cannibalism. Life was a jungle and the Eucharist was a part of it. She'd entered the convent to escape tribal warfare and she was surprised to be reminded of it, watching Buddy Holly munch his way through the Body of Christ.

After her breakfast, which she devoured, Philo was brought to the office by Sister Rosaleen. It was an efficient room, on the other side of the polished parlour. She sat in the chair provided and waited for the Reverend Mother. The chair had nice armrests. She placed her fleshy arms gently on them and splayed her fingers. It was reassuring to have something to hold on to. Philo closed her eyes and thought about what she might say to the Reverend Mother. She felt a blinding tiredness envelop her. She knew she had to stay awake and she knew she could conk out in one second flat, if she let herself. She decided to close her eyes until she heard the door open. That would be her signal to spring back to life. The click of the lock, the turn of the handle, the creaking of the hinge – any of those noises and she would open her eyes. She waited and waited, but there wasn't a sound to be heard – not in the convent, and not in her head. Just peace. Soundless peace.

When Sister Monica O'Donovan came into the room, she sat down and observed the sleeping Philo. The first thing she noticed were the fingers of her right hand; each had a letter just below the knuckle, making up the word 'MAMMY'. On her upper right arm, below the shoulder, was a tattoo of a heart. The name 'Tommo' had once been inscribed there. It was now covered by a bunch of flowers.

She coughed until Philo opened her eyes and came back to life.

—You must be tired, Sister Monica said.

—Not a bit; sure I never sleep. My eyes were heavy, that's all.

Sister Monica thought Philo sounded like Moore Street. She was from rural Cork herself, but she loved the genuine Dublin accent. She loved the dealers bawling out their songs from behind mounds of vegetables and trays of fish. Philo's gravelly voice was pure Dublin, pure Molly Malone.

—I understand you're homeless.

—That's true, Reverend Mother, I've nowhere to go.

Philo was glad she'd remembered to call her Reverend Mother. Some nuns were sticklers for things like that.

—So what brings you here to us?

It was a moment of truth. She wanted to get her children back but she didn't want to admit she'd left them. Bad enough she'd done it once, but this was the second time.

The first time she'd taken a train to Galway. She just threw in the towel, got out of the ring and left it to Tommo. It was a Friday afternoon. She prepared fish fingers and chips, the kids' favourite, and left them ready in the oven. A note for Tommo to explain that she wouldn't be back for a while. A note for the children to say they had to do what their father told them. She figured that, after four days on his own with them, he'd know what it was to run a home. He wouldn't be so quick to criticise and point the finger at dirty dishes and unwashed clothes, and he mightn't be so ready to put his face up to hers and call her a fat cunt.

But when Philo had returned from Galway she'd found the fish fingers and chips still in the oven. On finding the notes, Tommo took the children straight to Goldenbridge Orphanage and dumped them. Her plan had completely backfired. He got rid of them because he had to play a darts match. When she applied to get the children back, Social Welfare said she was an unfit mother due to her abandonment of them. It took her weeks to prove she wasn't deranged. The only deranged thing was having to 're-establish the family unit' as the price of getting her children back – having to live with Tommo, wash his clothes, cook his dinner and smile every time he called her a big fat cow, or worse.

Sitting there opposite Sister Monica, Philo felt it was Groundhog Day, but she wasn't going back to Tommo again.

She needed time to think her situation through. She was too impulsive, she knew that. She should have taken the kids, but she needed time away from them, too. The idea of a refuge for battered wives had crossed her mind but she wasn't ready to admit defeat. She was desperate for some approval, even if she had to lie to get it. There was nothing in the real world only trouble. She needed to be safe. The convent was the only place on earth she wanted to be.

—I've always wanted to be a nun, but I never had the balls to do anything about it.

She knew she shouldn't have said 'balls', and she kicked herself on the ankle for her indiscretion.

Sister Monica had seen many vocations, but never one like Philo. She looked forty-five (she was, in fact, thirty-two), she had a tattoo on her arm and another on her fingers, she didn't look like a postulant, and she was enormous. As she entertained these thoughts, Sister Monica was aware she was pre-judging this woman. Mary Magdalene, she reminded herself, was a prostitute and yet she got to wash and dry Christ's feet.

—Why have you waited so long? she enquired.

It was a big question and Philo didn't know if she could answer it in under six hours. She'd made a mess of her life, that was the simple truth, and she wanted to put things right.

—Ask and you shall receive, Philo said. I think that's lovely.

It was lovely. Philo's life had been one of non-stop giving, and now it was her moment to ask for something in return. God owed her that. She had stepped through the door of His convent and she wanted it to close forever behind her.

—We don't have many late vocations; it's quite unusual.

—I didn't know there was an age limit.

—There isn't. Not at all. You can be as old as you like.

—I'm thrilled skinny, Philo beamed. Not that I'm bleedin' skinny, no way.

She kicked herself again. She would have to cut out the language, she knew that: nuns weren't allowed to curse.

—When did you have the heart put on? Sister Monica asked, pointing at her arm.

—That was my first tattoo. Do you like it?

—I think it's very nice. Is it in honour of the Sacred Heart?

The truth was it honoured a right bollix, her husband, Tommo Nolan, but Philo couldn't say that. She bit her lip and restrained herself. The Sacred Heart was a much better explanation.

—I suppose you could say it's in honour of Our Lord.

—The Sacred Heart is Our Lord. They're one and the same.

—It's in honour of the two of them, so.

—No, they're not two separate persons, do you understand that?

—I have a confession to make, Sister. I was brutal at catechism in school, but I'm prepared to go back over it and learn it properly.

Sister Monica didn't think the woman before her would make a nun. But she had a duty to take her seriously. This woman deserved to be treated with respect, like anyone in trouble, and the Reverend Mother suspected it would take a little time for the truth to emerge.

—I have a form here I'd like you to fill in.

Sister Monica pulled it from a drawer in her desk and passed it across the table. Philo looked at it in dismay. She hated providing personal information. She was as she was, take her or leave her; that was her philosophy. Why did anyone need to know her age, weight and height – especially God, who knew without being told anyway?

—Take that home, fill it in at your leisure and bring it back to me.

—I don't have a home, Sister.

It didn't seem possible to Sister Monica.

—Have you no home in Dublin, no parents?

Philo knew she had to lie. She had to deny her children and that was hard. It was a bad thing, but out of it would come a greater good.

—I don't have anywhere to go. That's the truth. If I could stay here and fill in the form, I'd do anything for you.

Sister Monica knew she should refuse. She also knew she wasn't going to. There was something about Philo that drew her in. She was warm and direct, but there was vulnerability just below the surface. There was no doubt she was hurt but still fighting. In the circumstances, Sister Monica felt totally powerless to refuse her request. The family unit in the convent was normally reserved for mothers with children, but in this instance she was going to make an exception.

—We have a unit upstairs, she said. You can stay there for now.

Philo was relieved but didn't know what to say.

—I hope you're not in a hurry for this, she said. I'm very slow at the writing.

She took the form and folded it. It was a habit of hers, folding things, making them as small as she possibly could. She squeezed it into a ball and held it in her fist. She followed Sister Monica out of her office and along the corridor.

—I can't guarantee you a bed, Sister Monica said. We may get a needy family, and if we do, you'll have to vacate.

—Don't worry about me; I never sleep at night. I can walk the corridors and wash the statues, if I have to.

Sister Monica hoped she'd made the right decision by letting her stay. Walking down the corridor away from her, Philo looked like a human tornado, and Sister Monica just hoped she didn't get out of control.

Sister Rosaleen was put in charge of Philo. Since joining the convent, Sister Rosaleen had learned to practise the virtue of obedience – it went with the job and she'd become accustomed to it; now she had someone under her, and she had to admit it felt good. It was nice to issue an instruction and know that she was going to be obeyed. It gave her status, and she realised for the first time in a very long while that she liked the sound of her own voice and that she had more than the word 'yes' in her vocabulary.

Philo didn't have an obedient bone in her body, yet now she couldn't get enough of being told what to do. It gave her a sense of purpose and distracted her from thinking about the mess her life was in. She was so eager to serve, she didn't wait to be asked, but volunteered herself at every opportunity.

—Do you want me to drain the potatoes, Sister Rosaleen?

—Will I give a hand putting out the soup, Sister Rosaleen?

—Would you like me to give the floor a mop, Sister Rosaleen?

She ran from one end of the kitchen to the other in order to obliterate the life she was running away from. The kitchen, with all its busyness and distraction, was the perfect place to hide. It was manna and heaven rolled into one. Here, amidst a sea of food, she gorged herself, without guilt. First there was the oxtail soup – not even her favourite, that was Scotch broth, but a lovely thick oxtail that she stirred and slurped to her heart's content. Then there was the boiled bacon, covered in snowy fat that was a real delicacy. Most people cut it off and threw it away, but not Philo. She particularly liked a nice chunky piece that brushed off both sides of her throat on the way down; there was no finer eating moment she could think of. To finish things off, there was home-made apple tart and custard, a combination of tastes that was hard to better. All this was available to Philo in the kitchen. As the food secreted its way into her system, she knew she would sleep, and in that sleep she would forget her past just a little bit more.

The kitchen staff served out thirty-one meals onto plates, for the elderly people who came to the Day Centre and ate in the dining room; ten dinners were served in aluminium cartons for the meals on wheels. On the instruction of Sister Rosaleen, Philo doled out the potatoes for all these servings. After that, it was time for the kitchen staff to sit down and enjoy the fruits of their cooking. As a newcomer, Philo was in the spotlight as they ate, but she managed not to give too much away.

Miss Somers, the kitchen supervisor, had an unfortunate name; she always wore an expression like winter on her face. No one called her by her Christian name; she was Miss Somers all the year round. She didn't like competition, so she resented Philo from the off. At the table, she started to clear up before Philo was finished. She poured out the tea and then milked each cup in turn. Philo did not like people who took the liberty of milking her tea. It was very personal to her, the amount of milk she took, and she didn't like anyone who stepped across that line. She didn't want to start a row on her first day, so she bit her lip and raised the cup to her mouth with a smile.

It was then she realised how much she needed a cigarette. The old Philo would have asked for one on the spot, impulsive being her middle name. But the new Philo was practising servility and was determined to change her ways.

—Do any of you smoke? she asked.

The question was ridiculous, of course. The chances of Sisters Davina, Kevin and Rosaleen having cigarettes on them was less than zero. That left Miss Somers, who was anything but inclined to meet Philo's nicotine requirements.

—Did you say you were applying to become a nun? Miss Somers asked.

—Yes, I am.

—Nuns are not allowed smoke, you know that.

—No, I didn't.

11

—That's how they're so healthy. You never heard a nun with a smoker's cough, did you?

—No, as a matter of fact –

—They never get colds, cancer or bronchitis. They're so healthy they'd make you sick, if you know what I mean.

She was starting to seriously annoy Philo, who couldn't get a word in edgeways. With that, Miss Somers reached into her pocket and pulled out a packet of cigarettes. She opened it and withdrew one before crumpling the packet in her fist.

—I've only one left, sorry.

She lit up and blew the smoke into the air. Philo was possessed by an almighty urge to reach out and give her a clatter. She knew she couldn't, because she was on trial – and, apart from that, she knew the futility of violence. Nicotine was a powerful thing – as powerful as heroin, some people said – and withdrawal from it generated extreme emotional upheaval. If it hadn't been the start of her new life, Philo would have decimated her antagonist. Instead she smiled and turned to the holy hoodies on her other side.

—Is it true you're not allowed smoke? she said.

They looked momentarily bewildered.

—I don't think we are, Sister Kevin said.

—No cigarettes and no alcohol, that's the rule, Sister Davina added.

—That means, Sister Rosaleen said, pointing her finger, no more cigarettes for you.

Philo didn't like to be pointed at. All her life she'd been pointed at like the world's problems were her fault. She squeezed her fists into two tight balls and held her tongue.

Miss Somers continued to make clouds of smoke. She didn't inhale much, so they were thick balls of cotton wool. It was a wasted cigarette. What was floating in the air should have been floating in her lungs. Philo was a real smoker who sucked with pride, deep down into the pit of her stomach. She still believed Miss Somers would pass her the cigarette. It was an unwritten but universal law among smokers that a last cigarette was a shared cigarette. It cut across culture, creed and politics. You didn't deny a condemned man his final request, and you didn't deny a smoker a drag from your last cigarette. Philo waited in anticipation for what would be her final puff, before she put the cigarettes aside and embraced the religious life for good.

—We have to organise the dining room, Sister Rosaleen said. Come on.

The energetic nun was halfway to the door before she realised that Philo hadn't moved. She waved her arms, beckoning her.

—Come on, we have to sort out the tables.

—You want me to go out there? Philo could not conceal her horror.

—They're old folks, that's all. They're not going to bite you.

—I know what they're like. They're worse than vampires, they have fangs.

—You make them sound like monsters.

—They are fucking monsters.

The room gasped. Even the smoke seemed taken aback and shimmied away. Philo didn't care; she was genuinely horrified at the prospect of facing the old folks. She was from the parish: she knew many of them and they knew her. The convent was meant to be her refuge. She was safe in the kitchen, but to walk from there to the dining room was to walk the steps to the gallows. She wasn't ready for her execution, not just yet. She made her excuses and hid in the toilet for the best part of the afternoon.

Philo called around to Sister Rosaleen's room. It was nearly ten o'clock, but that meant nothing to Philo, who had no concept of time. Sister Rosaleen was saying her office when

Philo knocked on her door, entered and sat on the bed, eager to talk.

—You've every right to be annoyed with me. I'm a stupid bitch, Philo said.

Sister Rosaleen wasn't annoyed with her. On the contrary, she was delighted to have her around and thought her a breath of fresh air. It was just that night-time visiting was frowned upon: they had a vow of silence from eight in the evening and she needed the Reverend Mother's permission to break it. She tried to explain in a whisper, but Philo didn't want to hear.

—I know by the way you're going on that you're annoyed.

Sister Rosaleen got a piece of paper and wrote down on it, 'Vow of silence.' Philo pointed at the paper and then at Sister Rosaleen.

—You're not allowed to talk.

Sister Rosaleen smiled and nodded.

—I'll do all the talking, Philo said. You sit back and relax.

And she did. She talked, and Sister Rosaleen shook her head up and down and from side to side. Philo apologised for her disobedience. It was out of order and she deserved to be punished. She offered to prostrate herself and be whipped, and it was a surprise for her to learn that nuns didn't do that any more. She'd thought they had to. It seemed as important to her as keeping a vow of silence. She suggested a list of other possible punishments – from pouring ashes over her head to standing in a bucket of cold water – but Sister Rosaleen shook her head to them all.

Then there were the silences, long and beautiful, when she just stopped talking. She gobbled them up. After the madhouse screaming and shouting of home, they were a delicacy to savour.

—I love the fucking peace and quiet, she said. I just fucking love it.

14

Sister Rosaleen winced and Philo didn't know why. She was so at peace with herself, she didn't notice she'd cursed. Sister Rosaleen got her piece of paper and wrote on it, 'No swear words.' Philo was genuinely surprised.

—What exactly did I say?

Sister Rosaleen took up her pen and was about to commit the word to paper when she thought better of it. She looked up at Philo.

—What's the matter, can you not spell?

Sister Rosaleen started to laugh and tried to suppress it, which only made it worse. She covered her nose and mouth with her hands but it broke through, like steam from a boiling kettle. Philo joined in. Their laughter filled the silence around them in an unconscious, effortless way. This was real peace for Philo because it was the absence of war. She could never go back to what she had come from. Here in the convent, she had refuge and shelter without the stigma of being a battered wife. More importantly, she had love and respect; she had the community of nuns; she had Sister Rosaleen, who was her boss and a very kind one.

—I'd love my daughter to grow up like you.

Sister Rosaleen was surprised and touched.

—You have a daughter? she said, breaking her silence.

Philo had forgotten she could speak and got a fright.

—You have a daughter, Sister Rosaleen said again.

—No, I don't have a daughter. It was the truth: Philo had three daughters.

—If I did have one, I'd like her to grow up like you.

Sister Rosaleen couldn't remember the last time somebody had said something so nice to her. Most people avoided the subject of children around her. It was understandable: she'd taken a vow of chastity and would never have any. That didn't mean she never thought about it, though – about children, and what hers might be like if she had any. She was still a woman, and Philo had reminded her of that in the most tender, loving way. Her womb was still intact, it hadn't gone away, and Sister Rosaleen felt a renewal of pride in all of that. Thanks to Philo, she was proud to be a woman and a nun.

2

When Philo got up the next day, Sister Rosaleen took her on a tour of the convent. She started out on the roof garden, which was a collection of exotic plants in containers, looked after by Sister Xavier, who talked to them and prayed for them – but not today, because she was sick in bed with the flu. With so much devastation all around the North Wall, it was a genuine surprise for Philo to find the garden there, a piece of perfection at the edge of chaos. The nearby flats had been de-tenanted and were about to be demolished. They were a sad and sorry sight. The stairs and balconies where children had once played were silent and empty; the rooms that had contained so much life were only shells. Here on the roof, each plant had a label detailing its name, where it came from and the date it had been planted. The contrast couldn't have been more profound.

Philo could tell the plants were loved. They had a look that boasted of good care, proud leaves with a gloss close to a smile. What buds there were looked close to bursting; the camellias, particularly, were just about to flower. Philo could see God's hand everywhere. She looked across at the dying world of the North Wall, the silent flats that had once housed so many, the quays that had teemed with life. It was passing away and she was among flowers and happy to be there, happy to be out of it, so happy she wanted to cry.

From the roof, Sister Rosaleen took her down a ladder that led to the back of the oratory chapel. Standing in front of an oak-panelled wall, Sister Rosaleen slipped her hand into a slit, pulled a section of the panelling towards her and revealed a secret passageway that led to the back of the altar. They squeezed their way into the darkness and hauled themselves over the parapet until they were looking at the pews where the congregation knelt for Mass. It was so quiet they could feel God's presence.

—What do you think would happen if I popped up out of here during Mass tomorrow morning? Philo whispered. She leapt up and made funny faces, like a munchkin, at the imaginary congregation.

Sister Rosaleen convulsed with laughter and had to cross her legs to stop herself from peeing. Every time she thought of Philo's Viking head popping up during Mass, she collapsed in a heap. Philo joined in, but she didn't think it was that funny. She was laughing because Sister Rosaleen couldn't stop.

—I've a pain in my gee from laughing, Philo said finally.

'Gee' was Philo's favourite word in the whole of the English language. It was a slang term for the vagina, of course, and Philo used it mostly when she wanted to shock people. She liked to use it in the company of people she didn't like, especially if they were hypocrites like her father, her husband or the clergy. Sometimes she didn't think about it and it just slipped out, like now at the back of the altar.

—I've a pain in my gee, too, Sister Rosaleen said.

It was the first time Philo had heard a nun use the word and it didn't sound right. It seemed like a corruption coming from her lips. Philo didn't want to be responsible for turning Sister Rosaleen into a sinner like herself.

—I don't think you should be saying that word, Philo said.

—What are you talking about?

—I'm talking about gee.

—What's wrong with gee? It's your stomach, isn't it?

—No, it's not your stomach, it's further down. Philo pointed. Your gee is your vagina. It's your womanhood.

—Do you think it's a bad word?

Philo didn't know what to think. She had given her womanhood plenty of use before coming into the convent. Sister Rosaleen had never used hers, Philo suspected – she'd probably come straight from the fresh air of a farm (the red cheeks were a giveaway); she'd never had the shadow of a man fall across her. Philo was glad she herself had experienced sex before turning her back on it for good.

From the back of the altar, they wound their way down a circuitous series of corridors, back to the kitchen. The preparation of dinner for the elderly of the Day Centre was in full swing. Sister Davina, sturdy and sixty, was stirring the big pot of soup on the cooker; over by the sink Miss Somers was handing a jug of water to Sister Kevin, who was standing on a chair by the Burco boiler. It was pumping steam like a chimney. Sister Kevin lifted the flap and poured the water in. The diminutive nun (she was seventy and small) disappeared for a moment in a cloud of steam. Then she turned and handed the empty jug back to Miss Somers for more. It was as archaic a way to fill a Burco boiler as it was possible to imagine.

Philo offered to lift the boiler down off its shelf, but the others wouldn't hear of it. It was too heavy, they said; she'd strain herself lifting it back up.

—You can get up here if you like and do my job, Sister Kevin said petulantly.

Philo had no intention of hauling herself up onto a chair that might collapse under her weight. Instead, she lifted Sister Kevin like a doll and put her safely on terra firma.

—Just give me one minute, Philo said, and left.

She high-tailed it out of the kitchen and retraced her steps. On the roof, she found a length of hosepipe she'd spotted earlier. She brought it back to the kitchen and washed it. Then she attached one end to the cold tap and dropped the other end into the Burco boiler. A simple flick of her wrist, and water flowed out in a steady stream and fell into the belly of the boiler.

—Will I fill it to the top? Philo asked.

No one answered her. They were dumbfounded. For twelve years, since the Day Centre had opened, they'd made a human chain to fill the Burco boiler. Now Mammy Bear had arrived and shown them another, safer way to do it. She was an angel, an angel on horseback sent by God. Her sisters in Christ were ready to take her to their bosoms.

Miss Somers was the only one not impressed. She suspected the devil in all this. She felt threatened by the intruder. There seemed to be less air in the room with her about. The water continued to cascade into the boiler and for Miss Somers it was a siren, warning her of trouble ahead.

Sister Rosaleen spotted the danger and ordered her charge to follow her into the dining room. This time, Philo had no option but to obey.

She hid behind Sister Rosaleen as best she could, but it was impossible for someone of her size. They pulled the dining tables apart and stripped them of their tablecloths. From a sideboard, Sister Rosaleen took the games that formed the heart of the after-dinner activities. There were two decks of playing cards; a compendium that included draughts, Ludo and Snakes and Ladders; a set of dominoes; an American version of Monopoly that no one played with; a game called Mastermind that was played with small coloured pegs, most of which were missing; two editions of Cluedo, one pristine and one battered; a horse-racing game called Totopoly, a great favourite among the men; a game of Trivial Pursuit that no one bothered with because there were too many questions about the Royal Family; and a set of Junior Lego for children aged six to eight. In addition, there were magazines: *Ireland's Own, Hello, Image, Brides and Bridesmaids, The Listener, Golf World* (with two free tees still stuck to the cover), *The Sacred Heart Messenger, Far*

East, *Our Boys*, *In Dublin* and the *Sunday People* TV guide for programmes that had been aired eighteen months before. There was a method in Sister Rosaleen's madness, an order to the apparent chaos of where tables and chairs were placed; and, rather than try to decode it, Philo kept her head down and followed her lead.

Nan Cassidy, who lived four doors down from Philo's mother in East Wall, was leaning on her walking-stick talking to Granny Carmody. She knew it was Philo, but waited until she was passing and caught her by the arm.

—How are you doing, Philomena? I didn't know you worked here.

Philo opened her mouth and pointed at her throat to indicate that she couldn't talk.

—I haven't seen your mammy in ages. How is she?

Philo mouthed the words, 'I think she's all right,' but no sound came out. Nan Cassidy turned back to Granny Carmody.

—That's Sylvia Darcy's daughter – you know, that has the weight problem, four doors down from me.

—I believe she's an awful size.

—Oh, it's not funny, I can tell you. She can't even walk up the stairs, God love her.

—It must be an awful crucifixion, all that weight.

—I'd rather be in a wheelchair than carry all that weight, that's the truth.

Philo couldn't stand by and listen to any more of this.

—The wheelchair can be arranged, Nan Cassidy, she said through clenched teeth.

She brushed past the two women, nearly knocking them to the ground. Philo hated backbiting, especially among the elderly. They should be engaged in preparation to meet their Maker, not character assassination. It was true – her mother was an awful size – but that wasn't the point: it was enough to be fat, without people feeding off it like vultures. If she wanted to feed people, she could donate her fat to the chip shop on the East Wall Road after her death.

When the tables and chairs were in their final resting places, the congregation of old folks began to take their seats. They tried to make it look nonchalant, but it was a ritual as regimented as their religion. Nan Cassidy and Granny Carmody sat at a table with Barney Hughes, the Commandant, so called because he had served in the Irish Army. They played Cluedo together and didn't like intruders. They were very serious about murder. The Commandant won most days; he had the training for it, he was good at deduction and the women couldn't match him.

At the next table sat Cap Coyle, Mucky Mannion, Gracie Kershaw and deaf Olive Mulvey, who had a daughter of the same name with perfect hearing. Gambling wasn't allowed in the Centre, but they played Totopoly for money, using matchsticks, each one representing a ten-pence piece. They had strict limits: no one was allowed wager more than five matches a game, and you had to drop out altogether if your losses amounted to ten matchsticks, or a pound, in one day. They had tried playing for fun, in accordance with convent rules, but horse racing just wasn't the same if there was nothing at stake.

At the other end of the room, as far away as it was possible to get, sat Dina Sugrue and Minnie 'Mouse' O'Hara, the most feared duo in the Centre. They were physically small, with personalities the size of grizzly bears, and they both possessed tongues that could turn milk sour. They were usually joined by Ita Mullen and Chrissie Mongon, and the foursome made up a poker school that played for matches at fivepence each. Today it was draughts at their table, because half the poker school was absent due to a wedding.

Philo noticed Ninna Delargy sitting by herself and thought she looked pathetic. She was holding squares of Lego in her hand, trying to figure them out. Ninna lived alone in a house that straddled the canal right where it empties itself into the Liffey. There had once been a community of four houses there, but three of them were now derelict. They'd been built a hundred years before for families that worked the waterway. Ninna's husband, Matt, had been a lock-keeper. He had died in his early fifties; some said that when the canal finished for business, Matt did, too. Ninna had always looked like she was dressed for Sunday Mass; she had been known as a 'real lady' in the North Wall. That had changed when she'd been broken into and robbed. It knocked the stuffing out of her and she started to let her appearance go. It was her hair, more than her clothes: it had always been immaculately kept, and now it was dishevelled. Something in her had given up after her house had been invaded.

She stuck a number of pieces of Lego together and started to make a wall. She left a gap for something, possibly a door, and continued on. Philo marched over to where she was sitting and took her by the arm.

—Come on; you shouldn't be sitting by yourself.

—Let me finish the house first.

Philo could feel the resistance. She sat down with Ninna and helped her. Between them they found a door, a window and some slanted Lego for the roof. In no time, they brought it to completion: a plastic house with white walls, a yellow door and red roof-tiles. Ninna gave Philo a builder's self-satisfied smile.

—Would you like to play a game? Philo asked.

—That would be nice.

—Come with me and we'll sort you out.

She took her by the arm and brought her to the Cluedo table. The Commandant saw them approach and held up his hand, military style.

—We're in the middle of a game here, he said.

—She can join you in the next one, so, Philo said.

23

—There's only chairs for three at this table, Granny Carmody said.

—No room at the inn, is that it? Philo said.

The tension was immediate. All around, the other tables became aware of the awkwardness. No one offered; they all just stared. Philo drank in the blank stares of selfishness.

—There are magazines if she's on her own, came a voice from the crowd.

It was Cap Coyle. Before Philo wheeled around on him, he was sorry he'd said it. It sounded weak, like he was passing the buck, which he was. He picked one of the small wooden horses from the Totopoly game and held it up. It had the name 'Apollo' painted in white on the saddle, and below it the number 2. All the horses had names out of Greek and Roman legend – Hippolytus, Dionysus, Zeus, Aphrodite and Bacchus.

—It's a horse-racing game; I don't know if you'd like it, Cap said.

Ninna Delargy liked horses. She remembered them pulling barges along the canal when she was a little girl. They were Irish horses, great big drays, and one had been called Nelly, she was nearly sure – Nelly or Sally. Why was the horse in the game given a Greek name? she wondered.

—Would you like to play horse racing? Philo asked her.

Ninna didn't like everyone staring at her. It gave her a bad feeling. She felt her tummy heave, like when she'd been broken into. She would have said yes, only they were Greek horses and she didn't understand the names.

—I think I'll read a magazine, she said. I don't like to intrude.

She walked back to her chair with grace and poise. She was still a lady in Philo's eyes, surrounded by a sea of crabby old vampires.

—I hope you're well satisfied, Philo said. I'm glad I don't have to hear your confessions, that's all I can say.

24

No one spoke. Philo had pricked the collective conscience and their communal shame was palpable. She walked back to Sister Rosaleen, continuing with her invective.

—They go to Mass in the morning and they stab people in the afternoon. I hate that hypocrisy, don't you?

Sister Rosaleen nodded in agreement. She didn't have the guts to speak out, not with Philo holding centre stage, delivering her homily.

—You'd think at their age they'd learn to get on, Sister. You'd think they'd be an example to the generation coming up – wouldn't you think that?

Philo was in attack mode and couldn't stop herself. It helped that she was in a lousy mood, of course, due in no small measure to not having had a cigarette all day.

—No wonder this area is banjaxed, when the old folk can't get on with one another. I think it's sad, that's what I think; I think it's very sad.

The North Wall was a mixture of houses, flats, factories, coal sheds, timber yards, rail freight depots, oil terminals and all kinds of dock-related activities. It had been created by one of the great engineering feats of the eighteenth century, the creation of a buffer wall that extended the river out into the sea. This turned Dublin into a great port, and labouring men and their families came from all over Ireland to farm the river. At the beginning of the 1950s, twenty-four blocks of flats went up, making the North Wall the most densely populated area in the city of Dublin. It was dominated by Sheriff Street. On one side of it stood the faded grandeur of Seville Place, with its three-storied Victorian dwellings; on the other side was the River Liffey that separated it from the south side.

The North Wall had once been a thriving village at the edge of the city, bound up in and dominated by the river. No one could have foreseen, in its heyday, that it would become an urban wasteland.

The generation of old folks in the Day Centre were not responsible for this demise, but it saddened Philo that the divisions among them had made victory over them all the easier. They should be united, now more than ever; they should be taking down barriers, not putting up new ones. It sickened Philo to her core, because it reminded her of the ruins of her own life – ruins she was desperately trying to get away from and forget.

Sister Rosaleen couldn't help feeling the old folks deserved to have their knuckles rapped. They seemed almost glad their shortcomings had been pointed out to them, like bold children who know they've gone too far. There was no hint of protest; they'd erred and were repentant. Heads bowed, in silent reverie, they waited for forgiveness, waited for their sins to be washed away so they could become whole again.

Philo looked at Sister Rosaleen and knew she'd over-stepped the mark. It wasn't her position to lay down the law. She was only a wet day in the place; she was there to take orders, not give them; she was the skivvy.

—I'm sorry for giving out to yous, Philo said. It's just that I bleedin' love the North Wall.

Several voices rose up from the hall.

—You were right.

—We deserved it.

—We love the North Wall, too.

Dina stood up from her game of draughts.

—I'm proud to come from the docks. I was born here and I'll die here, and I can't think of anywhere else I'd rather die.

—You're not going to die just yet; sit down, Mouse O'Hara said.

Joxer Farrell, known for being a great lover of wakes, wanted to know who was dead. It took several voices to convince him that he wouldn't be going to a funeral in the next few days.

—I have an awful mouth on me, Philo said. It gets me into trouble all the time.

—It won't get you into trouble for telling the truth, Cap said, and everyone seemed to agree with him.

Sister Rosaleen had never seen the dining room so animated. It was good that people were talking, arguing, having their voices heard. Philo had lit a fire under them and it was a great opportunity to foster togetherness. Sister Rosaleen clapped her hands for attention.

—Why don't we say a decade of the rosary and offer it up for our intentions?

No one was interested in the rosary.

—Why don't we have a sing-song? someone shouted.

—Give us a blast of Al Jolson, Mucky, someone else chimed in.

—Go on, give us 'Mammy', Mucky, Joxer Farrell demanded.

All around the dining room, the request for Mucky to do his Al Jolson impersonation gathered momentum.

—'Mammy', Mucky! they begged. 'Mammy', Mucky!

Mucky Mannion's Al Jolson was legendary. His favoured approach was to slip quietly into a pub toilet, apply black boot-polish to his face (he always carried a tin with him when going out for a drink), make a grand entrance by falling onto one knee in the middle of the floor, and then launch into 'Mammy' at full throttle. In reality, the surprise had long gone out of it, but everyone played along out of respect for his showmanship.

Mucky could not respond favourably to the request because he never carried his tin of polish to the Day Centre, and he never, ever performed without his black mask.

—Why don't you give us a song, Philo? Dina asked.

—Yes, why don't you? several others asked, too.

It felt like Our Lady had appeared and demanded Philo should sing. They didn't want to hear excuses, it had been ordained, Dina had made the request on behalf of the pack and the congregation of wolves were not about to be denied. Sister Rosaleen added her voice to the chorus and, since Philo was under her command, she had no choice but to give in.

—I'd want a few jars in me before I could sing.

It was an excuse older than the Pyramids. Undaunted, Dina rooted in her bag for the naggin of brandy she kept permanently there. She turned her handbag upside down and gave it a little shake. The naggin of brandy slid out into the light, and with it came a salt cellar and a sugar bowl, the same as those that were on the dinner table.

—Take a slug out of that and whet your whistle, Dina said.

Philo observed the bottle. It looked inviting, but she knew if she let the brown liquid pass her lips she would have to have a cigarette. She declined.

—Seeing as I have so much in common with Tina Turner, I suppose I'll sing something by her.

The ones who knew Tina Turner laughed out loud, and the others wondered why it was funny.

—I share some very vital statistics with Tina Turner, Philo said. My wrist and her waist are the same size.

Philo held up her arm so they could see.

—We share a birthday, too – and there's other things, but I won't go into them here, they're not nice things.

Philo cleared her throat and launched into 'Simply the Best'. She sang it with all the passion of a Dublin pub on a Sunday night, when the women linked arms and swayed back and forth to the rhythm of one another's songs. Such was the intensity that pubs in the city had been known to leave the ground during such sessions.

The Tina Turner song was Philo's party piece. She'd adopted it as a personal anthem. It was about her; it celebrated her dogged will to put the past behind her and emerge as her own person, her own self. She moved with phenomenal grace for a woman of her size. Her feet touched lightly off the floor, like a ballerina's, her arms moved above her head like they were on strings, her hips flashed from side to side in a sway that was hypnotic. The sound that came out of her mouth would have blown Pavarotti out of the room. It rang through the building and brought people scurrying. First there was the kitchen staff, Sister Davina, Sister Kevin and Miss Somers, and after them assorted nuns who thought the old folks had gone crazy. They had gone crazy, and when they bellowed out the chorus, even the nuns found themselves with arms above their heads swaying disobediently to the insistent rhythm. At the finale, everyone cheered and clapped, and some of the men whistled in appreciation. There had never been an explosion like it before, there had never been such fun and there had never been such unity.

Philo, in compliance with tradition, announced that it was her noble call. She looked around for someone to pick and her eyes came to rest on Cap Coyle. He had a little lock-up store in Sheriff Street. She'd bought vegetables from him and knew his penchant for singing in the shop. He seemed a logical choice. There was Dina, too, of course. She had a vegetable shop, Get Fresh, around the corner in Dowdall's Lane. Philo had bought from Dina in her time as well. She had never understood or got involved in the ancient quarrel between Cap and Dina. She was too preoccupied with the here and now to be bothered by their vegetable war. Her main aim was to avoid conflict and bring people together.

—My noble call is Cap Coyle. Come on, Cap, give us a song.

There were lots of calls for 'hush' and 'order for the singer'. Inevitably, someone shouted out, 'One voice only, please.'

Cap stood up where he was and took off his cap. He held it in his hand and fidgeted with it. Singing in front of people was a serious business. He'd been schooled by his father,

3

From the opening note, Cap connected to something deep inside himself, and the passion of his voice made the world spin back forty years. It took everyone in the room along with it; all ageing disappeared and not a creaking bone or arthritic joint was heard, nothing but the joy in Cap's voice that conjured up the sunbeams of an Oklahoma summer.

That was how it was until he stopped mid-note. He looked down at Dina and became conscious of her, conscious of the present. He was suddenly engulfed in the sadness of their separation, and it made him feel old. They were enemies, they'd devoted their lives to mutual hatred, they'd grown up and grown old on it. Nothing could change that. History had dealt them a hand, and it would never be the summer again.

People thought he was pausing for effect, at first. Then the pause became a silence that seemed to go on forever. Cap looked lost, like a little child. Someone shouted out the next line of the song. He didn't acknowledge it, because the words were not the problem; the words, if anything, were a solution he couldn't face. They tried to give him encouragement, but he didn't need that either. He'd choked on the emotion and couldn't continue. He took his cap back from Mucky, put it on his stupid head, and sat down.

The sing-song continued, in a fashion, and everyone gave their all. It was the best day ever in the Day Centre. No one would ever forget Philo's take on Tina Turner, Granny Carmody's falsetto version of 'Down by the Sally Gardens', or Nan Cassidy's rendition of 'How Much Is that Doggy in the Window?' But when all the dust had settled, it was the memory of Cap stopping in mid-sentence that people would carry with them from the day. People suspected it had something to do with the vegetable war, but they weren't sure.

Cap was disgusted he'd let himself down. To start a song and not finish it was tantamount to spitting on his father's grave. Cap had worked as a singer-out on the docks. He used to stand above the cargo hold on the ship and sing out instructions to the winch man, who operated a crane from a blind position on the quayside. It was Cap's responsibility to ensure that the cargo came up cleanly, that it didn't hit off anything on its way and crash back down on the men below. He sang out the most banal instructions – 'Take her to the left and hold her steady' – and made them sound like they were melodies composed by Verdi. Now Cap's bad choice of song had led to his downfall in the Day Centre. Why had he chosen a love song when Dina was his sworn enemy?

Back behind the counter of his lock-up shop, Cap glowered at the vegetables like it was their fault. The Queens potatoes, with their beady black eyes staring up at him, particularly annoyed him. So did the cauliflowers, which reminded him he had the brain of an idiot. He put a sheet of newspaper across the potatoes to hide them and swapped the cauliflowers with the turnips. It provided only very temporary relief.

He tried hard not to think about Dina, but he couldn't get her out of his head. Starting that song, he'd seen her as she used to be: the best-looking girl in the parish of Saint Laurence O'Toole. No more than five foot two, she was a natural blonde with perfectly formed breasts and a posterior to die for. Cap used to encourage her to skip in front of him in the chip shop queue so he could ogle her at the counter. When she went to the altar to receive, she upstaged God and everyone else in the church. All the lads knew she would be the perfect ride, but no young man in the parish stood a chance with her. There were rumours of boyfriends in exotic, faraway places like Donnybrook, Ranelagh and Howth. She was a temptation, like Eve, to be admired from afar.

Cap remembered one Sunday morning when he'd been on his way up to receive Holy Communion and he'd seen Dina on her way back down. Her head was bowed, as it should be when you had God on your tongue. He was about ten yards from her when she looked up and caught him staring at her. He was going to look away, but she flashed him the biggest smile he'd ever seen. Her eyes were so intense it was like her spirit had entered him. No girl had ever done that to him before. Not even God had ever taken over his whole being and turned him into jelly. He was shaking so much he barely made it to the altar.

After that, when he wasn't singing out cargo, Cap was singing out Dina Barrett's praises. Gerry Sugrue was the same. Gerry and Cap had been best friends since their first day in school. Their fathers had also been best friends, and Bronco Coyle had been best man at Tom Sugrue's wedding. Cap and Gerry continued the tradition. They ate their sandwiches together, bought each other pints of porter in the pub, went to Mass and confession as a pair and shared everything from cigarettes to chewing gum and aftershave. The only thing they didn't share was girlfriends – but the sad truth was, they didn't have any. Neither of them could get up the nerve to ask Dina out, but every conversation ended up as a eulogy on one part of her anatomy or another.

Eventually Cap and Gerry got sick of listening to each other fantasising about Dina. That was when they tossed the coin – and Gerry won. Cap pretended not to mind, but his heart sank to his knees. He felt that Dina was his, and now he had to ask her for a date on behalf of his friend.

He walked up to her at the church railings and told her Gerry wanted to take her to a dance in Clery's ballroom.

—What's wrong with your friend that he can't ask me himself?

—I think he's shy, that's all.

—I don't like shy fellas; you can't trust them.

—I can vouch for Gerry. He's one hundred per cent reliable.

Cap pleaded the case for his friend, not knowing he himself was the one Dina fancied. She kept him talking for ages, feigning an interest in all sorts of things just to keep him there. Cap felt as stirred up by her as he had in the church; but Gerry was his best friend and he had won the bet, so Cap persevered. In the end, Dina agreed to go out with Gerry in frustration at Cap's lack of initiative.

From then on, Gerry Sugrue pursued Dina with the fervour of a zealot. He showered her with gifts. Anything exotic that came into the port of Dublin ended up on her doorstep. He was devoted to her. He worked for her, stole for her and prayed for her. She liked him and was flattered by the attention, but it wasn't love.

When he produced a diamond engagement ring one Friday night, she weakened and slept with him. Like all Catholic girls who sin, she got caught. There was no option but to marry him. History repeated itself and Cap played best man to Gerry, just as their fathers had done a generation before; only this time, the bride was marrying the wrong man.

As Cap sat in his shop dwelling on the past, it started to rain in Sheriff Street. It rattled like a machine gun on the concrete and ricocheted off the pavement into the lock-up. Cap closed the door against the attack. There was nothing left to do but sit it out. He detested rain. It recalled more bad memories. It was rain that had driven a wedge between him and Gerry. And it had cost him his job as a singer-out, too.

The tradition on the docks had been that work stopped when it rained and the men were paid 'wet time' at half the hourly rate. The stevedores wanted to change the custom, so they supplied waterproof clothing to overcome the problem. They might have reached agreement on the issue, only the stevedores deducted the cost of the waterproofs from the men's wages. The men, in return, refused to implement the plan. The stevedores retaliated by bringing in scabs to discharge the ships tied up in the port. These scabs instantly became known as 'aquanauts'.

It was 1951 and the docks erupted into full-scale war. All over the city, the aquanauts and their families were targeted by angry dockers. Men had their arms and jaws broken, but the lure of well-paid dock work continued to swell the ranks of the aquanauts. The more militant dockers wanted to take extreme action. As Cap hated violence, it was a difficult time for him. He hated what the stevedores were doing, but he couldn't square his conscience with cracking someone's skull open. At a union meeting held in the upstairs room of Campion's bar, Gerry Sugrue proposed they strap a concrete block to one of the aquanauts and drop him in the Liffey. The chairman of the meeting, branch secretary of the union Matt Kerrigan, ruled it out of order.

—I'm a paid-up member of the union, Gerry shouted. I'm entitled to be heard!

—You don't have a seconder, Matt Kerrigan shouted back.

—You're wrong there: I do have a seconder. Gerry turned around and looked at Cap. That's my seconder right there.

Since before he'd known how to blow his nose, Gerry had been Cap's protector. Anyone who wanted to pick a fight with Cap had to take on Gerry first.

—Put your hand up, Cap.

Gerry waited for his friend to respond.

—I need you to support the motion, Cap.

All Cap had to do was raise his hand.

—Are you going to second me or not?

—Gerry, you know I think this situation is wrong. Very wrong. But I can't condone murder.

The room burst into shouting, back and forth; tempers flared and insults were exchanged. Through it all, Gerry fixed Cap with a stare of betrayal.

—Thanks very much, he said quietly. Thanks for the support.

There was no shortage of men to back Gerry's proposal, but the chairman refused to take it, even after standing orders were suspended. The meeting broke up in disorder and Gerry led the hawks in a walkout. Cap knew he'd placed himself on the other side of the fence, so he stayed with the doves.

He went home and got into bed, but he couldn't sleep. At half-two in the morning, with rain lashing against the panes, there was a knock on his window. It was Gerry's familiar three taps, only they weren't taps, they were thunderbolts. Cap went to the door in his pyjamas and Gerry was standing there, very drunk.

—Come in out of that, Cap said.

—You don't tell me what to do. I'm my own boss, you understand?

—I know all that, but it's freezing, so get your arse in here.

—Don't tell me where to put my arse. You betrayed me.

—Come inside and we'll talk about it.

—I'm not welcome here.

—That's not true.

—You did a Judas, only you forgot to kiss me.

Gerry stuck out his cheek like he was inviting Cap to plant a kiss there. It was a strange invitation, because Cap wanted to make up with his friend, he wanted to throw his arms around him and say he was sorry, but Gerry's attitude made it impossible.

—Why did you do it?

Cap didn't have an easy answer.

—Why did you do it? Gerry asked again.

—I'm a coward, that's why, Cap said.

—Don't believe you.

—I don't like the sight of blood, my own or anyone else's.

—This has to do with Dina, doesn't it?

Cap was completely taken aback.

—You're jealous that I got her, isn't that it?

Gerry made it sound like he'd won her in a raffle. Even allowing for the drink, it was a strange way to express it.

—I know you fancy her, I know all that.

Gerry smiled over at Cap, but it was more of a leer. Could Dina have said something about the day in the church? Cap felt his face about to go on fire.

—You're jealous she's mine, that's why you went against me. I'm right – amn't I right?

—No, I'm very happy for you, Gerry.

—You're not happy for me, you hate me.

—Gerry, you've always been my best friend. I want you to be happy.

It may have been that in the deepest recesses of his soul Cap blamed his friend for taking Dina from him. He didn't know what he felt.

Gerry stabbed the air with his finger.

—Stay away from Dina and stay away from me.

—You're drunk, Gerry. Let's talk about this in the morning.

—I'm finished with you. No more talk – finished.

Gerry started to walk down the street, and one half of Cap wanted to run after him and say something that would heal the rift. The other half wanted to let him go, because if Cap revealed his true feelings about Dina it would cast a shadow over his friend's marriage and might kill their friendship anyway. There was only so much lying a person could do. He held his ground and let Gerry go. It was a decision that would have a profound impact on the rest of his life.

The aquanauts dispute tore the docks apart. Some say it was the beginning of the end of Dublin as a dockers' port. In its wake, the stevedores started to divert cargo through other ports, notably Drogheda, Arklow and Waterford. Gerry Sugrue never spoke to Cap Coyle again. They went back to work (having finally agreed to pay for their wet gear), but it was never the same. Cap sang out cargo but his heart wasn't in it. Gerry Sugrue treated him like he didn't exist. As a kid, he'd saved Cap from the bullies; now it felt like he'd turned into one, albeit a silent one. In the end, Cap took redundancy. With the money, he bought the lease on a lockup, which he called Christy Coyle's Fruit and Veg, but which was only ever known as Cap's.

The oul' wans of the North Wall had never had a singing vegetable man before, a tenor who could make sprouts and parsnips sound like champagne and caviar. Cap's shop became an instant success. They loved him singing out their change and dropping pennies and farthings into their purses with the panache of a Venetian gondolier. Cap's shop became a landmark in Sheriff Street and attracted an ever-increasing clientele.

The one customer Cap prayed would come into the shop was Dina Sugrue. He planned to make peace with her, but, unfortunately, he never got the opportunity. While he waited, the Sugrues sat in their flat and stoked the fires of resentment at his success. In the end, it was Dina who came up with the idea of giving him a drop of his own medicine.

Ten months after Cap's opening, Dina got her hands on a broken-down two-storey house in Dowdall's Lane. It had no electricity, no upstairs window panes and no water, but she was too anxious to damage her competitor to worry too much. With little more than a sweeping-brush and some candles, she readied the place. She hand-painted a sign and

Gerry nailed it to the wall over the door: 'Get Fresh', it read. Dina liked its double meaning. She was spoiling for a fight, and this was her public announcement to Cap Coyle that she was taking him on.

The war they'd started raged on for years, with Dina moving in over the shop so she could keep it open till midnight. It was the beginning of the end of her marriage to Gerry, who stayed living in the flats. Love had long since deserted their relationship, although their mutual hatred for Cap had held it together a few years beyond its best-by date.

While Cap and Dina warred, the community around them fell apart. In the days when Cap had sung out his cargo, upwards of five thousand men had worked on the docks. By 1973, the number of full-time dockers had dwindled to fifty-seven. In Sheriff Street alone, the post office, two butcher shops, two newsagents, two sweet shops, three public houses and a chemist's shop all closed their doors. Only a pub and the two vegetable shops survived. By the early nineties, when Dina and Cap had both turned sixty-five, there was no living to be made from vegetables any more. Many of the old stock had moved out of the area and it was fast becoming a ghost town.

Then Cap's closest friend, Mucky Mannion, had a stroke. When he got out of the hospital, Mucky came into the shop with a walking-stick and told Cap he was mad.

—That stroke's taught me something, Cap. These are hard times and you have to look after yourself. And let others look after you, too, if they're offering.

Eventually, Mucky persuaded Cap to accompany him to the convent for his dinner. They made their way at a more than leisurely pace, but when they got there, Cap nearly had a heart attack. Dina Sugrue was sitting at one of the tables.

Cap had kept tabs on her over the years, of course he had, but always from a distance. It was strange to be in the same room as her, eating the same food, from the same kitchen, the same pot; drinking the same tea, from the same cups, stored in the same presses. He thought about leaving, but he didn't want her to think she intimidated him. They were free dinners and he was as entitled to be there as she was.

Having survived one day and been the recipient of four nourishing courses of food, Cap decided he'd be mad to stay away. He made the Day Centre part of his daily routine, and at the same time kept a safe distance between himself and Dina.

Now he had made a total fool of himself by messing up the song. He'd looked at her just as he had in the church, and she'd turned him to jelly. Everyone had seen it, his friends and enemies alike. He was mortified. He'd made an ass of himself in front of Dina – the last thing on earth he'd wanted to do.

4

Philo was sorry she hadn't entered the convent at fifteen. She'd be a nun by now. As it was, she was in limbo – married with five children, and holed up trying to get away from them. She'd chosen that over a nervous breakdown. She wasn't sorry. Everyone deserved peace, however they got it. It wasn't too late for her. The war was over as far as she was concerned. She wasn't getting back into the ring with Tommo, no matter what.

She thought about Cap and Dina. They'd been at it for over forty years. That was longer than Philo had been on this earth. It sickened her to think a war could go on that long. At least they'd never had to live together, that was some consolation. She'd had to endure Tommo, forever wanting to get up on her and put his thing inside her. She'd thought her growing weight might put him off, but it only seemed to increase his sex drive. He used to fantasise that she was Tina Turner. He told her that one night when he was drunk – told her to hurt her feelings, but she was beyond all that. The one thing that did upset her was when he called her names in front of the children. She found that hard to stomach.

Her main aim was to hold on in the convent for as long as she could. She sat on the bed with the form in her hand. It felt worse than being back at school. It was impossible, in Philo's experience, to answer questions truthfully on a form. Her suspicious nature had been nurtured by the welfare system, where the simplest questions came fully loaded. Every answer was a potential bomb waiting to explode in your face.

She bit her pen and looked at the first question. *Discuss your relationship with God.* She had no idea where to start on that one. Her gaze went down to the second question. *Discuss your relationship with your parents.* She could have written a book on that, but she didn't have enough space. The next one was even worse. *Discuss your relationship with significant others.* That was too painful to go into. There were lots of significant others but Philo couldn't think about them right now. She had to look after herself; that was why she was here. Why did it always have to be about others? Why couldn't it be about her for a change?

She got so agitated she couldn't write a thing. Her brain was a colander and she couldn't hold an idea for more than ten seconds. She thought if she could sleep, an angel might appear to her and guide her. Hadn't the same thing happened when Our Lady was instructed to get pregnant? Philo didn't want to end up pregnant, no matter who the baby was for – and that included God. No part of her body was entering into the deal, end of story.

Philo knew she wouldn't sleep without food. Hard as she tried to put it out of her mind, the thought of the kitchen kept sneaking back in. In the end, she knew she would go mad if she didn't do something. She felt she would die if she denied herself food. She closed her eyes and thought about death.

Philo's favourite funeral was her own. She loved to picture her remains coming into the church and all the people shaking hands with her parents, telling them what a great woman she was. Her death was worth it, just to see the look on her father's face. Every time someone paid her a compliment, Philo whispered in his ear:

—Now, are you listening to that?

She loved egging him on and increasing his mortification.

—Say something nice about your eldest child, go on.

—She was a good daughter to me.

—Good? Is that all you can manage?

—She was a great daughter to me.

—That's a bit better.

—I don't know what I'm going to do without her.

—You dirty lying hypocrite, you never had a good word to say about her when she was alive.

After the funeral, it was back to the house for tea and sandwiches.

Food was Philo's obsession. Her craving for it infiltrated her whole being and had to be satisfied. Even in the convent, where she had no proprietorial rights on the kitchen, she felt she had no choice but to raid the fridge. She had to make the craving stop. She could delay it, but all that would achieve was a postponement of the inevitable. To put it off risked even greater gorging when she finally caved in. Over the years, Philo had learned that the best way to control her obsession was to satisfy it.

She made her way along creaky corridors. It felt as if God Himself were asleep. The large institutional kitchen was cold and unwelcoming. To counteract this, Philo lit the four gas rings with the sparker and turned them up to full power, then lit the oven and left the door open. Then it was straight to the fridge to see what was on offer.

There was enough milk to feed the babies of Ireland, but that wasn't much good to someone who needed a fix of meat. She pulled aside carton after carton until she hit the jackpot. It was a white paper packet, which she immediately suspected came from a butcher's shop. She opened it and there was layer upon layer of streaky back rashers. Beside them was a proud family of pork sausages, holding hands. It was produce from Kearns's Butchers in Parnell Street.

In next to no time she had eight sausages, six strips of bacon, two eggs and four tomatoes sizzling away in a pan of hot lard. While they were cooking, she threw the excess milk into a bowl of flour and made up a pancake mix. She'd let that sit for at least twenty minutes before introducing it to the pan. Next in would be the white bread, which would soak up the meat and tomato juices before it turned a crispy golden-brown.

Philo was salivating when she heard footsteps in the corridor outside. She ran to the kitchen door to lock it, but it didn't have a bolt or a key. She ran back to the cooker and took the pan in her hand. She turned around to see where she could hide it, and in that hiatus the door opened and Sister Rosaleen stood there, frozen in time like a photograph. They looked at each other in wonderment.

—Would you like a sausage? Philo said.

—Where did you get them? Did they come out of the fridge?

—No, I won them in a lucky bag.

—A lucky bag? Where did you get a lucky bag?

—I'm only joking. They came out of the fridge. I opened the door and they marched out and hopped into the pan. Will I put one on for you?

—That's tomorrow's dinner you're eating.

—There's loads left. I only took a few, look.

Philo held the pan out to her. Sister Rosaleen counted the sausages and rashers: eight of one and six of the other. It was a fair dent in the following day's supply.

—I can put them back, no problem to me; I don't have to eat them, Philo said.

It was a gargantuan lie. The sausages and rashers were covered in grease. There was no way they could be retrieved and used in a coddle, where the ingredients were boiled in water to make a stew – coddle was a great Dublin dish and a favourite among the old folks. Philo did her best to appear unconcerned at the fate of her fry, but she wasn't about to turn her back on the feast. She was a lioness with the scent of blood in her nostrils.

—You have to eat it now that it's cooked, Sister Rosaleen said. You can't put it back in the fridge.

—I can whip this off and put it on a plate, won't cost me a thought.

—Can you imagine if they were found in the fridge tomorrow? We'd have World War Three.

In the urge to satisfy her craving, Philo had forgotten about Hatchet-Face herself, Miss Somers. After two days in the kitchen, she knew how much of a tyrant Miss Somers was. It was possible she had the sausages and rashers counted. If so, there was only one solution.

—I'll go up to Parnell Street in the morning and replace these, Philo said.

—You will not. I'll take the blame if there's any trouble.

—No, you're not getting into trouble over my greedy gut, no way.

Philo scooped the fry to one side and threw the bread into the centre of the pan. She shook it over the flames and thought of hell. Some day she might end up there. She didn't mind; she'd put up with it as long as they had Kearns's sausages and rashers.

—I have something for you, Sister Rosaleen said, changing her tone completely. It sounded girlish to Philo's ears. She looked across at her and saw the hint of a bold smile.

—What is it?

—Guess.

—I haven't a clue.

—Guess.

—Is it something you can eat? A bar of chocolate?

—No, it's not chocolate.

—I'm not going to go through every type of food. Tell me.

—It's not food. You can put it in your mouth but it's not food.

Philo thought of toothpaste, which was the only thing she put in her mouth and didn't swallow.

—Do I have bad breath? Philo asked.

—You don't have bad breath, no.

—Why are you giving me toothpaste, so?

—I'm not giving you toothpaste, I'm giving you these.

Sister Rosaleen pulled a packet of cigarettes from her habit. She held them in the palm of her hand. There was a sparkle where the light caught the cellophane. Philo took the gift in her hand, like she'd never encountered the wonder of a cigarette pack before. The wonder wasn't in the pack, of course; it was in the act of love that had brought it to her.

—Where did you get these?

Her question went unanswered for a long while. She'd eaten her fry and was onto her fourth pancake before the truth finally emerged. Sister Rosaleen had gone to the oratory chapel and borrowed from Saint Joseph. In other words, she'd stolen his collection box. Then she'd left the convent and procured the cigarettes in a public house. In the process, she'd broken her vows of poverty and obedience. She'd also broken her vow of silence, but she didn't care. It was her way of saying thanks for the best day she'd had since becoming a nun.

Philo had never received an unconditional gift in her life. It felt strange not having to give something in return. She felt like she was worth something just for who she was. Her only experience of love was with her children, and that was different. Sex was supposed to be love but was usually a disaster. Sometimes she closed her eyes and imagined Tommo was George Clooney, but it didn't last long; the feeling of disgust was only ever the blink of an eye away. In fifteen years of marriage, Tommo had never bought her a bunch of flowers or a packet of cigarettes. The contrast with Sister Rosaleen, whom she'd known for two days, was startling.

Philo lit up and sucked the smoke down to her lungs. It felt better than an orgasm. She offered Sister Rosaleen a drag.

—You might as well be hung for a sheep as a lamb.

Sister Rosaleen refused at first and then threw caution to

the wind. She pulled on the cigarette and nearly coughed her guts up. She made a vow never to smoke again. Philo pointed out that she was good at breaking vows.

They sat in the kitchen until two in the morning, drinking tea and smoking. They went back over the day and talked about the future. They agreed the sing-song had broken down divisions and brought people together. Philo came up with an idea for a new game. It was so exciting that when they finally went to bed, to sleep on it and think it through, neither of them slept a wink.

They knelt together in the oratory the next morning. Buddy Holly celebrated Mass, but he seemed bored by the miracle of turning the bread and wine into flesh and blood. The late-night revellers, on the other hand, were excited at the prospect of turning the Day Centre into a chapel of love – a place where romance might begin and, with any luck, might end in wedding bells and honeymoons. They had decided to introduce 'Blind Date' to the old folks of the North Wall.

Philo leaned in and whispered in Sister Rosaleen's ear.

—I think you should play the compère.

—I wouldn't know where to start.

—You only have to copy the television. Just do what Cilla Black does.

—Who's Cilla Black?

In that exchange, Philo's fate was sealed. They couldn't have an amateur compère. Following on from her appearance as Tina Turner, she would play the part of Cilla Black.

Immediately after breakfast, Philo headed up town to replace the sausages and rashers. She borrowed Sister Rosaleen's overcoat and wore a black headscarf tight against her skull, turning her into a cross between a widow and a nun. She didn't want to be recognised. It was stupid, really, because she couldn't disguise who she was. Even as half a nun, she was one hundred per cent Philo.

She sauntered up Talbot Street at her ease. She was in no hurry; it was early and most of the shops were still asleep. At the top of North Earl Street, she turned right into O'Connell Street and headed towards Parnell Street. A group of cleaners were huddled at the glass doors of the Savoy cinema. Like most buildings on the main street of Dublin city, it had been given a plastic awning that took away from its grandeur and broke up the streetscape.

—How are you, Philo? someone said as she passed.

—I'm grand, Philo said, and kept walking. She could never walk through Dublin incognito.

The Savoy cinema put an idea into her head. A prize for Blind Date: two tickets in the back row of a Sunday night – very romantic. Maybe they could throw in a meal as well – next door in the Gresham Hotel, where else? Champagne on arrival, followed by a candlelit dinner. The Gresham was the oldest lodging-house on the north side. It boasted an old-world charm and was still much loved by the natives.

Philo was standing in the foyer of the Gresham, asking to see the manager, before she realised it. She was supposed to be reining in the impulsive side of her personality, but here she was letting it loose in O'Connell Street. When the manager came out, Philo explained her mission. She trotted out her demand and in return offered him the prayers of an entire convent – prayers, she assured him, that other hotels were queuing up for. Philo then launched into a history of the North Wall, and the manager had to interrupt her four times before he managed to shut her up.

—My father came from down there, he said. I'd do anything for the area.

He went off and came back two minutes later with a voucher in an envelope. Philo couldn't believe it had been so easy. She put the envelope in her pocket and kept her hand on it all the way to Parnell Street.

Johnny Hogan was behind the counter in Kearns's when she walked in.

—The dead arose and appeared to many. Where have you been hiding? he said.

—Up in Glasnevin Cemetery. I'm only out for the day. Have to be back in my grave by five o'clock.

Philo knew Johnny Hogan from his beatnik days. He'd been one of the Animal Gang from Corporation Street. She didn't like him. He was supposed to be tough, but he was a yellow bastard like most of them – brave in a gang, where he could hide. Now he didn't even have hair left; he was as bald as a baby's arse.

Philo didn't want him knowing too much about her business. She told him she was looking for bingo prizes and that sausages and rashers were high on her list. He gave her two pounds of sausages and a pound each of back rashers and streaky rashers. She told him he'd never go to hell with all the prayers being said for him. In her heart, she hoped that, wherever he ended up, she was in the opposite place.

She tucked the parcel of food under her arm and set off for the Abbey Theatre. The stage doorman, Pat Cowap, was a second cousin of her mother's. Philo had spent the nicest summer of her childhood on his family's farm and had famously decapitated a chicken with a rock during her stay. She had also learned how to milk a cow, but she'd never had a chance in Dublin to demonstrate her prowess. Philo figured that summer was the last time she could remember being truly innocent.

The Abbey Theatre, with its faded yellow bricks and complete absence of windows, looked like a nuclear shelter. It was the furthest thing from an abbey one could imagine. To the left of the stage door was a bell, and Philo pressed it. Pat Cowap opened the door, delighted to see her. He brought her into the green room and offered her a cup of coffee, which she declined. There was a rough-looking man sitting in a chair opposite; he had his hands across his face and looked like he was in great pain. Philo explained that she was looking for a black mask, the type that covered the eyes and made it impossible to see. Pat wasn't sure, but he set off to make enquiries.

There were leaflets on the coffee table, and Philo picked one up. It was an advertisement for a faith healer. Philo was surprised the Abbey was having such a thing; she'd thought it was just plays and the odd concert. Then she looked over at the rough man and made the connection.

—Are you here to see the faith healer? she asked.

The man dropped his hands and stared at her. He had sad, powerful brown eyes.

—I am the faith healer, he said.

Philo averted her eyes and saw the name 'Brian Friel' on the leaflet.

—Have you had much success, Mr Friel?

—I'm not Mr Friel – he's the author. I'm Dominic O'Neill, the actor. I play the faith healer.

She liked him, now that she could see him – and she'd heard of him, too. Maybe she'd seen him on the television. He was very masculine, the type of man she dreamed about – a George Clooney type, but older. She could definitely believe he was a faith healer and she told him as much. He started to giggle like a little boy, and his eyes lost all their sadness.

—Will you come and see the play? he said.

—I'll be in the front row, on my knees, staring up at you.

Pat Cowap came back into the green room and handed Philo a mask without eye-slits.

—It's silver, he said, that's the only thing.

Philo put it on over her headscarf to test it out. She couldn't see a thing.

—It's perfect, just what the doctor ordered.

Pat Cowap walked her around to the box office on the other side of the building and got her two complimentary tickets for the play. She set off for the convent, delighted with her morning's work.

Things got off to a bad start in the game of Blind Date. It was decided the women should pick first because they outnumbered the men twenty to twelve; it was a strange piece of logic, but sometimes force of numbers has its own moral imperative. The ladies, so called, put their names on pieces of paper and placed them in a hat, and the gentlemen, so called, did likewise in a separate hat. Philo put her hand into the first hat and pulled out a name. She unfurled the piece of paper and looked at the name in block capitals: DINA SUGRUE.

Philo cleared her throat and shouted out:

—Ninna Delargy, come on down.

She decided to make up for the disgraceful way Ninna had been treated the day before. Ninna made her way to the stage (no more than a cleared space at the top of the room) and sat down on the chair provided. Philo pulled the silver mask over her eyes.

—I don't like the dark, Ninna said, and pulled it off.

No amount of cajoling would convince her to play. Philo was only short of strapping her to the chair with ropes. She even bent down to her and divulged the contents of the envelope, all to no avail. Ninna sat where she was and repeated her mantra.

—I don't like the dark.

So Ninna was sent back to play with her Lego, and Philo pulled another name from the hat and looked at it: NAN CASSIDY, the bitch who'd made remarks about her mother's size.

—Dina Sugrue, come on down.

Sometimes two wrongs do make a right. Dina deserved her moment in the spotlight, even if she was a crabby bitch at times. She hobbled to the top of the room, plonked herself on the chair and pulled on the mask, delighted to be blind.

Philo warned the men to keep their mouths shut, to preserve their anonymity. Then she pulled three pieces of paper from the hat containing the names of the gentlemen. She opened the first one and read the name to herself – MUCKY MANNION. She pointed at him and waved him to a seat on the stage. Second to be picked was BARNEY HUGHES, the Commandant, who marched to the top of the room with the air of a man who had expected to be chosen. Third out of the hat was CAP COYLE, and when Philo pointed him out, he seemed reluctant to take his seat. In the end he made the long walk, secure in the knowledge that there was no chance he'd be chosen for the date.

Philo asked Dina for her first question. With hardly a pause, she shouted it out like she'd been rehearsing it for weeks.

—The only exercise I get is running up and down the stairs to my customers. What's your favourite exercise?

There was an expectant silence, broken by Philo, who roared at her.

—Who's that question for, Dina?

—That's for Number One.

Philo walked over to Mucky and bent down so he could whisper his answer to her. When he'd finished, Philo stood up and faced Dina.

—He says his favourite exercise is riding. He likes ... riding.

—That's very crude, Dina said. I don't like that.

There was embarrassed laughter all around the hall. Philo raised her hand, demanding silence.

52

—You have awful dirty minds. He's talking about horses: he likes riding horses.

Philo went over to the Commandant and solicited his answer. She turned to Dina.

—Number Two likes the firing range. He likes to shoot at the target and hit the bull's eye. I don't know if he fires blanks or the real thing, though.

She went back to the Commandant for clarification.

—You're safe, Dina, he only fires blanks.

—You've a filthy mind, Philo, Dina said.

Cap whispered his answer to her. She faced Dina for the third time.

—Number Three likes to swim. He's been at it since he was a kid. In the Liffey, the Canal, you name it – he's swum in them all. I'm sure he's gone skinny-dipping, too. Have you gone in your birthday suit, Number Three?

Cap shook his head vigorously.

—You're safe, Dina, he doesn't do skinny-dipping.

—Thank God for that.

The tension was mounting in the hall. Sister Rosaleen was glad she'd declined to compère the game. Philo was doing a great job. Her ability to make double meanings from innocent remarks had generated great excitement among the old folk. In their ordinary lives they were denied the right to be sexual beings; Philo, by making innuendo out of nothing, had restored that right to them. They couldn't wait for the climax, when Dina would choose her date.

Philo asked her for her second question.

—I suffer from room-or-toyed arthuritis. What ailments do you have and are they serious?

—You're looking for a boyfriend, Dina, not an undertaker, Philo said.

—I want to know if I'm getting a crock or not.

They all answered the question and gave themselves a

clean bill of health, leaving Dina no wiser than before. Philo issued a dire warning.

—You're down to your last question, don't waste this one!

Dina adjusted her position on the chair and stuck her chest out, delighted that she still had features to be proud of.

—I've never been on an aeroplane and I don't know that I want to fly. What would you do to make me? And that's for Number Three.

—Hold on a sec, Philo interrupted. It's much more likely you'll be getting a bleedin' bus for your date than a bleedin' aeroplane.

—There's no need for bad language.

Philo wanted to send her into orbit. Just a little uppercut under the chin, to send her out of the earth's atmosphere. She had to restrain herself. She thought of Cilla Black and she knew that Cilla would never do a thing like that – not in public, anyway.

—I like you, Dina, she said, not a lot, but I do like you. Now, do you still want to ask the stupid question about the aeroplane?

—Yes, I do.

Cap whispered his answer to Philo.

—Number Three says he's never been on an aeroplane himself, so you could just hold hands and be frightened together.

A spontaneous burst of applause rose up from the hall. It was a tender remark, certainly, but it was more its unexpectedness that drew the reaction. The suggestion that their hands would meet and intertwine struck a chord in the audience, even though it was fantasy.

—Number Two says he'd hold your hand, too.

There were howls from the audience; they figured the Commandant was trying to ingratiate himself by copying Cap. Philo had a hard time restoring order.

—Shut up for a minute, you shower of bastards – sorry.... Philo searched for an alternative word.

—We are a shower of bastards! someone shouted up from the hall.

—I'm not a bastard; speak for yourself! someone else shouted.

As the comments flew forwards and backwards across the hall, Philo solicited another response from the Commandant.

—He says he'd share a naggin of brandy with you, or as much brandy as it took to make you go asleep.

The old folks weren't convinced; they gave the answer no more than a lukewarm clap. The Commandant was taken aback and threw a dirty look at Cap, who shrugged his shoulders.

—Number One says that if you didn't want to get on an aeroplane, it wouldn't bother him. He'd just cash in the tickets and take you on the ferry instead.

The answer got thunderous applause. It was hard to know what Dina was making of all this from behind her silver mask. She seemed very still; maybe that was the result of her temporary blindness. Philo pointed out to her that it was time to make up her mind. The audience started to shout their preferences. The majority of voices were calling out for Number One and Number Two. When the shouting died down, Joxer Farrell stood up in his place.

—What's wrong with Number Three? he wanted to know.

The room burst into laughter. Cap stood up and took a mock bow. That only served to make people laugh even more. Philo restored order with a withering look.

—Do you want Number One, the ferryman? Or is it Number Two, naggin-of-brandy himself? Or do you want Number Three, the man who'd hold your hand? The decision is all yours, Dina.

Dina rose and a great hush descended.

—I was going to go for Number Two....

—Sit down, Dina, Philo said. We don't want the why, we just want the number, do you understand that?

—Yes, I understand that. I'm sorry.

—So who's it going to be? One, Two or Three?

—I'm going to pick Number Three.

There was a silence, and then the room erupted. It was as if some world tragedy had taken place – the assassination of a president, the death of a pope, the outbreak of a war. People felt they had to talk to each other, as if by talking they reassured themselves they were still alive. Dina Sugrue had just chosen Cap Coyle for her blind date. What did this mean for the vegetable war?

Dina pulled off the silver mask and looked across the stage. She found it hard to adjust to the light; she saw only three blurred figures. She wiped her eyes until they came into focus.

—Who's Number Three? she said.

Cap raised his hand slowly, in acknowledgement. Dina remembered the day he'd asked her out on behalf of Gerry Sugrue. Was this the chance to unravel the past and make a different map of the future? Was it an opportunity to heal a wound or to prise it apart and make it bleed even more?

Philo offered the envelope to Dina.

—Who wants to read out where you're going on your date?

Dina looked across at Cap.

—I can't go out with him.

—I can't go out with her.

—I'm only going to say this once. God is watching you; he's watching the pair of you.

Philo turned to the audience and willed them to clap, which they did. She turned once again to Dina and offered her the envelope.

—He's the one taking me; let him read it out.

She swivelled around and offered it to Cap.

—It's the lady's privilege to read the card, he said.

—What do you pair think I am, a carousel? Philo said.

She ripped open the envelope and pulled the voucher from it.

—First off you're going to the Abbey Theatre to see *Faith Healer*.

—What faith healer? they asked together.

—Don't worry, he won't put his hands near you; it's a play. After the Abbey you're going to the Gresham Hotel for a champagne dinner, followed by bed and breakfast for the night.

There were lots of oohs and aahs from the old folk.

—You'll be in separate rooms, of course. The only thing you have to do is come back here and tell us how you got on. That's assuming you don't kill each other.

It was hard to imagine such a public reconciliation taking place. It would have been more believable had they taken out guns and opened fire on each other. It was on the cards they'd both die on the date. Cap might strangle her or Dina might poison him. Instead of coming back to talk about the date, they might be coming back in coffins.

Still, it couldn't have turned out better for Philo. It was a perfect day, almost – until she looked down the back of the room and saw a man standing there. He waved at her and her feet turned to jelly. She grabbed hold of Sister Rosaleen.

—Save me, Sister – oh, please, save me.

Sister Rosaleen couldn't believe Philo was so frightened.

—What's the matter with you? You're shaking!

—That man down the end of the room is here to kidnap me. He's violent … please save me.

Sister Rosaleen did her utmost to convince Philo no one was going to kidnap her, but she was in no mood to be convinced.

—Who is he? Sister Rosaleen asked. Who is he?

Philo closed her eyes and shook her head. She couldn't talk.

—Tell me who he is! Tell me, Philo!

Philo said something, but it was such a mumble Sister Rosaleen couldn't make it out.

—You'll have to speak up. Who is he?

After a struggle, Philo got her voice back to an audible level.

—He's my husband.

—That man is your husband?

—Don't let him take me out of here, please don't let him take me.

Tommo Nolan was well built, square as the lorry he drove for Corrigan Transport. He was good-looking in the way that boxers sometimes are; he had a flat nose and a cauliflower ear that made him look like a man who'd been to war. The truth was he'd never been inside a boxing ring in his life, and the flat nose was inherited from his father. Tommo loved himself too much ever to put his life at risk. He had great stubble that made him look manly, and he had used it all his life to devastating effect.

As the old folks began to disperse, he walked confidently up the room. Philo grabbed Sister Rosaleen in a vice-grip.

Tommo smiled at the two women.

—I won't beat about the bush. I want you to come home, Philo, he said.

—I can't do that, I'm studying to become a nun.

He gave a little laugh and stifled it just as quickly. He knew her well enough to know when she was serious. Fifteen years of marriage had taught him that much. Philo took a step to get past him, but he easily moved to block her path. As he did, he noticed the tattoo on her arm, the bunch of flowers in the centre of the heart where his name used to be.

—I see you've blocked my name out, he said.

—It's in honour of the Sacred Heart.

—When did you get that done?

—I had it done in England. I'm only back.

Tommo reached out and grabbed her by the upper arms.

58

—Please, let her go, Sister Rosaleen said.

—I want you back, Philo. The kids want you back. We're a family, all of us together; that's how it's supposed to be.

—Where are your children? Sister Rosaleen asked, dumbfounded.

Philo could see the look of horror on the nun's face.

—She abandoned them and she abandoned me, Tommo said bitterly.

Philo pushed Tommo's hands away and ran out of the room. She ran down the corridor and up the back stairs. She opened the hatch that led to the back of the altar and crawled in. It had been almost a perfect day, and God had gone and spoiled it on her, just like he'd done so many times before. She put her head in her hands and cursed God for making a poxbottle of her, just when it seemed things were about to change for the better.

5

Dina had nothing in her wardrobe for going to the Abbey Theatre. She had only been inside the building once, and that had been at eleven o'clock in the morning when she'd needed to go to the toilet and happened to be passing by. She saw people going into it at night and they were all swank, fur coats and dickie bows and what have you. She didn't want to feel out of place because of wearing the wrong thing, and there wasn't much chance of her fitting in when she didn't have anything at all to wear, apart from the rags she stood up in. She was a vegetable woman and her wardrobe reflected that.

She cursed Philo for putting her in this position. Why did she have to start up a game of Blind Date? Had Dina been thinking, she could have put a false name down on the piece of paper and avoided this catastrophe. Bad luck to Philo for pulling her name out of the hat – and if there was worse bad luck available, Dina wished it on herself for picking Number Three. How could she have been so smug, sitting behind the anonymity of her silver mask, thinking she was having a great time when she was about to make the worst mistake of her life? Had she picked either of the other two, she'd have gone to the Abbey Theatre in her pyjamas and wouldn't have cared. But this was Cap Coyle she was going out with, Public Enemy Number One, and she'd rather die than give him a valid reason to criticise her.

There had been a time when she'd thought him boyfriend material. He was an innocent back then, and that was unusual on the docks, where most of the men were hard men. Dina knew she only had to stick her chest out to solicit fawning stares; Cap wasn't a gawker, and that appealed to her. He was shy, which was very attractive. She imagined she could teach him lots of tricks, and when he performed them, she would reward him and keep him loyal. He was cuddly and playful, like a pup, with not a hint of malice in him.

Short of writing out a manifesto that declared, 'I fancy you,' Dina couldn't inveigle Cap into asking her out. She told him she would love to feed the ducks in Saint Stephen's Green, and he offered to give her any leftover bread he had. The back row of the pictures came in for a mention, too, but he said he needed to sit up near the front because of his eyesight. She told him no one sat in the back row to look at the screen, and he changed the subject to variety shows, saying he preferred live performances to the cinema. He was so innocent he was delicious. She could have listened to him for hours – but she wanted a date first. In the end he did ask for one, but it was on behalf of his friend; and, in frustration, Dina said yes.

She fancied Cap, even after she married Gerry, and then things changed. Oh, how the worm turned. He sold his soul to the stevedores. He turned his back on Gerry and her and went with those who were trying to destroy the docks. Dina was so angry, she could have killed him. One Friday evening, she marched around to his fancy house on Coburg Place with only one thing on her mind – murder. Her youngest son, Brendan, was in the pram; he was ten months old at the time. She intended to put her hands on Cap's neck and choke him, but when he came to the door, he had a bar of chocolate in his hand for the baby. He held it out to Brendan and she slapped his hand away, full force.

—We don't want your chocolate! she shouted.

It flew out of Cap's hand and crashed against the wall. Dina raised her other hand and slapped him hard, across the face. He moved back and fell over the doorstep, landing on his backside in the hall.

—That's for what you done to my family, she said, and there's more where that came from.

The baby burst into hysterical crying, which added to the atmosphere of recrimination. It probably saved Cap from further violence, too.

—Don't cry, he's not worth it, Dina said. He's not worth one of your tears, son.

Her words, if anything, made the baby worse. Dina didn't care. He had his whole life to get over it. She wanted him to have a future. She wanted it to be on the Dublin docks, but she wasn't sure that was possible any more; no one was, after everything that had happened....

Dina shook the memory out of her head and looked at the racks of clothes in her wardrobe. There was a pink suit she'd bought for her grand-niece's wedding a couple of years back. She took it down and looked at it. She reckoned it was four years since she'd bought it (it was, in fact, ten years old) and the last time she'd worn it had been on a day pilgrimage to Knock with the Day Centre. Cap Coyle hadn't been on that trip, so chances were he hadn't seen her in it before. She draped it over the end of the bed and ruffled the skirt.

Someone came into the shop and shouted up the stairs.

—Come down here, Dina, I need carrots and onions for a stew.

—I'm closed. Come back tomorrow.

—You can't be closed; your door is open.

—Well, I am closed.

—What am I supposed to tell him when there's no dinner?

—Same as you told him the last time.

—Do you want it on your conscience if I get two black eyes?

—Go on, take what you need and pay me tomorrow.

—You'll get your reward in heaven, Dina.

—Well, I certainly won't get it here on earth.

It was Cissie Kennedy. After six o'clock and she didn't

have his bit of dinner on. Typical.... Dina was falling for the pink suit. It was slightly see-through. She'd have to wear something under it – a nice slip, maybe. There was a cream one; it had its own box, last seen down the bottom of the wardrobe somewhere. She pulled stuff out to get at it – a pillow, cotton sheets, two lampshades, a jigsaw, a roll and a half of unused wallpaper and a packet of paste – and came across a box, but not the one she was looking for. It was weather-beaten and quite heavy.

She brought it out, put it on the bed and took the lid off. Inside were mementoes of her wedding, photographs mainly. The first one was a black-and-white shot of her and Gerry on the steps of Saint Laurence O'Toole's church. She looked radiant in her royal-blue suit and matching hat with a veil. Her hands were clutching her bouquet like a trophy; she was all colour and life and hope, standing beside her man, the tall groom, Gerry. A second photograph caught her attention. It was Cap as the best man, standing next to her, with Gerry and the bridesmaid, Dina's sister Esther, on the other side. Someone had said something funny, because they were all laughing. It had had something to do with the ring; Cap had thought he'd lost it, until he'd found it hiding in his trouser pocket.

The photographs had occupied the wall over Dina's fireplace for many years, even after the marriage broke up. Then Dina heard Gerry was living with a younger woman, in Ringsend of all places, and she decided she'd had enough. Relegated to the bottom of the wardrobe, they'd stayed hidden with the other relics of her past.

She pushed aside a silk scarf and found a gold all-in-one. It had once been the most daring garment of the lingerie world. It was a bra, slip, knickers and suspenders, all sewn together to make a piece of erotic temptation. Under it was a pair of flesh-coloured nylon stockings with a seam up the back. Dina loved the feel of them in her hand. It brought her back to another life, before age had ravaged her, when she had a figure that made silk underwear tingle.

There was no one alive who could indulge in self-pity quite like Dina. She was the queen of crabby, and when the mood took her, she could make winning the lottery seem like an awful disaster. In such a mood she saw one side of everything, and that was the bad side. She confronted her image in the wardrobe mirror. Why was she going to sleep in the Gresham Hotel when she had a perfectly good bed in her own home?

She started to talk to herself. She put on her worst crabby face but thought it looked too cheerful.

—What are you looking at? she asked.

—That's what I'd like to know, she answered back.

She grabbed the worst-looking jacket she had and held it up to her.

—It looks disgusting.

—Then it's perfect.

She became Jekyll and Hyde by turns and couldn't decide which of them to send out on the date. When she thought about Cap and all he'd done to her, there was no contest. The injustice had been done not solely to her, but to her whole family. The only mystery was why she was going at all.

—You don't have to go.

—You do; you picked him.

Schizophrenia suited Dina. She played all the parts of herself with equal intensity. It was a frightening passion, worthy of the stage. She piled the pink suit onto its hanger and put it back in the wardrobe.

—Why should he see you all dressed up?

—All he deserves is a tramp.

The all-in-one was next. She picked it up off the bed to return it to its coffin. The soft material felt good. How much

64

better would it feel against her skin, against the sensitive parts of her body, her breasts and her groin? She'd always had a soft spot for delicate things.

—It would still look good on you, girl.

—You don't have the figure for lingerie, Missus.

In the mirror, she looked pathetic. The truth was she was riddled with arthritis and would never look good again. It was sad for her to be contemplating what underwear to put on; it was support tights and nappy pads she should be thinking of. She was an old person, going on seventy, a pensioner, deserted wife, abandoned mother, cripple, has-been, might-have-been, past her sell-by date, finished, as good as dead and almost buried. She was feeling sorry for herself, feeling pity strong enough to drink, recrimination strong enough to die for.

—You're as old as you feel, she screamed at herself. As old as you feel.

—You're not dead yet, not by a long way.

She could still make heads turn if she wanted to. Her chest stuck out at the memory, the cheeks of her arse tightened in harmony. Why should she settle for being a tramp when she was a queen? In the old days she could have had her pick of fellas, Cap Coyle included. It was an opportunity to remind him of what he'd missed out on, to give him a whiff of what might have been. Dina could only do that by looking her best.

The pink suit came back out of the wardrobe. She took the nylons and sprinkled them with perfume. Then she put her hand inside them, right down to where her big toe would go. God was talking to her through the lingerie. She knew that because she was at peace. She no longer had a trinity of Dinas inside her head directing her thoughts. She was one person, the parts of her all joined together, just like the all-in-one.

She stepped into the garment and pulled it up over her body, pushing her breasts into the waiting cups. The stockings felt good coming up over her skin. They clung tight and made her legs look curvy in just the right way. She clipped the suspender studs to the tops of her stockings, and it was a beautiful sound and one she hadn't heard in such a long time. The perfume rose up and made her smile. She was twenty-one again, beautiful and free; she was a queen.

Cap chose a trilby. He'd only worn it once before, to midnight Mass the previous Christmas. It had been a present from Mucky. Cap didn't like hats bought for him, because they were so personal and it was difficult to explain one's taste in them. People assumed that, because he wore caps, he liked all caps, which wasn't the case, not by a long shot.

He'd worn caps all his life. Eighty per cent of the body's heat went out through the top of your nut – he'd never forgotten that. To him they were the reason for his lifelong good health. He knew men who got colds every winter; they succumbed in October and didn't shake it off until March. There was one thing these men had in common, and that was the absence of a covering on their delicate heads. Cap never went without, winter or summer.

The only negative aspect was being given hats for presents. People bought hats for Cap and thought they were being highly original. In his time, he'd been bought berets, Scottish Highland caps, Russian fur hats, leather caps, Robin Hood hats, Frank Sinatra, Dean Martin and Sammy Davis Jr hats, woollen caps, flat caps and trilbies. And if someone bought you a hat, they expected to see you wear it, even though you might hate it with a passion. There was no such problem with socks, underpants or vests, because they were hidden. Hats offered no such reprieve. Cap's approach was to let the buyer see him in the hat once, and then put it away for good. He had a whole press full of orphaned caps, enough to start a costume shop.

For the modest man he was, he had an unusually large head. He was a size $7^5/_8$, when most people assumed he was under a 7. He wore three colours only – brown, blue and green – so, more often than not, people got it wrong on at least one count. Mucky was one of the very few who knew his size and colour preference.

The choice of hat was Cap's most important decision. He chose the trilby because it was serious, there was nothing casual about it; it made the right impression. Cap would never have worn it, for example, to go for a drink or a ramble. It had a history, so it would give him something to talk about if the conversation dried up. It was quite possible there would be silences during the evening, especially over the dinner. Conversation wouldn't matter during the play – in fact, it was bad manners to talk during a performance.

Cap had been to the Abbey once before, when it had been in the Queen's Theatre on Pearse Street. It had moved from there to its present home in Abbey Street, and he'd never been in the new theatre. He couldn't remember much about the play he'd seen and didn't recall the title. He had a definite memory of an IRA man hiding in an attic, and the British soldiers – perhaps they were Black and Tans – trying to get information from the landlady as to his whereabouts. Cap had been on the edge of his seat with the tension of it. The actress playing the landlady had been Eileen Crowe. Where had he stored that information all these years? he wondered. It would give him something to talk about if the conversation got difficult. That was two things he had now: the hat and the play in the old Abbey.

Cap stopped at Butler's newsagents on his way past, to buy sweets. His father had brought him to the opera sometimes, and they had always stopped at Butler's for sweets. It was cheaper than the theatre and had a better selection, too. The shop had gone to wrack and ruin over the years, but Cap spotted a nice box of Roses on the top shelf. He ordered them before he realised they might send out the wrong signal. Dina Sugrue was his date, but it wasn't real. The reality was that they hated each other and had done so since the troubles had erupted. Well, maybe it wasn't quite hate; Cap still felt something for her, but he couldn't put it into words. Sweets called 'roses' said too much. He declined the Roses and settled for liquorice allsorts instead. They were good sweets – fine sweets, in his opinion – but there was nothing romantic about them. They were the least romantic sweets in Butler's shop.

He got to the Abbey Theatre at seven o'clock, half an hour early. He and Dina had agreed to meet outside it at half past seven; they were too embarrassed to be seen walking together through the North Wall. Cap chose the main entrance for his first watch. He strode up and down the path, thirty paces each way, like a soldier on the battlements. He gave it ten minutes and then switched to the opposite path, outside the Plough bar. Ten minutes later, he found himself standing at the corner where Abbey Street and Marlborough Street meet, by the Flowing Tide pub. It was a good vantage point and covered all approaches to the theatre. He gave it another ten minutes there before the doubt started to kick in. Perhaps she had gone to the Gate Theatre by mistake. It didn't seem likely, however....

At ten to eight, he decided he'd missed her. She'd arrived at the theatre and slipped in unnoticed. There's a laneway at the side of the building, and people who know the city use it as a shortcut. That was what Dina had done, Cap decided, and so he abandoned his post at the Flowing Tide and bounded into the lobby.

It was packed with patrons. He started to wade through

the sea of bodies in search of her. It was debilitating, staring into people's faces and having to put on a stupid grin. Several people thought he was a programme-seller. He worked the ground floor and headed up the stairs. A portrait of Brendan Behan stared down at him from the wall. As Cap passed beneath it, he was sure he heard Brendan say:

—Chasing skirt at your age? Christ, you'd think you'd get bleedin' sense.

—I'm seventy-two next birthday and I'm not chasing skirt, Cap replied under his breath.

The ushers were telling people to take their seats. Cap was in a lather; he could feel the trilby glued to his head with sweat. He made one last foray out onto the street, ran down to the river and looked along the north quays as far as the Custom House. There was no sign of Dina. He went back to the theatre. It was just gone eight o'clock. He explained his predicament to an officious-looking woman with a walkie-talkie in her hand. She asked him for a description.

—She's a small woman with a.... He was about to say 'crabby', but he stopped himself. With a lovely old face and blonde hair to here.

He put his hand up to his shoulder. The woman advised him to take his seat and said they would keep an eye out for her.

Cap couldn't concentrate on the play, with the drama going on in his head. Dina had had a run of customers and couldn't close the shop – that seemed hard to believe. She'd eaten something bad and had diarrhoea – that, too, seemed lame. She'd had a crisis of faith and didn't want to come, just like the man in the play. Cap was praying for a miracle. He wanted Dina to walk into the theatre, take her seat and tell him she was sorry for being late. The longer the play went on, the less likely that scenario became.

Cap looked at the faith healer disintegrating on the stage and knew exactly how he felt. He'd been foolish to believe, that was all. It was a fantasy. The real world was a tough, hard place. By the end of Act I, all Cap wanted to do was go home and get back into his comfortable trench.

As Philo sat in the Reverend Mother's office, asylum was the only thing she could think about. It used to have a bad meaning, a house for the insane, but now it had a good meaning: shelter.

—I want asylum, Sister Monica, she said.

—You wanted to be a nun up until an hour ago.

—I know that, but I want asylum now.

She could never be a nun after Tommo had turned up. Married women were not allowed take vows. She was not eligible on any level. In fact, you couldn't get more ineligible than she was.

—You'll have to grant me asylum.

—You have five children to look after.

—I know that, Sister.

—You can't abandon your children.

There was that awful word, the one word Philo didn't want to hear. She tried to close her ears to it. She'd run away in order to save them.

—Your children need you, they need their mother.

Her home was a boxing ring. Up every day to another twelve rounds. In the red corner, Tommo Nolan, and in the blue corner, Philo and the kids.

—What are your children's names? Sister Monica asked.

Philo didn't want to say. If she named them, she'd see them, and if she saw them, she'd get upset. It was part of her survival strategy, not to see them. She'd practised it to perfection. If the thought of one of them entered her brain, she replaced that thought with a corresponding food. So for Jack, her eldest, she thought of jam; for Eileen, it was Easter eggs; Thomas became toast; Josie turned into jacket

70

potatoes; and Philomena, the youngest, was fresh fruit. Once Philo's obsession kicked in, thoughts of the children receded and the food took over. More than once, she had thanked God for the obsession that saved her from madness.

—What are their names? Sister Monica asked again.

—Well, the eldest is Jam –

—Jam? What an unusual name.

—No, sorry, Jack – Jam is a sort of a nickname. Then there's Eileen, Thomas, Josie and Philomena, who's called after me.

—Who's minding them now? Is it their father?

—That bollix is certainly not looking after them.

—They're not at home, then?

—He dumped them in Goldenbridge Orphanage.

Sister Monica had worked there, so memories of the place and of the children she'd looked after came flooding back. The Flynns from Kimmage, three curly-haired boys, ten, eight and six, steps of stairs – the youngest, David, with a cleft palate ... she remembered them with great affection.

—Why did you abandon them? she asked.

Philo would have preferred it if Sister Monica had scalded her with hot water or stuck a knife in her chest.

—I'd prefer if you didn't say that word.

—What word?

—The A-word.

—Abandon.

Philo nodded.

—I never wanted to leave them, but what was I to do? They were in danger. At least now they're safe.

Sister Rosaleen brought in a tray and looked over at Philo, all kindness. She poured out tea and handed the cups around. Sister Monica put a spoon of sugar in her tea, which was unusual – she normally only indulged on Christmas Day; the other three hundred and sixty-four days of the year, she offered it up for the lost souls. Philo took four biscuits and put three sugars in her tea. She crossed her fingers, waiting for an answer to her asylum plea. If it went against her, she'd end up back in hell.

—Is that husband of mine still here? she asked.

—He's sitting in the corridor, Sister Rosaleen said.

—Offer him a cup of tea, Sister Monica said.

—Make sure you don't spill it all over his lap, Philo said, and winked at her accomplice.

Sister Monica felt the sugar seep into her blood like a drug. She looked at Philo, mother of five, who'd come to take the veil – however bizarre that seemed – and had turned her convent upside down. Sister Monica wondered what she could do to help Philo put the fragments of her life back together, and as she wondered, she prayed for spiritual guidance to help her make the right decision.

Cap was furious that Dina had stood him up. He was so angry that he went, unawares, into the ladies' toilet of the Flowing Tide. A woman came out of a cubicle and saw him adjusting his hat in the mirror; she reported him to the bar staff, and he was asked to leave. He drained what remained of his pint in one gulp, slammed the glass on the counter and told them they could stuff their pub up their arses. It was most unlike Cap.

He set off down the north quays with destruction in his heart. As he passed the Custom House, an innocent seagull flew over his head and landed on the wall by the river. It gave a squawk that annoyed the hell out of Cap. He put his hand in his pocket, took out a liquorice allsort and threw it full force at the unsuspecting bird. It would have done damage had it connected, but Cap felt no tinge of remorse. He was not himself.

At the corner of Commons Street, his foot brushed against a rock. He walked on a few paces before he stopped, went back, picked it up and put it in his pocket. It would come in handy for breaking windows. No one was going to make a fool of him that easy. It was hard to believe he, a pacifist, was feeling this way, and it brought him right back to the aquanauts dispute. All his life, he'd sought out peace, but tonight he wanted war. He'd gone to a great deal of trouble and Dina had walked all over him. She'd trampled his emotions and dented his pride. She'd made him feel small, very small, and it was thanks to her he'd been barred from a pub. She wanted war, and he'd give it to her – he'd give it to her once and for all, to a finish.

He turned into Dowdall's Lane and felt he was stepping into No Man's Land. His gait shortened and he became fearful that at any moment he could step on a landmine and disintegrate. To his surprise, the door to the shop was open. He called out in a low voice.

—Anyone there? Anyone at home?

He stepped inside. Everything was familiar. It was a vegetable shop, just like his own. The produce was the same. The potatoes were Pinks and Queens – but they were hand grenades, too. This was enemy territory. The turnips were cannonballs and the cauliflowers were men's skulls.

Forty years of war and it was the first time he'd stood in her shop. He looked at the shelves, makeshift but ordered. There were mushrooms, carrots, onions, parsnips, Brussels sprouts, parsley and thyme. Five minutes and he could destroy this. It would just take his hands; five out-of-control minutes and he could reduce it to pulp, one vegetable seller to another.

He deferred that pleasure and headed up the stairs. On the landing, he pushed open a door to reveal the bedroom. There was a pink suit lying on the bed. Beside it was a box of what looked like photographs. The wardrobe door was open; Cap stepped into the room and jumped with fright when he saw his reflection in the mirror.

—Who's there? a voice asked, and he scuttled down the stairs like a frightened cat.

Halfway down, he realised the voice was Dina's. It had sounded like it was coming out of the wardrobe. What was she doing in there? He tiptoed back up.

—Is that you, Dina? he enquired.

He heard a sound. It was a low, pitiful moan.

—What are you doing in the wardrobe?

—I need help, came the reply.

He couldn't believe she was in there. He approached the wardrobe, and, as he did, he heard a moan from the other side of the bed. Dina was lying on the floor. Cap saw her legs first, nyloned and still, and then her lingerie-clad body. He was too embarrassed to do anything. She looked broken and hurt, like a discarded doll, and he didn't know what to do.

—Get me help, please…. I can't feel my legs.

He looked around the room as if the answer might be written on the walls. He wanted to lift her onto the bed, but a voice inside told him not to.

—Go around to the convent and get help.

—I think I should call an ambulance. How long have you been lying here, Dina?

—Just go to the convent, please.

Cap ran all the way to the convent. Sister Rosaleen let him in. He was out of breath and could barely talk.

—Hello, I need help, he said. Is Philo here?

Sister Rosaleen brought him to the office, where they interrupted the asylum hearing. Cap spluttered out his story, through a panic that was increasing by the second.

—Did you call an ambulance? Philo asked.

—She wouldn't let me.

—Call an ambulance, Sister Monica, Philo ordered. She was heading out the door when Sister Rosaleen blocked her path.

—Your husband is downstairs.

—That bollix is still here!

—Go out the back way, Sister Monica said as she picked up the phone.

The rescue party slipped out the back door and avoided Tommo. Philo led the charge down the street, followed by Sister Rosaleen with her habit hitched up over her knees and Cap, at the rear, with his hand planted on his hat to stop it blowing away. They looked strange, even by the standards of Sheriff Street. As they turned right into Dowdall's Lane, news of their appearance was already spreading among a people hungry for scandal.

Cap waited downstairs for the ambulance while Philo and Sister Rosaleen went upstairs to assess the situation. Dina was a veritable block of ice, having lain on the floor for three solid hours in her skimpy lingerie. Philo put a pillow under her head, threw a blanket over her and rubbed her hands to try and get some life back into them. She had never felt skin so cold on a living person before.

—You better have a good excuse, Philo joked at Dina as she rubbed her feet.

—I was reaching up to get a scarf from the top of the wardrobe and I fell off the bed.

—I believe you, there's thousands wouldn't.

—That's the gospel truth, Philo.

—Yeah, and they're going to make me Mother Superior of the convent.

—That's great news, I'm delighted.

By the time the ambulance arrived, a crowd of kids had gathered outside the shop. Cap was standing at the door, working hard to keep them at bay. A cheeky boy of about twelve was at the head of the pack.

—My ma sent me around to get carrots and onions.

—You'll have to come back tomorrow; the shop is closed.

—What are you standing there for if it's closed?

—I'm standing here for the good of my health. Now go home.

—You can't tell me what to do, you're not a policeman.

Cap turned his head away in exasperation, and the young wolves sensed weakness.

—You don't even own that shop, it's not yours.

—Go back to your own shop, you bleedin' robber!

Dina came down on a stretcher and saved Cap from the pack. On her way past, she smiled at him. It was the look in her eyes that got to him, a look that penetrated to his soul.

—Thanks, Cap, thanks for saving me, she said.

She was whisked into the back of the ambulance, and Cap felt terribly emotional. A great wall had divided them, it might be about to crumble – and she was being taken away. The worst of it was, he felt responsible. She'd had an accident trying to make herself beautiful for their date.

He ran to the back of the ambulance and grabbed the doors. He pushed on the handles, but the doors were locked. Cap started to panic. He pulled the handles outwards and the doors opened. He stood on the top step, and one of the ambulance men approached him.

—I'm going with her. She can't go on her own, Cap said.

—Are you her husband? the ambulance man asked.

—No, I'm her blind date.

—You're not related to her.

—I'm a friend. We go back a long way.

—I have to ask you to vacate this vehicle. You're not a blood relative. Please step down, sir.

Cap was ushered off under the watchful gaze of the swelling crowd. The kids had been joined by adults, drawn there by the piercing siren and the flashing lights. The crowd, at Philo's urging, pulled back to give Cap some room. He walked through them and the ambulance sped off up the lane. As people began to disperse, a young girl with a snotty nose stood in Cap's way. He looked down at her.

—My mammy says your vegetables are the nicest, Mr Coyle.

On another day, he'd have been flattered by the remark. In the circumstances, all he felt was sadness and loss. He'd spent half a lifetime at war, and for what? What had it gained him? Absolutely nothing. A compliment from a young girl that was, in fact, an indictment – of him, of Dina, of the North Wall and the entire dock community. It was on its last legs, and Dina had been taken away in an ambulance and he didn't know if he'd get another chance to mend broken fences with her.

Philo closed the door of the shop and slid the bolt across. She put the padlock on and clicked the mechanism into place. She turned and saw Cap. It hadn't been his night.

—Check that lock for me, Cap.

He walked over and, after a short struggle, pronounced it safe. He took the hotel voucher from his inside pocket and offered it to Philo. .

—I won't be needing that now.

—It's not the end of the world, Cap. Count yourself lucky: you had half a blind date. I'm Cilla Black and I had fuck all.

Cap couldn't help himself; he smiled. It was impossible to stay sad for long around Philo. She was too full of life to give sadness a chance. She was allergic to pain.

—If the worst comes to the worst, Sister Rosaleen said, you could use the hotel voucher yourself, Philo.

—You don't think the Reverend Mother will grant me asylum? I hope you're wrong. I hate hotels – getting in and out of them small bleedin' lifts.... I hate them.

Cap had no idea what they were talking about and didn't have the inclination to enquire. He bade them good night and set off for home. On his way, he put his hands in his pockets and felt the rock and the packet of liquorice allsorts, one for violence and the other for peace. He threw the rock away. At the top of the street, he sought out the snotty-nosed girl; after a few minutes, he found her. He showed her the sweets.

—Do you like liquorice allsorts?

—I don't know, Mr Coyle, I never ate them.

—Would you like to try them?

She nodded and held out her hand to him. He put the packet in her small, dirty palm and closed her fingers around it. He spoke in a slow, deliberate drawl.

—I want you to tell your mammy something. Will you do that for me?

—Yes, Mr Coyle.

—I want you to tell her that my vegetables are the exact same as Dina's. They're not nicer; they're the same. Do you understand that?

She nodded, wiped the snot from her nose with the back of her sleeve and put a sweet in her mouth. Then she turned on her heel and ran away. Cap watched her until she disappeared before he, too, turned around and headed for home.

6

After she made the 999 call, Sister Monica went to the oratory to enlist God's help. She'd made a decision to extend Philo's stay in the convent. On balance, she felt it was the Christian thing to do. She now sought guidance in relaying that decision to Philo's husband, Tommo. He'd been hanging around the convent for hours, like a man awaiting sentence. There was no telling how he would react. He was Philo's husband, after all, and he had rights. Those rights involved sex, which Sister Monica only knew about in the abstract. She knew it did strange things to men when they were denied it. As a species, they had a stronger sexual drive than women – she'd been taught that as a novice. She had also learned that there were men who were aroused by the thought that under every habit lurked a virgin waiting to be conquered. If worst came to worst, the advice given was that one should submit rather than resist, that compliance lessened the pain and trauma of rape.

Sister Monica felt uneasy. It wasn't rational; it was a gut thing. The convent was quiet, it was night-time and they were covered in a blanket of darkness. There were lots of unknown factors – she didn't know if Tommo had been drinking, had no sense of him as a father, didn't know if he was violent and hadn't met the children. She hadn't become Reverend Mother by being impetuous. On the principle that there is safety in numbers, she went straight from the oratory to rouse Sister Kevin and Sister Davina. They marched downstairs like the Three Musketeers for the confrontation with Tommo Nolan. They brought him into the office and sat facing him.

He couldn't have been more understanding and contrite. There were problems in the marriage, and he took his share of blame for that. He accepted that maybe he worked too hard and spent too many hours in the lorry. He was a good father and believed he could be better. He was sure he could improve if he got the chance.

—I want my family back, that's all I want – nothing else.

They looked at him, each in her own way. Sister Kevin thought it was very manly the way hairs grew on the back of his hands; it reminded her of her father, whom she had loved. Sister Davina couldn't figure out why she'd been hauled out of bed to come down and pass judgement on this caring man. Sister Monica was beginning to have doubts, but she didn't want to go back on her decision to let Philo stay.

—I think you should leave this with us, Mr Nolan, and we'll review the situation in a day or two.

—Nobody calls me Mr Nolan. I'm Tommo – plain, unvarnished Tommo.

Sister Monica thanked him for his patience but he brushed the compliment aside. He shook her by the hand and headed for the door. The Three Musketeers, individually and collectively, were very impressed. At the hall door, Tommo dipped his fingers in the holy water font and blessed himself before heading out into the darkness, alone.

Sister Monica went straight to Philo's room. Having listened patiently to the saga of Dina, Cap and the ambulance, she presented the case for Tommo. Philo was unmoved. None of the arguments – the sanctity of marriage, the gift of children, the beauty of companionship – none of them made a dent in her armour.

—I think he genuinely misses you, Philo.

—He misses his electric blanket, that's all.

Philo knew Sister Monica didn't get the reference.

—I'm something to keep him warm, that's all – something to get up on.

—He wants to be a father to his children. I think he deserves another chance.

—You can put me out, Sister, but I'm not going back to him. He charmed the knickers off me once, but I'm finished with being a punchbag.

It was impossible for Sister Monica to reconcile this scenario with the man she'd just met. Why would he hang around a convent all day, why would he pursue Philo the way he did, if he only wanted to beat her up?

—He is your husband, Philo, you can't deny that.

—You're right: I am married to the bollix, I can't deny it.

—He is the father of your children – you share that with him, too.

—He's not the father of all my children; you're wrong there.

Sister Monica should have seen it coming but didn't.

—He's not Jack's father. I had him for someone else.

Philo was running away from more than a violent husband. The time for half-truths was over and the time for disclosure was at hand.

The trouble started when Philo won a tattoo in a raffle. She was fifteen years old and wild. She brought the voucher to Jack the Scratch in Parnell Street. He put the heart on her arm and she ran home to show it off. Her mother thought it was nice but not very ladylike. Her father, on the other hand, hated it. To him, only prostitutes wore tattoos. He boxed the ears off her till she cried. Her mother tried to make the peace, as always, but it was no good. Philo was dragged screaming to the Mater Hospital to have it removed.

The surgeon examined her and said he could do something but it would take time and money. Money was the one thing that always brought Philo's father down to earth. The surgeon wrote the figure on a piece of paper; her father put it in his pocket, dragged her outside, gave her a few more clatters and told her she wasn't worth his hard-earned cash.

Philo ran down the street to get away from him. She hated him. Back to Jack the Scratch she went, and promised him a date if he'd put the letters 'M-A-M-M-Y' on the fingers of her right hand. Then she went around to Josie Cullen, her best friend, and stayed the night with her. Next day the pair of them stole onto the boat and ran away to Manchester, where Josie had cousins. They got jobs in a factory and spent all their spare time going to pubs and discos.

One Friday night a singer called PJ Proby came to town. He was famous for making his trousers split. Philo got drunk and decided she wasn't going to wait all night for the big event. So she jumped up on the stage and started to pull the trousers off him. The crowd cheered her on, but the bouncers didn't like her antics; she was physically lifted from the stage, carried out and dumped on the street. One of the bouncers took a handkerchief from his pocket and wiped his brow.

—Jaysus, you're a wild one, do you know that? he said.

Philo recognised the Dublin accent. She castigated him for being a turncoat and an informer.

—I'm a bouncer; we put out troublemakers. That's what we do.

—I'm Irish, like you, and the Irish should stick together, especially over here.

That night, Philo lost her virginity to Brian the bouncer. It was an unforgettable experience. It hurt before, during and after. She lost so much blood she thought she might need a transfusion. She was sickened by it – and she soon got sick of Manchester, too. So did Josie Cullen. They missed Dublin and their friends.

Philo arrived home to discover that Sylvia was pregnant. Sylvia was her mammy; Philo had started to call her Sylvia because she felt on a par with her for the first time. As the weeks went by, Sylvia started to show. Her stomach grew bigger and bigger; and as it did, so did Philo's. But she kept her secret hidden. She loved her mother, she loved Sylvia so completely that she couldn't tell her about her situation.

By the middle of September, Philo had decided to visit the doctor. The day she was to go, her mother went into labour and called an ambulance. Philo went with her to the Rotunda. When they arrived at the hospital, two nurses helped Philo down the steps and put her in a wheelchair. It never occurred to her to object. She felt that, if she didn't sit down, she would poo all over the road.

Philo was brought to a pre-natal ward and put lying on a bed. A young Indian doctor came in, asked for her name, told her to undress and then examined her.

—What age are you, Philo? he asked. He said her name funny, making it sound like it was Indian.

—I'm just turned sixteen, Doctor, she said.

—Can you give me a push, please? he asked her.

Philo put her hand through the bars of the bed and did her best to push the bed away from the wall.

—The brakes must be on, she said.

—I think you're a comedy person, the doctor said.

He put his hand in her vagina and felt around. Philo pulled back instinctively.

—You are two fingers dilated, he said. Your baby won't be long now, Philo.

For the first time, Philo admitted the truth to herself: she was going to have a baby. It caused everything inside her to increase – her heart rate, her pulse, her breathing, her anxiety – and she felt like a wreck. She wanted to get up out of the bed and go home, but she wouldn't have made it to the bus stop. So she stayed where she was and prayed for a miracle, only she wasn't sure what the miracle was.

As she was wheeled into the labour ward, she heard Sylvia's screams. In no time at all, she was screaming heartily along with her. They encouraged each other, like two athletes

83

running a marathon. If Sylvia let out a wail, Philo screeched one back to let her know she wasn't alone. It got so bad, the matron was sent for. She decided their screams were not real, that they were, in fact, putting it on. She issued an instruction for them to be separated. It was the first time in the two-hundred-year history of the hospital that a woman had been put out of the labour ward for faking it.

Philo was wheeled out to an annexe. She couldn't imagine how the baby's head was going to get out a hole as small as the one she had. She thought back to the night of awful pain when bouncer Brian had put his penis into her. He'd had to force it in, and that was just a penis. How could you compare a penis to a baby's head? She screamed her head off. No one came near her because they knew she was putting it on.

The baby didn't agree. He slid down inside her and tried to push his head out.

—It's coming, it's coming! Philo screamed out.

Ten minutes later, and two hours in advance of Sylvia, Philo Darcy gave birth to a son. The midwife cut the cord, washed off the goo and placed the infant at Philo's breast.

—There now, what do you say? the midwife cooed.

Philo started to cry. The midwife, who was childless after eight years of marriage, looked at her with envy.

—You must be so happy, she said.

—Happy? Philo repeated. My daddy is going to kill me.

That night, in Saint Gerard's ward of the Rotunda Maternity Hospital, Philo and Sylvia lay in adjacent beds with their babies. In one crib lay Philo's son, in the other her baby sister. She had never dreamed she would end up giving birth alongside her mother. She didn't like the feeling. She was still a baby herself. Sometimes, when her father was on the early shift (he worked as a bus conductor and was often out of the house by five in the morning), she snuggled in beside her mother in the bed. The folds of Sylvia's flesh were lovely, like a hot-water bottle, only better. Philo knew she could probably never lie beside her again, now that she was a mother. Her childhood was over. She was sixteen, with a baby of her own to mind.

—What are you going to call him? Sylvia asked.

—I don't really know, Philo said. PJ, maybe.

—PJ, Sylvia mused. Is that the name of the father, then?

—Sort of, Philo replied.

PJ Proby was as much the father as Brian the bouncer.

—This is my last, Sylvia said, so I'm going to call her Sally after my sister in Carlow.

Jack Darcy phoned the hospital at the end of his morning shift and was given the news of the double birth. He arrived there threatening to kill his daughter. When the young receptionist refused to tell him what ward Philo was in, he threatened to kill her too. Two hospital porters arrived and tried to calm him down. He demanded to know what ward his daughter was being held in. The porters tried to point out that it was a hospital and not a prison. He told them to go fuck themselves. At that point, the police were called.

Two guards grabbed Jack by the scruff of the neck and plonked him on the footpath. If he put a toe inside the hospital again, he'd be arrested and put in gaol. The news spread around the hospital like a bush fire. Philo breathed a little more easily knowing she would not have to face her father's wrath from the confines of her hospital bed. Five days later, mother and daughter left the hospital with their babies.

When they walked into the family home in East Wall, Philo held up her baby son.

—Your first grandchild, Da, she said.

—That child has nothing to do with me, he replied.

Philo felt totally rejected, but she did her best not to let him see she was upset.

—I was going to call him Jack after you, she said, but I'm not so sure now.

The day after they came home from the hospital, Sylvia

85

took Philo aside and told her that naming the boy Jack might be very good for family harmony. Philo would never have done anything to go against her mother. Sylvia was a saint, in her eyes, for putting up with her father. From that moment on, she started to call the baby Jack. It was the best thing she had ever done, because her father treated him like he was one of his own. It appealed to his vanity to have a grandson who would carry his name.

Philo was pleased to be raising her son at home, but she didn't like living under a curfew. She was sixteen years old with a bagful of wild oats to sow. According to her father, she wasn't entitled to an existence outside the home. He believed in a woman's place and all the rest of it. It wasn't for Philo, though. She only had to look at her mother to see where all that led.

After the birth of Sally, Sylvia took to sleeping on her own in the downstairs front room. The double bed had been brought down on her first night home from the hospital. She slept there with baby Sally and it was strictly off limits to everyone else, including her husband; Jack slept alone in what had once been the bridal suite. On the rare occasions when he ventured downstairs to exercise his marital rights, he found the door barred against him.

It proved effective as a means of contraception, but disastrous with regard to Sylvia's weight. The journey up and down the stairs had been one of the few bits of exercise she had engaged in. Now even that was at an end. She moved only from the front room to the kitchen and the kitchen to the front room, a distance of no more than thirty feet. Philo ran the errands to the shop, so even that walk was taken away from her. From morning till night, Sylvia lived in her dressing-gown and slippers. She snacked all day; there wasn't a moment when she didn't have something in her mouth or on the way there. The weight piled on until she looked like an inflatable castle.

Philo had to do something or she'd go insane. She couldn't stay in the house any longer, watching her mother getting fatter by the second. The key to her escape was her father, of course. She started to send him messages through the baby.

—I'm going to have to get a job, Jack, she'd say.

—Your place is here in the home, he'd say.

—I wasn't talking to you, I was talking to him, she'd say, pointing at the baby.

Then she'd take another tack.

—You're an awful bollix, Jack, do you know that? she'd say.

—That's no way to talk to the child, he'd say.

—Who says I'm talking to the child? she'd say.

—That's no way to talk to your father, he'd say.

—You're not my father, you're my gaoler, she'd say, and if I don't get out of this prison I'm going to do damage.

Finally, he relented, and Philo got a job in Pownall's through Josie Cullen. She stuffed eiderdowns with feathers and kapok. When they got fed up with the eiderdowns, they stuffed pillows for a break. The feathers went everywhere – down your back, up your nose, into your mouth, down your knickers; it was disgusting, but it got her out of the house, and that was the main thing.

Everyone in Pownall's sneezed from the kapok. They used to have sneezing competitions; the record was ninety-eight in one day. Philo was no good – it seemed to affect skinny people more. Instead of sneezing, Philo used to write notes on bits of paper and put them inside the pillows and the eiderdowns. She'd write stupid things like 'Twenty-six ducks died in the making of this eiderdown' or 'This pillow is not to be used for adultery.' If she was pissed off, usually with her father, she'd write, 'The person who stuffed this had the pox.' It passed the time to think of people finding them. It was a boring job, possibly one of the most boring jobs in the whole world, but it was better than being stuck in the house all day.

She walked Josie home every day after work. The journey took them along the north quays. They linked arms and sang pop songs and hoped that an impresario might discover them, the way the Beatles had been discovered in the Cavern. Most of the attention they received, however, was from dockers. It came in the form of wolf-whistles, mainly aimed at Josie. Philo and Josie ignored them as best they could, hoping it would encourage them all the more.

One day, the driver of a lorry lowered his window and whistled. They refused to look at him. He slowed right down to a crawl and whistled again. They stared resolutely ahead. He mounted the footpath with the truck and leaned out. He was close enough to touch them.

—Hey, gorgeous, what are you doing Saturday night? he asked.

Josie turned her head and stared straight at him.

—Nothing that involves you, she said.

—I wasn't talking to you, I was talking to your gorgeous friend, he said.

Philo turned and made a face at him. She saw he had a tattoo on his arm – it was a hook, line and sinker, one of her favourites. Above it, he had a massive anchor. And above that again was the green, white and orange of the Irish flag. She was in love straight away. She'd have got into the cab and driven off into the sunset with him, had he asked her. Not even Josie could have stopped her. But she had a child at home, and she couldn't just walk away; she couldn't abandon her son. Or could she? The thought struck Philo that young Jack would be better off without her. He would be better off being reared by Sylvia and Jack. They adored him, and he was already a part of their family. Her life lay with this stranger in the truck.

—I go dancing in the Galway Arms of a Saturday, if you're interested, he said.

—My Saturdays are very crammed; I don't know if I can fit you in.

The Galway Arms on Parnell Square was famous. No one went there for the dancing; everyone went for the fights. Gangs from Sheriff Street would take on gangs from East Wall. Dorset Street would square up to Smithfield. Most feared of all was the crowd from Corporation Buildings in Foley Street, affectionately known to their friends and enemies as the Animal Gang.

The fellas were searched for weapons going in. If they didn't have any, they were supplied. The walls inside were painted red to camouflage the blood. The place had a fearsome reputation, and at the same time it was impossible to get in if you weren't wearing a tie.

Getting out to the Galway Arms was a huge ordeal. Philo told her father she was going into the front room to talk to her mother. As soon as she stepped in there, Sylvia locked the door, and Philo put on her clothes and make-up before escaping through the window. When Jack came knocking on the door demanding his cocoa supper, Sylvia told him that Philo was asleep on the bed with the babies.

Philo was nervous going into the dance hall. Inside, though, all the girls gave her a wide berth. She couldn't understand why they were moving away from her. She spotted a girl she'd been to school with and went over to say hello. The girl's legs nearly buckled in her attempt to get away.

—Have I an infectious disease or something? Philo asked Josie.

—I think they're afraid of the tattoos, Josie said.

There was no doubt they made Philo look tough. Someone had started a rumour that she had a knife stuck down her knickers. Someone else said she'd had a kid for one of the Animal Gang and it was deformed. There were going to be killings, that was certain, and while nobody wanted to get hurt, nobody wanted to miss the slaughter.

The truck driver turned out to be called Tommo Nolan, and he asked Philo up to dance. It was a ladies' choice so she refused. He turned to walk away and Philo tapped him on the shoulder. When he looked around she curtseyed, the way she'd seen it done in the films.

—Excuse me, young man; can I have this dance, please? she said in a posh voice.

—Yeah, he said, and grabbed her by the waist.

—Have you no manners? she said. You're supposed to say, 'Thank you, Miss.'

He saw that she was serious.

—Thank you, Miss.

—You're welcome, young man.

They danced away onto the floor together, watched by everyone.

—Is it true you've a knife down your knickers? he asked.

—Is that your best chat-up line?

—Everyone is saying you're going to stab someone, he said. Is it true?

Philo stuck her nail into the small of his back.

—Don't move a muscle, it's pointing at your liver, she said.

Tommo didn't care if the knife pierced his flesh; he'd never been so excited in his whole life. Her big breasts touched him and he could feel his whole body expand to meet their invitation. He worked with hard men down the docks, but he'd never felt hardness like that which had taken hold inside his trousers.

—I'm only messing, Philo said. I'd never hurt you.

She relaxed her finger and he melted into her. From that first dance, they looked like a couple. It didn't matter that she was from East Wall and he from Liberty House (Animal Gang territory, not far from Corporation Buildings). She was Philo and he was Tommo and they went together like a bow and arrow. During that first date, they were talking about getting tattoos for each other. Philo showed him the letters on her fingers that made up MAMMY. Tommo asked her to be the mother of his children. She told him about Jack, her son, and he said that was his favourite name for a boy, apart from his own. Philo said she'd give him a son but not until after they were married. Tommo had a ring belonging to his mother (deceased), and it was back in his flat in Liberty House, but he wanted her to have it straight away. Philo couldn't give him an answer because she was bursting to go to the toilet.

As soon as she opened the door that said 'Mná', every girl in the toilets ran out, except for the girls in the cubicles. They stayed where they were, afraid to open the doors. No amount of reassurance would convince them to come out. Philo pleaded with them until she was about to go in her knickers. Rather than demean herself, she marched out of the ladies' and into the gents'. Her presence there caused a stampede.

When the fellas ran out of the toilets, the gangs in the hall thought they were being attacked. In an instant, every weapon known to man was produced, leading to the worst bloodbath ever seen in the Galway Arms. Through it all, Philo took a peaceful leak in the men's toilets, oblivious to the mayhem she'd caused. When she re-emerged, she and Tommo left the hall wrapped up in each other, the best-suited and most-feared couple in the whole of Dublin danceland.

Tommo walked her home to East Wall and couldn't believe it when she climbed in through the front window. They arranged to meet the following Saturday night; and when they did, Tommo gave Philo the ring by the railings outside the Galway Arms. Before she put it on her finger, she asked him to pull up the sleeve of her blouse. There, inside the heart, she'd had his name tattooed – TOMMO. He kissed her arm and she slipped the ring onto her engagement finger.

—Tell me about the father of your child. Does he dance in here?

—Let's get one thing straight, Philo said. You don't ask me about my past and I won't ask you about yours.

—I just want to know one thing, Tommo said. Could I stab your son's father in here?

—No, Philo said. He lives foreign.

They kissed until they didn't know whose mouth was whose any more. Tommo dropped the hand, but Philo slapped him on the Irish flag and told him he'd have to wait until they were legal.

—We'd better get married soon, he said. I can't wait.

—Well, I'm not stopping you.

—How about in two months?

—Two months? Philo repeated. How about two bleedin' weeks?

The priest wouldn't hear of two weeks until Philo threatened him she'd marry in a Protestant church and raise the kids as Anglicans. She didn't know what an Anglican was, but it did the trick: three weeks later, she and Tommo were married in Saint Laurence O'Toole's church. They had a one-night honeymoon in a bed-and-breakfast and took the next day off work to move Philo's stuff into Tommo's flat in Liberty House, where they set about making babies straight away.

Philo produced a daughter and called her Eileen, after her maternal grandmother. Then followed Thomas, who immediately became known as Young Tommo; after him there was Josie, named for Philo's best friend and bridesmaid; finally there was Philomena – Tommo named her, and Philo assented only after it was agreed her name would not be shortened to Philo.

Things between them were good for a few years. She laughed at his jokes and he laughed at hers. She looked forward to him coming home for his dinner and bringing stories from the docks with him. Then his father died suddenly, and Tommo started to change. Not that a death excused bad behaviour – it didn't – but Philo could trace the change in him back to that point. Of course, he must have always been like that; the death was just the excuse he needed.

Six years into the marriage, Philo realised she'd married her father. She'd run so fast to get away from him, she'd ended up in the same prison half a mile away. She had always thought that men with tattoos couldn't be bastards. It sickened her to have to admit she'd been wrong. Not only that, but the two bastards, Tommo and Jack, got on like a house on fire. They seemed to fan the flames of nastiness in each other.

The night of baby Philomena's second birthday was a prime example. They were walking back across the bridge from Philo's mother's when Tommo started in on her.

—I hope you don't end up like your mother, he said. She's an awful bleedin' size.

—My mother is pleasantly plump, that's all.

—She's an elephant, for Jaysus' sake, and you're heading in the same direction.

It was the same name-calling Philo had lived with growing up, and it was the thing she'd most wanted to get away from. Jack called Sylvia a cow, right into her face, and made cow sounds when he did it. Sylvia never reacted to his taunts, and it had always driven Philo mad to have to witness her ritual humiliation. Now the poisoned chalice had been passed to her. She looked at her children and wondered if they were thinking the same horrible thoughts she had as a child. She didn't want to create a scene with Tommo in front of them, especially not about her size. She realised, in that moment, that her silence was a repetition of her mother's silences down the years. Not only had she married her father; she was becoming her mother.

—Can you not see how fat your mother is? Tommo continued. She's as fat as a bleedin' cow.

Philo stopped in her tracks, turned the pram around and headed back across the bridge. It took a minute before Tommo's boozy brain copped on to what was happening. He ran after Philo and tried to grab her by the arm, but she shook him off and kept walking.

—Where are you going?

—I'm going where I'll get some respect.

She was lying, of course. There was no way she could go back to her mother's, because her father wouldn't let her do that. He would never come between a husband and wife, never do anything to upset Tommo. 'You've made your bed, now lie in it' was his all-time favourite expression.

Philo wanted to run away. She wanted to get away from this man who'd insulted her. Tommo was enraged that she'd do this, humiliated that she'd go back and seek shelter in Jack's house. He ran after her and slapped her across the face. Then he grabbed her by the hair and tried to force the pram and her to turn around. Philo thumped him on the arm for his trouble, and he upped and kicked her, full force, in the backside. By this stage, the children were starting to cry, and young Jack was in the middle trying to separate Tommo and Philo.

—Leave my mammy alone! he pleaded. Leave my mammy alone!

—Don't pull my mammy's hair! little Eileen screamed.

Tommo pulled Philo along the footpath, away from the East Wall. She held on to the pram for fear it would topple over.

—Tell the children where we're going, Tommo yelled. Go on, tell them!

—It's all right, kids, we're going home.... Philo tried to calm them.

They moved in a frightening convoy across the bridge towards home. Tommo only released his grip on Philo's hair when he was sure her feet would continue to move in a westerly direction. They cried their way up Seville Place, past the church where they'd been married. They cried along the North Strand, where they'd walked on their way home from the Galway Arms. Tommo held Young Tommo in his arms and tried to comfort him. Jack held Philo's hand and looked at the pram-wheels making their way towards Liberty House. Eileen sat up on the pram and wiped the snots from Philomena's lips, which only two hours before had blown out the candles on her birthday cake.

Philo gave as good as she got in the rows that followed. She suffered a few black eyes and dished out a few as well. Tommo was stronger than her, and he could hit and run like Muhammad Ali; she was slow because of her size, and it wasn't always possible to get her retaliation in first, which was the only way to fight him. In the end, she couldn't take it any more and ran away to Galway. That was when Tommo took the children to Goldenbridge Orphanage and left them with the nuns.

Philo came home because it was the only way she could get the kids back. There was peace for a while, but it was brittle and shaky. Six months after her repatriation, the ceasefire broke down. They were watching a wildlife programme on television and Tommo made a disparaging remark about animals who abandoned their young. Philo responded by castigating human beings who dumped their children in orphanages. She was immediately sorry she'd said it and turned around to apologise. Tommo's hand was already in mid-flight, and she received a slap on the mouth. Her first impulse was to hit back but she managed to control the urge. Later on, she was glad she had: it was over quicker that way.

That established a pattern. When Tommo erupted, Philo took her dose of digs with dignity and in silence. Because of that, he couldn't seem to keep it up for very long. It protected the children better, too. There was less shouting, fewer broken dishes, fewer black eyes and fractured limbs. Dignity and silence – the two words that kept the family together.

That was how it was until young Jack, not yet twelve years old, started getting into trouble. It began with him staying out of school. Tommo tried to ground him at weekends as a punishment.

—You're going to get an education and that's that, Tommo said.

—You can't tell me what to do; you're not my father.

Philo pleaded with her son to reform himself. It seemed to work for a while; he went back to school and seemed to be getting on all right. Then tragedy struck. When Jack was fifteen, he was chased by the police one night in a stolen BMW. All over the city he drove it, at a hundred miles an hour. Eventually he crashed it into some railings and was taken, unhurt, from the wreckage. His passenger and navigator, Mickabird Stynes, suffered a broken leg.

Philo waited in Store Street Garda Station until Jack was released. When he emerged from the holding cells, she couldn't contain herself; she slapped him on the face.

—What are you hitting me for? he said. You should be hitting that pig you live with.

—What are you talking about? He provides for you, doesn't he?

—Why do you sit there and take the digs off him? Jack said. Why do you sit there and not hit back?

It was the end of the world as Philo knew it. She had tried to protect her children from the violence, but her silence had only fed it. Her son was a joyrider, and if he didn't kill some innocent bystander or himself, he would certainly kill her. Children were supposed to be innocent, but hers were

96

corrupted. Her world was falling apart. It made no sense to keep it together any more. She was only making it possible for more heartache and tragedy to befall her. She didn't know what to do but run.

She went to Manchester in the hope of finding Brian the bouncer, Jack's father. For three days she visited her old haunts, though many of them were now gone – the club where she'd pulled the trousers off PJ Proby was now a graphic studio. She wandered around Piccadilly and Belle-vue. She went out to the Old Trafford football museum because she remembered Brian saying how much he loved Manchester United. The city felt like a cradle; it gave Philo a respite.

Searching for Jack's father was like looking for a needle in a haystack, but it was at least that. In Dublin there was nothing, only an abyss. Even if she found him, what would it reveal? What would it do to save Jack? Philo didn't know; but while she searched, there was hope – miniscule, infinitesimal hope. For five days, its faint glimmer kept her alive. For five days she nurtured it, until it finally flickered out and she returned to Dublin and knocked on the convent door seeking shelter.

7

Philo knew she had to step out of the convent and face the world again. The children were waiting to see her. Not jam, Easter eggs, toast, jacket potatoes and fresh fruit – it was Jack, fifteen; Eileen, thirteen; Thomas, eleven; Josie, ten; and Philomena, nine. They were Philo's flesh and blood. She was going to visit them, but they wouldn't be coming home with her. Neither would she be staying.

It was a painful situation, and the only thing she could think of to lessen the pain was chocolate. She was making a list of the children's favourites in her head when she realised she had no money. Then she remembered her children's allowance: the previous month's instalment had gone uncollected. She cashed it in at the post office and headed for the nearest sweet shop, where she bought in sixes, one for each of the children and one for herself. On the bus, she started in on her own stash – she ate a packet of popcorn, two plain chocolate bars, a bar of Fruit and Nut, a Snickers bar, a Mars and a Moro, all washed down with two cans of Diet Coke. Philo put great store by diet anything and justified many a chocolate binge with her belief in the magical power of low-calorie drinks.

The Goldenbridge nuns greeted her like one of their own – which, in truth, she nearly was. The children were brought to her in the visiting room. Philomena, the baby, refused to come through the door; she stayed out in the hallway. As a result, all the initial attention went towards her, and the sadness they all felt at not seeing one another for over three weeks was dissipated. The others tried to cajole Philomena, but Philo knew it was best to let her come around in her own time. She exchanged hugs and kisses with Eileen and Josie, but Young Tommo held back against the wall.

—You're not too big for a hug, are you?

He shrugged his shoulders to show he didn't care.

—When are we getting out of here? he asked.

Philo didn't have an answer. She held her arms out to him in invitation.

—Come here and give me a hug.

—Are you not going to tell me?

—A hug first, come on.

He went to her and she embraced him. She held on to him, determined he would feel every inch of her love. Young Tommo felt her flesh and melted against its warmth. It was the safest place in the world. He'd missed her special smell; none of the nuns had it. Philo planted her lips on his neck and blew gently, making lovely, squelchy sounds. Young Tommo half-heartedly tried to pull away, but he didn't want to succeed; it was his favourite game and it made him laugh in a way that involved his whole body.

—Who's a vampire? Philo asked. Who's a vampire sucking blood?

—You are! he squealed. You're a vampire!

At that, Philomena came bounding into the room to demand her place on the vampire's knee. She tried to push her older brother from his perch.

—Suck my blood, Mammy – do it to me!

Philo replaced Young Tommo with Philomena and sucked her neck until all her defiance and anger dissolved in vampire kisses. She licked her baby daughter until the spit in her mouth dried up and she could lick no more. Then she made the four of them sit on the floor for their chocolate surprises. It was then she asked where Jack was.

Eileen was the one with the news. He'd been sent to another place, more suited to a fifteen-year-old boy who was

99

robbing cars. It was called the San Francisco Boys' Home after a refuge in America that took in boys who were sleeping rough. Philo was very unhappy that he'd been separated from his brother and sisters. She wanted them kept together, at all costs; the last thing she wanted was her family broken up even more than it already had been.

In no time they were covered in chocolate – apart from Eileen, of course. She was so neat and tidy, just like her grandmother Sylvia. Her silver chocolate wrappers were spread out neatly before her, like they were going to be used again. Maybe she was going to make Christmas decorations with them; she was very artistic. Josie, on the other hand, was a mess. She'd made the mistake of drinking her Coke first, and now she had no liquid left to wash down her chocolate. The peanuts from her Snickers bar were refusing to pass by her tonsils, despite the best efforts of her dry mouth. Philo noticed she was struggling. She popped the can she'd bought for Jack and gave it to Josie.

—How come she's getting another can? Philomena wanted to know.

—It's my can and I'm giving her a sup, Philo said.

—Can I have a slug?

—Me too, I want a slug.

—I want a slug if she's getting one.

—You can all have a slug when you finish your own.

Suddenly, the race was on to get a free slug. They went at their drinks and battled one another to finish first. The only certain outcome was trouble. Philo had experienced it many times. Trying to share out a can evenly among five children was a feat beyond the wisdom of Solomon. Measuring it out into cups didn't work, because you couldn't see the level of the liquid, and glasses weren't an option because Philo never managed to have more than three glasses in the house at any one time. The only thing that made sense was to measure the slugs. In her house, a slug was three seconds from the time the liquid hit your lips. Of course, some people tried to cheat, especially the boys. More than once the can had had to be yanked from their lips and had ended up spilling onto the floor, leading to more rows.

Young Tommo was the first with his hand up for a slug. To Philo's surprise, he played by the rules: before she got to 'three', he took the can away from his lips and passed it on to Eileen. She passed it on to Philomena without taking a slug. When Philomena was finished she passed it on to Josie, who said she'd had enough. They were all on their best behaviour, and, in her heart, Philo knew why.

—When are you getting back with me da? Young Tommo asked.

Philo drank down the dregs of the can. Then she took a paper hanky from her bag and handed it to Josie.

—Wipe your mouth with that or you'll have the nuns giving out.

—I don't care if they give out; they don't own me, Josie said.

—Well, I do, so wipe your mouth.

Young Tommo repeated the question. Philo wanted to hide. She wanted to disappear. She would never knowingly hurt her children, but that was what she'd done and was about to do again. She looked at her son and tried to think of toast, but it was useless. He was flesh and blood, breathing, before her.

—I'm not getting back with your father. I can't live with him any more.

It would be nice to be somewhere, stuffing her face with food, Philo thought. She wanted to be anywhere but where she was. For a moment she thought she was going to cry, but that was the last thing they needed. They needed her to be strong. They needed to feel she would look after them, come what may.

—I want to live with me da as well as you, Young Tommo said.

—Is that what you all want? Philo asked.

She looked at Eileen, her eldest daughter, and wondered what was going on inside her head.

—I don't want him calling you names, Eileen said.

That sentence summed up Philo's marriage. Of all the people in the world she deserved respect from, their father was number one; and she couldn't think of anyone who disrespected her more.

—I don't like my daddy when he calls you a big fat cow, Josie said.

Philomena was the only one who hadn't spoken.

—What do you think? Philo asked her.

—I don't like when he says 'Moo' and you start to cry.

—When did you ever see me crying? Philo said, laughing at her. You never saw me crying, did you?

She had done everything to protect them – she had learned to take blows in silence and to cry without tears – but it hadn't been enough. They'd seen her invisible tears, there in her laughter when she turned the worst things into jokes. They remembered the day the electricity man had come to turn off the light and she'd made him laugh so much he fell off the ladder and sprained his ankle. He told her she was a tonic, but he still had to disconnect her supply. When Tommo came home from work, the house was bathed in candlelight and Philo was making shadow puppets on the wall with her hands. The children thought it was better than the television and invited their da to join in, but he said it was enough to have one stupid cunt in the house. The fun went out of it fast, and they were all reminded they had no electricity and no television. Tommo had called Philo names, and she had taken it in silence and made toast at the fire with bread stuck on a fork.

—Maybe if you lost weight he'd stop calling you names, Young Tommo said.

Philo was cut in two by the remark.

—I like myself just the way I am, thank you very much, she said.

It was a lie. She didn't like herself. It was hard being fat. It was hard carrying around suitcases full of rocks. She blamed it all on her thyroid, which she'd inherited from her mother. She made fun of her weight; that was how she survived. Philo made no connection between her size and the food she put in her mouth. It was in her genes, it was who she was, and there was no escape. She hated that thyroid almost as much as she hated Tommo. Someday she would submit herself to the surgeon's knife and have it removed. There was no sign of the weight going down by itself. It only went one way, and that was up. Having children had destroyed her altogether. When Jack was born, Philo had been a lovely, trim one hundred and sixty pounds. By the time the baby, Philomena, came along, she'd risen to over two hundred pounds. The last time she'd stood on the scales, she'd been over two hundred and forty. If she got to two hundred and fifty she would do something about the situation. Two hundred and fifty was going to be her line in the sand, her Armageddon, her apocalypse, her execution date. She hadn't stood on the scales in months – she'd avoided them like the plague – but in her heart she knew her time was up. Young Tommo's remark had served to remind her she was at the point of no return.

—It's bad manners to talk about a lady's size. If I was in India, I'd be worshipped.

—I don't think you're fat, Mammy, Josie said.

—I like you just the way you are, Eileen said.

—Will you bring us more chocolate tomorrow? Philomena asked.

—Not if you're going to insult me, I won't.

Young Tommo knew it was meant for him.

—I'm sorry, Ma, it just came out.

—That mouth of yours will get you into trouble one of

these days. Remember, if you can't say something nice about a body....

—Don't say anything at all, they piped up in unison.

It was one of those old clichés Philo had taught them from when they were babies. Ironically, she never practised it herself. She was incapable of keeping her mouth shut, ever. She was a clown who laughed at the world to shield herself from the pain of her obesity.

She hoped the children would not grow up to be like her, the girls in particular. She remembered her own childhood and the promise she'd made never to grow fat like her mother. She'd spent half her life trying to shut out the insults her father threw at Sylvia, and she'd spent the other half absorbing the same hurts from her husband. It was a cycle, vicious and vindictive, and Philo wanted to break it. There was no plan, she had no strategy, her actions were spontaneous and anarchic; she just never wanted to be called a fat cunt again for as long as she lived.

Seven o'clock came and it was time for her to leave. She'd have loved to stay and get them ready for bed, but the orphanage had strict rules surrounding that. Indeed, it was unusual to have unsupervised visits like the one Philo had just had (the norm was for a member of staff to be present at all times), and that was down to it being second time around for all concerned. The staff knew Philo's form and that she was no danger to her brood. That said, the children, Philomena in particular, weren't happy about having to stay in Goldenbridge. Before they had time to get really upset, Philo promised she'd be back the following day with lots of chocolate surprises.

The San Francisco Boys' Home was in a quiet little avenue off Amiens Street. There were no bars on the windows, which surprised Philo. She'd expected a steel door at the very least, but it was a bright-yellow wooden one with brass fittings and a silver 2 at the top. Every light in the two-storey house was on. Even the doorbell was illuminated.

Philo pressed it, and a young man wearing an apron opened the door. It was the first time in her life she'd seen a boy so attired. He greeted her with a smile, brought her into the hall and screamed out at the top of his voice:

—Brother Felix, it's for you!

Moments later, a man with a beetroot face appeared before Philo. He was small, with glasses that magnified his eyes, making them look too big for his face. He purred with enthusiasm, like a toy that had been wound up and was anxious to uncoil.

Philo introduced herself and asked about Jack. The veins in Brother Felix's face lit up.

—Jack is a champion, he's a champion.

Philo sought to clarify the situation.

—I'm talking about Jack Nolan, she said. He's a car thief.

Brother Felix laughed.

—Come on, follow me, he said, and walked off down the hall.

He opened the door to the kitchen. There, standing at the sink with his back to Philo, was her son Jack. He had a wire brush in his right hand and a potato pot in his left. He brought them together and scrubbed for all he was worth. Philo watched in disbelief. Then she stepped back out to the hall and whispered to Brother Felix.

—He's washing fucking dishes.

—You're not happy with that? he said through a frown.

—Not happy? I'm over the bleedin' moon. I can't get him to wash a cup at home.

Philo went back into the kitchen, crept up on Jack and put her hands over his eyes.

—Guess who?

—It's me ma.

Jack got suds all over her neck when he embraced her, but Philo didn't notice. She was delighted to see him and he was delighted to see her, but there was an unease.

—I can't talk to you now, Ma.

—Why not?

—I have to finish these, it's the house rules.

—I'll give you a hand, so. Come on.

Philo picked up a tea towel, but Jack reached across and grabbed her hand.

—You're not allowed, Ma, you're a visitor.

She looked across at Brother Felix, who grinned.

—He's the boss, Mrs Nolan.

Philo was delighted to be put in her place.

She waited in the sitting room for Jack to finish. He joined her there almost immediately.

—What do you think of ET? he asked her.

—Who's ET?

—Brother Felix. We call him ET on account of his eyes.

People weren't responsible for their appearance; it came from God. Brother Felix had been born with eyes that were too big for his face. Philo had been cursed with a faulty thyroid. It wasn't acceptable for her to be called a fat cow, and it wasn't right for him to be called ET.

—It's not right calling him names like that.

—He loves us calling him ET; he gets a laugh out of it.

—He's a Brother and he deserves respect.

Jack explained that Brother Felix wasn't a real Brother. He'd been a Benedictine monk, got too attached to the wine they made and ended up an alcoholic. He had gone into a treatment centre, where he'd met some drug addicts from the inner city. They helped him get well, and he came out of the centre determined to work with young people in trouble. That led him to the San Francisco Boys' Home, which had just opened its doors. Felix had started off as a volunteer. He was in charge now, but you would never know, because the boys made the rules. The house was run on a very simple philosophy: it was a refuge, and you could stay as long as you kept the rules.

Jack was learning to be a mechanic. Every day he went to work at nine o'clock. They had a garage at the back of Saint Laurence O'Toole's school; it had been donated by a widow, Mrs Clarke, who loved the Benedictine monks. She especially loved Brother Felix, but she didn't know he'd left the order. In the vicinity of the garage, consequently, he was Brother Felix, Father Felix or simply the Monk.

They stripped cars and put them back together again. So far, Jack had learned about carburettors (how to clean them), clutches (how to replace them), what to do when the transmission failed, how to put in plugs, points, brushes (in the starting motor), accelerator and brake cables, front and back brake pads, exhaust pipes, radiators, water pumps and a million other things he was too excited to remember. Black Bob – so called because he was always covered in oil – was their supervisor, and he helped them turn out cars in top mechanical condition. On Sundays they brought the souped-up machines to the car track in Santry and raced them. Jack could only drive against the clock because he wasn't sixteen yet and didn't qualify for a provisional licence. But his birthday was only four months away, and he was counting down the days to his first official race.

—I should have abandoned you years ago, Philo said. Look at you; you're a miracle.

—It wouldn't have done any good, Ma.

—Why do you say that?

—ET only takes you in if you're over fifteen.

It was time for Jack's chocolate surprise. Philo poured the mound of food from her bag onto the coffee table. It was enough to feed an army. She brought out several cans and stood them shoulder to shoulder in front of him. Having shared out his earlier can among the other four, she had gone back to the shop for more supplies. Believing that Jack was in some sort of juvenile prison, she'd gone overboard with her purchases.

She started to divide it up – one for you and one for me. It was going to be her second picnic of the day. Her eyes roamed across the chocolate undulations and came to rest on a Snickers bar. Her hand reached out, and she tore the wrapper off in transit and put the fat chocolate stick in her wide-awake mouth. She sucked on it and stared across at Jack. He returned the stare without moving.

—What are you staring at? Take your pick.

He normally bounced into action when Philo issued a command. He didn't move a muscle.

—We're not allowed to have our own food.

—What are you going on about? It's only chocolate.

—We have to pool everything we get. It's the house rules.

No one in the house was allowed have anything that made him superior to anyone else. All gifts, including food, were pooled and shared out on Friday evenings after the weekly house meeting. It was a practical sort of communism. It encouraged collective responsibility and nurtured a spirit of giving amongst the boys. It was a charter that turned potential troublemakers into potential citizens.

Philo thought it was a royal pain in the arse. Sitting there with a Snickers bar stuck in her mouth and being stared at. Wanting to suck the peanuts out of it and being made to feel like a criminal. Her son sitting across from her with his two arms dangling down by his sides. He might be in a labour camp, she thought, but she wasn't joining him.

She was happy for Jack – more than happy; she was overjoyed. He was on the road to a career, when it had looked like he was heading down a one-way street to prison. The San Francisco Boys' Home was the best thing that had ever happened to him. She finished the Snickers and pushed

Jack's share across the table to him. She returned her own stash to her pocket. If Jack wanted to bequeath his goodies to the house, that was fine, but she wasn't in the mood to let hers go – not just yet.

Jack took her on a tour of the house. He shared a bedroom with five other boys. There were three sets of bunk beds. His wall was splattered with pictures of cars and racing drivers. Beside them were his own hand drawings of engine parts festooned with arrows, and a cartoon of a face labelled 'ET (Felix the Monk)'.

Philo had spent five days in Manchester looking for Jack's father. She'd gone there out of desperation. She'd traipsed around Piccadilly in search of an illusion, unaware that back home in Dublin Jack had, for the first time in his life, found a man he could look up to. It wasn't lost on Philo that Brother Felix had called him a 'champion'. It filled her with pride to have him praised, and she felt validated by it, too. How different all this was from home! There were no champions there – only fuckers, little fuckers, bastards, big bastards, pigs, dirty pigs, swine, elephants, big fat cows and fat cunts.

It was nice to put her mouth on ceasefire and follow her son meekly around. They ended up in the kitchen, where Jack offered her a cup of tea. It was another welcome first. They were joined by Brother Felix, who apologised for ignoring them. He'd been on the phone to another distraught parent.

—Will you have a cup of tea, ET? Jack asked.

—I will if you're making it, he replied.

Philo was offended by the nickname; she couldn't help it.

—You don't mind him calling you ET?

—Not at all. I look like him, don't I?

It was just the eyes. Brother Felix didn't have a skinny neck or a funny voice, and his beetroot face was all wrong for ET. It was an insult to compare him to an extraterrestrial. Without the glasses, no one would have done it. Philo would never have described him as good-looking, but he was attractive in a way that went beyond appearance. The more she looked at him, the more beautiful he became.

—You're not looking for a house-mother, are you? she asked.

Brother Felix laughed at her question, like it was the most outrageous thing he'd ever heard. Philo laughed, too, but deep down she was deadly serious. Her accommodation situation, to put it mildly, was depressing. She couldn't go home to Tommo, and her prospects as a nun were looking shaky.

—I don't suppose you're married, she said.

—No, I never met the right girl.

—Where were you when I was looking for a husband?

—I was probably swimming in a vat of wine.

Philo left the San Francisco Boys' Home on a high. Jack was in a good situation. Instead of being arrested for stealing cars, he was servicing them. She'd expected to find him in prison, but he was living in a place that was more of a home than the one he came from. It made Philo sad, because it was a glimpse of what life could be like. She'd had the privilege of seeing her son interact with a real father, and it made the awfulness of life with Tommo all the more intolerable and obscene.

She wanted the children back. She wanted them all together under the one roof with her. But something good had come from their abandonment. She had been lashing herself over it, but now she could put down the whip. They were all safe and had beds to sleep in. Philo thanked God, Buddha, the Goldenbridge nuns, the North Wall nuns and Brother Felix for her change of fortune. For the first time in weeks, she thought of her children and didn't immediately try to banish the thought. She stayed with it, luxuriated in their cheeky faces and felt hope. She'd forgotten what it felt like, but now that she had it back, she didn't want to lose it again.

Philo walked across the railway bridge that linked East Wall to the rest of the city. There was a bounce in her step. The trains rattled away beneath her, busy pulling cargo in their stop-start fashion. She loved that sound, the metal thud of colliding carriages followed by the slow roll of the wheels; it seemed so deliberate, so welcoming, like they wanted to embrace one another. The footpath seemed to push against the soles of her feet in rhythm with the clashing of iron. There was a strange, beautiful harmony in the world and she felt supported by it.

She reached the brow of the bridge and started to descend. Her legs moved faster going down the hill. It reminded her of coming home from school and running all the way, breathless. She had loved crashing through the door and getting the smell of hot soup in the hallway. She was looking forward to seeing her mother again. It wasn't going to be easy explaining the events of the past few days, especially if her father was there. She had hope in her heart, though, and that counted for a lot.

Her feet took her right into Irvine Terrace. The house was on the left, the last on the row, number 10, next to a disused piece of ground called Loydier's Plot. To its right, a set of concrete steps ran up to a bridge known locally as Johnny Cullen's Hill. Halfway up the steps, there was a man sitting with his head bowed, like he was examining the concrete, or feeling sick. As Philo made her way down the terrace, the man looked up and saw her. She felt her heart stop. It was Tommo.

She felt as though she was coming face to face with an angry dog. She could brave it, or she could turn and walk away. The most important thing was not to let him sense her fear. She walked with purpose towards him, and he started down the steps in her direction. She needed to get inside her mother's house to be safe. She arrived at the door and reached up to knock.

—Don't knock, please – I need to talk to you.

She couldn't recall him saying 'please' before, in fifteen years of marriage. She became conscious of her hand and took it down.

—I want us to get back together again. You, me and the kids.

Philo had no reason to disbelieve him and no reason to comply.

—I've had it, Tommo. I can't take any more.

He put his hands up in a gesture of surrender.

—I won't ever hit you again. On my father's grave, I'll never raise another hand to you.

She'd been taken in by promises before. She was afraid of this man, her husband, but it wasn't his fists she feared, it was his tongue.

—I miss you, Philo. The house is no fun without you.

That was it, she thought: he had no one to make fun of. All her life, people had hung around her because she was game for a laugh. From the time she could walk, people had thought she was hilarious. She was sick and tired of making people laugh.

—That's very sad, Tommo, it really is.

Philo was being tongue-in-cheek.

—What are you talking about?

—You not having fun. You should employ a comedian to entertain you. You'll find one in the Golden Pages, under 'Funny'.

—Why would I do that when I have you?

—Except you don't have me.

—Please, Philo, I'm begging you, come home. It's useless without you.

It was a red-letter day. 'Please' and 'begging' in the same sentence, plus an admission that he was useless. Philo was mildly flattered that he wasn't threatening to pull her back home by the hair. There was a definite change in his tone, but she wasn't going to be duped by it. He didn't have the children at hand to blackmail her with. He had dumped them in Goldenbridge, and it had backfired on him. She felt empowered to say no because the children were safe. All she had to think about was herself, and that was a liberation.

She decided to kick for touch.

—I'll give you my answer in writing.

—What are you talking about – a letter?

—Exactly.

—You've never written a letter in your life.

—Congratulations; you'll be the first to get one, so.

Philo smiled at him and knocked on the door.

Tommo didn't know how to respond. It was an unexpected development from his perspective.

—Why are you writing a letter when you can just tell me?

She wanted to send him a letter. It would begin, 'Dear Bastard,' and it would end with the words, 'Your Fat Cunt no more.'

—I need time to gather my thoughts, Tommo, she said.

Sally, Philo's fifteen-year-old sister, who shared a birthday with Jack, opened the door. Philo stepped inside, relieved to be getting away from Tommo, for now.

Sylvia was in the front room tearing wallpaper off the walls. It was three months since Philo had seen her, and she seemed to have doubled in size. Sylvia, when she looked at Philo, had the same thought. Neither of them mentioned it.

—Why are you stripping the wallpaper? Philo asked.

—I don't like that awful brown; it makes me depressed.

—You should get someone to help. It's too much for you.

113

Sylvia had no intention of letting anyone near her room. It was her retreat and she intended to keep it that way. Her husband, Jack, was well capable of decorating a room. So were the boys, Anthony and Brendan (Tony and Bren, both born on 12 May, a year apart, and always referred to as 'the twins'), but Sylvia didn't want them meddling where she slept. In any event, they were married and had their own lives to lead. Sally was too interested in teenage magazines and boy bands to bother with interior decoration, even though she got on with her mother. It was therapeutic, stripping away wallpaper, taking off the layers one by one and getting down to the plaster.

—I could come around and give you a hand, Sylvia.

—You've enough on your plate with five children to look after.

It was the perfect opening for Philo, but she couldn't take it. Standing in the room with her mother, she was a child again, a doll in a doll's house, cocooned and smothered in love. It was impossible to unleash her bad news.

—I have loads of time, honest, Sylvia.

—No, I need the exercise; it's the only bit I get.

It was as close as Sylvia came to admitting she was losing the battle with her size. She weighed over three hundred and fifty pounds, and when she moved, the room seemed to heave under the strain. She wasn't tall – five feet four and a half – and she resembled a globe. Her neck, with its layers of double chins like frozen jelly, looked like the Arctic Circle; it was matched by the folds of flesh that fell from her ankles and hung over her shoes like layers of ice. Her breasts hung down her front and bobbed about like icebergs.

—I'm working in the convent with the old folks, did you know that?

—How would I know anything when I never see you?

—I help out with the dinners and the activities. You should come over; you'd enjoy it.

—I'm only fifty-five, you know. I'm not an old folk.

—The walk across the bridge would do you good.

—I'd never make it; they'd have to shovel me up. No, I'll stick to the wallpapering.

Philo watched her pick at the wall with a kitchen knife until her father came home from work. He changed out of his busman's uniform while Sylvia put out his dinner on the kitchen table. He asked after his namesake, Jack, as he always did, and Philo wanted to tell him the good news but restrained herself in time. After dinner, Sylvia buttered him a slice of bread and poured out his tea. She put in three spoons of sugar, stirred vigorously and topped it off by measuring out two spoonfuls of milk to give it a dark-brown hue. It was all part of the ritual of their lives that satisfied Jack's need to be waited upon. He was, indeed, the lord and master of all he surveyed.

Philo remembered, as a teenager, telling her mother to 'let him milk and sugar his own fucking tea'. She had been put out of the house for her indiscretion and had ended up sleeping in the coal shed. She'd spent so much of her life trying to change them, always taking her mother's part and never understanding why Sylvia stayed with him. And here she was, a marriage and five children later, trying to navigate the waters of separation from Tommo, and it was killing her.

She watched Sylvia waddle over to the press and take out her jar of slimming tablets. She shook two Colfax onto her palm and drank them down with her tea. Sylvia swore by the power of the pink capsules. She'd been taking them for over twenty years. It was all part of the delusion that kept her from going insane.

Philo didn't want to go back to the convent. She waited until her father and Sally went to bed before asking her mother if it was OK for her to stay.

Sylvia was taken aback.

—You're not leaving the children with Tommo, are you?

It was Philo's second opportunity to tell the truth.

—They're staying out with Josie in Tallaght.

—She's looking after your five as well as her own?

It sounded unbelievable – it was unbelievable – and Philo was at her wits' end trying to construct a credible lie.

—It's just the girls; the boys are at home with Tommo.

It was an awful lie – giving her husband jurisdiction over the boys – and it made her want to wash her mouth out with soap.

—I'm glad you didn't leave the girls with him. I don't trust men, any of them.

Philo knew that it was Jack, her father, Sylvia was referring to. He was the man she didn't trust, the one who had made her wary of all men. She'd spent a lifetime protecting Philo from him, not always with success, but always with passion.

Philo snuggled into bed beside her mother. It had been a long day. She was tired, but she didn't want to sleep; she was at ease and wanted it to last. It might be a long time before she felt this way again. It was so quiet she could hear Sylvia breathe. Night-time usually spelt trouble for Philo, the smell of burning rubber and the screeching of brakes on stolen cars. Tonight, Jack was safe, and she was safe too. She joined her hands and said her prayers.

—*Now I lay me down to sleep,*
I pray the Lord my soul to keep.
If I should die before I wake,
I pray the Lord my soul to take....

It was hard to believe she had once been inside her mother. Ten pounds and two ounces, she'd been, when she slid out into the world. It was miraculous, considering the size they both were now. Philo unjoined her hands, put one around Sylvia's middle and held it against her stomach. She thanked God for her mother's womb. She was the fruit of it, so she thanked God for her own womb, too.

She tried to imagine the wombs of all the different women

she knew. She put a fruit in each one. Josie Cullen was skinny so she got a banana. Dina was small so she got a grape. Red-faced women got peaches and fat-arsed ones got pears; jaundiced women got mangoes and well-endowed ones got melons; crabby women, gooseberries, and women with moustaches, coconuts; pale women, lychees, and fat women, pumpkins.... The combinations went on and on and brought Philo to the deepest, fruitiest sleep she'd had in years.

She was lost in a dream jungle when she heard what sounded like an animal caught in a trap. It woke her up. She listened and thought it might be a cat outside the window. She sat up and cocked her ears. It wasn't a cat; it was a human cry. It took a moment before she realised it was Sylvia.

—What's wrong, Ma? Are you having a bad dream?

—My arm is stuck, Sylvia whispered. I can't get it back.

Philo looked across and saw her mother's right arm hanging out of the bed. She jumped out and went around to retrieve it. As soon as she touched it, Sylvia screamed out in pain. Her arm was in spasm, like the limb of an athlete with cramp. Philo massaged it, and gradually it began to ease and she could move it again. Philo lifted it back into the bed, but she could tell Sylvia was afraid it might fall out again. She lifted her right breast and eased the arm in under the folds of flesh.

—I need you to promise me something, Philo, Sylvia said.

—I'll do anything you want, Sylvia, anything.

—Do something about your weight.

Philo hated her fat, just like she hated her mother's, and this was the first time she had been asked to acknowledge that.

—If you don't do something about it, I'm going to come back and haunt you. Do you hear me? I'm going to come back from the dead and make a show of you.

Sylvia started to talk about her funeral. They'd never

broached the subject before, and Philo was amazed to hear her go through the details with great precision. She wanted a plain oak coffin, nothing fancy. Nobody was to make speeches about her in the church. Her body was to be cremated, not buried; her ashes to be thrown off Howth Head so she could fly through the air like a bird; her flowers to be placed on the altar of Saint Laurence O'Toole's church; her wedding ring to be given to Philo and her engagement ring to Sally; her savings in the Post Office to be divided equally among all the grandchildren.

Philo hoped her father would go first. It was terrible to think in those terms, but she couldn't help it. Her mother deserved a few years on this earth without her crown of thorns. Nobody deserved it more. They were macabre thoughts, yes, but she enjoyed giving them space in her head, where she could work out all her retributions.

—Look at me; I'm like an elephant, Sylvia said.

—It's only your thyroid. You can go in and have it taken out.

Sylvia gave a derisive snort, as if the illusion wasn't worth maintaining any more.

—You're not going to end up like me. I'm not going to let it happen, even if it kills me, do you hear?

Philo heard her but didn't respond. For one night, at least, she wanted everything back the way it had been when she was a little girl, before she grew fat and the world turned ugly.

8

The Day Centre was bursting with excitement. Everyone had come to find out about the blind date. They wanted to know how the odd couple had fared at the Abbey Theatre and, more importantly, afterwards at the Gresham Hotel.

They arrived at the Centre only to be confronted with the tragic events of the night before. There was no Dina, no Cap, no Philo and no scandal. All they had was Sister Rosaleen and the story of the ambulance. She recounted the drama, delighted at the role she'd played in it. She even found herself embellishing it here and there. When Nan Cassidy asked her how many people had gathered outside Dina's shop, she paused and said two hundred when she knew in her heart it had been no more than fifty.

Cap arrived for his dinner, drawn and pale. He hadn't slept. Normally it wouldn't have bothered him; he could survive on just a few hours. At two in the morning, he'd poured himself a large whiskey and knocked it back in one go. He'd thought it might induce sleep, but it had had the opposite effect. An hour later, at three o'clock, he'd found himself on patrol in Dowdall's Lane, making sure Dina's premises were secure. From there, he'd walked up to Sheriff Street and inspected his lock-up. He had gone home, satisfied, but sleep wouldn't come.

He'd poured himself another large whiskey. He'd never been a drinker and didn't know why he was indulging in it now. He was looking for courage; that was the truth of it. All his life he'd been afraid of conflict. Throughout his childhood, Gerry Sugrue had been his minder. At the first sign of trouble,

Cap had run to him for protection. It was sad for Cap to reflect that at seventy-one years of age he was still a weak man. The possibility of turning that around was there before him, and he had to find the courage to grasp it with both hands.

As soon as he arrived, Cap was pounced on by Chrissie Mongon and Ita Mullen, two of Dina's cronies. They'd been absent and missed the game of Blind Date. They wanted to know what he was doing, going out with their friend. Before he could answer, Granny Carmody interjected, wanting to know every detail from the time he'd left his house until he'd discovered the injured Dina on the floor of her bedroom. Minnie O'Hara, who sat at Dina's table, wanted to know what he'd been doing snooping around Dowdall's Lane. Nan Cassidy expressed surprise that he hadn't gone around to the Gresham Hotel and had his dinner on his own. Mucky Mannion said that it was the luck of the gods Cap hadn't used the voucher, and that Dina would be dead only for Cap's unselfishness. Joxer Farrell wanted to know who was dead, and they all had to shush him up. Then Ninna Delargy stepped in.

—Give Mr Coyle some room. Can't you see he's still in shock? she said.

It was the formal use of his name that sounded funny to Cap. He looked at Ninna. The hairs on her head seemed sculpted into place. He wasn't to know she'd spent the entire morning washing and drying her hair. There was something brittle about her, a doll-like vulnerability. He didn't know she'd spent the whole of the previous night crying over him. She'd got into bed and pulled the blankets up over her head, blocking out the light – the darkness didn't frighten her. It could have been her at the Abbey Theatre with Cap, if only she'd been brave enough. It could have been her living it up in the Gresham Hotel, if only she hadn't been so silly.

Ninna did her best to protect him from the pack of wolves, but it was no good.

—What possessed you to go down there? Ita Mullen asked.

—Did you get a message from God? Mucky wanted to know.

—He wasn't saying his prayers, he was snooping around, Chrissie Mongon said.

Cap had wanted to put a brick through Dina's window for standing him up.

—I just happened to go that way on my way home, he said. It was an accident.

He hadn't walked down Dowdall's Lane in over thirty years. It was a poisoned little street that he avoided at all costs.

—That's not on your way home, Chrissie Mongon said.

Cap felt a hot flush sweep up his face to the top of his skull. It got trapped under his cap and trickled back down whence it came.

—It's not on my way home, no, he said.

—You went there on purpose, Chrissie Mongon said.

—Yes, I did, I went there for a reason –

—You went there to spy on her, Minnie O'Hara butted in.

—No, I didn't....

—Why did you go there, so? Ita Mullen asked.

—I went there to ask her why she'd stood me up.

It was a version of the truth that seemed to satisfy the majority.

—She stood you up because she hates you, Ita Mullen said.

There was real venom in her tone. Cap felt threatened by it; he wanted to hide.

—No, she was getting ready and she slipped, he said.

—That's what you'd like to believe, Chrissie Mongon said.

—That's the truth.

—She'd do anything to avoid you, that's the truth, Minnie O'Hara said.

—She stood you up, Ita Mullen said.

Cap knew it wasn't true. They hadn't seen the look on Dina's face when she came out on the stretcher. They hadn't heard her kind words.

—She hates you with a passion, Ita Mullen said with finality.

Dina's cronies retreated to the far end of the room and sat waiting for their soup to arrive. Cap started to doubt himself. Could it all have been a plan to avoid him? Ninna Delargy took hold of his arm and gave it a squeeze. Cap acknowledged it and turned to walk away, but the Commandant stood in front of him and blocked his path. He put his hand to the side of his head and stiffened it in salute.

—You saved her life, soldier. Congratulations.

—Thanks, Barney, Cap said. Thank you for that.

Ninna watched it all, delighted that the date had fallen apart. She sat by herself, as usual, but she didn't feel alone. After the soup was served, she walked over to Cap and told him she'd like to be included in the racing game, if that was acceptable. Cap consented, and she walked back to her table delighted with herself.

At the far end of the room, the cronies laughed out loud at something. Cap felt it was at his expense. He stood up and walked down to them.

—I want to say something, he said.

They stopped eating and looked up at him. The other tables, too, went silent.

—I don't hate Dina, do you hear me?

The cronies made no reply.

—I'm asking if you hear me.

—Yes, they mumbled in reply.

—I don't hate her.

He wanted to say more about how he felt, but it wasn't appropriate.

—When I want to know what she feels, I'll ask her. Is that clear?

—Yes, they mumbled again.

—I don't need you to tell me. I will ask Dina myself.

Cap turned abruptly and walked back to his seat. In the silence, Mucky started to clap, and then the others joined in with a generous round of applause.

Philo was lathered in sweat. She cursed every granite step at the front of the Mater Hospital, and she cursed the baggy knickers that let rivers of perspiration escape down the fronts and backs of her legs. She stopped by the entrance doors to get her breath back. She would have to do something about her weight, as soon as she got organised. For today, the crisis was accommodation.

She'd been to the housing department that morning. In front of an official of Dublin Corporation, she'd declared herself homeless. When he asked her for a current address, she gave it as care of the convent. He wrote it down on a form and passed it through the hatch to her. For one glorious moment, Philo thought she was going to get something there and then; but the official just asked her to fill in her details and warned her that false or misleading information would result in permanent exclusion from the housing list and/or a fine. She wanted to scream, but instead she scrunched up the form and stuffed it into her bag. She'd marched out of the housing department in a temper, which was a mistake, because it had increased her body's metabolism and made her sweat more.

She headed into the lobby of the Mater Hospital and looked for a Toilets sign. There wasn't one to be seen. Undaunted, Philo headed for the nearest ward. She found Saint Joseph's – a men's ward, but she didn't care; needs must. She slipped into the toilet, locked the door, stripped off her coat and blouse and draped them across the bath. She searched for toilet paper and found a box of cut squares that came out one by one – just her luck. She pulled out a handful and dabbed under her arms, across her shoulders and under her breasts. Then she hitched up her skirt and dried under her knickers and down along her legs. By the time she was finished, the toilet bowl looked like a papier-mâché factory. When she flushed the toilet, the paper collected in the S-bend and the water rose up and spilled onto the floor. Philo was starting to mop it up with a towel when a patient knocked on the door, demanding access. He was so insistent that she had no alternative but to open the door and evacuate her position as quickly as her legs would carry her.

She returned to the lobby and enquired after Dina. The porter asked for a surname. Philo had to think for a moment.

—I think it's Sore, she said. Dina Sore.

—Dina Sore, the porter repeated. He flicked through his ledger of patients. Dina Sore, Dina Sore … I don't think we have a Dina Sore.

—I hope not, Philo said. They're extinct.

The porter looked at her and got the joke. He was not pleased. Philo was sorry for her prank. She was sorry she'd played it on this humourless version of homo sapiens.

—It's Sugrue, Dina Sugrue, she said, trying to look penitent.

It took him eleven minutes to find the name.

—Third floor, end of the corridor, Unit 4, he said.

—Plus two, Philo said.

He looked at her like she was a Cyclops.

—Unit Four Plus Two, 'The Concrete and the Clay', she said, and walked off.

They were a pop group from the sixties, one-hit wonders. Philo and Josie used to sing their song. Philo loved the line, 'the concrete and the clay beneath my feet begins to crumble'. She often found herself singing it for no reason. Maybe it was because her life was in that line. She sang it going up in the lift and along the corridor.

When Philo turned in to Unit 4, the first thing she heard was Dina screaming. A doctor and a nurse were by her bed, trying to calm her down. She had two big bandages, one on either foot; they were so big, her feet looked like skis. The nurse was trying to convince her to let the doctor cut the bandages open.

—Oh, Philo, save me, please save me! They won't leave me alone!

—It's only the doctor and the nurse, Dina. They're trying to help you.

—No, no, no, they're trying to cut me up – save me, Philo, please, save me!

Philo exchanged looks with the medics. It was obvious they had no solution. She took the initiative and sat on the side of the bed. Dina snuggled against her, as if shielding herself from attack, and Philo patted her on the back of the head as though she were an upset child.

—I brought you a surprise, but I'm not giving it to you if you don't do what you're told.

Dina squeezed hard into Philo's flesh.

—I'll do anything you tell me, but keep that doctor away from me.

—I have to check your wounds and make sure they're healing properly, Mrs Sugrue, I have to do it, the doctor said firmly.

—If you don't let Doctor do it, I'll have to send for Matron, the nurse added.

Philo could feel the fear in Dina's touch. She was going on seventy and behaving like she was seven.

—She's just afraid you'll cut her little piggies, Philo said.

Dina pushed her face right in under Philo's armpit and squeezed even closer.

125

—Is that what you're afraid of? Philo asked her.

—Yes, she replied.

—I won't let them hurt your little piggies, Philo reassured her.

The doctor put his hand on Philo's shoulder.

—Can we talk outside, please? he said.

His tone was soft but serious. Philo released Dina back down onto her pillows, gave her the white sheets to hold on to and went out to the corridor.

Despite the intense heat, the news sent a cold shiver up Philo's spine. Dina had lost three toes from her right foot and two from her left. The damage had been done in the hours she'd spent on the bedroom floor: hypothermia had blown its evil breath on her and cut off the blood supply to her toes. There was a possibility she might lose more. It was important that the doctors examine the wounds to see how they were healing. That would tell them a great deal. They didn't want to sedate Dina, because of her age, but they would if she continued to resist them.

Philo was overcome with guilt. She and her stupid game of Blind Date had been the reason for this catastrophe. No matter how many times she swore to change, no human force could prevent her mouth from opening and spewing out its bullshit. She wished she could be in a hospital bed waiting to have her mouth stitched shut. But she wasn't; it was Dina lying there, looking up at her with those intense, pleading eyes of hers. Philo couldn't abandon her, not now – not after the part she'd played in putting her there.

Philo went back to the bed. She cupped a hand under each of Dina's feet and lifted them gently into the air.

—We're going to cut open these bandages and I want you to be still, do you understand that? she said.

Dina looked at her from under her lids.

—As long as you do it.

126

Philo looked at the doctor and the nurse. There was an almighty silence. Then the doctor stepped forward and ran his finger across the front of the bandage.

—I want you to cut across here, he said.

He handed the scissors to Philo. She slipped one of the blades under the bandage and started to cut. The sharp edge slowly crunched its way across the muslin sea. She withdrew the scissors and did the same on the other foot. The doctor pulled the flaps apart to have a look, and Dina immediately jerked her leg back. She looked to Philo for support, but it wasn't there.

—Either you let him look or you get a needle in the arse, Philo said.

The warning produced an immediate change of heart. Dina stuck her leg out like she couldn't wait to have it examined. Smiles broke out around the room. The doctor shone his light on the foot, and Philo arched over his shoulder to get a look. It was sad to see the gaps where Dina's toes should have been. The ones that remained looked lost, like dancers without partners. The nurse cleaned the wounds, pushed white ointment into the gaps and replaced the bandages. The doctor made notes on his chart, thanked Dina for her co-operation, told her she was on the mend and then briskly left the ward.

Philo sat down, determined to make the best of a bad situation.

—You're a very lucky woman, she said. You must have been saying your prayers.

—I'm in hospital, Philo. How is that lucky?

—You're bleedin' steeped; you could have lost your fingers. Look at them.

Dina did as she was commanded. She held up her fingers and examined them.

—Why am I looking at my fingers?

—You could have lost them, that's why. Think of all the things you do with your fingers.

—Like holding a cigarette, do you mean?

—Exactly. And weighing out your vegetables.

—Putting money in the till and giving out change.

—Picking your nose and flicking the snot.

—I don't pick my nose; I'm a lady.

—There's a million things you do with your fingers. You do fuck all with your toes.

—What have my toes got to do with my fingers?

—If you had to lose one, what would you pick – a finger or a toe?

Dina looked at her bandaged feet. She hadn't thought too much about what lay beneath the muslin – not until that moment. She had no feeling from the knees down. Her feet felt detached from her, like they belonged to someone else.

—Have I lost one of my piggies? she asked.

Philo was determined to stay optimistic, but Dina's pathetic, hurt little face was making cracks in her resolve.

—You've lost more than one, Philo said.

—How many little piggies have I lost?

—You've lost five altogether. Three from your right and two from your left.

Dina collapsed in a wail. The air left her body and was replaced by sobs. Philo wrapped her up in an embrace and rocked her. She pulled out a few squares of toilet roll she'd nicked earlier, gave them to Dina and told her to blow her nose. Dina managed a small nasal clearance and Philo congratulated her like she'd just ridden the winner of the Grand National. Dina tried to say something, but she was too choked up to get the words out.

—What good are piggies anyway? Philo went on. They're a fucking nuisance, to be honest. I have two ingrown toenails and you wouldn't want them. I'm telling you, Dina, they have me crucified. I went to that chiropodist in Fairview and I had to give him a bag – he nearly got sick on me. Never saw anything like them. I've blisters on my little toes the size of saucepans. Do you get corns, Dina? Do you?

—Sometimes I do.

—I'm slaughtered with them. Tried to cut them off and they broke every scissors I had. I feel like tearing the guts out of them sometimes. They're worse than piles.

Dina held her hand out; it took Philo a minute to realise she needed more tissue. She had none left, so she slipped into the toilet and brought out a handful of squares. She fed them to Dina until she'd cleared her nostrils and dried her eyes.

—Thank God you're here or I don't know what I'd do, Dina said.

It was hard to wrest compliments from Dina, and Philo would have been flattered had she not felt so guilty.

—You're better than a daughter, Dina said.

It was nice to receive unsolicited praise. Dina had a daughter, Florence. When Philo had been in junior infants, Florrie Sugrue was in fourth class. They were aware of each other but had never been friends. Philo wondered if Florrie knew about her mother and the state she was in. Rather than raise the subject and disturb the equilibrium, Philo indulged the compliment that had her on a pedestal.

—I was hoping you'd do something for me, Dina said.

—I'll do it if I can.

—I have some regular customers. They'll be looking for their vegetables.

Philo held her hand up to stop her.

—You want me to open the shop for you.

—An hour in the morning and an hour in the evening, that's all.

There was only one alternative, and that was Cap's. Dina was afraid to hand him an advantage; even on her sickbed, she was afraid to lose customers to him.

—I'll get someone else if you can't do it, Dina said.

—I didn't say I wouldn't bleedin' do it, did I say that?

—I'll pay you. I don't expect you to work for nothing.

—It has nothing to do with money.

Philo was wondering how long they'd keep Dina in. It was a serious thing to lose toes, and they might have to amputate more. She'd be confined for several weeks. They couldn't let her out until the wounds healed. They looked pretty raw, from what Philo had seen.

She thought about the shop. There were advantages to taking it on. In the short term, it could solve her accommodation crisis.

—You'd want me to open in the morning, Philo said.

—Yes, I would.

—That means I'd have to stay over.

—Only if you wanted to.

—If I'm going to do the job, I'm going to do it right. What about your daughter Florrie? Philo asked.

—What about her?

—I don't want to be stepping on anyone's toes, that's all.

Philo and her big mouth; she'd done it again, done it in style, as she always did. But Dina didn't seem to notice; she continued with her train of thought unbroken.

—She has no time for me. She's a daddy's girl, always was and always will be.

—I suppose I can't refuse you. I'll do it.

Dina smiled like a well-fed cat. Philo opened her bag and was greeted by the form from the housing department. She pulled it out of the way, and there was the form from the convent for becoming a nun. Under that were the ten Woodbines she'd brought as a surprise. She handed them over, and Dina remarked how lucky she was not to have lost her fingers.

That afternoon, Philo went out to Goldenbridge to see the children. She told them about her new job as a vegetable woman, but they weren't very interested. They wanted to

130

know when they were getting out and where they were going to live. Philo showed them the form from the housing department and told them it was their passport to a new life. They were immune to promises that usually turned out to be false. Philo fed them their chocolate surprises and they stuffed their mouths instead.

Accommodation wasn't such a big issue for Jack, but he was delighted for Philo. 'Delighted' was the buzzword in the Home for the week (it had been 'grateful' the week before), and the boys were encouraged to use it as much as possible. Philo's news made it easy for Jack. He was delighted on every front – delighted she was making the break into vegetables, delighted she was getting away from her pig of a husband; there was no other word, he was delighted. Philo herself was delighted, but she wondered could he not use some other expression the odd time.

—Like what, Ma? Jack asked.

—Like thrilled bleedin' skinny, Philo said.

—Bleedin' is a curse and we're not allowed to curse.

—Well, thrilled skinny, then.

Brother Felix came into the room and was delighted to see her.

—Thrilled skinny to see you, too, Philo said.

—I haven't heard that expression since I was a kid, he said.

—Well, I'm delighted for you, Philo said.

—I'm delighted, too, he said.

—So am I – I'm delighted, too, Jack said.

The three of them smiled at one another.

—We're all bleedin' delighted, so can we stop bleedin' saying it? Philo said.

Brother Felix laughed. Philo told him about Dina and he commiserated over her toes. When she revealed that she was now in charge of the shop, he almost said he was delighted for her but stopped himself in time.

131

—I'm excited at your promotion, he said.

Jack was excited, too. He had a car ready to race. He'd worked on every bit of it and had it in mint condition. He was going to give it a solo run at the track on the Sunday and he was, well, delighted with himself.

By the time she got to Dina's, Philo was exhausted. She'd bought a large single of chips and two smoked cod. She sat at the rickety kitchen table and broke open the white wrapping paper. The chips were swimming in vinegar, just the way she liked them. She picked up a handful and let them drip onto her tongue before dropping them into her mouth. They disappeared down her throat at great speed. There were five pieces of cod in all, two large and three small ones. She picked up a large piece and bit into it. There was half an inch of batter heaven, crispy brown on the outside and soft underneath. She was drooling over it when her teeth met the pure, orange flesh of the fish. It was a double assault on the taste buds, and she surrendered to it.

She knew she would sleep. It was the reward for eating. Her body would ingest and her mind would shut out reality. The vinegar would course through her veins while her body recovered its strength. Philo licked her salty fingers and retired to the bedroom. There was rubbish strewn here and there, but she didn't care. She stepped over the box of Dina's mementoes and lay down on the bed. The weight of the world descended on her eyelids.

Just as they closed, she caught sight of a cobweb on the ceiling, above the light. She tried to shut it out of her mind, but it wouldn't go. The thing Philo feared most in life was spiders. She'd rather face a crocodile than a spider. She imagined one landing on her face. It was the way they moved that frightened her. The black ones with the thin legs were the worst.

She opened her eyes and looked up. There were families of cobwebs on the ceiling, reaching into the dark corners. The spiders were waiting for her to fall asleep before they trooped out to view her tender flesh.

She got up and went in search of a vacuum cleaner. She opened every press and drawer in the kitchen, to no avail. What she did find was cups, saucers, knives, forks, sugar bowls and salt cellars, all remarkably like the ones used in the Day Centre. Not wanting to entertain thoughts of Dina as a thieving bitch, Philo concentrated on finding a vacuum cleaner. The best she could do, however, was a sweeping brush.

She brought it into the bedroom and raised it over her head to the ceiling. As soon as she made a sweeping motion, two spiders landed at her feet. She left the room at the speed of light. Before she knew it, she was on her way to her mother's.

When she got to Irvine Terrace, her father opened the door, surprised to see her. Sylvia was in bed taking a nap. Jack asked after the children (his namesake in particular) and wondered why Philo wasn't at home serving them up their dinner. She asked for a loan of the vacuum cleaner and immediately got a refusal. That was Jack: paranoid about his possessions and about letting them out of his sight. She was about to tell him to stuff it when he dragged the vacuum cleaner out from under the stairs and warned her to return it ASAP. She draped the hose around her neck, took the body under her arm and set off over the bridge once more.

Philo hated men. It stemmed from her father. Everything in him was rigid, like a straitjacket. He never seemed to care how she was feeling or what was going on in her head; all he cared about was making judgements. She could never measure up to anything in his eyes. Everything she touched was a failure. It had never crossed his mind to wonder why she needed the vacuum cleaner; nothing could be allowed to disturb his routine. His world was sacrosanct.

Philo remembered an incident from her childhood. Her father had been a conductor on a single-decker bus at the time, the number 3 route from Ringsend to Santry. When they introduced the double-deckers, he put a rope across the stairs on his bus and refused to let the passengers up. When the bosses asked him what he was doing, Jack told them he'd take down the obstruction when they paid him to work two buses. He nearly lost his job over it. It was a funny story in the pub among his friends, but they didn't have to come home and live with him. Bad as he was on the buses, he was four times as big a bastard in the house.

Back in Dowdall's Lane, Philo cautiously entered the bedroom and searched for a socket. There was one to the left of the bed. She tried to insert the plug, but it wouldn't go in; she examined the socket and saw that it had only two holes, but that there were three bits sticking out of the plug.

She stood up to ponder her situation and realised that she was swimming in sweat again. She went to the bathroom to dry herself off. Fortunately, it was well stocked with toilet roll – and it wasn't the cheap stuff, either; it was the same brand they used in the Day Centre. So was the soap that sat on the sink and the towel that hung from the rail. All of Dina's possessions came from the convent.

Philo thought about a bath, but the water was freezing. She boiled a kettle on the gas, poured it into the sink and washed herself down. She rooted around in Dina's drawers for fresh underwear until she found a large pair of knickers. They wouldn't even come up over her knees. She had no choice but to revert to the sweaty ones, having dried them off with a towel first. No matter about the suffering; her priority was getting rid of the cobwebs. That meant finding an adaptor or changing the plug. Philo headed out the door, bound for town.

Along the way, she passed Cap's lock-up store. It was closed. Her gut instinct was to call round to his house and give him the news. He was one of the few good men she knew – straightforward and honest, with not a devious bone in his body. But time was against her. She walked at good speed as far as Clifford's in Talbot Lane; it was a television repair shop, but the assistant had an adaptor and gave it to her for half nothing. On her way back, she went the long way so she could call in on Cap.

He lived in a cottage at the back of the boys' school. It had been in the family since his grandfather, Christy (after whom he'd been named), had moved there in 1892. The row of cottages had been built by a local wine merchant for his employees. Cap's father, Bronco, had purchased their cottage outright, and when he died he had left it to his son. It had been beautifully maintained down the years. The hall door and windows were the original timbers, preserved in mint condition because Cap had painted them every year without fail. The exterior elegance was matched by a tidy interior. Cap had been a bachelor all his life, but despite the absence of a woman it was a house with a feminine feel, and in summer there were always fresh flowers in the window-boxes.

Philo turned left into Coburg Place. As she approached Cap's house, the hall door opened and Ninna Delargy stepped onto the footpath, followed by Cap. He pulled the door closed after him and made sure it was locked. They were turning to walk down the street when Cap spotted Philo. He became very flustered and embarrassed. Philo stared at the geriatric Romeo who'd been caught with his trousers down. She felt nauseated, thinking of Dina's missing toes.

—I'm walking Ninna home, Cap said.

—I can see that, Philo replied. I haven't lost my eyesight, thanks be to Jaysus.

—Mr Coyle is a proper gentleman, Ninna said.

It wasn't the word Philo would have chosen. All she saw

135

and felt was betrayal. Dina in her hospital bed, and Cap entertaining another woman in his home. The thought of him running his fingers through Ninna's permed hair came into her head and she couldn't get it out of there. He was guilty, she knew that by his body language, and she was gutted.

In fact, Cap's only crime was that he had been at home when Ninna called. She'd come around with the offer of tickets to the Abbey Theatre; she'd asked Cap to accompany her. She felt sorry that his previous visit had been so botched up. Cap, touched by her concern, brought her into the house. It was a terrible mistake. He offered her a cup of tea and she drank it at the rate of one sip every twenty minutes. An hour after she arrived, she still had half a cup to go. At one point Cap tried to take it, but Ninna wouldn't let it go. The other difficulty was that he couldn't shut her up. It was hard to believe this was the same shy woman who kept to herself in the Day Centre. She told him all about her childhood, her family, her marriage and her need for a loving companion. In the end, Cap had put on his overcoat and told her he'd walk her home.

—How is Dina? Cap asked Philo. Have you heard any news?

—She was alive the last I heard, Philo said.

—I was going to go up and see her. Do you think that would be all right?

—The way things are right now, maybe you should leave it.

Cap wanted to say more but couldn't. Philo wanted to imagine the worst, and did. In this atmosphere of mutual misunderstanding, they parted. Cap walked Ninna to her home on the canal and Philo went back to Dowdall's Lane.

She plugged in the vacuum cleaner and made spiders homeless by the thousand. Her thoughts were on the vegetable war. She had always blamed Dina for starting it, but now she wasn't so sure. She was consumed with rage at Cap. She'd wanted to believe in the possibility of a peaceful future, to believe that men and women could coexist without destroying one another. If the old folks were fighting, then what chance was there for Jack, Eileen, Josie, Young Tommo and Philomena? Philo had put a lot of hope in Dina and Cap. She didn't want to take sides, but she was being forced to.

She lay down, and, despite the strength of the emotions doing battle inside her, she slept the sleep of the dead in Dina's bed.

9

It was the middle of the night. Philo woke with the taste of cobwebs in her mouth. She was alone and motherless. She looked at the wall for a crucifix, thinking she might be in the convent, but all she saw was a strip of torn wallpaper. She looked around for something familiar and thought she saw a dog stretched out on the floor, looking up at her. Who did she know with a dog? She couldn't think of a single person. Then she realised it wasn't a dog; it had a trunk. A second later, she realised it was a vacuum cleaner, and a millisecond after that she knew precisely where she was.

She wouldn't sleep again, that was certain. She got up to make tea and wash the taste from her mouth. On her way from the bed to the door, she tripped over the vacuum cleaner and nearly broke her neck. She kicked out at it like it had misbehaved. In the kitchen, she lit the gas ring and filled the kettle, then brought them together in the interests of making tea. Knowing that a watched kettle never boils (it was another of Sylvia's favourite expressions), she went to her handbag and brought out the form from the housing department.

It looked intimidating, with its obstacle course of white spaces and black boxes. Philo started in the top left-hand corner with the long version of her name, Philomena, in block capitals. That was followed by her married name, Nolan, and after that the names of her children and their dates of birth. It was slow, painful work, but her family history started to take shape on the page. She filled in her maiden name, Darcy, and her parents' Christian names, Sylvia and Jack – in that order, her mother first, taking pride of place for once. Her mother's maiden name was next, and as she wondered why they needed that, the kettle started to whistle. Philo did her best to ignore it.

—Hold your whist, can't you see I'm busy?

She was navigating the section on lone parents, trying to work out if she was legally separated or not. She put a tick for 'yes'. Satisfied, she went on to the next section, which asked for the name of the court that had granted the separation decree. She flung down her pen in temper and roared over at the kettle:

—It's all your fault, you whistling bastard!

She got up and removed it from the gas.

—You're starting to annoy me, do you know that?

She put two tea-bags in a cup, poured boiling water on them and plunged them with a teaspoon until they were well and truly drowned. A strong cup of tea was the only thing that calmed her nerves. She added three spoons of sugar and drank it black. It was half pleasure and half punishment. It woke her up but left a taste in her mouth that was worse than the cobwebs. The form was the real object of her rage, and she wanted to pummel it into powder, but it wasn't hers to pummel.

After the tea and a cigarette, Philo went back and put a line through the 'yes' box on legal separation. It didn't look very neat, so she continued working away with her pen and turned it into a black solid that looked like a coffin. She filled in the rest of the form, and by the time she was finished, the first flickers of daylight were starting to steal in through the window. It was time to get washed and dressed before heading to the housing department with her masterpiece. In the absence of hot water from the tap, Philo refilled the kettle and kissed it, grateful that she hadn't done it any permanent damage.

She left Dina's and headed up town. It was eight o'clock when she arrived at the office in Jervis Street. The building was closed tight. Philo was so anxious to return the form, it had never occurred to her to check the opening time. A blue-on-white sign in the window read, '10 to 12.30 and 2 to 4'. She banged on the door, more in frustration than in hope.

Her only option, apart from waiting two hours, was to post the form in the letterbox. She didn't have an envelope. She sat on the front step, leaned the form on her knee and wrote 'EMERGENCY CASE' in block capitals across the top. It looked good, she thought. She added two coffins, one on either side. Now she wasn't so sure. She decided she'd come back later.

As she rose to go, a security van pulled up alongside her. The window rolled down and a man in uniform looked straight out at Philo.

—Are you looking for something? he said.

—A two-bedroom house on the north side, she said. Do you have one?

The security man was lost for words. Finally, he managed to splutter out:

—We had a report of someone acting suspiciously. It wasn't you, was it?

—Acting, me? I go to the Abbey Theatre if I want to see acting.

He turned away and spoke into his walkie-talkie. Then he drove away. Seconds later, the door of the housing department opened and the night porter stepped out. He looked like a man on the point of a heart attack.

—Was it you banged on the door, Missus? he asked.

—I was only trying to leave in this form. I'll come back later.

The night porter relaxed, delighted it wasn't a break-in. Philo turned to leave and he shouted after her:

—I can take that, if you like.

Mission accomplished, Philo walked back to Dina's via the twenty-four-hour shop and bought sausages, rashers,

140

eggs, butter and bread. There would be plenty of time for breakfast and a snooze before she had to open the shop. It was hard to believe she was stepping into Dina's shoes.

The previous day, in the hospital, she'd played down the importance of toes. Reflecting on it now, she realised how important they were for walking. It was the toes that gripped the ground and stopped you from falling over. Every time a foot went out, the toes acted like a buffer. It was an automatic thing.

Philo looked at the feet of the people trundling through town and tried to imagine what would happen if they were toeless. There would be a lot of people crawling to work, she concluded. Toes were much more important than she'd given them credit for. Dina still had half of hers left, and they might be a very important half – the difference between walking and not walking. Half a loaf was always better than no bread.

There were five people waiting outside Dina's shop when Philo got back, among them Chrissie Mongon, Ita Mullen and Mouse O'Hara, Dina's cronies. The thirst for information was insatiable. Two of the cronies (Mouse O'Hara being the exception) had called up to see Dina the night before. They'd only been let stay a few minutes, as Dina had been given sedatives and was ready for sleep, but it was enough time for them to ascertain two things: one, that Philo had saved Dina from the doctor by taking the scissors off him; and, two, that she'd actually seen the site of the amputations.

—This shop doesn't open until ten o'clock. You may as well go home for an hour, Philo said.

—We're not here for vegetables, we're here for news, Chrissie Mongon said.

—Well, I'm not a bleedin' gossip, so you can fish some-where else for news.

—Just tell us what it looks like, Philo, Ita Mullen said. Does it look awful?

Philo opened the shop and they all trooped in after her. She was halfway up the stairs when she realised someone was behind her. She turned around and saw Chrissie Mongon following her.

—These are living quarters up here, Philo said, and they're private.

Chrissie Mongon said nothing, just walked back down the stairs without a hint of guilt in her gait. Philo went to the kitchen and put the shopping on the shelf beside the sink. She half-filled the kettle and put it on the gas, then returned downstairs with the intention of getting rid of her customers as quickly as possible. Chrissie Mongon, Ita Mullen and Mouse O'Hara were sitting on boxes, behind the counter.

—I hope you're comfortable, Philo said.

—Yes, we're grand, they replied.

—You wouldn't like a cushion or anything, would you?

—We kept the cushion for you, Ita Mullen said.

There in the corner was the throne Dina sat on – a faded brown leatherette armchair. It looked like it had been made for a leprechaun. The legs had been sawn off, so it sat very close to the ground. In the middle was a cushion that looked out of place because of its newness.

Philo looked at the armchair and looked at the cronies. She knew it would crumble under her weight.

—You're very bleedin' thoughtful, she said sarcastically.

Two other women had arrived and were standing outside the counter. Philo recognised them: they were from the new houses in Oriel Street.

—What can I do for you, ladies? Philo asked.

—She must be in an awful state, the poor woman, one of them said.

—Her toes gone just like that; she must be very sore, the other one said.

It was gossip time, and Philo wanted to surrender to the word 'yes'; she wanted to put it on a poster and hold it up for all to see. But she tried to concentrate on the task in hand, to focus on the role she'd been given by Dina.

—What vegetables would you like?

There was a pause as they contemplated the question.

—Would you like some carrots and onions?

—Do you know what I think? one of the women said.

—You're thinking potatoes, Philo said. I can tell by your face.

—I think you can get toes replaced nowadays, she said with conviction.

That opened the floodgates, and the company went at it like seasoned professionals. One of the women had seen on the television where a man had had his finger sewn back on when he'd cut it off with an electric saw. Someone else had heard of a lion tamer getting his arm re-attached. They'd all seen the man in America who'd had his penis cut off, and he deserved it, too, but it was a miracle of science the way they'd stuck it back on again. Surely if they could save a penis they could save a toe. If they could make false teeth and grow hair on Elton John's head, they could do anything. Someone had heard they were giving pigs' hearts to human beings, and they drew the line at that. A transplant too far, that was.

Philo felt like she was at a medical conference. She closed her eyes and all she could see were people with missing limbs. Sylvia without an arm, sleeping peacefully. Tommo with no eyes, throwing blindly at a dartboard. Her father, headless at the back of a bus, and the passengers screaming. She opened her eyes and there were two more women in the shop, eager to contribute to the growing mountain of medical knowledge.

—Do you want vegetables or are you here to gossip? Philo asked.

—We're here to gossip, one of the women said.

—Well, you can buy first or you can get out of here, Philo said. And that goes for all of you.

She rolled up her sleeves like she meant business, and suddenly a new attitude permeated the room. One of the women from Oriel Street ordered a half-pound of carrots, and such was the silent stare Philo gave her that she changed her order first to two pounds and then to three. In addition, she bought five pounds of potatoes, three onions and a turnip, none of which she needed. With the purchases on the counter, Philo stared at them and realised she didn't have a price list.

—How much does Dina charge for carrots? she asked.

—Thirty pence a pound, Chrissie Mongon replied.

—Well, I'm not a charity; they're sixty pence a pound from today.

Philo doubled the price of everything and there wasn't one dissenting voice. In fact, everyone seemed delighted to be paying more. It might have been out of sympathy for Dina and her lost toes. Ita Mullen was getting her change (she was the last to be served) when Philo thought of the uncooked breakfast that was waiting for her upstairs. At the same time, she remembered the kettle.

She dropped the coins and bounded up the stairs. As she did, the acrid smell of burning metal assaulted her nostrils. When she reached the kitchen, the kettle was doing a jig on the ring, looking like it might explode. She knew not to touch it. She picked up a sweeping brush and, with the handle, hauled the kettle from its perch.

—You wouldn't whistle when it was needed, you bastard you.

She'd forgotten to put the cap on the spout. As a result, she'd fried the kettle. It was black and brittle as charcoal. She put it down on the table and it started to burn the wood. Quick as a flash, she moved it to the sink and dropped it in. The water it touched quickly vaporised and hissed away into space. Philo wished she could fuck off into space along with it. She wanted to be anywhere but where she was. In bed with Sylvia, her knees tucked up under her mother's fleshy bum and her arm draped across her warm stomach.

It took the kettle ten minutes to cool down. Philo picked it up with a damp cloth and brought it downstairs. The three cronies were still sitting on their perches like wise old owls. She put the remains on the counter for the post mortem.

—What is it? Mouse O'Hara asked.

—It's Dina's kettle, Ita Mullen said.

—Was a kettle but is no more, Chrissie Mongon said.

—She won't be able to make a cup of tea when she gets home from the hospital, Mouse O'Hara said.

Philo felt doubly guilty.

—Do you know where she got it? she asked.

—The convent, they all chirped.

Philo was taken aback at the frank admission. She would have expected Dina's friends to be a little more circumspect.

—She got it in the convent, did she? she repeated.

—That came from the convent, definitely, Chrissie Mongon said.

—Like everything else, Philo added. And you three needn't look all innocent; I know what you're like.

—I don't know what you're talking about, Mouse O'Hara said.

Philo was not going to be taken in.

—I'm talking about everything that's up them stairs. Cups, saucers, toilet rolls.

She stared at them like a lawyer in full flow.

—Soap and towels as well. All stolen out of the convent. Sugar bowls and cutlery, too.

The three cronies had no defence.

—You wonder where the kids of the area get it – and you robbing the nuns blind, all of you.

—Dina won that kettle in a raffle, Chrissie Mongon said.

—You needn't try and change your story, Philo said.

—Last Christmas, the nuns had a raffle and Dina won the kettle, Ita Mullen said.

—Sister Rosaleen pulled her number out of the hat, Mouse O'Hara said.

—It was the third prize, a whistling kettle, Chrissie Mongon added.

Philo wanted to be dead and in heaven. Unfortunately, she was alive and in the middle of a dung heap.

—Why didn't we hear it whistling before it got burnt? Mouse O'Hara asked.

Philo wanted to stuff what remained of the kettle into her own mouth. She wanted to superglue her lips together so she could never speak again. She felt totally humiliated. She wished they would pick up the vegetables and throw them at her. She was the village idiot, after all. She had attempted to reveal a bad side of Dina and had ended up with egg on her own face. Since she couldn't disappear, she decided to retire upstairs. As she left, she turned and spoke to the cronies.

—If you mention anything about what I said just now, to anyone, I'll cut your tongues out, do you hear?

—Yes, we hear you, they mumbled.

Philo walked slowly up the stairs and put on the fry. She cooked everything she had – eight sausages, ten rashers and six fried eggs. When they were cooked, she stuffed them into her mouth with abandon. She lay down with a beautiful taste in her mouth, put there by the mix of bacon and fried bread. It was working its way down her throat when she was disturbed by shouts from downstairs.

—Come down here, Philo, there's a man to see you.

She thought they were pulling her leg.

—Is he good-looking? she roared down.

The silence was deafening.

—Well, his mother thinks he's beautiful, Chrissie Mongon said.

Philo got out of bed and headed down, intent on giving

them a tongue-lashing. She bounded into the shop and there was Brother Felix, looking decidedly out of place. Philo didn't know what to say, didn't know what to call him, didn't want to give anything away; in her state of confusion, she said:

—Brother. Monk. Felix. Jaysus.

The three cronies were delighted. It wasn't every day an exotic stranger came into Dina's, especially one with four names who reduced Philo to blabbering.

—Is that your brother? Chrissie Mongon asked.

—I must say he doesn't look like you, Ita Mullen said.

—That's the Monk, he's famous, Mouse O'Hara said.

—Are you the Monk? Chrissie Mongon asked. Are you really him?

Brother Felix laughed. The Monk was a famous criminal in Dublin, an elusive figure known by name but rarely seen in public.

—No, he's not the Monk, he's Felix, Philo said.

—You should be called the Cat, if you're Felix, Ita Mullen said.

—Well, I was a monk one time –

—Don't tell them your business, Philo interrupted, unless you want it broadcast all over the area.

It was important that she see Brother Felix alone. She told the women to get out of her shop. Chrissie Mongon tried to point out that it wasn't her shop, and this enraged Philo altogether. She picked up a handful of tomatoes and threatened to splatter them. They started to move to the door, but not fast enough for Philo; she discharged a tomato, and it whizzed past Ita Mullen's head and exploded against the cement wall. (She had missed deliberately, but they weren't to know that.) A second tomato took up firing position in her hand. They all covered their heads and made a hurried exit.

Out on Dowdall's Lane, the complaints started. Philo told them to write them down and she'd pass them on to Dina. She shut the door and offered Brother Felix Dina's throne,

147

which was more his size than hers. She sat on a sack of potatoes.

—I know Jack's done something, so spit it out, Philo said.

—Jack's done nothing.

Brother Felix gave a nervous laugh, which Philo read as an admission that she was right.

—He's after wetting the bed, is he?

Philo could think of no other reason why this man was sitting in front of her. Jack was a serial bed-wetter. She'd tried everything to stop it: she'd cut out liquids before bed, she'd tried getting him to pee in the middle of the night, she'd set alarm clocks for him, but nothing worked. She'd had his kidneys checked out, too, and they were in perfect working order.

—I know what he's like; you don't need to cover up for him.

—Jack doesn't wet the bed, Brother Felix said. I'd know if he did, believe me.

—Why are you here if it's not trouble? Philo asked.

—I'm here to buy vegetables.

—Stop bleedin' messing, now. I'm a bit old for having my leg pulled.

Brother Felix took a list of vegetables out of his pocket and started to read it out. It had been compiled by the boys in the house. When they'd come to choosing a messenger boy, Brother Felix had volunteered himself for the job. The boys had been suspicious of him – and they'd been right: he had an ulterior motive, and as he worked through the list with Philo, it began to emerge.

—It would mean an awful lot to Jack if you came out to the racetrack on Sunday, he said.

Philo hadn't given it a thought. She'd been so caught up with other things – her housing crisis, Dina's toes, running the shop – that she hadn't focused on Jack at all.

She felt that she'd failed him again. Sometimes she looked

at him and wished that she'd given him up for adoption. He was so full of anger, there were times she feared he would burst into flames with the rage inside him. He might have had a better chance with two parents who wanted him; it might have calmed him down. As it was, he'd grown up with a stepfather who was useless. Philo had berated Tommo over the years, but it wasn't solely his fault; she was to blame, too. There were times when she had made excuses for Jack when what he needed was discipline and a firm hand. He had that in the Home. She'd seen it with her own two eyes – he had rules, discipline, responsibility and respect, things he'd never had before. Now that he had them, he was making something of himself. It filled her with guilt that she hadn't provided them for him earlier in his life.

She couldn't admit any of this to Brother Felix, of course – she couldn't confess to being a bad mother; so she went on the offensive.

—I didn't know I was invited. You never bleedin' told me.

—I'm bleedin' telling you now, so you better bleedin' come.

Philo knew the curses were for her. It wasn't every day someone went to that kind of trouble to make her feel at ease. It nearly made her blush. Brother Felix was a thoughtful man. He knew how to get the best out of people. He'd succeeded with Jack, and now he was working his magic on Philo.

At that moment, Tommo walked into the shop. He'd been on Philo's mind a minute earlier and now he was standing in front of her. That happened to her a lot: she thought of someone, walked around a corner and there they were. It was usually a nice surprise, but this time it was an unpleasant shock. The worst of it was, she had no escape.

She stood up, and Brother Felix followed suit. There was an awkward silence. Philo didn't want to introduce the two men. The word 'husband' felt like it might stick in her throat.

She'd gone beyond having a husband and being a wife. There was no going back to that. She couldn't and wouldn't introduce Tommo as her husband, so she stood there with her voice smothered inside her.

—I need to talk, Philo, Tommo said, and then added, in private.

Brother Felix knew who Tommo was by osmosis, and knew he shouldn't be there. He came out from behind the counter, made some excuse and headed for the door.

—What about your vegetables? Philo said.

—It doesn't matter, they'll wait.

—You're not going home without them.

—There's the list; I'll call back for them after.

Philo didn't want him to go, but she couldn't stop him, not in the physical sense. She wanted him to know that she was afraid, and yet she didn't want to appear vulnerable in front of Tommo.

—I'll have them ready for you before twelve. Will that do?

—Take your time, there's no hurry, Brother Felix said, and left.

If Tommo killed her, she'd be found soon. Philo consoled herself with that thought. Tommo let his eyes wander around the shop. He wanted to appear as relaxed and informal as possible.

—Who's your man when he's not shopping for vegetables? he said.

—He's a customer, that's all.

—Is that who you left me for?

—No.

—Is he your new fancy man?

—No, he's not my fucking fancy man.

It was an instinctive response and it brought Philo right back to the early days with Tommo. They had been in the pub one Sunday night, Philo in a corner with the women and Tommo with the men on the other side of the room. Some

Dublin pubs had snugs that separated the men and women, but not this one. About nine o'clock, May Flaherty started the sing-song. She was a street dealer from Moore Street and she kicked off the singing every week with her version of 'My Child'. After May, it went around the circle of women before becoming a free-for-all that embraced the entire pub. By closing time, the women linked arms and swayed to the beat of songs by Elvis Presley, Frank Sinatra, the Everly Brothers, Buddy Holly and the Beatles.

On the Sunday night in question an over-zealous cattle man, Git Cummins, broke into the circle of women between Philo and May Flaherty. They tried to bypass him, but he had a neck like the jockey's proverbial. He burst into a version of the hit from *Grease*, 'You're the One that I Want'. He performed it complete with all the moves, like he was Dublin's answer to John Travolta. As it was exclusively directed at her, Philo played the Olivia Newton-John part, right down to bouncing her arse off Git's on the chorus. Their double act brought the house down. Everyone in the pub thought they should team up immediately and turn professional.

When they got home that night, Tommo accused Philo of leading Git Cummins on. He further accused her of making a show of him in front of the male clientele of his local. Philo brushed it off, saying it was the drink talking, but Tommo was in no mood to be brushed off.

—That little fucker is your fancy man, isn't that so? he said.

Philo couldn't believe it. To be awkward, she agreed with him.

—Yeah, he's my fancy man, that's right.

At that, the heavens opened and the digs rained down like a monsoon. She decided never to go to the pub with Tommo again. Of course, she'd relented in time, but she'd never given her heart fully to the sing-song again. The only thing she was allowed to give her heart to was Tommo; that was the Golden Rule. She wasn't allowed to flirt with other men, ever.

The reference to Brother Felix as her 'fancy man' put Philo on edge. She kept a close eye on Tommo as he inspected the walls and ceiling of Dina's shop.

—I don't know him. Is he from around? Tommo enquired.

—You needn't worry, he's from outer space. He's an extraterrestrial. They call him ET.

It took a moment for the penny to drop. When it did, Tommo smiled at her; he pointed at his eyes and nodded in recognition of the observation.

—I presume you didn't come here to buy vegetables, Philo said.

—No, I came to tell you I'm off the drink.

—Good for you. You'll be able to save a fortune, so.

—I joined Alcoholics Anonymous. I'm serious about giving it up.

Philo thought it was funny but she didn't want to laugh. There was a saying about closing the stable door after the horse has left, and it seemed to fit, even if she couldn't remember the exact words. It made her think of herself as a horse, running mad through the North Wall, with people running after her shouting that Tommo had given up the drink. She couldn't figure out what had put these thoughts into her head, but they were nice thoughts. It was good to be a horse, especially with no jockey on her back.

—I know I have a problem and I know it's the drink, Tommo said in a penitent voice.

Philo thought her ears were playing tricks.

—Are you saying you have a problem? she asked.

—Yes, I am.

—You never have a tape recorder when you need one. Can I write that down and get you to sign it?

This was another red-letter day – Tommo admitting he had a problem. Philo thought it was his mouth, more than the drink. He'd even started warning Eileen, Josie and Philomena about their size.

—Have you been to see the children? she asked.

—No, I have to concentrate on myself. It's a selfish programme.

When Philo heard the word 'programme', she thought he was going to be on television. It wasn't something she'd have thought possible. Why would they want to make a programme about Tommo, unless it was to make people turn off their sets?

—If I'm to get sober, I have to do it for me. I can't do it for anyone else.

—They told you that in Alcoholics Anonymous – not to visit your children?

—No, not exactly.

—Did they tell you to give up darts as well?

—What have fucking darts got to do with it?

—That's what takes you down to the pub, isn't it? You always said it was the darts made you drink.

Tommo didn't jump in; he seemed to consider what Philo had just said.

—I did blame the darts, didn't I?

—Yes, you did.

—Hats off; you're right about that.

Philo couldn't believe she didn't have a witness to verify this – an admission by Tommo that she was right. If it was Alcoholics Anonymous that had brought this about, then she wanted to praise it to the skies. The 'selfish' lark, she didn't understand. What was wrong with giving up drink for someone else, after all? Wasn't it a good thing for a man to give up booze for his wife? Or his children? Tommo was selfish enough as it was without getting encouragement from Alcoholics Anonymous.

—I want you to come home, he said. I'm fed up living on my own.

Philo knew what that meant. He was fed up living off smoked cod and chips from Fusciardi's. He wanted the feel of fresh underpants and the taste of home cooking again.

—I have a roof over my head and I'm happy, thanks be to God, she said.

—You can't live here forever. Your place is at home with the kids.

He was correct, of course – she couldn't live in Dina's – but he'd forgotten to add that it was his fault things had turned out the way they had.

—It's my fault things have turned out like this, he said.

How could he read her mind like that? It made her sick to her stomach. She averted her eyes from him, but the feeling persisted. She tried to empty her head but found it impossible to think of nothing. She thought of the horse to distract herself. She saw it running down the docks, free and wild.

—I can understand you wanting to be on your own.

Philo's stomach was somersaulting into her mouth. Tommo was inside her head, renting rooms in her brain, and she wanted to get him out of there.

—Just come home with the kids. I'll move out. I'll stay in a bed-and-breakfast.

—You don't want to live with me, is that it?

—I want the kids to have a mother.

—But you don't want them to have a father.

—I want to get sober first.

Philo was more confused than ever. She'd let herself be sweet-talked into staying with Tommo several times before. Yet this seemed different. He'd never talked about giving up the drink before. That was a first. There was something different about him and she couldn't put her finger on it. He'd been a selfish bastard throughout the marriage (and probably all his life) but he'd never admitted it. Now he was owning up, and she couldn't decide if it was real or a game. If it was genuine, then it was a miraculous transformation.

Hundreds of times she'd prayed that he'd change, all to no avail. Why should she believe in miracles now? Why should she go back into the lion's den on the basis of a feeling that could be wrong? The odds were he was still the same miserable streak of manhood she'd fought so hard to get away from. For all she knew, he wanted her back because he didn't like sleeping on his own; he missed her warm, juicy body next to his in the middle of the night.

—You miss me, do you?

Tommo nodded.

—You miss getting your Nat King Cole, am I right?

He was taken aback.

—It has nothing to do with sex. I can do without me Nat King Cole when I have to.

It wasn't his reply that surprised her (though he was a man who couldn't go two days without sex); it was the softness of his tone. Any criticism of him, however mild, was usually met with a sledgehammer. Philo was intrigued; she would have liked to take it further, but she ran the risk of appearing too interested in him, at a time when she was trying to detach. In particular, she'd have loved to ask him what he'd done with her wages for the four weeks she'd been out of the house.

For the thirteen years they'd been together, Tommo had used money as a weapon. Like most things, it had started off as a joke. Every Thursday evening (Thursday being payday), she had to ask him for her wages. He never handed them over without being asked. It was a playful thing, in the early years, and often ended up with Philo tickling him until he surrendered her money. As the marriage deteriorated, it became a major source of conflict. There were many times, particularly when Tommo had been drinking, when Philo had to beg for it on her hands and knees, literally. There were many occasions when she'd gone without, rather than demean herself. In the end, though, she always had to ask, and there was nothing Tommo enjoyed more than playing Mr Generous to her outstretched hand.

She was thinking of Thursday evenings and being made to beg. It made her want to drive nails into his hands and feet. It was a cogent reminder of the life she'd left behind in the house of Nolan.

—Are you all right for money? Tommo asked.

Philo couldn't understand how she was having a thought and he was reading it.

—I have some money here, if you need it.

He took out a small brown envelope and held it in his hand. It was a miracle, but it had come too late for her. He'd pissed on her too many times, and the stench of it was still in her nostrils.

—I don't want your money. I can manage.

—It's not my money, it's yours, so take it.

There was something about refusing money that went against the grain. There were always things you wanted and couldn't afford – clothes for the kids, curtains for the windows, a washing machine that didn't break down. Money was something that was always useful. Many's the good dinner Philo had cooked for Tommo and ended up dumping in the bin, but she'd never throw out money. The only time she could imagine refusing money was in exchange for sex. She'd never sell her body, not for a million pounds. Well, she'd be tempted by a million if it was strictly a once-only effort. That would have been years ago, when she'd had a figure. Since she'd piled on the weight, there was no way she'd take off her clothes; she'd never expose herself, never let her naked flesh be gawked at. She would never prostitute herself for the measly wages that were in the brown envelope before her. She wasn't taking payment from Tommo so he could tell her when to open and close her legs. He could go and pay for his Nat King Cole; he could get a brasser, as far as she was concerned.

She opened Brother Felix's list and examined it.

—I have a couple of orders to get ready and I don't want to be ignorant, so if you'll excuse me....

She picked up a handful of carrots and threw them on the weighing scales, mumbling to herself.

—Eight pounds of carrots ... what have we here? Six – that's two more....

Tommo stood his ground. He wanted to argue with her, but he knew it would do no good. He'd been told by the people at Alcoholics Anonymous to avoid strife, particularly on the domestic front. He'd got annoyed when he was told that, because he didn't understand what 'domestic' meant. So he'd had to ask someone, which was a new experience for a man who thought he knew everything.

They'd told him it would take time and not to force things. He watched Philo weighing the vegetables and tried to remember the serenity prayer, but it wouldn't come. All he could recall was the slogan 'HALT' – hungry, angry, lonely, tired – four feelings he'd been told to avoid. He was about to fall at the hurdle marked 'angry'. He was lonely, too. The flat was empty without Philo and the kids. He'd never known emptiness like it. He wanted them back, but he had to put his sobriety first. First things first: that was another of the slogans.

He went to the door for air. The three cronies were sitting on the window-ledge outside. It was obvious they'd been earwigging, because as soon as Tommo appeared, they jumped. A queue of women had formed behind them, stretching down the lane. At the rear was a man, looking out of place and uncomfortable. It was Cap Coyle.

Tommo wondered why they were there. He wanted to ask them but resisted.

—You have a fan club out here, he shouted in to Philo.

Philo threw her eyes to heaven.

—You're a big hit with the aul' wans of the North Wall.

Philo stepped out onto Dowdall's Lane and thought she was being set up for 'Candid Camera'. Not wanting to be the butt of anyone's joke, she got her retaliation in first: she announced that the shop was closing for the rest of the day. Amid the protests of the would-be shoppers and gossipers, she went back inside and put the finishing touches to Brother Felix's order. Moments later she emerged with a cardboard box of vegetables and pulled the door closed behind her. She set off towards the Home, watched by a bewildered and disappointed group of women.

There was Cap, too, of course, as bewildered as anyone else. He ran after Philo and caught up with her at the corner of Seville Place.

—Let me carry that for you, he said.

—It's a wonder you're not ashamed to show your face around here, Philo said, after what you done.

Cap stood directly in front of Philo and blocked her path.

—You're talking about me and Ninna Delargy, aren't you?

He launched straight into an explanation of what had transpired between them. It was more than an explanation; it was an attack on people who judge by appearances, it was a robust defence of old-fashioned manners. He had behaved towards Ninna like a gentleman, because that was how he'd been raised; she had no place in his heart, that was reserved for another, and he was not a flirt or a gigolo, he was a one-woman man; he didn't know if he was chasing rainbows but he didn't want to get hurt, he'd spent a lifetime nursing resentment and hate and he was afraid of his own feelings, of making them known, because he didn't know if he could cope with being rejected twice in the same life, this life, the only life he had – he didn't know if he could cope with being rejected again.

—Jaysus, I'm glad you got that off your chest, Philo said. Keeping that bottled up could kill you.

It was true: heart attacks and strokes had been caused by less.

—You're telling the wrong person, Cap. You should be telling Dina all this.

—I don't know if I can tell her. I'm too old-fashioned. I can't change my ways. It's how I was brought up.

Philo didn't understand him. She couldn't conceal her feelings for very long. If she felt something, she said it. She never stopped to think of the consequences. Even if she didn't say anything, it was obvious; she was an open book. She felt it was time for Cap to stop playing the gentleman and wear his heart on his sleeve.

—You have to take chances in love. It's the name of the game, Cap.

—She's married to Gerry Sugrue. They have a family. She's another man's wife.

Philo was touched by his concern, but she wanted to strangle him. He was a man with a troubled conscience, doomed to paralysis. Dina and Gerry Sugrue hadn't been a couple for over twenty years. The marriage was dead. Gerry Sugrue would never in this life charm the knickers off Dina again.

—I suppose you're worried they won't get on, Philo said.

—Who won't get on? Cap asked.

—The kids.

—What kids are you talking about?

—The ones Dina had for Gerry and the ones she's going to have for you.

Cap didn't like sarcasm, but on this occasion it hit home. Philo pushed the box of vegetables at him. Cap threw the box up onto his head and held it with one hand, like a true vegetable man. Philo headed off in the direction of the San Francisco Boys' Home and Cap followed, arguing all the while about love and responsibility, until their voices became a blur under the noise of the railway bridge at the top of Seville Place.

10

When Philo arrived to see Dina, she found her transformed. They'd transferred her from a private room in Unit 4 to a public ward in Unit 1. As she entered the ward, Philo could hear Dina regaling the other patients with stories. Less than six hours in her new bed, and she was surrounded by a conference of cronies who fed off her gossip like it was plasma. It was a great gift, honed over forty years on her leatherette throne in Get Fresh.

Philo was under the spotlight immediately.

—That's who I was telling you about: that's Philo who's minding the shop for me, Dina said.

—Jaysus, I'd love to take you home with me, one of the women said.

—You can come and work for me any time, another butted in.

—I hear you're a great woman for a sing-song, said a voice from the corner bed.

—It'd take more than a tune to liven up this sad place, said a woman who had to pull her oxygen mask off first.

—She's only saying that because she has a voice like a crow, said the woman next to Dina.

Sixty seconds, six patients, all sick and with something to say. It was more inclusive than a parliamentary debate in Dáil Éireann. Dina was propped up by her pillows, cracking the whip and keeping everyone in order, oblivious to any physical pain or missing body parts.

—How are the toes? Philo asked.

—If someone hadn't told me they were missing, I wouldn't know.

Could it be she was drugged to the point where she didn't feel any more – her senses were numbed and she wouldn't know about pain until feeling returned? Or maybe it was just that she was high on the company, after the loneliness of being on her own. There was no doubt her recovery had been spurred on by her co-conspirators in Unit 1.

—You're in great form, Philo said. The drugs must be working.

—It has nothing to do with drugs.

—That's disappointing, because I was going to ask you for some.

Philo pulled a chair in close and sat on it.

—They're going to let me home; I spoke to the Matron. Isn't that great?

—It's great so long as you can manage. You don't know if you're going to be able to walk or not.

—They won't let me home on my own; I have to have someone minding me.

—They're going to give you a nurse? That's great. I have five kids and I get fuck all except abuse.

—I have to have my own home help. It's not a nurse.

—That's a job for your daughter. Get her up off her arse and give her something to do.

Dina's pallor changed and she reverted to her old crabby self.

—You wouldn't inflict her on me. She's useless.

—She's still your daughter.

The tea trolley arrived, steered by a woman in a blue plastic coat who announced her presence to the world like the world had better listen. She poured from the large silver pot into the six waiting cups, then put two Bourbon Cream biscuits on each saucer before distributing them around the ward.

—Is there a spare cup in that pot? Philo asked. She was gumming for a sugary cup of tea.

—Refreshments are for patients only, Miss Plastic Coat said, delighted with her pronouncement.

If she'd said it in a nice way, it wouldn't have mattered, but her tone bothered Philo; it bothered her a great deal. She never liked to feel she was being bullied, especially by someone from her own class, which this woman was.

Just then the Matron arrived and Dina introduced the two women. Matron couldn't believe this was Philo – the woman who'd taken over the shop, the nurse who'd tended Dina on her bedroom floor, the woman who'd cut open her bandages for the doctor, the person who'd told Dina the true extent of her injuries.

—I'm delighted to meet you, Philo. I feel like I know you.

—Have you been spreading gossip about me? Philo jokingly asked Dina.

—I don't gossip, I'm not that type of person, Dina answered.

—I'm so glad you're going to be looking after Dina when she goes home, Matron said.

Philo looked at each of them in turn, certain that if she opened her mouth she'd say the wrong thing. There was a look of conspiracy tinged with terror in Dina's eyes.

—Would you mind repeating what you just said, Matron? Philo asked.

—I'm delighted you're going to be looking after Dina for us.

—You're my home help, Dina said. I put your name on the form.

—I'm very glad you asked me before you did that, Philo said.

—You'll get an allowance. It's money in your hand. None of it's for me, it's all for you – isn't that right, Matron?

—You'll get the carer's allowance, of course you will.

162

Philo didn't care about the monetary reward. She only cared that she was being emotionally blackmailed. All she could see were strings attached to her heart and Dina pulling at them for all she was worth. It was making a strange kind of music, and Philo didn't like it. Nurse Philo; it wasn't how she saw herself. Dina's daughter had the perfect name for a nurse, Florence; but she was useless at everything, according to her mother.

There was Sylvia, too, who needed care and attention. Philo had more reason to be concerned about her mother – her weight and lack of exercise – than she had about Dina. Apart from her toes, Dina was in the best of health, and she'd live to be a hundred and eight. She was the type of woman who was allergic to coffins. There was a breed of such women in Dublin – they were small, skinny and bad-humoured, ate very little and lived mainly on booze, cigarettes, sweets and gossip. Such people were to be found in every Day Centre, nursing home and hospital – they loved corner beds and wheelchairs, any solid vantage point from which to observe and complain. They always attracted a coterie. People felt they were lucky and hoped that, by association, the luck would rub off on them, too. The skinny complainers, sad to say, always outlived their listeners by talking them to death. There was no way Philo was going to let that happen to her. She had too many people depending on her to let Dina lead her down that path.

It was obvious Dina was going to walk again – why else would they let her out of hospital? She just needed tender loving care for a few weeks, and Philo was being asked to provide it. She was honoured to be asked, in truth, and it was just the kind of Christian act that might bring her a change of luck. Perhaps her name would mysteriously float to the top of the housing list, she thought. The more Philo considered it, the more she had to admit the plan had some attractive points.

But it was important for her not to appear too eager.

—I hope you can walk, because I can't bleedin' carry you, she said.

—No one is asking you to carry me. Amn't I entitled to a walking wheelchair?

—First I ever heard of a walking wheelchair, Philo said.

—She means a Zimmer frame, Matron said.

—A Zimmer frame, exactly, and I'm entitled to one.

—I suppose you have to fill in a form to get one of those, Philo said, like everything else in this country.

She said it in jest, but she knew immediately from Matron's reaction that it was the terrible truth. Another black-and-white obstacle course to be negotiated before an entitlement could be gained. What would Dina have to do to secure the Zimmer frame? Perhaps she'd have to bequeath her body to medical science – or maybe they'd just hold on to a part of her, her lungs or her brain or her heart. Philo had filled in so many forms that they owned her, lock, stock and barrel. She was leasing her body from the State until she died.

—I have a form for the Zimmer frame in the office, Matron said, and I have the carer's form, too.

Philo had one last chance to pull out. But she couldn't look at Dina and say no; it wasn't possible. She looked around the ward at the faces smiling back at her. Bless them, but they had no idea; they would all be dead before Dina. They wanted Philo to say yes because they wanted their Queen of the Gossip to be cared for, just as they themselves wanted to be looked after.

Philo saw Miss Plastic Coat beyond the door, feigning disinterest as best she could. She knew from the angle of her neck that she'd been eavesdropping to beat the band.

—Filling out forms is thirsty work, Philo said. I'd kill for a cup of tea.

Matron turned around and clicked her fingers, as Matrons do. Miss Plastic Coat came running into the room.

—Get Philo a cup of tea, please, Matron said.

Miss Plastic Coat stood there for a moment, frozen to the spot. Philo could hear her grind her teeth from where she was sitting. She'd always hated people grinding their teeth, but not any more; now she loved it.

—Don't forget the Bourbon Creams, Philo said. I'd love a Bourbon Cream.

It was a small thing, a cup of tea; on the scale of things it was a small victory. In a world that conspired to defeat her at every turn, it was sweet all the same. If half a loaf was better than no bread, then a crumb was better than nothing at all. Holy Communion was nothing more than a morsel of bread. The secret that unlocked doors was to be found in the smallest things. On reflection, Philo thought, it was a major victory, not a small one. She deserved respect, and it was right and proper for her to get it wherever she could.

She got the cup of tea, and it cheered her; so did the Bourbon Creams that got stuck in her teeth. On her way out, she went to the office and signed forms that made her an official carer and a guarantor that Mr Zimmer's frame would be returned after use. Philo wasn't sure that Dina would ever walk again unaided. On the assumption that she would live until she was all talked out at a hundred and eight, it was certainly a long-term guarantee to give. By that stage, Philo herself would be going on seventy. That was the same age Dina was now. Philo didn't ever want to be that old.

She put it out of her mind as best she could and headed out to Goldenbridge, happy to have something that brought her back to the here and now, even if it was a bucket of shit.

As always, the children wanted to know the time and date of their release. Young Tommo, in particular, wanted to know if Philo had seen his father. Rather than lie, she told him she had, and that he was trying to get help for his drinking.

165

—Does that mean he's stopped? Young Tommo asked.

—Yes, I think it does, Philo said.

—Are you going to get back with him, so?

Philo wanted to say yes, because it was so hard to disappoint the children all the time; it was head-wrecking to constantly tell them what they didn't want to hear. There were only so many times you could throw chocolate at their questions. Not that it was chocolate; today she'd brought apples, oranges and pears – the nuns liked to encourage healthy eating. But it wasn't good to stuff the children's mouths to prevent questions, even if it was with fruit.

—I'm bringing you out for the day on Sunday, Philo announced. She'd already cleared it with the nuns.

—Where are we going? Are we going on a bus? they wanted to know.

—Are we going to see Granny and Grandad?

—What time are you collecting us?

—What time do we have to be back?

A hundred questions, a thousand hopes.

—Is Jack coming, too? Eileen asked.

—Yes, Jack will be there as well, Philo replied. That was as far as she wanted to go.

—Are we going to Dollymount to collect winkles? Josie asked.

—No, we're not going to Dollymount. It's a surprise.

—Are we going to Howth to look at the jellyfish? Philomena asked.

—She's not going to tell us, it's a surprise, Young Tommo said.

A thousand questions, a million hopes. They had something to look forward to, for the first time in a long while. They begged her to tell, but she wouldn't relent. It was better to keep it a surprise. If she told them, the magic of it would disappear. This way, it left them with an expectation, with mystery. It would be a better week for them this way.

166

It was raining when Philo got back to Dowdall's Lane in the late afternoon. She was glad, even though she had no umbrella; it meant there was no queue waiting to be served. She opened the door of the shop and was surprised to see two letters on the ground. One of them was small, a brown square with no stamp – just her name in block capitals, underlined. It felt like money, and it was: crispy new notes wrapped in a sheet of paper, and just one sentence.

It's bad manners to refuse your wages. Tommo.

One hundred and eighty pounds in twenties, brand-new notes in sequence. Was this part of his plan for a new beginning? She looked at the writing: it was primitive, like a caveman's, there was nothing refined about it. She'd fancied rough men when she was younger; she'd thought unshaven, hairy men were attractive, masculine, and she'd imagined she could live with a wild man because she herself was wild. After a few months Tommo's wildness had amounted to not doing the dishes and refusing to learn how the washing machine worked. He played darts and claimed it was the working man's hunting – hence the name 'arrows' for the bits of plastic he threw at the treble twenty.

Philo figured this was the first time she'd received her wages without having to ask for them. Maybe he had changed because the poison that fuelled his madness, alcohol, had been taken away. He'd never written to her before; this was the first epistle of their marriage. It wasn't very romantic, but by Tommo's standards it was a love poem. The one word noticeable by its absence was 'love'. He'd signed off, 'Tommo', but he'd put nothing in front of it – nothing soft, nothing from the heart, nothing to make Philo feel special; nothing except three weeks' wages that hadn't been begged for.

The banknotes felt powerful in her hand. She was glad she'd rejected them earlier, because now she had them without having had to put her hand out for them. The notes went into her pocket and felt warm, like a little electric blanket.

The second letter looked more official; it had one of those plastic windows that warned of bad news inside. Strangely, there was nothing in the envelope. Philo turned it over, and on the back was a handwritten note from Sister Rosaleen.

4 p.m., Tuesday. Social worker from the Eastern Health Board called to see you. It seemed important. Miss you lots. Regards, Rosaleen. S.A.G.

It was a beautiful script, every word sculpted like it had been designed by God himself. It was definite *Book of Kells* material. No one had ever written to Philo that they missed her. She'd never had anyone sign 'regards' to her in a letter before. They were simple, beautiful words – even the 'S.A.G.' (Saint Anthony Guide) was moving – and it wasn't even a letter, it was only a note. She'd married the wrong person, and the wrong sex, too. It should have been a woman she'd tied the knot with thirteen years earlier, a woman like Sister Rosaleen – or plain Rosaleen, as she'd written on her note. No, it wasn't a note; it was a letter, the best letter Philo had ever received. She folded it and put it carefully in her bag.

She hadn't given a thought to who the social worker was or what she wanted. It struck her that it might have to do with Dina. Perhaps it was the Zimmer frame department – and hats off to them if it was; they certainly didn't hang around. Or maybe it was something to do with the carer's allowance? Knowing Dina's luck, she probably had the whole of the Health Board running after her trying to fix her up with entitlements.

Philo didn't bother going upstairs. She pulled an old newspaper from under the counter (Dina used them for wrapping vegetables), put it over her head and set off for the convent in the rain. The Day Centre was closed for business so she used the main entrance. Sister Davina answered. By the time Philo got inside, the newsprint was running down her face, making her look like a zebra.

—There was a woman here asking all about you, Sister Davina said. I think she was from the Health Board.

—I hope you said nice things about me, Philo said.

—You needn't worry, I praised you to the skies.

As they walked down the corridor together, two kids came hurtling towards them. They managed to step out of the way of the first one, a girl of six or so, but the second, a boy of about eight, crashed into Sister Davina and sent her sliding along the floor on her bum. The children had just moved into the family unit upstairs, and although they'd been warned not to run in the corridors, the lure of this polished skating rink had proved too much. Fortunately, Sister Davina had landed perfectly on her padded posterior and had come to no harm. Philo hauled her up at the same time as she admonished the children.

—Don't run in the corridors or you'll fucking kill someone, do you hear me?

The children hung their heads.

—You could have killed Sister Davina, do you know that?

—We're sorry, they said.

—And what are you going to do from now on? Philo said.

—We're going to walk.

—Show me how you're going to walk.

The brother and sister set off at a snail's pace, holding hands, the echoes of their quiet steps reverberating around the convent.

—That's more like it, Philo said. That's how to walk in a convent.

She turned to head into the office and there, framed in the doorway, were Sister Rosaleen and Majella Kiernan, the Eastern Health Board social worker. She was plain-looking, with just the faintest hint of a moustache, and her eyes seemed sympathetic. Philo made a quip about the Zimmer

169

frame to get things going, but nobody understood what she was talking about. This visit had nothing to do with Dina and everything to do with Philo. On it would depend the future custody of her children. The interview, or rather the investigation, by Majella Kiernan was part of an evaluation to establish the parenting needs of the children.

They sat in the office and went over the history of the marriage. Philo had wanted to keep Sister Rosaleen there for moral support, but everything had to be by the book. It was strictly a one-to-one encounter. Majella Kiernan took extensive notes, writing in her ledger, without emotion, like she was making an important shopping list.

Philo went over everything from Jack's conception to dancing with Tommo in the Galway Arms, marrying him within a month, the births of their four children, the start of their rows, his jealousy, the physical and verbal abuse, his addiction to darts, their sex life, his addiction to alcohol, the first time she had abandoned the home, the second time she had abandoned the home, the current status of their marriage, her mental health, his mental health, the mental health of the children, their safety, her safety, the dangers posed to her by Tommo, the dangers posed to Tommo by her, the dangers posed to Jack, the dangers posed by Jack, the dangers of joyriding, turning joyriding into something useful, the importance of ET, the solo trial at Santry, pet names and nicknames, verbal abuse, fat cows and fat cunts, judicial separation, maintenance money, accommodation, abandonment, crisis.

She was exhausted by the effort. Her biggest mistake had been abandoning the kids, and when confronted with it she tried to ameliorate it by saying she had left for the sake of family peace. Majella Kiernan kept on using the A-word, so Philo changed tack and referred to Tommo's abuse every time the A-word was mentioned.

—I don't see any physical evidence of abuse, Majella Kiernan said.

—What about mental abuse and torture? Does that not count?

—It's very hard to gauge that. It's not like a black eye or a broken arm.

—I've had them in my time, but Tommo's very cunning; he knows not to mark me.

She was sorry he hadn't beaten her up, the cowardly bastard. If she'd known how much scars would have helped her case, she'd have provoked him. There was a set of darts he kept on the sideboard – they were his prize possession; he'd scored one hundred and eighty with them in a darts final and the team had won the Leinster Shield because of it, because of him, Tommo the Great. If Philo had done anything to disfigure those arrows, he'd have disfigured her. It would have been so simple. She could have donated them as a prize to a sale of work, and it would have turned him into an out-of-control caveman. A good hiding would have been guaranteed. She could even have offered particular parts of her body for the slaughter – the eyes, the nose, the mouth.

On reflection, she could still do it. What was to stop her getting back with Tommo in order to provoke him? She didn't want to, of course, but that was hardly the point. He'd been pursuing her, begging her to go back to the family home. What was to stop her giving in to his pleas and going back? From there to a good hiding was simplicity itself. The only problem she could foresee was the drink. It might not be so easy to provoke him if he was still off it. Without alcohol he was a lamb; you'd never believe he could turn into the Incredible Hulk. The solution to that was to spike his tea. A good drop of whiskey, plenty of sugar and he'd never know. It was a shame to have to plan this way, especially when he was attending Alcoholics Anonymous. And there was always a possibility the plan could backfire. If he was taking anti-booze tablets, spiked tea would make him violently ill. He could end up spewing his insides all over himself and all over

Philo, too. There were no prizes for guessing who'd clean up that mess.

—If you get custody of your children, Majella Kiernan said, what guarantees do we have that you won't abandon them again?

—It wasn't the children I abandoned, Philo said. It was Tommo.

For the first time in the interview, Majella Kiernan didn't write anything down. The truth of Philo's comment seemed to get to her; it registered in a way that went beyond the need to record it. She let down her guard and looked at Philo with compassion and concern. Philo had the sensation of something moving in her direction, a tide turning. By way of information, she told Majella Kiernan that Tommo hadn't been out to Goldenbridge to see his children, not once. Majella Kiernan recorded that, and Philo was delighted.

—I don't know why I'm surprised, because that's the type he is, Philo said.

She was deflated when Majella Kiernan pointed out that it wouldn't come down to a decision between her and Tommo. It wasn't a custody battle; it was more complex than that. For now, the Health Board was just gathering information; there would be no decision in the short term.

—How are you financially? Are you managing? Majella Kiernan asked.

Philo was taken off guard.

—I'm doing fine. I have the mickey money.

—What's the mickey money?

—The children's allowance.

It took a moment for her to understand.

—Your husband is not giving you anything, I presume?

The spanking new banknotes were sitting in Philo's pocket, and she knew that if she denied their existence they would burst into flames and betray her.

—He gave me money, but I'm going to give it back.

—Why would you do that? You're entitled to it.

—I don't want anything of his.

—He's still your husband, and what's his is yours.

Philo liked Majella Kiernan; she liked the way she put things, simple and direct.

—What's his is mine, Philo said.

The twenty-pound notes started to feel more at home in her pocket. The tide was definitely on the turn, and thoughts of a shopping spree were washing over Philo.

—I like your tattoo, Majella Kiernan said, pointing at her arm. You should get another one.

—I have one on my leg, Philo said.

It was actually on her thigh, and it wasn't one she showed, for obvious reasons. She'd had it put there to celebrate the birth of her eldest daughter, Eileen. It was a rose, pink for a girl. Tommo had chosen it. Philo pulled up her skirt and revealed it.

—It was supposed to be a climbing rose, but I was robbed, she said.

—What kind of a rose is it?

—Well, it's not a climbing rose, because if it was it should be halfway up my arse by now.

Majella Kiernan smiled and Philo pulled down her skirt. It was nice to be able to share a joke with a social worker. It wasn't every day that happened.

—I'd love to get a tattoo, but I don't have the guts.

Philo tried to convince her to take the plunge, but Majella Kiernan thought her employers might take a dim view. Underneath that conservative exterior was a Gothic personality trying to get out. Vampires and crucifixes were her thing, but the need to pay rent kept her impulses in check. Philo suggested she put one in a place not open to public view, namely her back or her arse. Philo wrote down the name of the tattoo parlour, Jack the Scratch, and his address in Parnell Street.

While she was doing that, Majella Kiernan filled out an appointment card for Philo to see the chief psychiatrist, Matthew Kelly, the man who would assess her mental health in relation to her suitability as a parent. He had a reputation for being tough but fair. Majella Kiernan warned Philo to wear something that would hide the tattoo on her arm, just in case.

11

Cap Coyle set out for Ringsend. He hadn't been there since he'd played Under-16 schoolboy football – Sheriff United against a local team called Bolton Athletic. The rivalry was tribal – north of the Liffey versus south of the Liffey; two legendary dock communities, the North Wall and Ringsend, separated by a mutual distrust deeper and wider than any river. For thousands of years, the communities on both banks had worked the river for a living, and they'd fought wars for the privilege.

Cap hopped on the number 3 bus outside Clery's in O'Connell Street. It had been fifty-four years since he'd been to Ringsend, and yet he knew the number of the bus to take and where it went from. He couldn't remember yesterday's headlines, yet he could recall a bus journey he'd made over half a century before. The modern number 3 trundled across the bridge and turned left into Townsend Street, just as Cap expected it to. He'd entered at the front, whereas the old method had been to hop on at the back, with the conductor yelling at people to enter on 'both sides of the bar, please'. Now there was no conductor and the driver was voiceless behind a floor-to-ceiling shield of perspex.

Cap went upstairs for the view. It used to be you could smoke on the upper deck, but they'd outlawed that, too. As the bus headed down along Pearse Street and over Grand Canal Bridge there wasn't a smoker's cough to be heard. In the old days, discarded packs of Capstan, Player's, Sweet Afton, Woodbines, Churchill's and Wills Gold Flake would be everywhere, and not a health warning on any of them –

nothing only the promise of a satisfying smoke and hours of happiness. It was a guaranteed road to success. The man with the cigarette always got the girl. Cap had never taken to them, he couldn't swallow the smoke; but Gerry Sugrue lived on Players, always had one dangling, always. It proved the theory, because he was the one who had got Dina.

Approaching Ringsend, Cap sat upright to take it in fully. The bus struggled to the brow of the hill, and in that moment before descent, when it seemed suspended in time, Cap witnessed the shocking reality: Ringsend was intact. It was a village and it was alive. People were coming and going, out of pubs and into the church, out of the church and into the chipper, out of the launderette and into the shop; a man was walking a dog; a woman with books under her arm looked like she was heading to a library. This was not how it was meant to be. Old villages were supposed to atrophy and die. Why should Ringsend escape the plague when Sheriff Street had been wiped out by it?

He sat where he was as the bus swept down through the village and around the bend into Irishtown. There was only one stop in Ringsend, and Cap did not get off. He was shell-shocked. He stayed with the bus as it made its way out onto the road at Sandymount Strand. The houses were magnificent, like the sea they looked out on – individual as the waves and proud as the swell. Cap looked across the bay towards the north side. Nothing of it could be seen; it was hidden by the land mass. It wouldn't matter if it just slid away and disappeared.

The number 3 parked at Saint John's Protestant church, and the driver bawled out that it was the last stop. Cap stared at the mahogany notice-board in the church grounds. The times of worship were written on it, and at the bottom was a quote: 'The apocalypse is nigh.'

The driver appeared at the top of the stairs.

—Are you all right, Mister?

—I'm fine; I just missed my stop. I'll get it on the way back.

The driver took a packet of cigarettes from his pocket and offered Cap one.

—We won't be leaving here for ten minutes. You're welcome to have a smoke.

—It's all right; I don't indulge.

It was a funny word, 'indulge', and the driver had never heard anyone refuse a fag like that before. He traipsed back down the stairs, and ten minutes later they were on their way back from Sandymount. Cap came downstairs and sat in the seat by the door. He got off at the stop opposite the Catholic church, the only stop in Ringsend village.

He had no idea where Gerry Sugrue lived, but he figured it was in one of the Corporation flats opposite the chipper. He walked towards the entrance. There were eight blocks stretching off into the distance. Was he to knock at all the doors until he found Gerry? Cap retraced his steps, back towards the bridge. There were three pubs together on the incline and he chose the one in the middle, the Oarsman, because it looked the oldest. His enquiries there were met with suspicion and he was pointed elsewhere.

In Fitzharris's pub he was more devious. He simply asked if Gerry Sugrue had been in that day, to which the barman replied that he hadn't.

—I was going to leave something here for him, Cap said, but maybe I'll bring it around to him instead.

—If it's money I wouldn't leave it here, the barman said.

—What number does he live in? Cap asked.

The barman shouted to a customer at the far end of the bar. They couldn't figure out the number, but between them they were certain Gerry's was the fifth cottage on the left-hand side after Cambridge Road.

Cap thanked them and left. He could feel his heart beating faster. It was pumping him into the future, but his mind was in the past. He remembered the day they had tossed the coin and he had lost. He should have made his feelings known then. He had let himself be ruled by his head. He was going to see Gerry because he wanted to reverse all that. He had to do it now, before it was too late.

Within minutes, he was standing outside the cottage and he wanted to run away. Why was he afraid? He'd crossed the Rubicon to get there, and now he didn't know if he could knock on the door. He didn't know if he had the courage to see it through. He was looking for an action to make him appear strong. It was a charade, and seeing his blurred reflection in the glass of the door made him painfully aware of his cowardice. He was about to abscond, and he would have, only someone came out of the cottage next door. It forced Cap's hand, literally. He reached up and knocked.

A figure came down the hallway and fiddled with the lock. The door opened, and an old man with a newspaper under his arm stood there. He was wearing black glasses, one arm of which was missing so that they hung lopsided. His hair was gray and a little overgrown. He had on a cardigan (buttoned in the wrong holes), slacks and well-worn slippers. Cap had brought the image of a much younger man. There was no doubt this was Gerry Sugrue, none at all, but he looked like a pensioner.

—Are you who I think you are? Gerry said.

—I think I might be, Cap said.

—If I said you were Cap Coyle, would I be right?

—One hundred per cent right, you'd be.

—I knew it was you before I opened the door.

Cap looked puzzled.

—I could see the hat. Once I saw the hat, I knew it was you.

Cap put his hand up and took it off, in deference.

—You're still wearing the hats.

—I have to confess I am. Still keeping the head covered.

Gerry brought Cap in, but he refused to take off his coat. They went down to the kitchen at the back; despite the warm May weather, Gerry had a turf fire on the go. They sat in chairs opposite each other and Cap declined the offer of tea.

—So who's dead? Gerry asked.

Cap didn't understand the question because he wasn't expecting it.

—That's why you're here, isn't it? Someone is dead.

It was a logical deduction and one Cap himself would have made had the positions been reversed. No one was dead, but they still went through a list of all those who'd passed away from years ago. Cap played for time; it was all he could do. He complimented Gerry on the cottage and on how well he was looking, and came back to the cottage again. There was much talk of Sheriff Street and how the old neighbourhood was finished and just waiting for the obsequies.

—You got out in time, Cap said. You saw it coming.

—I had to go. I couldn't live with Dina any more.

It was the perfect opportunity, but Cap couldn't find the words; he couldn't break through the barrier he had around women and courtship and love. He had forced himself out to Ringsend, to the confrontation with Gerry, he was sitting across from him, and he couldn't bring himself to say that he wanted Dina, that he'd always wanted her, that she should have married the best man and not the groom.

—I've always regretted that we fell out. I'm sorry that happened, Gerry.

—It's all water under the bridge as far as I'm concerned, Cap.

The lack of bitterness was real. So was the awkwardness that existed between them.

—If we'd stood together we might have saved the docks, Cap said.

Gerry disagreed, and for a moment it looked like a row

might develop, but they quickly papered over the cracks. They were old-age pensioners, making peace; there was nothing to be gained from resurrecting past disputes; all that stuff was dead and buried.

—I still want to say I'm sorry. I think I got it wrong back then, Cap said.

—You're saying I was right, are you?

—Yes, something like that.

—You came all the way out here to tell me this?

Cap smiled to hide the lie.

—You found me after forty-odd years to tell me I was right about the aquanauts? Is that what you're saying? Is it?

Cap became aware of how hot he was, sitting in the glow of the fire with his overcoat on.

—No....

He squeezed the rim of his hat, and the perspiration from his fingers melted into the fabric.

—No ... it's not that....

—Are you in some kind of trouble, Cap?

—Not trouble as such.

—You're dying? You have cancer, have you?

—No, I don't have cancer.

—You don't have cancer. You're a lucky man.

—Yes, I am lucky. Have you cancer, Gerry?

—No, I bought too many daffodils; I'm exempt.

Cap hadn't had a conversation like it in years. It brought him back to when he and Gerry had been young men. He'd gone through life and made many acquaintances, particularly in the shop, but he'd never found a pal like Gerry, someone who could read his mind and prick his conscience.

—No one is dead and you don't have cancer; it must be woman trouble, so, Gerry declared.

Cap opened the top button of his shirt.

—Who is she? Do I know her?

—Yes, you do know her. It's Dina, Cap said.

180

Contrary to Cap's expectations, Gerry had no problem with Cap making advances on the woman who was still technically his wife (and the mother of his three children). Their marriage was only in name; Gerry had no feelings for Dina on any level, good, bad or indifferent. He had no opinion on their potential union. In truth, he thought Cap was insane, but he left that unexpressed. He had relationship problems enough of his own – Vera, his companion and his junior by fifteen years, was off at the bingo, and although Gerry was expected to be at home on her return, Cap's visit was just the excuse he needed to get out to the pub.

They welcomed Cap back to Fitzharris's, glad to receive his custom on a slack Tuesday night. He and Gerry drank pint for pint, and later, when their ancient bladders couldn't take any more porter, they matched each other in whiskey and peppermint. By closing time, they had bridged a fifty-year separation and were reconnected. It felt good for Cap to talk to someone who didn't pass judgement on him. It let him be a little boy again.

Standing on the bridge in Ringsend waiting for the last bus, Cap wanted to ask Gerry a parting question. It was the question that had brought him there in the first place. Gerry was probably the only man in the world he could ask, and it still felt too shaming. Cap wanted Gerry's permission to bed Dina, that was true; but it wasn't the whole truth. There was something much deeper and much more difficult than that.

It was what to do when he got Dina there, in the bed, beside him. The awful truth was that he didn't know what to do and he'd never had someone he could ask. He was a hopeless virgin, that was the core of it – a seventy-one-year-old man who'd never had sex. He was too shy even to seek out a prostitute. He wanted to know what to do; he had to find out what was expected of him. That was why he'd sought out Gerry Sugrue, his old friend, and now he couldn't ask; he was too ashamed. He was light-headed from all the liquor and he couldn't bring himself to ask for help. He was a pathetic, lonely virgin, doomed to failure.

The number 3 bus came roaring around the corner. The two men embraced and held on to each other, pinched each other's skin. The bus driver waited patiently, but in the end he sounded the horn. Cap stepped on without bothering to show his pass. The driver let it go.

Cap sat at the back of the bus and waved out the window at his old pal. In a matter of seconds, Gerry disappeared behind the hill, and Cap was on his way back to a deserted village that was falling apart.

12

Business boomed at Get Fresh. The numbers of people coming through the door grew in proportion to the hike in prices. There was no strategy to it, no rhyme or reason; Philo simply thought of a number, doubled it and added ten. People were outraged, naturally, but they were prepared to pay because Philo was good fun. Not only did she increase business by doubling the prices, she managed to buy cheaper, too, because she bought in greater bulk. The wholesaler, Frank Rooney, was more than happy to knock money off the increased orders. In truth, he'd have reduced prices anyway, because he enjoyed dealing with Philo; he loved the banter, he had no other shopkeeper like her.

Sister Rosaleen called, but it wasn't to buy vegetables. She wanted to give Get Fresh the custom and had suggested it to Sister Monica, who had said it was a decision for Nan Somers. Miss Somers's antipathy to Philo was all too obvious; Sister Rosaleen didn't need to have it confirmed.

The shop was packed and alive with gossip when she called. In seconds, it all went quiet, and people bought their vegetables and left.

—I must get you around here more often, Philo said. You're better than a bouncer.

—Is that good or bad? It's bad, isn't it? It has to be bad.

—No, it's good, as a matter of fact. Here, suck that.

Philo offered her a Conference pear from a batch that had come in that morning. Sister Rosaleen took it and put it back on the counter.

—I hate pears, she said.

Philo could tell that she was in bad form.

—They're very good for your digestion, she said.

—There's nothing wrong with my digestion.

—They're good for your complexion, too, lots of Vitamin C.

—I can't stand pears, all right?

—What side of the bed did you get out this morning?

—I didn't get out any side of the bed.

—How did you manage that?

—I didn't go to bed last night.

Not being able to sleep would make an antichrist of anyone.

—Why did you not go to bed? Philo asked.

Sister Rosaleen looked for a moment like she was going to cry.

—Don't tell me that nuns' disco was on again. No one in Sheriff Street gets a wink of sleep when you lot start that racket.

Philo started to twist on the spot, hands and hips, an imitation of the dance made famous by Chubby Checker. With the movement, she sang out the inane lyrics. She tapped Sister Rosaleen on the elbow and pulled her by the arm, but the nun was not for dancing.

—I'm having a crisis of faith, Sister Rosaleen said.

It was a cry from the heart that brought Philo to a stop.

—Are you fed up being a nun?

—I don't know if I have a vocation any more.

—Maybe it's lost and you'll find it again.

Philo suggested a swop, the vegetable shop for the convent; she was trying to make light of it, but Sister Rosaleen didn't see the funny side. She'd lost her sense of humour as well as her vocation. All her life she'd wanted to serve God, and now she felt trapped by Him. His refuge had become her gaol.

—What brought all this on? Did you have a fight with someone?

Sister Rosaleen shook her head.

—The Mother Superior, was it?

—I didn't fight with anyone.

Her tone was very agitated.

—Maybe you should have a row with someone, Philo said. It might clear the air.

—Who would I have a row with?

—You could have one with me, if you want.

—You're the last person I want to have a row with.

—I don't believe that. You're annoyed with me and that's why you didn't sleep last night. So what did I do to annoy you? I must have done something.

The truth was, Philo had abandoned Sister Rosaleen. She'd left her to her own devices in the Day Centre, left her without help or direction. After the sing-song and the game of Blind Date, life would never be the same again. The old folks had tasted real excitement and weren't content to pass the time playing silly board games and doing juvenile jigsaws any more. Philo had brought them together and made a community of them. She'd engendered a spirit reminiscent of the old days, when they'd had a village at their doorsteps, before progress had made rubble of their streets and homes. And Sister Rosaleen, unfortunately, didn't have the skills to perpetuate what Philo had started. Hard as she tried with the old folks, they just didn't respond to her. The only solution was to get Philo back, but Sister Rosaleen didn't want to ask her; she was only too aware of what Philo had on her plate and didn't want to make more demands on her. The result was that she felt useless as a person and as a nun.

—I'm not very good at my job, that's what's annoying me.

—You're a crap nun, are you? Is that why you opened

your door to me? Bought me cigarettes when I was down in the dumps?

—I stole that money from Saint Joseph.

—Good for you. You're supposed to give to the poor.

It went backwards and forwards in a prolonged game of good nun, bad nun. The more it went on, the more confusing it became, until Sister Rosaleen ended it by accepting that she wasn't good or bad but somewhere in between.

The question remained of what to do with her disgruntled clientele in the Day Centre. Philo suggested bingo, and Sister Rosaleen thought it was a good idea until she realised someone had to call out the numbers and Philo wasn't volunteering for the job.

—We'll have to get a bingo caller, Sister Rosaleen said. I can't do it.

Philo wasn't having any of it. She put Sister Rosaleen through her paces, starting with Paisley's drum, number one; unlucky for some, thirteen; key of the door, twenty-one; all the threes, thirty-three; Sheridan's door, forty-four; seventy-seven Sunset Strip; two fat ladies, eighty-eight; and so on up and down the numbers ladder. Sister Rosaleen couldn't remember it all, but Philo persisted with her. It wasn't easy stepping into the shoes of a bingo caller, in a city of divas and doyens of rhyme in smoky halls from Killester to Whitehall and Inchicore to Crumlin. They were seasoned professionals who knew how to build tension, surveying numbered balls and leaving pregnant pauses that almost brought on childbirth or heart attacks. It would take Sister Rosaleen time to compete with the élite, but she had to start somewhere and the Day Centre was as good a place as any.

Before they left the shop, Philo threw a selection of vegetables together and wrapped them in newspaper. They would make a suitable prize for a line across but probably wouldn't do for a full house.

—We can do without prizes, Sister Rosaleen said.

—You can't do without prizes! Philo snapped back.

—Why can't they just play for the fun of it? she asked.

It was time for the facts of life. Just as babies were made by reaching a climax, so it was with bingo: it was a cauldron of tension where the players invested great emotional energy in order to experience the orgasm of shouting, 'Bingo!' Without the climax, it didn't exist. The exultation of the winner was balanced by the moans and groans of the losers. It was a sort of Judgement Day, a nirvana for the winners and hell for the losers. Every new game offered the prospect of salvation and the near-certainty of damnation. It was compulsive and addictive.

—I can't do it on my own, Sister Rosaleen said. I need you with me.

It was a request Philo could not turn down. They left the shop and headed for the convent. On the way past Noctor's pub, they went in and secured twenty cigarettes for the prize fund. They would have to raid the convent for the rest. There were bound to be tins of beans and peas in the kitchen presses, and toilet rolls, of course.

Sister Rosaleen thought it a very odd suggestion.

—Wouldn't they have toilet rolls at home?

—Yeah, robbed from here, Philo answered, by a bunch of thieving swine.

Whether toilet rolls were robbed or not, Sister Rosaleen couldn't believe they'd be of interest as a bingo prize.

—Did you ever wipe your arse with broken glass? Philo asked.

—No, Sister Rosaleen answered in disbelief.

—If you had, you'd know why the convent toilet rolls get robbed all the time.

The old folks were delighted to see Philo back. She'd been absent for four days and it felt more like four weeks. They bombarded her with questions – how long was she going to stay, when were they going to have another sing-song, how were things in Get Fresh and, of course, how was the patient, Dina? Conscious that she was there to build up Sister Rosaleen and push her to the forefront, Philo kept her answers brief. She told them that Dina was expected home on Monday and that the house was getting a spring-cleaning on Sunday, if any of them were free. A few volunteer hands went up, and Philo suggested they call at twelve o'clock. Then she remembered Jack was racing his car on the Sunday.

—We better make that Saturday, she said. I'm going to Santry racetrack on Sunday.

Not only did they want to know what was happening at the racetrack, they wanted to accompany her.

—You're all very welcome, she said. The 16A bus goes right to Santry, and you can get it in O'Connell Street.

They didn't want public transport, they wanted to make an outing of it. One of their own was making his racing debut. Even if he was a recently retired car thief, he was Philo's son, and they had more in common with him than they had with Our Lady of Knock, whom they had visited on their last outing together. They didn't really care where they went; it was more about finding a good pub and having a sing-song on the way home.

The bingo game hadn't been played with in years. Sister Rosaleen set herself up at a table and busied herself counting the numbered balls to make sure they were all there. There was a small wire cage and a board, both of them the worse for wear. Philo distributed the bingo cards around the room. There were twenty-eight players and only sixteen cards, so Philo asked people to double up and play together. Nobody made a move, apart from Ninna Delargy, who was only too happy to pull in beside Cap Coyle.

—If you don't double up we just won't play, Philo said.

It produced a miraculous response: people teamed up like happy worker ants. Sister Rosaleen gave the cage a twirl and settled herself down, nervous as hell.

—Eyes down, game on, she bellowed, as Philo had instructed.

There were all sorts of shouts from the hall – people weren't ready, others needed to put their glasses on, more needed pencils to mark off their numbers. So Sister Rosaleen gave them another minute before she put her hand in the cage and started the game.

—First ball out is all the threes....

—Thirty-three, they chimed back in unison.

Sister Rosaleen hadn't expected them to answer, and she was surprised and delighted. It was like the Mass, only more spontaneous. Bingo was a strange liturgy. There was no Eucharist, the reward was mercenary, and yet the atmosphere in the room was spiritual.

Philo walked between the tables and chairs, waiting for a check. She was delighted with Sister Rosaleen taking her first steps on the road to becoming a bingo caller, her voice growing in confidence with every ball out of the cage.

—On its own, the Holy Trinity, number three.

Philo loved the way she brought her own experience to bear on the numbers, stamping her vocation on the bingo balls. She could feel the excitement mount as the players got closer to a line across.

—On its own, number six. Two fat ladies....

—Eighty-eight.

—Key of the door....

—Bingo!

Not just one voice, but several:

—Bingo!

—Bingo!

Voices raised in triumph, all around the room.

—Bingo!

—Bingo!

They were coming from every corner. There were eight tables with hands raised in victory. Ninna Delargy, looking like she'd just won a husband; Cap, mortified at their success. Nan Cassidy and Granny Carmody, unhappy they were sharing with so many. Chrissie Mongon and Ita Mullen, victors who'd have a story for Dina on her return. Mucky Mannion, playing on his own, with his hand up, too. Philo started with him and called the numbers back to Sister Rosaleen. They tallied perfectly. Then she moved on to Olive Mulvey and repeated the exercise. The numbers were exactly the same as Mucky's.

A further check revealed that all eight winners had the same set of numbers. The bingo cards were photocopies of one another. It might have been sabotage, it might have been an innocent mistake, but someone had made gelignite of the bingo game.

The game was aborted and the prizes distributed. Granny Carmody went first, and chose a tin of pineapples with as much delight as if she'd won the tropical island they came from. Ninna Delargy picked a packet of tea-bags, beaming because it gave her the perfect excuse to invite Cap around to her house. Nan Cassidy chose a tin of beans and balanced it on her head as she walked back to her chair. Cap went last, by choice, and was left with the assortment of vegetables Philo had thrown together, the last prize in the world he needed. But he was pleased because he saw it as an omen. He'd been given something of Dina's, and he would reciprocate, in time.

Fourteen people left the Day Centre better off than when they had come in. They went home with the spoils of war, from tinned peas to toilet rolls, cigarettes to diet yoghurt. They hadn't managed a full house but they were satisfied with their line across; the winners and the losers, all were happy – apart from Sister Rosaleen.

She was gutted. Nothing in her religious life had given her the satisfaction she'd experienced calling out the numbers. Nothing before had connected her so dynamically to the lives of her charges. For once, she wasn't apart from them, watching over them; she was of them and they were of her. She hadn't wanted it to end, and now that it had, she couldn't wait for it to start again. She was addicted.

Philo found the vacuum cleaner staring back at her like a cross teacher. She should have returned it, but she couldn't face the prospect of dragging it back across the bridge to East Wall. Apart from that, she needed it for the big clean-up. There'd be hell to pay for holding on to it – not that her father ever hurt the feelings of a vacuum cleaner by using one, but that wouldn't stop him delivering a State-of-the-Nation speech on the evils of borrowing. It was time for Philo to negotiate an extension to the loan.

As soon as she arrived home, she could feel the chill winds blowing down the hall at her. There was no greeting. Her mother turned away from her and went straight into the front room. She straightened the blankets on the bed and fluffed up her pillows with solid right jabs, like an angry boxer.

—What's wrong, Ma? Are you fighting with me? Philo said.

—I'm not fighting, no. What makes you say that?

When Sylvia didn't offer her a cup of tea on arrival, that meant she was fighting with her. She bustled about some more, keeping her back to Philo.

—It would be nice to be told things, that's all, Sylvia said.

She was in cryptic mode, and that was serious.

—Will I put on the kettle, Sylvia?

—You can do what you like.

This had nothing to do with the vacuum cleaner; it was more serious than that.

—What's annoying you, Sylvia? Is it something I done or something I didn't do?

—What you do is your business and what I do is mine.

This verbal tennis could go on forever. Philo decided to try and break the ice.

—I'm putting on the kettle.

—Nan Cassidy knows more about your life than I do, Sylvia said in a hurt tone.

It stopped Philo in her tracks. She thought back to earlier that day and the game of bingo in the Day Centre. She couldn't remember if Nan had won a prize, but maybe she'd called in to Sylvia on her way home to show it off. It was terrible to think this situation might have been created by a packet of tea-bags or a tin of pineapple chunks.

—How come Nan Cassidy gets invited out to Santry on Sunday and you wouldn't think of inviting me?

Philo felt nausea wash over her in waves.

—I'm your mother and Jack is my grandson.

Philo couldn't think of a suitable response; nothing that formed in her brain made any sense.

—Would you like a cup of tea, Sylvia?

—I'd like to know what I done, that I'm not invited.

—Maybe you'd like a diet biscuit with that?

—Jack is driving in a Grand Prix race and I'm the last to know.

—It's not a Grand Prix; he's driving on his own, against the clock.

—How come I'm not invited? What's wrong with me that I don't get asked?

—You are invited. That's what I came around for. I came to invite you.

Philo was thinking hard. She didn't care what lies she told as long as they extricated her from the mire she was in.

—I wanted to surprise you, she said, but that stupid cow is after spoiling it on me.

Had she been wired to a lie-detector machine, it would have exploded.

192

—How am I going to get out to Santry? Sylvia asked.

—On the bus.

—You're joking me. I can't get on a bus.

—Why can't you get on a bus?

—A bus to Santry, from O'Connell Street?

—What's wrong with that?

—Look at my legs. I can't walk to O'Connell Street.

—Who says you've to walk anywhere?

—It's hardly going to come and get me.

—Would you be surprised if it did?

—The 16A bus is not going to come down here and stop outside my house.

—Did I say I was going to surprise you?

—Yes, you did say that.

—Well, be ready on Sunday, 'cause a bus is going to come down here and collect you.

With that pronouncement, Philo went out to the kitchen and put the kettle on. She'd have to hire a bus. Thankfully, she had her wages from Tommo to pay for it. It was a small price to pay for the gaffe she'd made. In many ways, it was a blessing in disguise. She could turn it into an outing for everyone – the children, her mother, the old folks, Brother Felix, her sister Sally, and anyone else who wanted to go, including her father, although she secretly hoped that he was working. Getting Sylvia out of the house would be a good thing. Once she experienced a day out with the old folks, she might develop the taste for more. It was sad that she'd become a recluse.

Philo scalded the teapot and poured the steaming water out the spout. She heard Sylvia come into the kitchen behind her.

—I'm going to give Sunday a miss, if that's all right, she said.

—No, it's not all right. You're going. I've paid for the bus.

Philo looked at her with determination. Sylvia made some reference to having nothing to wear.

—If you have to go out of here in a sack, you're going.

Sylvia sighed and mentioned her pink cardigan and cream skirt as the only suitable clothes she had. The argument was over and she would be going. Philo was delighted for her mother and sad for herself. It meant she had to reveal the truth about where the children were. So far, she'd kept it from Sylvia; it was painful to distress her, and the reality of the children would do just that. Yet it would be good to have it out in the open. Secrets were shaming things and Philo had nothing to be ashamed about. She'd never done anything to harm the children; she'd always done her best, in her own mad way. Ideally, she'd have waited until she had them back before telling her mother. Her hand had been forced by Nan Cassidy, but she only had herself to blame for issuing reckless invitations at the Day Centre.

Philo poured out the tea and put two of Sylvia's sugar-free diet biscuits on the saucer. They sat across the table from each other. Sylvia offered Philo a biscuit, but she declined.

—You can eat as many as you like, it says on the packet.

The wrapper promised succulent eating with no weight gain. Looking at her mother, Philo couldn't think of anything that had failed so abysmally.

—They won't do you any harm. Have one.

Her optimism was infectious, so Philo took one. One bite and she remembered she hated them. Not only did they not work, but they tasted horrible into the bargain.

—I think they only taste good if you've suffered from the menopause, Philo said.

Sylvia had put up with them for years because she expected to suffer in life. Unlike most martyrs, however, she never complained. The state of the world bothered her, but she was an optimist with regard to her own life and always found something positive to focus on.

—I want you ready at twelve o'clock on Sunday, Philo said. We collect you and then we go to Goldenbridge.

—I thought we were going to Santry.

—The children are staying in Goldenbridge for a few days, so we have to collect them there.

Philo tried to ease Sylvia into the mess that was her life – a place of housing lists, forms, daily visits to orphanages and boys' homes, convents, nuns, Zimmer frames, vegetables, bingo, blind dates, joyriding, and racetracks – but the softness of the introduction couldn't muffle the shock. Philo tried to keep it as humorous as possible, but Sylvia saw nothing funny in any of it. Her only concern was the children. For her, there was nothing positive in the break-up of the family. No matter how bad the situation, children were better off with two parents, and no amount of nuns could make up for that.

—I have peace of mind; that counts for something, Philo said.

—You have it at someone else's expense, Sylvia replied.

It felt like a knife in the chest.

—Others are suffering for your peace of mind.

Philo had spent the previous weeks focusing on a solution that would bring her and the children back together without Tommo. She'd done that by blocking out their upset as best she could. One comment from her mother and she was overwhelmed with guilt. She felt like a complete and worthless failure.

—We've always suffered at the hands of the men, Sylvia said. That's never going to change.

—It's the name-calling, Ma – I can't put up with it any more.

—You have to.

—I don't think I can.

—That's the price you have to pay, same as me. We all pay a price; none of us gets away free.

Sylvia stuffed the last of the biscuit in her mouth and washed it down. She believed what it said on the package, because she had to; that was her delusion. Like the blubber of a seal, her mounds of flesh were her layer of protection. They shielded her from the pain of the world.

Philo looked across at her and knew she was looking at her own future. She was three-quarters of the way there. What harm was there in going all the way? Not for the first time, the omens were telling her to get back with Tommo. She'd made a mistake leaving the family home; it had reduced her to a person without value or rights and robbed her of her children.

—I've been praying to Padre Pio and he never lets me down.

Padre Pio was Sylvia's hero. She could ask him for anything as long as it wasn't for herself. Only for that, she'd have lost the weight years ago. He'd have taken stones off her.

—What are you asking Padre Pio for now? Philo said.

—I've been praying to him for Tommo.

—That bastard doesn't need your prayers.

—We all need help, we can all do with intercession.

—He's an abuser. He'll never be any good.

—It's the drink, Philo. I'm asking Padre Pio to help him give up the drink. I didn't succeed with your father, but maybe I will with Tommo.

Philo had never really believed that you could ask a dead person for a favour. The casual way her mother invoked the name of Padre Pio caught her off guard. She made him sound like someone who lived four doors down and called in to have a chat with her twice a week. Sylvia was very isolated, and this was her one true friend. She'd asked Padre Pio to do a message, and he'd gone and taken the drink out of Tommo's hand. Philo wasn't sure what this said about Alcoholics Anonymous. The truth was hard to determine. Padre Pio and Alcoholics Anonymous would have to fight it out between themselves.

In the meantime, Philo decided to say nothing about

Tommo and the drink. She didn't want to give Sylvia a heart attack. She took the middle ground and asked for a Padre Pio leaflet instead. If it worked for Sylvia, it could work for her. She didn't know what she was going to ask him for, but she looked forward to making a list of possibilities and playing around with it, in her head, before coming to a decision.

Christy Furlong, the gate-man at the Santry racing track, was sure the bus was lost. The approach to his turnstile position (fifteen years and never missed a Sunday) was a dirt road that didn't allow for speed. A cattle-gate was attached to the side of the turnstile, and Christy had it in the locked position, because all the cars for that day's racing were inside the compound. He came out onto the dirt road, held his hand up policeman-style and brought the bus to a halt. It wasn't every Sunday he had a bus to deal with. Indeed, he'd never had a bus before, not in all the years he'd been minding the gate. That was how he knew it was lost.

He inspected the front of the bus, took a long look at the registration plate, and indicated to the driver to open the door. A gush of air and Christy was hopping up the steps, buoyed by his success.

—You took a wrong turn there. Where are you headed for?

—Santry racing track, said the driver.

—I know this is Santry racing track, but where do you want to get to? What's your destination?

—Our destination is Santry racing track.

Christy Furlong looked at the faces looking at him. They were a strange collection.

At the front was a woman who was the full width of two seats. She was puffing for air, surrounded by children who were pulling at every part of her. In her hand she had a bag of sweets, and she was feeding the children like they were monkeys in the zoo. Behind the fat lady were lots of old, wrinkled faces, women wearing scarves and men with hats. At the back, side by side, were another huge woman and a nun, laughing together at some shared joke. To Christy, they all looked like they were from a hospital, or a nursing home. Then it struck him that they could be patients from the asylum in Portrane. Its proper name was Saint Ita's Psychiatric Hospital, but nobody called it that. Christy thought he was being set up for a practical joke, but it wasn't going to succeed. He wasn't going to be taken in by the blank expression on the driver's face, either.

—Go back out onto the main road, take a left and follow the signs for Portrane.

—Portrane?

—That's right, Portrane.

—Do you think I'm mad? said the driver

—In a word, yes, I do.

It was just about to get heated when Brother Felix appeared from nowhere, jumped up onto the bus and welcomed them all to the circuit.

—You know these people, ET? Christy Furlong said.

—Yes, they're here to support Jack Nolan.

Christy ran like a man with a dose of diarrhoea, opened the gate at speed, disappeared into his turnstile and hid. The bus edged its way in and parked behind a steel container that functioned as an office, a meeting point, the stewards' room, a first-aid bay and a sweet shop. Brother Felix took Philo's crowd to a reserved enclosure, which was a grassy hill cordoned off by a few grey ropes that had once been white. A couple of barrels connected by planks represented the seating arrangements. Sylvia was glad to relieve the pressure on her feet, but the remainder of the North Wall contingent, twenty-eight in all, looked down on the racing from their standing positions.

It was primitive and noisy, with the smell of oil and burning rubber everpresent. There was a definite honesty about the whole thing. The track was formed by a cement wall on one side and, on the other, row upon row of worn-out tyres. In the centre, the in-field, drivers and mechanics were making last-minute adjustments to their cars. The roar of the engines was deafening. Philo spotted Jack with Black Bob, his supervisor; she called out to him, but he couldn't hear her.

A man with a microphone made an announcement; it was impossible to make out a single word of it, but the cars all went quiet as a result. He spoke again and the words crackled through the battered speakers.

—The Golden Dragon to the starting line, please.

—That's Jack's racing name, Brother Felix said.

Young Tommo got very excited. This was much better than a Sunday in the orphanage. He clapped his hands above his head, in rhythm, and started to chant: —The Gol-den Drag On, the Gol-den Drag On! Eileen, Josie, Philomena and Sally joined in, and so did Philo and Sister Rosaleen. By the time the car got to the starting line, young and old were at it. For Sylvia, it was the most exercise she'd had in months.

Jack took his yellow Opel Kadett on a warm-up lap. He did his best to block out the world by pulling his helmet fast against his ears. Coming around the final bend, he put his foot to the floor and took the flag. As he headed down towards the first bend, he imagined the police were on his tail; he'd pulled off a bank robbery and was looking at fifteen years if he was caught. It focused his mind. He was putting his joyriding experience to good use, going up and down through the gears like someone possessed by a spirit. Having worked on the car, he knew what every part of the engine was doing at every second – the pistons pumping for all they were worth, the spark-plugs firing the internal combustion, the oil lubricating it all and the water preventing it from boiling over. The temperature gauges were trembling and the sweat was running down his neck onto his shoulders, making them tickle. There was no way any pig in a uniform was catching up on him, not now, not ever.

He was almost there. Coming into the fourth bend, he went down into third; coming out, he pushed into fourth and headed for the line. He took the flag and released the accelerator, letting the car decrease speed rapidly on the run-down lap. He loosened his helmet and lowered the window. Looking over at the grandstand, he saw a crowd of people going mental – and they weren't baying for his blood. He brought the car to a stop by the in-field gate and got out. The man with the microphone gave out the lap time.

—Ladies and gentlemen, that was a 56.7-second lap and a new under-16 track record for the Golden Dragon.

The grandstand turned into a bull run. Young Tommo led the charge, followed by the others, children first and then Philo and Sister Rosaleen, with the old folks bringing up the rear. They surrounded Jack and hoisted him up onto the shoulders of Brother Felix and Black Bob.

—Michael Schumacher! said Brother Felix. He's a young Michael Schumacher!

—Michael Schumacher? said Philo. Who the fuck is Michael Schumacher?

They carried the triumphant Jack to the stewards' room, where he signed the book for his record-breaking lap. His brother and sisters were all over him. To them it was as good as if he'd won the world championship, but Jack brushed their compliments aside like it was nothing at all. He gave each of them a go of his helmet in turn, except for Eileen, who didn't want one.

—You're getting very grown-up, do you know that? Jack said to her.

In truth, he was the one who had matured. Just weeks earlier he'd been an out-of-control joyrider who wet the bed. He'd come a long way in a very short time.

Sister Rosaleen organised the group back onto the bus. They'd seen what they'd come for, and the noise and the smells were overpowering for the more delicate souls like Olive Mulvey and Ninna Delargy. Not that they were going home – far from it: the day was only beginning, and they had to find a good pub in which to have their sing-song.

Mucky Mannion made himself scarce and slipped into the gents' toilet. It was no more than a concrete trough, with an outlet at one end where the bubbles and cigarette butts gathered. There was no roof on it, which meant that the foul odour could at least escape before it choked the pissers. He took the boot polish from his pocket and started to apply it to his face. He did it carefully, with a rag, to stop it getting on his hands. There was no mirror, so he used the little square one he carried in his wallet. Satisfied with the application, he put the polish and rag away, took out the white gloves and slipped them over his splayed fingers.

Christy Furlong came into the toilet. He noticed the white hands first. His gaze brought him from there to the black face with the piercing blue eyes. His first thought was that he'd crossed over to the other side. He didn't know if it was heaven or hell, but he wasn't waiting around to find out. Not even the overwhelming urge to urinate could compete with the desire to be out of there. So, bladder bursting, he made his way back to the haven of his turnstile.

There was one person missing, and Sister Rosaleen wasn't leaving without him. Cap assured her that everything was fine, and that the errant Mucky would appear once the bus got going. And so he did. As the driver headed out the gate and down the dirt road, Mucky jumped in front of the bus and brought it to a stop. He hopped up the steps and fell to one knee in the middle of the aisle before launching into his Al Jolson show. First song up was 'Mammy', and in seconds he had them all singing along, walking a million miles for one of her smiles.

—That's especially for you, Sylvia! Philo shouted from the back seat.

The sing-song went on uninterrupted until they reached the sea at Donabate. It continued in the Bay Arms, a pub that overlooked the beach. Sylvia sat outside and watched the children jump off the sand dunes dotted along the strand. The orange sun was setting behind them. The sea was calm and Lambay Island looked like a giant sea creature, floating in the distance. It had been a perfect day. It was almost a perfect evening. Later on, the children would return to Goldenbridge, and it broke Sylvia's heart to imagine it. Her thoughts turned to kidnapping, but it wasn't really viable – not with a husband like Jack. There was always Padre Pio, the only man she'd ever loved, but she didn't want to overburden him. She'd come back to him later, when the time was right.

Philo came out of the pub and sat beside her on the wall. The only sounds were the playful shouts of the children and the waves breaking on the sand. Freedom and innocence, side by side with orphanages, boys' homes and body fat. Everyone had their own ball and chain. For now Sylvia and Philo had freedom, too, and it was enough that they had it.

—It was a nice day, Ma. Did you have a nice day?

—I had a lovely day, daughter, the loveliest.

13

Dina came home on the Monday afternoon to a clean house. Philo's army had been in the previous Saturday and had gone through the place like a dose of salts. They'd turned up with polish, rags, buckets, caustic soda, Brasso, odour-buster, flowers, mops, chamois cloths, Silvo, dustpans, toilet rolls (stolen, bought and won), washing-up liquid, plungers, mouse poison, bubble bath and a 'Welcome Home' sign. At one point, there were so many people in the house it was like a train carriage in rush hour. People newly arrived couldn't get in the door; they were queuing down the lane like they were at a grotto.

Philo opened the upstairs window to address the crowd below. She placed her hands on the ledge and leaned out. The image of Jim Larkin, the great labour leader, came into her mind: on Bloody Sunday in Dublin, he'd stolen into the Imperial Hotel and from an upstairs window he'd addressed the crowd in O'Connell Street. From the time Philo could speak, her father had regaled her with stories of Larkin and how he'd come to raise the Dublin working class from their knees. As she looked down onto Dowdall's Lane, his words echoed in her ear: *The mission I have come to preach is the divine mission of discontent.* She felt like roaring it out, but she resisted; it was Clean-up Saturday, not Bloody Sunday.

So she came up with a plan to divide the work into two shifts. Those who were on the ground floor and the street were sent away to come back later. Those who remained, spurred on by Philo, attacked the house with gusto. The result was that not a corner or a surface, a door or a ledge had got away without being washed twice. The house was cleaner than the day it had been built, with an array of smells that competed with one another in the welcoming stakes.

Dina didn't know what to think. As soon as the ambulance men carried her through the door, she could see things were different. The shop was suffused in light because the windows that had been caked in years of grime were translucent again. Not that the presence of light bothered her – it didn't. As she went up the stairs, her nose was on fire with the smell of furniture polish. It brought her back years and she was glad of the time travel. The upstairs was a complete revelation; it looked like it had been brought back from the dead. It was full of colours and textures she'd never noticed before. How could she have lived there and not noticed the cast-iron fireplace with the recessed blue tiles; the cornices and the ceiling roses; the door panels and the brass handles, restored to their golden hue; the sideboard with the cut-glass vase full of the most beautiful flowers; the wall with the 'Welcome Home' sign draped across it? None of these things displeased her, even if the familiar had been made to look strange.

—You must have been up all night cleaning the place, Dina said.

—You must be joking; I did that in an hour, Philo said, with her tongue firmly in her cheek.

—An hour? You must have been going like the clappers.

—Not at all, I didn't even break sweat.

Dina looked around at the transformation and knew it didn't make sense.

—You were at this morning, noon and night, Dina said.

—I'm your home help, not your bleedin' slave.

—Did you pick the flowers?

—No, an admirer sent them.

—You're a married woman, Philo, you're not supposed to have admirers.

Philo waved at her to make sure she had her attention. She lowered her face to Dina's level and spoke slowly.

—It was an admirer of yours. They were bought for you, not for me.

Dina knew Philo wasn't going to tell her without being asked. She didn't want to give her the pleasure, especially if the flowers had been sent by the nuns or one of her cronies; she didn't want to fall for that.

—Do you know what I'd love? Dina said.

—You'd love to know who sent them flowers, Philo answered.

—No, I'd love a cup of tea.

Philo got up to make it, and Dina called her back. After she'd been confined to a hospital bed for days, the pleasure for Dina was in making it herself – standing in her own kitchen, filling her own kettle with water, putting it on the gas and watching it boil. She'd been waited on hand and foot, and now she wanted to do something under her own steam. The bandages were still on her feet and walking wasn't easy. She put her hands on Philo's waist and they moved like two clunking train carriages towards the kitchen. Philo found it hard to judge the speed.

—Am I going too fast for you? she asked.

—I'm just afraid I'll kick you, that's all.

Philo turned around and faced her.

—Let's do it sideways, so.

Immediately it felt better, because they could see each other. They fell into a rhythm: a step with the kitchen-side leg, followed by a drag with the trailing leg. They moved across the room towards the kitchen, without the slightest concern about when they'd get there. Dina's hands moved into the dancing position. It happened effortlessly. Philo counted out the steps, one-two-three, and Dina started to hum 'The Anniversary Waltz', a hum that soon found the real words, a song she hadn't sung in thirty years. They reached the kitchen door, but instead of going through, they reversed back across the room.

—Are you sure you're up for this? Philo asked.

Dina didn't want to lose her place in the song; she just kept on singing.

—I don't want to waltz the legs off you, that's all.

Dina looked so frail in her bandages, and even though Philo knew she'd live to be a hundred and eight, she didn't want to overdo things on her first day home. When the song ended, they were further away from the kitchen than when they'd started.

—You're a lovely dancer, do you know that? Dina said.

Not knowing what to do with a compliment, Philo said nothing.

—I can't remember the last time I danced like that, Dina went on. I'll have to do it more often.

—You'll do what the doctors tell you.

—Fuck the doctors, I'm sick listening to them. Come on, dance me to the kitchen till I have a cigarette and a drop of brandy.

Dina had been severely lectured about smoking and the effect it had on her circulation, never mind the danger to her lungs. In the hospital, she'd been as compliant as a mouse, promising a complete revolution in her lifestyle. Back home in the arms of Philo, she wanted to be her old self as quickly as possible. She was happy in her life – more than happy; she was ecstatic. She had the shop, her cronies, the convent and a home help. Her living quarters were like a new pin and she'd taken up ballroom dancing. She was reborn.

The kitchen was mercurial. Drawers that had been stuck for years were sliding in and out again with great poise. The sink, which had been blocked since the invasion of the Vikings, was discharging water with speed and zest. The leak in the tap had been solved by means of a rubber washer, thanks to the Commandant – indeed, he'd been responsible for all the plumbing odd jobs. The grease on the cooker had vanished under the deadly combination of Granny Carmody and Mr Muscle. The cutlery and crockery, a good deal of it stolen from the convent (and some from hotels), had been washed, dried, polished, and put back in clean presses and drawers.

Yet the first thing Dina noticed was the burnt-out kettle. Philo had left it on the cooker to remind herself to get a new one. With so much to do around the homecoming and the race day in Santry, she'd forgotten.

—What happened to my poor kettle?

—I burnt the arse out of it, that's what happened.

—It had a little whistle like a choo-choo train; did you not hear it?

—I was downstairs in the shop trying to earn some money for you.

Philo put most of the emphasis on the 'you'. It seemed to work: Dina held her fire. Philo put some water in a saucepan and lit the gas. Boiled water was boiled water. A saucepan did the job as well as any other vessel. A whistling kettle didn't make the tea taste better, no matter what Dina or anybody else thought. Philo took out two cigarettes and lit them. She handed one to Dina, who put it in her mouth and puffed out smoke.

—I loved that little kettle.

It was as though she'd lost a child.

—I loved everything about it.

Her whole demeanour was pathetic.

—I'm going to miss it terrible.

—Look, I'll organise a funeral for the kettle, if you like.

—That might be nice.

—I wasn't bleedin' serious. You can't bury a kettle.

—I hate seeing it deformed, that's all.

Philo couldn't take any more. She put the kettle in the bin.

—Cap Coyle brought the flowers, she announced.

It didn't register with Dina. It was a peace offering from her old enemy, but it meant nothing. She was lost in a reverie, going back over her whole life with the kettle and wondering how she would get on without it.

—They're very romantic, don't you think?

Dina was sucking on her cigarette like it was a lollipop, pining for her lost kettle.

—The lilies have a beautiful scent, do you get it?

Philo was wasting her time. The flowers could have been bought by Jesus Christ and delivered by John the Baptist, and Dina wouldn't have cared. Cap Coyle wasn't in her thoughts. Dina had come home to a beautiful house, and all she could focus on was the piece of burnt-out metal. She couldn't see beauty anywhere. Philo decided to let her be a crabby bitch for her first day back in reality. Not that she was in reality; she was in a fantasy world, and maybe she'd stay in it forever if she wasn't brought back to earth.

—Come on, you lazy bitch, make the tea like you promised, Philo said.

Dina looked angelic in her cloud of white smoke.

—Why am I a bitch? she asked.

—You're not sitting on your arse all day; there's work to be done. You said you'd wet the tea.

—I did, too. I haven't had proper tea in ages.

—No pot makes tea like your own pot.

It was one of those Gaelic expressions that didn't quite make it in the translation to English. Philo had picked it up from her mother. *Níl aon tinteán mar do thinteán féin*: there's no hearth like your own hearth. The Gaelic was off-beat and musical; it had great rhythm and pace. Perhaps Dina felt the same thing with the kettle, a connectedness to the tinkers of old. It wasn't that long since they used to come and repair buckets, basins, kettles, all manner of household stuff.

According to folklore, they brought good luck with them as long as you crossed their palms with silver. The whistling kettle might have been Dina's link to that world, a world that had passed and was gone.

Dina made the tea and Philo watched her.

—Would you like to put out the sugar and milk? Dina asked.

—No, do it yourself, Philo replied.

She sat on her arse, delighted not to be of assistance. Dina, likewise, was delighted to be doing it all. It confirmed that she was independent, that she could manage on her own, at least to the extent of feeding herself.

—Are you comfortable sitting on your arse? Dina asked.

—It's my favourite place in the world, thanks for asking, Philo replied.

Dina put three spoons of sugar and plenty of milk in the tea before handing it to her. Philo, in return, lit two more cigarettes and handed one to Dina. They puffed and slurped for several minutes. They observed the silence between them like it was a house rule. When she was finished, Dina brought her cup to the sink and dumped it in.

—Cap brought the flowers, is that right? she said as nonchalantly as she could.

Philo was surprised she'd absorbed the information.

—The very man, the one and only.

—Brought them in person, did he?

—No, he sent a ghost in a white sheet.

—He could have had them delivered.

—Well, he didn't. He turned up carrying his own flowers.

—Did he come up the stairs and see the place?

—You hardly think I left him standing in the lane.

—Thank God you'd cleaned the place, so.

Philo tried to explain about the clean-up. The idea that an army of her friends (and enemies) had converged on her house and crawled through it, hoovering up her dirt, was not something Dina could easily come to terms with. It was an invasion of her privacy and there was no point in pretending otherwise. She asked for a list of all the people who'd crossed her threshold, and Philo told her to go fuck herself. She was shocked to be spoken to that way by someone who was being paid to look after her. On the other hand, she couldn't imagine herself being looked after by anyone else. Philo wasn't just a home help; she was a saviour. Dina held her peace and said nothing.

At ten o'clock they retired to bed. For Dina, it was like having a radiator under the blankets; the heat came off Philo in waves. Dina snuggled into her and felt like she was being toasted.

—You're lovely and warm, do you know that?

—I must be starting the menopause, Philo said.

—You're not old enough to be starting that.

—I probably got it off you. It's highly contagious, you know.

Dina moved away and then realised she was having her leg pulled. It was lovely to have someone to talk to in bed. She hadn't had that since Gerry had left.

—I'm sorry for being a crabby bitch, she said.

—That's all right, you're forgiven.

—I'm an awful complainer, amn't I?

—Sometimes.

—I hate myself for being a moan. Do you hate me?

—Sometimes.

—You're not going to walk out on me, are you?

—No, I'm going to roll over and smother you.

—I wouldn't blame you. If I was you I'd do the same thing.

—Have you made a will?

—No.

—I won't smother you, so.

—Why not?

—I wouldn't get a penny out of you if you died tonight.

—What makes you think I'll leave anything to you in my will?

—I'm your home help.

—That means you look after me.

—That means I can torture you.

—I'd tell on you, I'd scream out for help.

—Not if you had a sock in your mouth and your hands were tied.

Dina thought about it. She was completely at Philo's mercy, as vulnerable as a newborn infant. She couldn't remember that far back, had no memory of the cot or the cradle, so she had nothing to compare it to. The only strong feeling she could summon up was loneliness – the awfulness of being on her own, lying in this self-same bed and wondering where her family had gone to and whether they were alone too. These were only ever empty thoughts, because there was no one there to share them with.

—It's lovely to talk, Philo.

—You needn't try and butter me up.

—I know you wouldn't put a sock in my mouth.

—You're right, I'd use sticky tape instead.

Philo was determined not to let Dina fall into the poor-me's and drag her down along with her. If she let herself be pulled into a pessimistic spiral, she might not get back out again. She needed to stay focused on a solution to her problems.

—Can you hear that radio? Philo said.

They both listened. It was raining outside. The drops were heavy on the roof-tiles, but the strains of a voice could be heard, singing. Philo turned around to face Dina.

—Did you leave the radio on? she asked.

—That's not a radio, that's a human voice, Dina said.

It was some poor soul in Dowdall's Lane, making his way

home, bawling his song out against the elements. It was pitiful. There seemed to be a plea in the voice, a demand to be heard. Then, suddenly, Dina realised it was directed at her; and a moment later she realised who the singer was.

It was sad to reach the age of seventy-one without ever having done it. There were certain things in life that were assumed – knowing how to ride a bicycle, being able to bless yourself, drinking a pint on coming of age – and Cap had experienced those. Putting one's penis into a vagina (at least once in your life) was a birthright of all males, in the city of Dublin anyway. Cap had worked with men on the docks who openly discussed vaginas, comparing their elasticity, wetness, shape, hairiness and muscle strength. He'd picked up a certain knowledge from these situations, but it wasn't the same as doing it. Someone could describe riding a bicycle, but nothing prepared you for putting your feet on the pedals, pushing with all your might and straining to keep the quivering mass of metal from falling down on the ground. Ending up on your arse was all right at age ten, but not at seventy-one.

Cap suspected there was more to it than the crude mechanics he'd heard described on the Dublin docks. It was what went before that bothered him, getting into the right position; the build-up. All his life he'd wondered about it and never had the courage to ask. He'd kissed a girl from the Avenues one time, Kathleen Burke. It was under the railway bridge in Seville Place. He'd got very aroused and put his hand on her breast, but she'd slapped it away like that was an indictable crime. His body was bursting with desire, but permission for it to act was resolutely withheld. It had ended on a sour note, too. They were dancing in the Four Provinces ballroom, a slow set, when Kathleen Burke asked him if he was carrying a beer bottle in his trouser pocket. It took him a moment to realise she'd felt his penis against her leg. In his embarrassment he'd denied all knowledge of a bottle.

—Well, whatever that is, keep it away from me, she'd said.

He'd felt rejected and humiliated. He'd led with his manhood and been ridiculed for it. Maybe he was just unattractive to the opposite sex. He thought there might be an odour from him that women found repellent. Perhaps his penis was too big – or, worse again, not big enough. Women required something from him and he couldn't give it; that was the core of it. Cap had lived in fear after that, petrified to ever take a chance again.

He'd learned to live with his paralysis. He rose to an occasional wank, and that got him through for years, but that, too, had petered out to nothing. He didn't know if his machinery was still in working order, but he suspected it would rise to it if the occasion was right. What really mattered was what women expected of him. He never wanted to make a fool of himself in that regard again. He'd heard talk in a pub one time of a sex video that was like a training manual. The people in it were real, as opposed to actors, so nothing was faked; it was actual sex. He thought it would be useful, but he had no video player. It was an expensive item to purchase to watch one video. What if he bought the machine and then found that the video didn't exist? Or that it wasn't available in Ireland? He'd feel worse than he had with the beer bottle in his pocket.

He decided that a book might be a safer option. Entering Eason's bookstore on the O'Connell Street side, he started on the right-hand wall and worked his way around. Every Irish book and author known to man was there, but not a hint of sex among them. He went through fiction, biography and poetry and ended up in maps of Europe and the world. From there it was on to art books; there were a few interesting nudes, but no instructions. Psychology and philosophy promised to unearth the meaning of life but there wasn't a copulating couple between them. The health section was next, and Cap was about to bypass it when he spotted a book on fertility and how to improve it. He was flicking through it when he saw *Secrets of the Kama Sutra* two shelves down.

He'd never seen such a collection of pencil-like penises in all his days. The women were flat-chested and looked as though they were offering it up. It was the diameter of the penises that fascinated Cap. It made him feel good about his own member, which was humongous by comparison. He thought back to the night of the Four Provinces: at least Kathleen Burke hadn't accused him of having a pencil in his pocket. There was nothing approaching a beer bottle in the pages of the *Kama Sutra*, and, for the first time in a long time, Cap felt proud of what he had.

The Joy of Sex was next. On the front cover it promised a gourmet guide to lovemaking. Inside, it was packed with text and illustrations. The book opened with starters, went on to main courses, moved to sauces and pickles and ended with problems. Cap went straight to the last chapter and was reassured to read that neither men nor women lose their sexual function with age. It was just what he wanted to see.

A woman's voice asked him if he required any help. He turned around, and a cross-looking shop assistant stared at him like he'd exposed himself. He declined her help and brought the book to a cash point. The girl at the till couldn't take for it because it wasn't wrapped in cellophane; she held it up and shouted for someone to bring an unopened copy of the book.

—What's the name of it? a voice roared out.

—*The Joy of Sex* by Alex Comfort, the cashier roared back.

Cap stood there with the money in his hand while the

entire shop stared at him in a mixture of disgust and admiration.

The book was written in the form of a sex alphabet. Cap spent the next few days learning it by heart. That was how they'd done it when he went to school: learning was by rote, and once something was committed to memory it was there forever. The illustrations were the only thing that put him off. The man, with his long hair and beard, looked like a Jesuit priest, only nude. The woman was much more friendly-looking and got to dress up an awful lot. Cap's new knowledge, from anal to voyeurs and buttocks to wet look, reassured him greatly. He felt that no surprises could be thrown at him and that he'd never be made to look a fool again.

Foreplay was the key. Women wanted a slow build-up. They wanted to be fêted. Men were over-anxious and impatient. Women really cared who their partners were, men much less so. Cap wasn't really after sex. He'd like it once before he died, certainly, but it wasn't everything to him. He cared about Dina as a person. He'd fought a war with her because it was better than staying neutral. He hoped that she found him attractive. He couldn't expect to experience what he'd read about in *The Joy of Sex*, but he'd done his homework and was prepared for all eventualities.

As he was sitting in the pub with Mucky one night, talking about the great footballers of yesteryear, he realised he was not going to advance things with Dina from a bar stool. Cap berated himself and thought about the opera. All his heroes were men who took action, they were doers, they were decisive. They proclaimed their emotion through song – love, sorrow, hatred, revenge, patriotism – and brought it to a level unmatched in any other form of expression. Cap had cried more times in the Gaiety Theatre than he had in Glasnevin Cemetery.

He bade Mucky good night and stepped out into the teeming rain. He had the protection of his hat and was thankful for it. He thought of Ulysses on the stormy Mediterranean, chasing after Helen of Troy. He decided not to go home. With the wind at his back, he was swept along to Dowdall's Lane. Dina's house was in darkness, but Cap didn't care; he opened his mouth and started to sing, 'Oh, What a Beautiful Mornin' '. He was determined to sing it, whether Dina heard it or not. The song was in praise of the sun, the earth, the cattle and the corn; all of God's goodness was in it, from Ireland to America, and he was adding his voice in celebration, even if he was a little drunk, or more than a little drunk. The notes came from deep inside and beat their way up past the raindrops, towards the window.

In the middle of the second verse the light came on. Seconds later the window flew up and Philo leaned out.

—I don't know about a beautiful morning but it's a lousy fucking night, Cap.

He didn't respond, except to raise his arms and continue singing. Nothing was going to deflect him from his purpose. From the bed, Dina listened and knew it was for her. Over the years she'd had her collection of boyfriends, but none of them had ever serenaded her in the middle of a rainstorm.

—Romeo is down here looking for you, Philo said. Will I send him home?

Dina was content to listen. The mixture of music and rain was perfect. It made her feel sexy for the first time in years. She'd thought she'd lost it but it was still there, smouldering away, waiting to burst into flames.

The song came to an end. Dina clapped spontaneously and stopped herself just as quickly.

—Are you going to play hard to get or are you going to talk to him? Philo asked.

—I can hardly talk to him from here.

Philo came over to the bed and took her, jockey-back

216

style, across the room. She eased her down at the window and Dina looked out at the saturated figure below.

—You'll get double pneumonia standing out in that, Dina said.

—It doesn't matter; I'm free, Cap said.

—I didn't know you were locked up.

—I've been locked up for years.

—Sounds to me like you're drunk.

—I am. I'm celebrating.

—What are you celebrating?

—Seeing you.

—You're not drunk, you're mad.

—Thanks be to God for that.

The river of rain ran down the insides of his sleeves to his armpits, and from there down his body to his legs and out the bottoms of his trousers. He was a human drainpipe. The only dry part of his anatomy was his head, and so long as the top of his nut remained that way, he felt invincible.

—You look like Gene Kelly, Dina said.

—What do you mean, look like him? I am Gene Kelly, Cap said.

He started to dance in the puddles, and the words to 'Singing in the Rain' flowed naturally. Dina sang along with him, but they didn't get past the chorus – not that it mattered. Cap hummed and splashed and soaked up half the rain in Dowdall's Lane.

—Are you going to sing and dance there all night? Philo roared down.

—Only if you want me to.

Philo turned to Dina.

—You'd better say something to him, he's not listening to me.

—I can't tell him what to do.

—Well, he didn't come around here because he fancies me!

—He has a mind of his own. I'm not his keeper.

Dina was lapping up the attention, and Philo had to admit it was preferable to the pair of them scratching each other's eyes out. She'd had no idea, when she'd initiated the game of Blind Date, that it would end up like this. The Irish weather spoiled everything, of course, and Cap looked like he was going to drown. Philo was happy to play the home help but she didn't want to end up as an undertaker. Dina was smitten and oblivious to any apparent danger. Philo knew she had to get the drunk Cap inside.

She got the house keys and threw them down to him, but unfortunately he missed the catch. It took him a full five minutes to find them. By the time he got himself inside and up the stairs, he was saturated to the point where all he could do was shake like a dog. Philo got a towel and sent him into the bathroom to dry himself off.

He draped the wet clothes over the side of the bath but kept his hat on. He stood on the new rug (a homecoming present from Dina's cronies), started with his face and worked his way down. His penis was totally limp and he gave it a good rub to bring it back to life. It reminded him of the *Kama Sutra*, and that made him laugh. He was nervous about standing naked in a strange place but delighted to be drying himself off with one of Dina's towels. He was conscious that it had rubbed off her body, too. He draped it around himself and closed his eyes. An event from long ago came to mind: Dina standing at the church railings, her breasts alert and inviting; him walking across to her and asking her for a date.

Cap opened his eyes and looked in the mirror to embrace the moment. His hat was stupid, dripping water onto the rug. He took it off and put it on a shelf. The talcum powder looked straight at him. He sprinkled it over his body and rubbed it in. After his night singing and dancing in the rain, he was dry again. He was smelling good, too, and ready to rejoin the company. The only problem was he had nothing to wear – not a pair of socks, underpants or a vest. He wrapped himself in the towel and came out. He explained his predicament, and Dina thought it was hilarious.

—I can't walk home in my pelt, he said.

—You'll have to sleep in the bath, Dina said.

—You don't have any dry clothes, do you?

—Unless you want to put on knickers, a skirt and a blouse, Philo said.

He didn't reject it out of hand. Cap knew from his manual that lots of men wore women's clothes. There was F for Fetish and T for Transvestite. It was a turn-on for some men to wear knickers, stockings, suspenders, garters, and negligées. Most men tried it at some time in their lives. Cap had never been presented with the opportunity and didn't want to seem like a prude, certainly not in front of Dina.

—Would you like my frilly knickers or my plain cotton ones? Philo asked.

Cap thought about his response. He was aware of Dina's eyes burning into him.

—I'm very shy, he said, but if you forced me….

—We're not going to force you, no way, Philo said.

—If you put a gun to my head, I'd go for….

—The frilly ones, Dina said.

—Yes, the frilly ones, Cap repeated.

The two women looked at each other, amazed.

—It's good to know that, Philo said, but it would take ten of you to fit into my frilly knickers.

—My frilly ones wouldn't go around your waist, Dina said.

—I'll have to sleep in the bath, so, Cap said.

Philo decided to put on a fry. She wasn't that hungry, but she wanted to give the pair of them time alone. Before she left for the kitchen, she told Dina to show Cap how she got around without her Zimmer frame.

—I will not, Dina shot straight back.

—And that man brought you those lovely flowers, Philo said as she left.

Without Philo as a go-between, the atmosphere was awkward. Cap became aware of Dina's bandaged feet and Dina got the waft of talcum powder. Neither of them wanted to make the first move, so they sat there in silence. Then they both spoke across each other.

—The lilies are lovely, Dina said.

—I'm sorry about your toes, Cap said.

—It's nothing.

—Yes it is. It's something, believe me.

—It's nothing, believe me.

The awkwardness, real as it was, couldn't conceal the desire. It felt like a taste, something from long ago that had been pushed down deep inside and was now looking for light and a reprieve.

Cap looked relaxed on the outside but he was trembling inside. It was one thing to memorise a guidebook; it was altogether different to be sitting in a room with a real, living woman, minus your clothes. He felt so vulnerable he wanted to retire to the bath and go to sleep. His stomach was churning and he didn't know what to say or what to do. And yet, he'd been waiting for this moment, preparing himself for it. It was probably the last chance he'd ever get. He had to make a move and he had to live with the consequences of that, come what may.

The courage he'd felt earlier, buoyed by the drink, had left him. He told himself to be positive. The *Kama Sutra* came into his mind. He had a lot going for him, but he had to believe it. The time for initiative was at hand. His moment of truth had arrived.

He stood up and the towel fell off. Dina looked away.

—For God's sake, cover yourself up, she said.

Cap looked at her and looked at the towel. He was in no hurry. This was who he was, and if she didn't like it, it was too bad. He wasn't an exhibitionist, but he wasn't ashamed either. He'd been made to feel that way once before and he wasn't going to take it this time.

—Look at me, he said. This is who I am.

He held out his hands to reinforce the point.

—This is my body and it's the only one I have.

Dina was looking at the ground. Cap held his position and issued the invitation to her once again.

—Look at me.

She craned her head and accepted his strange offer. It was a long time since she'd seen that part of a man. She'd forgotten there were so many bits involved. It was nice to remind herself how it all went together. To her eyes, it looked very impressive.

—Do you like what you see? he asked.

—I like it very much, she replied.

Cap bent down and retrieved the towel, still shaking but delighted that he'd stood up for himself.

—Show me how you walk without the frame, he said.

There was an authoritative air about him that Dina hadn't seen before.

—I'm not going to take no for an answer, he said.

—Getting pushy in our old age, are we? she said. She wanted him to be pushy. She wanted him to be forceful and strong.

—Do you want me to drop this towel again? he asked from behind an impish grin.

She stood up and held out her arms, like she was accepting an offer to dance. He took a solid hold and they began to move across the floor. From the kitchen, Philo started to sing 'Delilah' as their steps became a dance, Cap in his towel and Dina in her dressing-gown, the sound of sizzling sausages mixed with 'my my my's and one-two-threes, their bodies moving left to right and closer together so that by the end of the song they were almost in an embrace.

Cap lifted Dina's chin up with his hand and kissed her gently. The pressure of their lips gave way and they exchanged tongues, a gentle pushing in and out like ships docking and undocking, before Dina slipped hers under Cap's top lip, an unexpected move that wasn't in the manual.

Philo turned her sausages and peeped out. It was beautiful to behold and she crossed her fingers for good luck. The vegetable war looked like it might really be at an end. The North Wall was almost finished, and it was sad that Cap and Dina couldn't have settled their differences when the place was alive; but it was better late than never, as the old cliché had it. They were a version of Romeo and Juliet but one that didn't end in failure, at least not yet.

It gave Philo hope. Anything was possible, but you had to have hope. Her own situation wasn't beyond redemption, perhaps. Optimism was a child of God and pessimism the progeny of the devil. Philo didn't usually allow herself to think too much about favourable outcomes, because of past disappointments. It suited her far better not to think at all. Looking at the duo exchanging kisses triggered a feeling that all was not lost, that things might come right in the end, just as they apparently had for Dina and Cap.

At the end of the kiss, Cap asked Dina to stand on his feet. It was a game he'd played as a child, a million years ago. Dina looked down at his bare feet. She put up one bandaged foot and then the other. Cap placed his hands on her hips and held her firm. He took one exaggerated step and then another. They moved like giant puppets, across the room and into the kitchen, where Philo thought they were funnier than the Keystone Cops. From there it was across the living room and into the bedroom, where they fell, accidentally on purpose, onto the bed. They lay beside each other and laughed their hearts out, like they were seventeen and unfettered. Without Cap having to give it a second's thought, he was where he always wanted to be: he was in bed with Dina.

By the time Philo emerged with her fry, the bedroom door was closed. The sounds coming from inside it were hard to describe. The only thing she could compare them to was one of those wildlife programmes on the television. The high-pitched screams of female monkeys always made it difficult to judge if they were being killed or having the time of their lives. Whatever Cap was doing made Philo jealous. She'd had sex dozens of times but never made those sounds. Cap must be very experienced, she thought.

The sounds from the bedroom mellowed. The screams turned to licking sounds. What part of the anatomy was on the receiving end of this, Philo wasn't sure. She'd never been licked herself. The only thing she'd ever received from a tongue was abuse. Philo lay down on the couch, closed her eyes and tried to imagine all the nice things a tongue could do.

14

Philo wore a blouse with long sleeves when she went to see the Chief Psychiatrist, Matthew Kelly. She loved her tattoo but she was sick of not having her children. Every afternoon she trundled up to Goldenbridge to be with them, and when she left she did a good job of pretending it didn't hurt. The children knew she wasn't an ordinary mother. Most parents who came to visit were quiet as mice and behaved like they were ashamed. Philo was a grizzly bear who roared like everyone had better take notice of her. She wore everything on the outside – her heart, her soul, her guts, her tattoos – and everyone thought she was wild. It was a great way to be for playing games and going on outings, but it was a bad way to be for filling out forms and getting out of institutions.

Young Tommo asked, every single day, when they were coming home. He didn't mind missing the odd football match, but now whole leagues were being won and lost in his absence. Josie and Philomena wanted to be back in their old school and in their old beds. Eileen was a model of patience, but even she was beginning to wilt. After the day at the racetrack and Donabate, she had realised how much she missed her granny and her brother – even though Jack was only her half-brother, to her he was as full a brother as you could get. All this transmitted itself to Philo and made her determined to resolve matters once and for all.

The long sleeves went against her nature. Her instinct was to fight against authority in whatever guise it presented itself. She'd been at it with her father since she was ten years old. Up until then, she'd thought he was God and behaved for him like one of his angels. Anything she was asked to do, she performed with grace and a smile. Then he sent her to the devil and it all changed.

Every Thursday after tea, Jack dispatched her across the bridge with the Vernon's Football Pools and money in a sealed envelope. She brought it to a house on Portland Row off the North Strand. The row was a short hill, but every step Philo took on it felt like a mile. At the top end stood a red-brick convalescent home that cast a huge shadow over everything below it. The house nearest the tall gable wall of the home, number 2, was the one she made her way to. It belonged to the devil, a man they called Uncle Sam Harris though he wasn't, in fact, related to her in any way. The house had bushes growing wild around the hall door, giving the impression that it was lost.

Philo remembered his hands the most, because the hair grew right down to the knuckles and used to scrape against her skin when he put his finger in her nookie. He stretched it so that she would grow up to be a proper woman and when the time came she would deliver her babies without any pain. He always had a lollipop for her to suck while he stretched her nookie. They were the expensive lollipops, too, from the shops up the town, each one with its own multicoloured wrapper that made an effect like a kaleidoscope when it was being twirled off. Even as a child Philo knew she should say no to the lollipop, but she couldn't. Every Wednesday night she said a prayer going to bed, and every Thursday she went to Portland Row to refuse the lollipop. As soon as he twirled the rainbow in front of her eyes, she caved in. Once she had the lollipop in her mouth there was no going back. All she could do was concentrate on sucking the hard sweet and extracting the flavours with her tongue. That way she could blot out his hairy hand and his dirty poems.

Mary had a little lamb
Its fleece was black as charcoal

225

And every time that Mary stooped
The lamb looked up her arsehole.

She was going on thirteen when she decided to make a stand. It was just after she started bleeding. She was sure his hairy hand had something to do with the blood. In order to stop it, she had to remove the temptation of the lollipop. The only way to do that was to stop going to his house. That meant standing up to her father, and she did. On the Wednesday night she prayed that the right words would come out of her mouth the next day.

—I'm not going to Portland Row any more, she said.

Her father wanted to know why, and she wouldn't say, except to repeat her mantra that she wasn't going. After five minutes of this, her father got into a rage and clattered her. He pushed the envelope into her hand and forced her out the door. Philo walked as far as the North Strand, looked up Portland Row and walked back home. She threw the envelope on the table and braced herself for more clatters; but she got a tongue-lashing instead, which was worse. Her father called her a lazy pig, like her mother. It was the first time she'd defied him, the first time anyone in the house had stood up to him and lived to tell the tale.

It turned her from his special messenger into Public Enemy Number One. Every opportunity to put her down and call her names, he took. Every pound of weight, every inch on her waistline, he greeted with a smirk and a comment. Unlike Sylvia, Philo didn't take it lying down. She preferred to risk violence rather than be a sacrificial anything. She wouldn't kow-tow to any authority – not God, her father, Dublin Corporation, the Eastern Health Board; she wouldn't give any of them her allegiance, because they weren't worthy of it.

The Chief Psychiatrist, Matthew Kelly, was going to be an exception, however. She wasn't going to give him any cause to put a black mark against her name. When the Pope had come to Ireland in 1979, the crowd had sung that he had the whole world in his hands, but he didn't have Philo's world: that was a privilege that belonged to the Chief Psychiatrist. Her answers to him would determine if she was sane enough to be a mother to her children again. Philo knew her Achilles heel was her mouth. She had to protect herself against it. Whatever came into her mind, she had to say the opposite. In the run-up to the interview she practised asking herself questions, biting on her tongue and counting slowly to ten. She ended up with a mouth full of sores.

Matthew Kelly had a fuzzy beard that was black in the centre and grey at the edges. He wore a brown corduroy jacket, a fleck shirt and a red tie. He looked intelligent, like those late-night presenters on Open University. Philo suspected he was a socialist, but she thought it a bit of a contradiction that the beard hid most of the red tie from view. Why bother sporting it if you were going to block it out? She counted to ten and the urge to comment on it passed.

—How did you get on with your father? he asked.

It wasn't a question she'd rehearsed.

—I was his little angel as a child, she said, and then he turned against me.

—What brought that about?

—I don't understand what you mean.

She understood perfectly. The conversation was heading in the direction of Portland Row, and she didn't like it. Not since she was thirteen years old had she set foot in that street. Over the years since, she'd found ways to avoid it. It wasn't always easy, because it was an artery that linked the North Strand to Ballybough and the rest of the north side. The question immediately brought back memories of sucking lollipops while having her nookie stretched.

—What caused your father to change towards you? Matthew Kelly asked.

She'd nearly have revealed the secret to get her children

back. Not another soul knew of her childhood shame – not her best friend Josie Cullen, and not Sylvia. Why should she tell a stranger? A man with a beard who might not believe her? An outsider who might presume she'd led him on? It had to be some evil inside her that had precipitated what had happened. She had to keep that part of herself hidden so that it would never raise its ugly head again. Silence had protected her all the years, and she wasn't about to break it now.

—I was his eldest and I think he wanted a boy, a son and heir, someone to carry on his precious name.

—Did you look like him as a child?

—Thank Jaysus, no. I'm like my mother.

—Does that make you happy?

—Of course it does. I love my mother.

—You love her more than your father.

—I hate my father, I told you that.

—He was the dominant one, your father.

—Yes.

—You stood up to him?

—I defied him, yes.

—Could your mother not stand up to him?

—No.

—He's too strong for her, is he?

—He has a vicious tongue.

—Why do you want to be like your mother?

—I love every inch of her.

—She's a weak woman who can't defend herself.

—She's a lovely person inside. She's a lady, a real lady.

—Why do you hate your father?

—I hate him for his abuse.

—How did he abuse you?

Whatever about being Chief Psychiatrist, Matthew Kelly was definitely chief head-wrecker. Philo hadn't had an opportunity to count to two, never mind ten. It was the way he switched back and forth that got her going. His manner was gentle and his voice was soft, but that didn't stop him being a razor blade. The questions sliced her open. She was sure he could see right into the thinking part of her brain. If so, he knew all about her and Uncle Sam Harris. It was as though he'd been looking through the window when she was having her nookie stretched. It was like he'd been there when she tried to tell her father what was going on.

—He looks at me funny, she'd said to him.

—What's wrong with that? He doesn't have horns, does he? her father had replied.

—He teaches me to say bad words like arsehole and cunt.

—Well, don't repeat them in this house.

—I don't want to go back there.

—You have to.

—He has dirty, hairy hands.

—I don't want to hear it. You have to go back.

It turned out that the 'pools money' was, in fact, repayments on a loan, and Sam Harris wasn't an uncle, he was a moneylender. Her father must have suspected what was going on, and still he'd sent her there, week after week and month after month. He was supposed to protect her and instead he had sent her into the lion's den, just so that he could appease his blood-sucking moneylender. Philo had repaid the loan with her flesh. No amount of lollipops could make up for that. And no clever questions were going to force her to divulge it. Matthew Kelly was smart and had brought her back to Portland Row. She'd taken him on a guided tour of the street, but her secret was staying resolutely in the shadows where it belonged.

She was conscious that her evasions made her look like a ditherer. The purpose of the interview was to prove her sanity, to demonstrate that she was a fit mother, and she felt like a drowning woman splashing around for a lifebuoy. Hard as she tried, she couldn't get onto terra firma; she always ended up, by one sloshy road or another, back in the quagmire of her family's past.

—When did you last tell your father you hated him? Matthew Kelly asked.

—Oh, I tell him all the time in case he forgets.

—When did you last tell him you loved him?

Philo felt like she'd been hit with an uppercut from Muhammad Ali. Instead of landing her on her bum, it made her hysterical. Events from her past played out like a film in her head. She was standing on the wall at Howth pier with a fish in her hand. Beside her was her father, with a fishing rod in one hand and his other hand on her shoulder. She was small and skinny, just like the mackerel. He was so proud she'd caught the fish that, instead of throwing it back into the sea, he took it home to Sylvia and showed it off. She remembered how proud of her he'd been that day.

—It was back when I was a skinny little thing. I must have been about ten.

Matthew Kelly looked down at his chart, checking something.

—That's over twenty years ago, he said.

He wrote something down like it was important. Maybe it was hard for him to believe she'd ever been skinny. Looking at her now, no one could ever imagine she'd once been skin and bone. Perhaps he was wondering why she'd piled on the weight. If he thought she was fat, what would he make of Sylvia? Philo had a photo from last Christmas in her bag – her and Sylvia by the tree; they looked like beached whales. She had one of her Confirmation, too: a small body on top of matchstick legs. If she had one unattainable dream, it was to be that size again. Her body had been perfect before Sam Harris put his finger in and started poking around. He'd started her on the lollipops, and once she'd developed the taste for sugar, she couldn't stop. No matter how much she stuffed down, it was never enough.

230

Had Sylvia been abused? The thought had never crossed Philo's mind before. This was the first time she'd made that connection – their stories were the same. So what did that make of the overactive thyroid, the theory that Sylvia's weight problems were the result of a genetic flaw? Maybe it was a tale of convenience because the truth was unsayable? Bad as it was for Philo to have had her nookie stretched, an unwanted hand pushing its way into Sylvia was a thought too painful to bear.

—Does your father make fun of your size? Matthew Kelly asked.

—Yes.

—Is that why you hate him?

—Yes.

She'd put on the fat to protect her secret. Sylvia had done the same. It was time to put it out in the open, perhaps. There were three daughters to think of – Eileen, Josie and Philomena. Philo loved them as intensely as she loved Sylvia. She felt an almighty urge to have them near her. It was an emotion she didn't permit, because it was too powerful; she couldn't allow herself to be overwhelmed. It was imperative to maintain a calm exterior. She didn't know what to say, so she just opened her mouth and let the words take flight.

—Do you think I'm mad? she said.

—No, I don't think you're mad.

She was relieved. The Chief Psychiatrist thought she was sane, even if she wasn't sure herself.

—I think you're running away from your problems instead of facing them.

She could sing that if she had an air to it. Words by Philo Darcy to music by Matthew Kelly.

—Do you think I'm a good mother? she asked.

—You're not a bad mother.

—Why did I abandon my children?

It was the first time Philo had used the A-word in relation

231

to what she'd done. It meant making herself vulnerable, and she couldn't remember the last time she'd done that in front of a man.

—I fucked up big-time, I know I did.

She was laying herself bare because she didn't know what else to do.

—I'm sorry I ran away, I really am.

Her honesty appealed to Matthew Kelly. He had no reason to doubt her sincerity. Had she been playing a part, he would have detected it straight away; he'd sat in his chair too long to be fooled by insincerity. He knew there were underlying issues, and he was certain they went back to Philo's family of origin, long before she was married and had children of her own. But he wasn't God; he couldn't force her to talk, however much he thought it would help.

—I'm not going to get them back, am I? Philo said.

—What makes you say that?

—I'm not a fit mother.

He looked down at the papers in front of him again. It was as if he'd written the answer somewhere and had forgotten what he'd decided. Philo could see a red box at the bottom of a page. From her upside-down position she could make out the word 'RECOMMENDATIONS'; there was handwriting, too, but she couldn't decipher it.

Matthew Kelly turned over several pages before he found what he was looking for. He put his finger under the words and ran it across the page.

—It says here you visit your children every day. Is that true?

—Yes.

—How do you get out there?

—I get a bus from the quays, the 21A.

—That's not the action of an unfit mother.

For the first time in the interview, Philo allowed herself a smile. It wasn't an ordinary smile; it was a great big ugly one.

She could feel the tears welling up behind her eyes. There was a box of tissues on the desk, and she reached across and pulled one out. She blew her nose and at the same time sucked the tears back to where they belonged.

—They're going to offer you a house in Kilbarrack, Matthew Kelly said.

Philo thought she'd misheard. She asked him to repeat himself.

—A three-bedroomed house in Kilbarrack, he said.

—My family are all around the North Wall, she said. I'd be lost out there.

—Well, maybe a break from your family would do you good.

Philo had never dreamed of moving out of the inner city; and, apart from herself, there'd be war with the children. New streets, new schools, new friends ... it wasn't something they'd embrace gladly.

Matthew Kelly explained his decision. He was prepared to facilitate a reunion on a trial basis. Majella Kiernan, the social worker, would visit the children twice a week to see how they were getting on. Philo would report to Matthew Kelly on her progress and state of mind. It was to be a situation for ongoing assessment. Philo wanted to give it a try, but she didn't know if she could move out of the area where her heart had always been.

Attendance soared at the Day Centre. It was incredible the way people who'd been incapacitated somehow found the will to make the trek there. From the four corners of the parish and beyond they came. They came in groups, they came alone, widows and widowers; some took up their crutches and walked there. It wasn't for the food they came; it was to catch a glimpse of the vegetable lovers, Dina and Cap.

There was the lure of bingo, too. Nowhere in Dublin

boasted a game like Sister Rosaleen's. There was no entry fee and the number of prizes meant there was every chance of a win. Philo spread the word around the area, so everything that 'fell off the back of a lorry' ended up as a prize. On one occasion, a consignment of electric drills was dumped at the front door and the lorry driver (Josie Cullen's brother, Paddy-whack) was arrested in the grounds of the convent while trying to make his escape. After that the call went out for smaller prizes. Lots of bananas, tins of corned beef, varieties of breakfast cereal and sides of smoked salmon followed. It was the healthiest bingo game in the city of Dublin, if not the world.

It wasn't the lovers that brought Sylvia. After the outing to the racetrack, she'd realised how isolated she'd become in the house in East Wall. She loved bingo but didn't like crowds because they stared a lot. That was the price she had to pay. In order to get there on time, she allowed herself an hour for the walk across the bridge, stopping several times along the way to catch her breath. At the church, she slipped in the side door and stood at the back to say a few prayers. She was always afraid that if she knelt down she wouldn't be able to get back up again.

Dina and Cap looked like the first couple over seventy to discover they had working sex organs. Cap, with his perman-ent grin, was the embodiment of delayed gratification. Fifty years he'd waited for sex, and when it came, it tranformed him.

Dina was a walking version of the Mona Lisa, one hundred per cent smirk. She never asked Cap where he'd honed his technique; she assumed he'd been practising for years on some of his female customers. Up until that night, she'd thought her ears were for listening and her lips were for saying prayers. When he said he was going to find her clitoris, she thought he was looking for the elastic on her knickers. When he found it, she thought her soul was leaving her body and going home to heaven. Despite three children, she'd never had an orgasm. When it came, it felt like she'd been touched on the shoulder by God Himself.

Not everyone was enamoured. Dina's cronies had made a profession of bitching about Cap. They'd spent countless nights in the downstairs shebeen stoking the fires of bitterness and keeping the vegetable war alive. Now, because of one moment of orgiastic madness, they were being asked to extinguish the past. They figured Dina had been in so much pain after her amputations that her mind had been led astray by pleasure. They said nothing and hoped that Cap would blow away and disappear. On the contrary, he started to become a fixture about the place, and the cronies found it harder and harder to woo Dina down from her pleasure dome at the top of the stairs.

At every opportunity, they were nasty to Cap.

—Do you not think you're a bit old for her? Chrissie Mongon said.

—She needs a toy boy, not a pensioner, Ita Mullen said.

—How many women are you seeing on the sly? Mouse O'Hara said.

Cap just smiled and went about his business.

—I know what you need, Ita Mullen said.

—We all know what you need, Mouse O'Hara said.

—A woman who can bear you children is what you need, Chrissie Mongon said.

Cap would nod at all their insights and suggestions before setting off up the stairs to look after Dina.

—Did Dina not tell you? he said. We're going to adopt.

In no time, the word was out that Cap and Dina were looking for a Romanian orphan. When Cap was confronted with the story, he said it was only half-true because they were, in fact, looking for a baby of Chinese origin.

He was in Noctor's pub, buying Dina cigarettes, when a voice behind him called out:

—You dirty aquanaut!

He hadn't heard anyone called that for years, and, despite the passage of time, it still carried the power to hurt.

—I'm talking about you, Coyle. You're an aquanaut and the son of an aquanaut.

It was Peter Mongon, Chrissie's brother and an old docker himself. Cap paid for his cigarettes, tipped his hat and left. When he reached the shop, the cronies picked up where they'd left off.

—There's going to be trouble with Gerry Sugrue, Mouse O'Hara said.

—Gerry Sugrue is still her husband, Chrissie Mongon said.

Precisely because he had nothing to fear from his old pal, Cap put on the air of a man about to be sent to the gallows.

—You don't really think he'd come after me? Cap said.

—There's no thinking about it, Chrissie Mongon said. It's certain.

—You're trying to put the wind up me, that's all, Cap said.

—You know the sort of temper Gerry Sugrue has; you'd want to watch out, Ita Mullen said.

—Watch out for what? Cap enquired.

—Well, a knife, I suppose, or a bottle on the back of the head, Mouse O'Hara said.

The cronies wasted no time before exploiting this perceived weakness with Dina. She brushed it off, initially, but then became concerned because the cronies were so animated. She brought it up with Cap and he told her about his trip to Ringsend. She couldn't believe he'd sought out Gerry Sugrue. It seemed so old-fashioned, the knight heading off to confront his adversary. She loved the feeling it gave her; it made a princess of her.

—Do you love me? she'd say to him.

—I love every inch of you, he'd reply.

—Do you really, really love me?

—I love the ground you walk on.

They laughed over that, because Dina didn't walk very much any more. Around the house, Philo gave her a jockey-back for convenience. Going from Dowdall's Lane to the convent Philo and Cap carried her, one on either side. Then Cap bought a pair of roller skates and adapted them to fit her bandaged feet. That meant they could wheel her and she could stop along the way to chat with neighbours and friends.

The cronies were put out by the new seating arrangements. They felt demoted now that Cap and Dina were the centre of so much attention. People stared at the nonchalant way Cap would drape his hand across Dina's shoulder and caress the lobe of her ear with his fingers, the turn of her neck arching back like a swan's in response. There were so many tendernesses between them, provocative in their simplicity. He would take one of her legs, lift it into his lap and rub her calves with his palms until his hands were burning with desire to move further up. Then there was the bingo. Cap had the knack of pushing his card across, just as he was about to check; and making the victory Dina's. She would respond by slipping her hand onto his thigh and giving it a squeeze. Philo noticed it as she checked back the numbers with Sister Rosaleen. So did everyone else in the dining room. It made Ninna Delargy cry, because she had missed her chance. She'd willingly have given up her toes to have her legs caressed and her ear stroked. There wasn't a woman in the Centre who wouldn't have made the same sacrifice. Even the cronies were beginning to come around. The vegetable war had sustained them, but love is more infectious than hate.

Several displaced residents came back to check out the love nest. Among them was Skinny Sullivan, who'd left the area ten years before. Philo had met him out in Kilbarrack. She'd gone there to check out the area. She'd spent a morning traipsing from the road where she was being offered a house to the shopping centre and back again. She wasn't overly impressed; the best she could say was that it was better than an orphanage. She was mulling over the situation when she saw Skinny holding up the wall of the bookie's shop.

—How are you, Skinny? she said. Do you like it out here?

—It's massive, daughter, only bleedin' massive.

Skinny had no head for names, so he called every female 'daughter' and every male 'Tommy'.

—What's massive about it? Philo asked. It looks shite to me.

—Don't be fooled by looks, daughter. Kilbarrack has everything.

—It doesn't have the River Liffey, or O'Connell Street, or Noctor's pub.

—No, but everything out here is electric, including the gas.

—How can the gas be electric?

All Skinny could manage was a wink, like it was a secret too precious to divulge. Philo told him she might be his neighbour soon, and he warned her never to leave the inner city unless she was evicted.

—I thought this place had everything, Philo said.

—It doesn't have romance, he said, and winked. The news of Dina and Cap had reached Kilbarrack.

Philo invited Skinny to the convent for his dinner. He refused at first, but then relented for old times' sake. They travelled in on the bus together and everyone was delighted to see him, until he checked in under thirty-three calls to win the snowball game. The prize was a day return for two to Holyhead and six free bottles of wine, courtesy of B&I Ferries. Skinny badgered every woman in the Centre to go with him, but without success; he even tried his luck with Sylvia, but she gave him short shrift. In the end, he accepted that he'd have to bring someone he knew from Kilbarrack.

Two days later, Philo met Skinny's travelling companion.

She arrived at the Centre with Dina and Cap, as usual. The first person she saw was Sylvia. She was in conversation with two men, one of whom was Skinny. The other man looked familiar. Philo stood staring at his profile, knowing she knew him but not wanting to make a move in his direction. Her eyes were on his lips, which were moving a lot, and she could hear Sylvia laughing. He had an ugly mouth that was hard to take your eyes off. He must have been telling a joke. Philo couldn't hear it but she didn't like Sylvia having to listen to it. Sylvia didn't like foul language or anything coarse, especially not 'arsehole' or 'nookie' or anything in that vein; she was a lady, she wouldn't put up with anything like that.

He was older but it was him, unmistakeably him. He didn't need to turn around, but he did, and there he was, looking straight at her with a big grin – she could have done without the grin; she could nearly have ignored him only he was laughing at something, his little rhymes and his cursing competitions and his big, hairy hands.

—Do you know who this is? Sylvia asked.

There was a silence while they waited for Philo's answer.

—It's Uncle Sam Harris, Sylvia said.

—He's not my uncle, Philo said.

—How are you, Philomena? he said.

Philo just stared; there was nothing else she could do. Her legs were shaking and she didn't want him to see that she was afraid.

—Sam is coming on the ferry with me to Holyhead, Skinny said.

Philo's first thought was that it might sink. It was a long time since a ferry had gone down in the Irish Sea, so a maritime disaster was overdue.

—We're neighbours out in Kilbarrack, Skinny said. His chalet is next to mine.

It was twenty years since she'd stood in his house in

Portland Row and had her nookie stretched. He was an old man but the lips were still the same. He leered at her, secure in the knowledge that their secret was intact.

—How many children do you have, Philomena? he asked.

—That's none of your business, she said.

It was a simple question. It was an invasive question, too.

—Don't be so rude, Philo, Sylvia said.

How easy it was to steal a child's innocence and not get caught.

—If you don't tell him, I will, Sylvia said.

—Tell him nothing.

—What's the matter with you, Philo?

—There's nothing the matter with me.

—Tell him about Jack and Eileen –

—No.

It was on the tip of Philo's tongue to let it out. But what if she lost control in the telling? What would her friends in the Centre make of her then? What if she failed to wipe the grin off his face? What if he denied it and was believed? She was better off pinning her hopes on the ferry going down, or him going overboard and being lost at sea. It was a risk-free option; it was safer, much safer than raking up the past and presenting old wounds for inspection.

Sylvia took her aside and wanted to know what was wrong.

—What's upsetting you? Is it Sam Harris?

—No, Philo lied.

—Did he do something on you?

—It's not him, Ma.

—If it's not him, it's someone. Is it me?

—How could it be you, Ma?

—What is it, then? I know when you're upset.

Sylvia took Philo's hand and stroked it. It reduced her to being a child with a grazed knee. Any moment now, Sylvia would produce the magic iodine from her bag and make her white skin turn purple.

—It won't get better keeping it all bottled up inside, Sylvia said. What's bothering you?

—It's my weight, Ma. I'm sick of being fat, that's all.

It was a convenient way out. Their excess pounds kept all other issues at bay. For half an hour they moaned into each other's cups and pledged to do something about their weight. They discussed a new diet. Sylvia promised to give up potatoes if Philo did the same. They'd exchanged vows like it many times before.

The trays started to come in from the kitchen, and the smell of bacon and cabbage filled the dining room. Philo went out to give the kitcheners a hand. The white bacon fat was floating in the pot, alone. It would end up in the slop bucket, which was an awful shame. She hated waste, couldn't stand the notion of food being thrown away while people starved in the world. She spooned it into her mouth and slurped it down. The potatoes were there, too, but she left them alone because of the promise she'd made. It was the least she could do, in the circumstances.

Relocating to Kilbarrack was out of the question. Just as Philo had spent half her life avoiding Portland Row, she would never again set foot in Kilbarrack. Walking past the chalet where he lived – and having her children do so – was not something she could countenance. She could live with her secret, but not with that.

The alternative was to go home. Sylvia had been encouraging her to give it one last try. It was hard for Philo to embrace the idea, because everything had been about getting away from Tommo; how could she return to him when nothing had changed? Except that Tommo had stopped drinking, of course. That was something she couldn't ignore and didn't want to.

In the end, the conspiracy of God, Padre Pio and Sylvia was too much to resist. Philo couldn't look at the children and tell them there was nothing she could do.

It was time to toss a coin. Heads for going back to Tommo, tails for staying where she was. It came down heads. Philo did the best of three, and going home to Tommo won again. At least he'd be sober; she consoled herself with that thought. Most of their rows came when he was drunk. She had nothing to lose by talking to him. That was the first step: put it on the table and see what he had to say.

It was strange to be walking back to Liberty House, the block of flats where she'd been held hostage all those years. When she reached Amiens Street, she walked straight across the road against the traffic. Just as she reached the far side, a motorcyclist stopped in front of her. She thanked him and he pulled off his helmet. It was Tommo.

—Where are you going? he asked.

—Up to the flat to see you, she said.

—Fuck off.

—All right, then, I will.

—No, I didn't mean that.

—Where did you get the bike?

—I bought it.

—Fuck off.

—All right, then, I will.

—I didn't mean that; come back.

—Hop up.

Philo looked at the bike and looked at Tommo. It was a Honda 50.

—I'd rather walk, she said.

—I'll give you a lift.

—I don't have a helmet.

—You can borrow mine.

—Thanks, but no thanks.

A passing car driver lowered his window and shouted at them.

—Get in off the road if you want to have a conversation!

—Fuck off, poxbottle! they answered together.

It was the first time for years they'd spoken in unison. Their life had been one of chronic disagreement, black for white and all the rest of it. Their children had been conceived in the lulls between rows. They were being made to pay for the sins of the parents. Philo wondered if she had the right to take another huge gamble with their futures.

Tommo had been on his way to the chipper when he stopped the bike. Philo agreed to meet him back at the flat. He doubled the order, and when he got back, Philo had two hot plates, knives, forks, tomato ketchup, salt, pepper and vinegar waiting on the table.

—Do you want your cup of tea now or after? Philo asked when he walked in the door.

—Seeing as we're doing it in style, I'll have it now, he said.

So Philo poured it out, and they ate their smoked cod and large singles with not an uncivil word between them. At the end of the plate-licking, Philo explained her mission. The children were coming out to her on a trial basis and they'd been offered accommodation in Kilbarrack.

—The house has everything OK. All mod cons – electricity, gas, piped television, everything.

She wanted Tommo to think that she had choices. He did, and it upset him.

—I get the bleedin' picture, he said.

Her preference, she explained, was to keep the children at home, in the inner city, but she couldn't do that if Tommo was there; he'd have to move out.

—I offered to do that before, he said.

—Yeah, I know you did.

Naturally, he was intrigued about why she'd come around.

—How long would you want me out for? he asked.

—I don't know, we'd have to see.

Giving up his bed for a while wasn't such a great sacrifice for Tommo, if it meant getting back with Philo and the kids in the future. It was hard graft living on your own, no one to talk to. Now that the pub was no longer an option, the loneliness was permanent. The meetings of Alcoholics Anonymous were a help, but you couldn't bring them home. Putting down the glass had given Tommo a new perspective and made him determined to bring the family back together at the earliest opportunity.

He took a cigarette from his top pocket and lit up.

—This is your home, this is where you and the kids should be, he said.

He pulled the smoke hard into his lungs and scrunched up his face.

—I can move out, he said.

He released the smoke and immediately sucked on the cigarette again, like his life depended on it. He held it out to Philo.

—Do you want a blow? he said.

There was a time she'd gladly have accepted, in the days when drugs had seemed innocent, before heroin came and destroyed so many lives. Philo enjoyed marijuana then, and liked the effect. Then drugs started to kill, and she could never distinguish between hard drugs and soft drugs – in truth, she didn't want to. She brought the curtain down on her own use because it was easier that way. Tommo continued to dabble, and Philo let it go so long as he didn't do it in front of the kids. In truth, she preferred him stoned to drunk, because he only seemed to abuse her when he was drunk. When he was stoned, he got all lovey-dovey and wanted sex. She preferred being his juicy teddy bear to being a stupid fat cunt.

—You're not supposed to do that in the house, she said.

—The kids aren't here, he said, and smiled like an errant schoolboy.

That was true, but if they were coming home she didn't want the smell about the place. It was a new beginning; she didn't want any hangovers from the past, just fresh air and healthy living with no rows. Tommo was off the drink – that was a good thing – and maybe he'd give up the hash, too. Philo didn't want to raise it as an issue just yet. Everything had gone so well, Tommo was a changed man and there was so much hope for the future.

Tommo took another pull and offered the joint to Philo again.

—It's a peace offering, he said.

It was a strange new world when Tommo Nolan was talking about peace. It wasn't so much the words as the tone of his voice, gentle and soft like a fresh-faced priest's. *Let us offer each other a sign of peace.* That was the invocation at the end of the Mass, the moment when people shook hands. It was a ritual stolen from the Native Americans, and one which Tommo was restoring to its rightful context with the joint.

—You can't refuse the peace pipe, he said.

Philo reached out her hand and took it. She didn't want to bring bad luck by refusing it. Tommo had acceded to her demands without a fight, and it was important to acknowledge that in some way. She put the filter to her lips and pulled in the smoke. The rush to her brain was immediate and made her dizzy.

—You need something to take the edge off, he said. We all do.

She'd forgotten how powerful it was. Once you inhaled,

there was no question of pulling back, or slowing down, as you might with alcohol. You succumbed to it and that was that. Philo felt good being transported out of her own world. She looked at Tommo and he smiled at her, and she felt safe. She pulled on the joint, happy to tap into its power. As the smoke charged down to her lungs, her problems seemed to evaporate. Things were starting to go her way. It was a welcome change. She took one last pull and handed it back to Tommo, but he refused it with a smile.

—It's all yours, he said, and laughed.

All her life she'd craved the love of a decent man. Tommo had made her feel good about her size, in the early days, before he'd turned. It was good to remember him speaking well of her; it made her feel loving towards him. And she wasn't sure if it was the change in him due to his not drinking, or the change in her due to being stoned, but whatever the cause, it beat being at war, beat it hands down. *Let us offer each other a sign of peace.* If Cap and Dina could end their hostilities, why not her and Tommo? Enemies could love; and Tommo wasn't her enemy, he was her husband. She had loved him, once upon a time, and the fairytale wasn't over yet.

—I'm sorry about the tattoo, she said.

She could never restore his name, and now she was sorry. Her head was dizzy with love and she wanted to reach out and heal everything in her life, because the hash was so powerful and she'd forgotten how lovely it was, and how sexy, but most of all it put everything into perspective because it let her float above it all. It was a wonderful new perspective and Philo wanted to share it with Tommo, but her lips were dry and she couldn't get the words out.

Tommo leaned over and kissed her arm. Philo knew she should fight him off, but she had no energy for it; she only had space for being positive. Her children were coming home and their father was turning back into the man he had once been. She planted a kiss on his lips, and the saliva from his tongue made her mouth wet once again. He started to roll another joint and he invited her to partake of it, and Philo accepted because she was desperate to keep the fairytale alive.

15

Dina was delighted when Philo broke the news about the children coming home. Orphanages had their place, but children were better off with their parents. It was good they were coming home to familiar surroundings, where they would have Philo at hand to look after them, get their meals ready and wash their clothes.

—Is Tommo going to stay with them at night? Dina asked.

—Not if I have anything to do with it.

—Who's going to mind them while you're here with me?

—What are you talking about?

—You can't leave them on their own, Philo. Someone has to stay with them.

Dina couldn't hide her disappointment when she realised she was losing Philo. She couldn't imagine life without her.

—You're better than a hot-water bottle, do you know that? Dina said.

—Jaysus, I'm glad you pointed that out to me.

—I'll probably get pneumonia without you.

—And it'll be my fault, is that it?

—I didn't say that.

—Get yourself an electric blanket.

—I don't believe in them.

—You don't have to believe in them, they're not a religion; all you have to do is plug them in.

—I'd be afraid I'd go on fire. I don't mind how I die but I don't want to go up in flames.

It was the hole it might burn in her purse that was

bothering Dina. Electric blankets weren't cheap to run. Philo had trebled her turnover in the shop, quadrupled her profits and was still waiting to have a penny of it put in her hand. Not that she wanted it – she didn't – but it didn't escape her notice. Dina was a miser who wouldn't part with a penny if she didn't have to. It was a condition and there was a name for it, but Philo couldn't think of it offhand. It wasn't kleptomania, although Dina had that one as well. 'Tight-arsed' was close but not right. Philo was thinking about Dina's stinginess when she remembered something.

—You don't pay electric bills, she said. You get it for free.

—I'm an old-age pensioner, I'm entitled to it.

—An electric blanket wouldn't cost you a tosser.

—I'd still have to buy it.

—You're probably entitled to a free one.

—It's not the same.

—What are you talking about?

—It's not the same as having you in the bed. You're a person. You don't just keep me warm; you talk to me, you give out to me – you're my home help.

Philo was quick to point out that sleeping over wasn't in her job description. She'd done it because it suited her, and now it was rebounding on her.

—I'll still come around to see you every morning, Philo said.

—I don't get afraid in the morning, I get afraid at night.

This was news to Philo. She'd never seen Dina afraid.

—What did you do before you had me? Philo said. You slept on your own for years.

—I wasn't on my own.

Philo was taken aback. She tried to imagine Dina's secret companion but couldn't form a picture of him.

—Who was he? Do I know him? she asked.

—It wasn't a he.

—Was it a she, then?

—No, they were my friends. They kept me safe, but you hoovered them up.

—You're talking about fucking spiders! Philo spluttered.

Dina loved them. Big ones, small ones, hairy ones and skinny ones, spiders had been her friends for years. It was her mother who'd told her not to harm a spider or she'd never have an hour's luck. On the other hand, her house would always be safe if she gave shelter to God's creatures. Signs on it, she had never had a break-in from that day out. The spiders must have known her home offered asylum, because they had taken shelter in it like welcome refugees. At night they would come out from their hiding-places and spin their webs. Dina loved to watch them and became an expert in their methods of entrapment; it was her blood sport, and she couldn't deny the thrill when a fly got stuck and the spider danced out in a frenzy to make the kill. She imagined herself as the spider and her enemies as the flies. She made up names for her eight-legged friends and never raised a hand in anger to brush any of them aside. That was before the holocaust had wiped them out. It had left her nothing but a white ceiling, cobweb-free and barren. She had no one for company, no one to keep an eye on her and ward off the evil spirits.

—You could always ask Cap to stay over, Philo suggested.

Dina's face lit up at the mention of his name.

—We wouldn't like to give scandal, she said.

Scandal? The word had become defunct. There had been a time when it was beaten from pulpits like a drum. Now the Church had become the giver of scandal and the banging of that drum had ceased.

—Scandal? Philo repeated. How would Cap staying over do that?

—I have family. Cap has friends. People talk.

—So?

—We have to be careful.

250

—Well, let me tell you, Dina, everyone knows he's riding the arse off you.

That wasn't how it was with Cap; it was different. Dina couldn't explain because she still carried huge guilt about taking pleasure from sex. Not that it was sex – it was the part that went before it; Cap called it foreplay and she called it Christmas. How could she tell Philo that Cap spent hours brushing back the hairs on her fanny so that he could get a good look at her clitoris? He'd discovered it, so she could hardly stop him. She couldn't believe how beautiful it was to be looked at – to have a man stare at her and see the wonder on his face; it deified her. She'd always fancied that her breasts were her best features and that down below was something ugly, something that bled, something that should be hidden away. The attention from Cap had changed all that. She felt adored. She felt that her vagina belonged to her, that she owned it. She ran her finger all around and poked inside like a child with a new toy. She opened it out and displayed it. She even put a circle of lipstick around it as a surprise for Cap. He licked it off with the pleasure of a schoolboy attacking an ice-cream cone. Dina had never known feelings like these.

—You're not going to deny that he is riding the arse off you? Philo said.

Dina was not about to deny or confirm anything. Her position was delicate. She was going to miss Philo in the bed but she had no intention of replacing her, not with an electric blanket and most certainly not with Cap. All she could do was sleep with the window open and hope that the spiders would return at the earliest opportunity.

The homecoming was going to be very emotional for Philo. It was a new beginning and a last chance. She felt like she was going on trial and any moment a voice would come over a loudspeaker and say, 'Don't do that, that's not what proper mothers do.'

Sister Rosaleen helped her get the place ready. They washed the bedclothes, cleaned out presses, polished shoes and so on. It was back-breaking, sweaty work. Sister Rosaleen got so hot she had to change out of her habit and veil and into a pair of Tommo's overalls that Philo found for her.

—You missed your vocation, definitely missed your vocation, Philo said.

—Why do you say that?

—You look like a car mechanic.

—I might look like a car mechanic, but I don't feel like one.

—What do you feel like?

Sister Rosaleen paused and then, with a giggle, said:

—I feel like a bingo caller.

—That's a funny vocation for a nun.

—I know, but I love it. I only call out bingo numbers because of you – I'll never forget that.

Philo got the veil and put it on her head. It was four sizes too small for her.

—How do I look? Philo asked.

—You look like a doll.

—I don't feel like a doll, I feel like a nun. I would have made a good nun – what do you think?

—You would have made a brilliant nun.

Philo was delighted with the compliment. She'd always looked on the religious life as the thing that bestowed the most respect on a woman. It should have been motherhood that was honoured, of course, but it wasn't.

—You could have made a good wife, too, you know, Philo said.

—Or even a good husband, Sister Rosaleen replied, indicating the overalls.

—Where were you when I was looking for a man, that's what I want to know?

And so the cleaning and banter continued until it was time for Philo to leave for Goldenbridge.

The children noticed that Philo was wearing a blouse, a skirt, tights and shoes when normally she'd have on a T-shirt, tracksuit bottoms and runners. She had decided it was important to look like a mother, that her appearance sent out an important signal. The days of looking like a house slob were over; she wanted to display a feminine, maternal side. It didn't matter that the shoes pinched her toes and the tights made her sweat; she wanted the children to see a proper woman when they looked at her.

—Why are you all dressed up? Josie enquired.

—Are you going to a funeral? Young Tommo asked.

—Do you not wear tracksuits any more, Ma? Philomena wanted to know.

It surprised her how much they noticed and made her glad she'd gone to the trouble.

—I want to look nice, that's all, she said.

—You look great no matter what you wear, Ma, Eileen said.

Not satisfied, they pestered her for a better reason. It was Eileen who quietened them down and made them listen. She'd been protecting her siblings in Goldenbridge, that was clear. In that short time, she'd physically and emotionally filled out; she'd become an adult. It flowed from her like sap from a tree.

—I don't want you to end up big and fat like me, do you hear? Philo said to her.

It was Sylvia's admonition to her, the warning she had issued every week of her life. Philo had sworn she would never repeat it to her own children, and here she was with the words flowing freely from her lips.

—Whatever size I'm meant to be, that's the size I'll be, Mammy, Eileen said.

She was thirteen, the same age Philo was when she stood

up to her father and refused to go to Portland Row. She hoped her daughter would never have a dark secret like that to carry. That was her one wish, the thing she wanted more than anything else in the whole world.

Philo stood up and looked at the children.

—Do you want a surprise? she asked them.

—Yeah, yeah, yeah, yeah! rang out the chorus.

—What would be the best surprise you could get?

—Easter eggs, Young Tommo said.

—New clothes, Josie said.

—A pet rabbit, Philomena said.

—It's none of them, Philo said.

—Getting out of here, that would be the best surprise, Eileen said.

Philo looked at their expectant faces. She had so much wanted to make it a surprise, and now that the moment had arrived, the tears welled up and choked her words.

—Are we getting out of here? Eileen asked.

—Are we, Ma? Young Tommo chimed in, followed by the others. Are we getting out of here?

Philo nodded her head, and they all sprang to their feet and engulfed her with hugs and kisses like nothing she'd ever experienced before. Then they charged back to their dormitories and packed their belongings in seconds. Minutes later they were on the 21A bus, heading back to their lives in the inner city. Josie, Philomena and Young Tommo sat in the front seat upstairs, while Philo and Eileen remained below.

—They treated you OK in Goldenbridge? Philo asked Eileen.

—Yeah, the nuns were lovely.

—No one abused you?

—What do you mean?

—No one made you do anything you didn't want to?

—Are you crazy, Ma?

—I'd better not answer that or I might incriminate myself.

—Well, you're not crazy. You taught us to stand up for ourselves. No one is going to make us do anything we don't want to.

Philo wished she could bottle Eileen's words. Whatever else, her children seemed like they were maturing into proper adults. It filled her with so much pride she could have burst.

Sister Rosaleen and Jack were waiting for them at home. For one terrible moment, the children reacted like they were back in Goldenbridge, until Philo explained the situation.

—She only looks like a nun, Philo said. She's a car mechanic in real life.

—Not true, Sister Rosaleen said. I'm a bingo caller.

With that, she left for the convent and Philo turned her attention to Jack.

—You needn't think you're too big for a hug. Come here.

—Save it for later, he said.

—I want a hug now, so come here.

He resigned himself to the inevitable. As he did, they heard the sound of a key in the door. The clunk of metal on metal was followed by the turn of the lock. The door was pushed in and Tommo stood there. He slapped his thighs and held his arms out. Josie, Young Tommo and Philomena dropped what they were doing, ran to him and jumped all over him. Eileen followed them at a distance, but Jack held his ground. With the younger ones hanging off various parts of him, Tommo struggled across the threshold into the room.

Philo found it impossible to feign enthusiasm. He had gate-crashed the homecoming. It wasn't part of her plan to have him around on their first night home. What message did that present to the children? That everything was as before and nothing had changed? They were delighted to see him and she was happy for them, but she was furious he'd turned up without permission. She felt like he'd crept in and spread a noxious gas all around the flat.

She should have asked him to surrender his key. Possessed

of it, he could come and go as he pleased. It gave him a right of entry that was appalling.

—Why did you not come up to see us? Young Tommo asked.

Out of the mouths of babes, thought Philo.

—I was working the whole time, Tommo said.

—You should have driven your lorry up to Goldenbridge, Philomena said.

—You could have crashed it into the gates, Josie added.

Tommo didn't know where to look or what to say. The children were asking him to account for his actions, and he didn't have the answers. He looked across at Philo as though she'd put them up to it.

—Would you like lemonade and crisps? Tommo asked.

Their 'yeah's rang out and they bounced on him like he was an inflatable castle. He had to appeal to Eileen to save himself from being punctured by their enthusiastic limbs.

—Is it all right to get them lemonade and crisps? he asked.

Philo wanted to stick pins in him, but she smiled and said it was fine. After he left, Young Tommo started a chant that the others picked up and turned into a raucous anthem.

—Lem-on-ade, lem-on-ade! they bawled.

—Have yous unpacked? Philo asked three times before being heard.

They were dispatched to their bedrooms to get started. Jack, meanwhile, came over to give her a hug and said he had to go.

—Don't leave because of Tommo, she said.

—It's not that; I have an early start tomorrow, Jack said.

—Don't lie to me, son. I know why you're going.

—I don't like lemonade and crisps, that's all.

—I'd really like for you to stay the night. Would you not do that for me?

—If I stay I'll wet the bed, Ma, he whispered to her.

It was the first time Philo had seen Jack make himself vulnerable. His usual reaction to things was aggression, which he'd learned from Tommo, of course.

—Brother Felix told me you'd stopped, she said.

—I want it to stay that way, he said.

—Of course you do, she said. I understand that.

Tommo had called Jack names because of the bed-wetting. Encouraged by this, the others had made fun of him, too. Philo had thought there might be a reason why he wet the bed and suspected he had weak kidneys. Now she could see quite clearly it had been because of Tommo.

Jack left, and Philo went into the girls' bedroom. They were standing on the double bed belting each other with pillows. It was nice to see them being bold, but as soon as they became aware of her presence, they stopped.

—What are yous doing? she asked.

—Nothing, Ma, they replied.

—Yous weren't doing nothing.

—We were having a pillow fight, Eileen said.

Philo held her hand out and Eileen put the pillow in it. She banged each of them in turn over the head. Within a minute, a full-scale war was in progress. Young Tommo heard the commotion from his bedroom and came running. In a flash, he was in the middle of it, but he was no match for his mother, who pummelled him and his sisters into weary submission. By the end of hostilities, there was a snow covering of feathers everywhere – on the floor, the beds, the window and the dresser. There were feathers up noses, too, in mouths and ears and stuck in clothes. After their exertions, nobody had the energy to clean up. They lay sprawled out, spitting and sneezing in harmony with one another, weary from combat.

Tommo let himself in on his return.

—What the fuck happened here? he asked.

Philo wanted to tell him that it was none of his fucking

business, but if she said that, there was bound to be a row. Her whole purpose had been to get away from the fighting and the shouting and the name-calling. Here she was, not a night back home, walking on eggshells around Tommo. Her intuition told her not to pick a row. In a short while he'd be gone and it would be the start of the rest of her life. She could change the locks and keep him out. All she needed was to get through the drinking of the lemonade and the eating of the crisps, and everything would be fine.

She got cups from the kitchen and put them on the table. Tommo threw the crisps around and then took a naggin of vodka from his pocket and offered it to Philo.

—I got that for you, he said.

—I don't want any drink in the house, thanks all the same.

—Please yourself, he said, and put the naggin in his pocket.

—Where did you get the vodka? Philo asked.

—I got it in the pub with the lemonade and the crisps.

—You were in the pub?

His look was sufficient confirmation.

—Did you have a drink? she asked.

—Of course I had a drink. It's not every day a man's wife and kids come home.

Philo wanted to deliver a kick to Tommo's groin that would send his prick up into his stomach, where it would never be seen again. She wanted to ensure that his sperm would never again contribute to the misery of the human race.

—Are you happy to be home, kids? he asked.

—Yeah, they replied through the crunching of crisps and the swallowing of lemonade.

Philo swept the feathers into a pile, to take her mind off the fact that Tommo was back on the drink. She had no option but to kill him. If Padre Pio couldn't help him, nobody could. Her plan was to murder him in bed. With any luck he'd ask if he could stay the night, and she'd agree. She'd encourage sex and beg him to get up on her. With her legs open and him in between, she'd take her sharpest knife and plunge it into his chest.

She went out to the kitchen and opened the cutlery drawer. There wasn't a knife among the paltry selection that would guarantee success. She switched her thoughts to smothering him. A good pillow was all that was required, but there wasn't one left. She searched the presses for rat poison and found some. It looked like grains of wheat. How would she administer it? The only possibility was to put it in the vodka. How would she relieve him of the bottle without giving herself away?

Her thoughts were thus occupied when Eileen came into the kitchen with the dirty cups and the empty crisp bags.

—I'm going to bed, Ma, I'm exhausted, she said.

Philo took her cue and put them all to bed. Young Tommo was the only one to offer resistance, but Philo cajoled him easily enough in the end.

—I'd better be on my way, Tommo said when they were alone.

—Stay as long as you like, I'm not running you out.

He was taken aback at the tone of Philo's words.

—Mickser will be waiting up for me; I'd better go.

Mickser Cummins was his best friend, and Tommo was going to stay with him until matters with Philo resolved themselves. Tommo seemed anxious not to have Mickser worrying, but Philo suspected his hurry was to get back to the pub.

—I take it you're back on the drink, she said.

—That was just a little celebration. I'll be off it again tomorrow.

Philo let him out, disappointed she wasn't going to have an opportunity to murder him. She should never have shared that joint with him. It wasn't possible for her to take pleasure in his company. Somehow he took that as permission to abuse her. As soon as she let down her guard with men, she was in trouble. Reefing the trousers off PJ Proby: disaster. Sucking lollipops in Portland Row: humiliation. She would never drop her defences in front of a man again. She had to keep them away. Outside of every fat woman was a skinny man trying to get in. She had to zip herself up. Batten down the hatches. Change the locks. Make herself an island.

16

Everyone had agreed to meet at the wrecking ball. The foreman in charge had wanted to start knocking down the buildings at seven in the morning, but he'd been persuaded to put it back to eleven so that the old folks could witness it.

The Corporation flats had stood for over forty years. They had to be knocked down because the ground they stood on was too valuable to have people living there. Whatever took their place would be part of the new economic boom engulfing the city – what people were calling the Celtic Tiger. That didn't make it easy for the residents of the Day Centre, many of whom had raised their families there. They remembered the flats going up. At the time, they had been the promise of the future, the new high-rise living with communal rubbish chutes, the like of which no one had ever seen before. The old folks were about to witness that promise being returned to dust. It felt like they were coming to bury a child. They had no choice but to come; they hadn't spent forty years of their lives there to turn their backs on the place now.

Philo got the kids out to school that morning without too much difficulty. Her first port of call was Dowdall's Lane, to collect Dina. There were plenty of others who could push her, including the three brass balls (the name Philo had bestowed on the cronies), but Dina always insisted on having Philo at hand any time she was being moved.

—I'm your home help, not your bleedin' transport manager, Philo had said to her more than once.

The shop door was closed when Philo arrived. She let herself in, but she knew from the eerie silence there was no one about. A quick check up the stairs confirmed what she had sensed – Dina was gone.

Philo headed down to the viewing area at the corner of Sheriff Street and Guild Street. A large crowd had already assembled. Philo was talking to Sister Rosaleen when Chrissie Mongon interrupted with the news that Dina had been taken to hospital the night before. Cap had called the ambulance, and this time he had gone with her.

Eleven o'clock came, and the foreman started bawling out instructions to the man in the crane. He, in turn, pushed and pulled at levers, causing the metal ball to rise slowly into the air. There was no adornment; it was as primitive as bare-knuckle boxing. The metal fist moved backwards and forwards, sizing up the target. It glided by an old pigeon loft but made no attempt to strike out; it was a dry run, a *danse macabre*, a show of strength before the real thing.

The tempo built. The ball moved in a great arc across the empty eyes of the buildings and then suddenly, surprisingly, changed direction and delivered a body blow into the centre of the staircase. The bricks and ironwork held their own for a brief moment before they bent double and collapsed. The ball retreated and delivered another sickening blow. It kept at it, wave after wave, until it rooted out the staircase and everything surrounding it.

It was impossible to watch the defenceless building being battered to death and not be affected. The old folks looked on in silence. Many of them turned and walked away. Their past was turning to powder, and it was too hard to watch. It was better to carry the memory of it alive than to see it reduced to rubble.

They returned to the sanctuary of the convent and ate

their dinners, punctuated by the dull thud of the wrecking ball outside. Sister Rosaleen set up her bingo table, but there was no enthusiasm for it. There was no sign of Sylvia. Philo was torn between going to the hospital and going to her mother's. On the basis that Dina had Cap for company, she set out for East Wall.

She knocked on the door and shouted in through the letter-box.

—Come on, Sylvia, open up.

She looked through the front bedroom window and made out Sylvia's shape on the bed. She rapped on the window several times, but there was no sign of movement.

Philo became very concerned.

—Come on, Sylvia, they're going to start the bingo without you.

She didn't know what to do. Something terrible was wrong. Her hand continued to pound against the glass, and in the end it cracked.

—I'm going to break in this window if you don't answer me, Sylvia!

Philo went back to the door, grabbed the handle and the knocker and shook it like it was a person, capable of understanding her words.

—Open up, you bastard, open up!

Mr Matthews, the next-door neighbour, came out to see what was going on. Philo barked out words that didn't make any particular sense, but Mr Matthews understood enough to go out the back, scramble over the dividing hedge, enter the back door, come down the hall and open the front door. He stood aside to let Philo through.

—Will I phone for an ambulance? he said.

—Yes, Philo replied without looking at him.

She opened the door and stepped into the bedroom. Sylvia looked so peaceful, like she'd fallen into the perfect sleep.

Philo wanted her back; it wasn't right she should slip away without having a conversation.

—Don't go now, please come back – I don't want you to go away, do you hear me – I don't want you gone, Sylvia … Sylvia … Sylvia….

She called her name over and over and over.

—It's Philo, Ma … Philo … Philo…. Can you hear me?

It was hopeless and she was hopeless, too, looking at her mother, who might come back if she did something instead of sitting there watching her slip further and further away. Philo needed to do something, she needed to get up off her arse. She knelt up on the bed, put her two hands squarely on Sylvia's chest and started to push. She didn't know what she was doing – she'd only ever seen it on television – but it got hearts going again, she was sure of that.

She kept at it for several minutes but there was no response. It was time to try something else. She bent over and put her lips on Sylvia's. They were so cold compared to her own. She blew long and hard and in no time she was out of breath; she didn't know if she could keep going. There was no alternative. Three more breaths and she'd go back to the chest. She climbed over Sylvia again and brought her fist down hard on her chest. Maybe she could fool her heart into starting up again. If she could give it one jolt hard enough, just one. With all the strength she could summon, she clasped her hands and slammed down. Sylvia's body moved under the force. Philo waited for a response.

—Beat, you fucker.

Nothing came, nothing but remorse that she'd hurt her mammy. Philo lay down on her and started to cry.

—Don't go, Mammy, please come back, please please please come back….

She lay there and cried her heart out. In the distance, the *thump, thump, thump* of the wrecking ball at its deadly work continued, to be overtaken, finally, by the shrill siren of the ambulance as it made its way across the bridge towards the East Wall.

Everything about the funeral was contentious. It started with the row over where Sylvia was to be buried. Jack wanted her to go into the Darcy family plot in Balgriffin Cemetery. Philo insisted that she was going to be cremated.

—I'm not making ashes of your mother. It's no way for a lady to go, and your mother was a lady, a real lady.

—She's a lady now, when she's dead?

—She was always a lady.

—Why did you call her a fat cow and moo at her when she was alive?

—We're not talking about that, we're talking about the funeral arrangements. I want to give her a headstone with her name on it.

Philo thought about the hypocrisy he'd inscribe on it. *Deeply regretted by her loving husband. A devoted mother and wife, sadly missed.* Headstones were the source of awful public lies. They were a hypocrite's charter.

—How did you treat your wife? saith the Lord.

—I gave her the most beautiful headstone, saith the lying husband.

How much better it would be to proclaim the truth. *A weary wife, abused and ignored over many years. Sadly forgotten by the one who never had a good word to say about you.*

The thought that upset Philo was not her mother's coffin going into the ground, but Jack's coffin going in on top of her. To have him there for all eternity – it wasn't going to happen. If Philo had to make a funeral pyre of the house and torch it, then so be it, amen. Sylvia was going to have her wishes respected and that was that.

Jack knew the argument was lost, but he couldn't be seen to back down.

—She'd still be alive only for you, he said.

Philo was shocked.

—I killed her, is that what you're saying?

—Walking to that bingo every day – she wasn't able for it. She was only doing it to please you.

For once Philo didn't have a reply. She was hurt and upset by him, feelings she didn't allow in the normal course of things. Only this wasn't normal. The most important person in her life was dead and she stood accused of her murder. There was truth in the contention, of course, and that was the nub of the problem for Philo. The results of the post mortem would take six weeks to be known, but everyone suspected it had been heart failure brought on by the strain of walking back and forth across the bridge every day. As always with her father, Philo had to appear strong and not let him see that she was upset. She had to stay focused and not let him trample over Sylvia's wishes the way he had when she was alive.

They waked Sylvia in the house, and she looked lovely in her blue jacket and white blouse. The family were all together under the one roof for the first time in years. Philo's brothers, the twins Andrew and Bren, whom she hadn't seen since Christmas, six months before, were there, with their wives, Lilly and Marie, and their children, two apiece, John Paul, Sorcha, Sinéad and Laurence. There was Philo's baby sister, Sally, although she was a baby no more; she shared a birthday with Jack and they would both be sixteen soon. These things, small details that united families, became important around funerals. Philo was so glad her own children were not still in Goldenbridge. Upset as they were at their granny's death, it helped that they were around and part of the grieving process.

Sylvia was laid out in the front room in a plain oak coffin.

Philo had gone to the undertakers and helped prepare the body. She didn't want her mother laughed at, not in death. She could imagine outsiders looking at the folds of her flesh and thinking it was funny. Preparing the body was a way of bearing witness to Sylvia's humanity and protecting her dignity.

The choice of coffin had been another source of conflict between Philo and Jack. Sylvia was too big for any of the standard-issue ones. There was no problem making one to fit, except that she was as wide as she was tall; if they constructed it around her shape, then it would come out square. To give it a coffin shape they would have to exaggerate her height. The undertakers suggested making it seven and a half feet long, and Jack objected on the grounds that it would make her look like a giant. Philo argued that it was better than putting her in a square coffin. In the end, they'd compromised on seven feet even.

Everyone commented on how peaceful she looked. People always said that, but this time it happened to be true. There was a complete absence of struggle on Sylvia's face.

—She was ready to meet her God, Ninna Delargy said.

—She's a saint now, Granny Carmody said.

—She makes a beautiful corpse, Nan Cassidy said.

More nuns came to pay their respects than you'd find in a convent.

—She's with the angels now, Sister Monica said, with the angels in heaven.

—Just look at her, Sister Davina said. You can tell she's with God and his holy angels.

—She's with the blessed and holy angels, Sister Xavier said.

Sister Rosaleen was next. She was too upset to say anything. She took Philo's hands and squeezed them in hers. Philo bent over and whispered in her ear:

—The next nun who says she's with the angels, I'm going to burst her.

Sister Rosaleen tried to suppress the laughter, but it ended up in tears streaming down her face. Philo put her arms around her and gave her a hug. She noticed Cap at the far end of the room, offering his condolences to Jack, and made her way across to find out the news about Dina.

—I'm very sorry for your trouble, Philo, he said.

—And I'm sorry for yours. How is she?

Cap shrugged his shoulders and looked away.

—She's not good, Philo, not good.

—How bad is not good?

Death always came in threes. Perhaps it was reaching out to embrace Dina. It would be a terrible thing for the old folks if the angel of death were to touch two of their number, leaving the rest to ponder who was going to be next.

—Is she dying, Cap? Philo asked.

It was the same awful question Cap had asked the doctor. At ten o'clock in the morning, after they had held hands all night in Casualty, Dina had been admitted in a flurry. Everything had been peaceful and then she suddenly became an emergency. One moment she was with him, the next she was gone. He paced the waiting room and the corridor and the concrete steps outside, waiting for news. At three o'clock the doctor found him and brought him to his office.

—This is not a good situation, not good at all.

—Is she going to die? Cap asked, his voice trembling.

The options were very stark. The doctor explained that Dina had gangrene. That was the cause of the blackness on her feet.

—We can amputate and possibly save her life, or we can leave things as they are and she may die.

—You're talking about her legs.

—Yes, from below the knee, both legs.

Cap tried to imagine what that would do to her. It seemed a violation too far. Waking up with no legs could kill her.

—I'd like your permission to proceed, the doctor said.

It wasn't his to give. This was a life-or-death decision and not his to make. Gerry Sugrue was still Dina's husband. But the truth was, Cap was closer to her than a husband. He wanted her alive, no matter what bits were poisoned and had to be cut away. He couldn't do a Pontius Pilate; he couldn't wash his hands and walk away when all he wanted to do was hold hers.

—I'm her lover, Doctor, he said.

It was the first time he'd used the word. It was an honest description. He was her lover.

—I want to keep her alive, whatever that takes.

Cap had made the only decision he could. It was the same decision he'd make every time: he would always choose to have her, to keep her alive at any price.

Philo looked at him, waiting for a reply.

—She's not going to die, is she? she asked again.

—No, she's going to be all right, Cap said.

It wasn't the time to tell Philo about the amputations. She had the loss of her mother to contend with; it wasn't fair to burden her with more bad news. Cap knew that if he started to talk he would get upset. Dina had lost her legs but she was still alive, still breathing. Philo would never see her mother again. Tears for Sylvia were the only legitimate tears; the tears for Dina would have to wait. He knew Philo would want to know and had a right to know. He also knew that he couldn't tell her.

With that in mind, he turned to the coffin and kissed the corpse. He made his excuses and went off to find a suitable messenger who could bring Philo the news, and the first person he clapped eyes on was Sister Rosaleen.

The day of the funeral began in awful fashion and went downhill all the way to the finish. Philo and the immediate family took up the front pew in Saint Laurence O'Toole's church. The Mass had begun when Tommo marched up the aisle and wormed his way into the row beside her. It suited him to play Happy Families in front of the congregation. With her father to the right and him to the left, she had the smell of stale drink in stereo.

Philo took Communion and prayed that Sylvia was happy. She was in heaven, of course, and Philo knew that. She thought about the soul. It was supposed to be weightless, but Philo couldn't imagine that. People compared it to an astronaut in space, but that wasn't very appealing, having to spend eternity locked up in one of those suits. The concept of angels was much nicer, but it was hard to imagine a pair of wings strong enough to get Sylvia up off the ground.

By the end of the day her body would be cremated, and soon after Philo would scatter her ashes from the top of Howth Head. She'd won the argument with her father, but the children had been much more difficult to convince. They knew their granny was dead but they still thought the flames would hurt her. Eileen and Jack had put on an air of understanding because they thought it was the adult thing to do. It was largely pretence, however; in their hearts they'd have preferred a regular burial. Philo had sat them down and tried to explain how hard it was for Sylvia to carry all that weight, and how she didn't want to go to heaven and meet God looking like that. They had understood why their granny wouldn't want to be reunited with her old body if she could have a new one instead. It was still awful what she had to go through to get it.

—Does that mean you want us to cremate you, Ma? Eileen asked.

It was always Eileen who cut to the quick.

—I'm not going to do it, Ma, Josie said.

—Neither am I, Philomena said.

—None of us are, Young Tommo said.

—If that's what Ma wants, we have to do it, Jack said. We have to respect her wishes.

—Why can't you not be fat, Ma? Josie asked.

—Why can't you get thin before you die? Young Tommo said.

Philo had to lose the weight; if not for herself, then she had to do it for the children. Walking behind the coffin as it left the church, she asked Sylvia for help.

Ma, stop me turning into an elephant.

The church was packed with all her friends – some she hadn't seen since school, others she'd worked with in Pownall's – but Philo looked straight ahead because she knew if she made eye contact she would cry. She focused on the coffin and kept her eyes there, determined that hers would be a regular size when her time came.

Ma, stop me turning into an elephant.

Outside in the church grounds, people milled around to shake her hand. Jack couldn't believe his wife had such a circle of friends. It was a great source of comfort that so many people had taken the time to offer their condolences. Tommo hung close and held out his hand for comforting, too. At one point he put his arm on Philo's shoulder, but she gave him such a withering look that he quickly withdrew it.

The wrecking ball had ceased its pounding for the funeral Mass, the workmen paying their respects in a simple, dignified way. Philo looked across at one point and saw the crane-man remove his hard hat and bless himself. It was a gesture she would never forget.

Nor would she ever forget what happened next. Across to her right, by the side of the hearse, she saw Sam Harris shaking hands with her daughter, Eileen. He was talking to her, because she was nodding her head in response. Philo broke off what she was doing, walked across, took Eileen by the hand and, without a word, dragged her away. Then she rounded up the rest of the children and got into the mourning car.

Ma, stop me turning into an elephant.

She wanted it to be over. The sooner they were up in the crematorium and done with the formalities, the happier she'd be. She shouted out the window for her father to join her. They pulled out of the church grounds and headed over the bridge into East Wall. They stopped outside the house and observed a minute's silence before heading off to Glasnevin Cemetery. In the distance, the wrecking ball went back to pounding the heart, liver and lights out of Sheriff Street.

A large crowd packed into the small crematorium chapel in Glasnevin. It took six funeral attendants to lift the coffin onto the conveyor belt in front of the red silk curtains. The priest read out the prayers for the dead and sprinkled the coffin with holy water. It was the moment of departure, and Philo started to sob. She'd held herself together for the sake of the children, but she had nothing left to stop the tears. It was her mammy in the coffin and she'd never get to lie beside her and feel her warmth again. It was the final goodbye in this life, and in that moment it felt too much to bear.

The priest put his hand to the side of the lectern and pushed a button. Everyone looked across at the coffin. It started to move, then came to a stop; it moved again, about two inches, and stopped again. Half a dozen times it seemed it would finally go, and on each occasion it stopped. It bobbed up and down and then sat still, like it had given up the effort. The squeal of the conveyor belt was followed by the smell of burning rubber – it was like Sheriff Street on a bad Saturday night. The priest had no idea what to do.

Philo bent down and whispered to young Jack to go up and switch off the conveyor belt, but at that moment Tommo walked boldly up to the front of the chapel and gave the coffin a shove. It started to make its way towards the opening behind the curtains. Philo watched and suddenly realised that the coffin was too wide to go through. It edged its way into the jaws of disaster as Tommo stood there, like the fool he was, conducting the catastrophe.

Jack made his way to the altar, but before he could press the button to stop the belt, the coffin struck a granite iceberg. The side panel cracked in two, and Philo screamed when she saw Sylvia's arm appear. The priest quickly draped his black coat across the hole in the coffin. At the back of the church, one of the undertakers, in panic, smashed a glass panel that set off a fire alarm. People ran for the doors. The evacuation took less than ninety seconds to complete.

The mourners gathered outside, in shock.

—This is all your doing and I hope you're satisfied, Jack said.

—I'm sorry, Da, really I am.

It was the first time Philo had apologised to him since she was twelve years old. The last thing she'd wanted was to turn the cremation into a circus.

—Why didn't you let me put her in the ground like a Christian?

Philo thought the whole thing was a sick joke on God's part. To add insult to injury, it started to rain.

—I'm sorry for everything, Da.

She was falling apart with the pressure. Why was Sylvia doing this to her? The cremation was for her, and now everything was conspiring against it. What sort of a message was that to send from heaven?

The six undertakers, aided by two workmen, carried the coffin out the side door of the church. The priest's coat was still draped over it. The rain fell and bounced off the varnished wood. Philo remembered a saying of her mother's: 'Happy the corpse that the rain falls on.' She hoped it was true, because no one else at the funeral could be described as anything other than traumatised. The men went in what looked like a tradesman's entrance at the rear. It was a sad, undignified exit. The saddest.

The post-funeral refreshments were served in the North Star Hotel at the top of Sheriff Street. There was the usual mix of soup, sandwiches, tea, beer and whiskey. Sister Rosaleen took Philo aside and broke the news about Dina's double amputation. Initially, Philo was angry that Cap had kept it from her, but it didn't take her long to see that he'd done it for her own good.

She was starting to come to terms with the news when Tommo appeared before her, buoyed by the free drink. Before she had a chance to tackle him, he got his retaliation in first.

—I was only doing my best, he said. You can't ask for more than that.

—I hope you die roaring, Philo said, and the sooner the better.

—I don't intend going, not for a good while yet, but when I do go, I think I'll go into the ground.

—It couldn't happen to a nicer person, Philo said, and walked away from him.

He followed her and asked if she wanted a lift home.

—You're in no condition to drive, she said.

—I do all my best driving when I'm relaxed, he said.

—I'm not going with you in that state.

—Please yourself.

Tommo set off down the quays, bound for Mickser's house. The rain had stopped and the roads had dried off. There wasn't a puff of wind about; it was the perfect evening for driving. He came off the bike on the north quays near Campion's pub and fractured his skull on the metal bridge. There were no other vehicles involved. When they found him, there was just a slight trickle of blood from his mouth. He'd driven into the central stanchion of the bridge and died instantly.

17

Philo cried openly at Tommo's funeral for the sake of the children. No matter how much of a bollix he'd been to her, he was still their father; they'd lost him and they were grief-stricken. You only get one da in your life and Tommo was theirs. She tried to console them with the idea that he was with the angels in heaven, the very thing the nuns had said to her and for which she had wanted to burst them. It was hard to watch the kids suffer and not say something.

—Does that mean he's with Granny? Philomena asked.

It wasn't what Philo had in mind, but what could she say?

—Is he really up in heaven with Granny? Josie asked.

—Where else would he be? Philo said.

—He could be in purgatory, Josie said.

—My da's not in purgatory, Young Tommo said.

—If he's anywhere he's in heaven, Eileen said.

—That's if there is a heaven, Jack said.

It was less a question and more a statement. For the second time in a week, they were being confronted with the appalling vista that death was a full stop with nothing after it.

—How can there not be a heaven? Young Tommo asked.

—Same as there's no Santy, Jack said.

There was a compelling logic to Jack's argument, expressed with all the certainty of youth. The implication, of course, was that none of them would ever see Tommo again. Philomena burst into tears and couldn't stop, despite the best efforts of Philo and Eileen. As soon as she seemed to be stemming the flow, another flood came from somewhere to engulf her.

—Don't mind him, Philo said. There is a heaven.

—I hope you're satisfied now that you've upset her, Eileen said to Jack.

Hard as he tried, Jack could feel no sorrow at Tommo's passing. All his life he'd been made to feel less than whole by Tommo's constant reminders that he was a cuckoo in the nest – half-brother, stepson, bastard, waster, bed-wetter and joyrider. He was glad to be the last of those because he was good at cars; he'd proven what he could do with the lap record out in Santry. Getting away to the San Francisco Boys' Home had been the saving of him. No one there ever told him to stop talking through his arse. He could express opinions without being threatened.

A week away from Tommo and Jack had decided there wasn't a God. There was only birth and death and then it was over, that was it, curtains. Religion was just another invention to keep him in his place. He wasn't going to be a sheep any more. There was no God and no heaven. How could there be a place to reward bastards like Tommo?

Having said that, it wasn't the time to start an argument on the subject with his nine-year-old half-sister. Jack bent down to Philomena and took her chin in his hand.

—Of course there's a heaven, he said.

—I don't care about heaven, she said.

—We all care about heaven. They have everything up there, he said.

—Do they have football pitches? Young Tommo wanted to know.

—They have loads of football pitches, Jack replied.

—Does that mean they have swimming, too? Josie asked.

—They have every sport under the sun, Philo said.

—You said there's no Santy, Philomena said.

In that millisecond, everyone realised Philomena's problem did not concern the existence of heaven.

—Did I say there was no Santy? Jack said.

—Yes, you did, Philomena answered emphatically.

—Then I'm stupid, amn't I?

—No, you're not stupid.

Jack was playing for time.

—Anyone who doesn't believe in Santy is stupid, he said.

—Jack is right, Eileen said. There is no Santy in heaven, there's only a Santy down here where we are.

—Is that true, Ma? Philomena asked.

Philo looked at Eileen in wonderment and awe. Where had she got her brains from? It wasn't from her, and it certainly wasn't from Tommo. Eileen was such a rock of sense. All Philo had wanted from life at her age was to get away from her father and go mad. She'd run so fast she'd met herself coming back wearing a different set of manacles. She looked at Eileen and wanted to be her. The only person she'd ever wanted to be before was Sylvia.

She'd lost her mother and found her daughter. It was the nicest feeling she'd had since she was a little girl, before the world had stepped in to corrupt her. She'd believed in Santy back then, a feeling of hope and trust and magic, and she had it again now. It had come to her through Eileen, who made her feel proud to be her mother and her friend. Philo looked at all her children, delighted they were reunited and a family once again.

—Is it true? Philomena asked again.

—It's the truth, the whole truth, and nothing but the truth, Philo said.

At the graveside, the children cried profusely. Philo did, too; she thought of Sylvia to bring on the tears. It was strange to be standing there watching Tommo's coffin going down, so soon after the events of the cremation. The story of that day had gone all around Dublin, and people who had been nowhere near Glasnevin were claiming to have been present when the coffin split its side. One account had it that the red curtains went on fire and blackened the entire chapel. It was only a matter of time before someone put it around that Sylvia was still alive when the denouement came. Whether it had been a catastrophe or not, Philo couldn't be sure that Sylvia hadn't orchestrated the whole thing. The imprint of a guiding hand was all over it. And she'd done it in answer to Philo's prayer.

Ma, stop me from turning into an elephant.

Sylvia wanted nothing more than for Philo to lose weight, and she'd used the cremation to embarrass her into action. She was working through the children, too. It was Josie who let the cat out of the bag when she said that they were all giving up chocolate, sweets, biscuits and ice-cream. Philo was intrigued about why they were giving up such treats so soon after coming out of Goldenbridge.

—Why are you giving them up? she asked.

—We just are, Josie said.

—You're giving them up for no reason, are you?

—We don't like them any more.

—How long are you giving them up for?

—A long, long, long, long time.

—That sounds like you're giving them up forever.

Josie tried to imagine what that would be like, and Philo could read the disappointment on her face.

—We might go back on them when you get thin, she said.

Philo immediately committed herself to the task. She had run out of excuses. Her children would eat chocolate again, and ice-cream too. They would not suffer because of her size. The weight was coming off and that was the end of it. There would be no more fat and no more comfort eating. Late-night rashers and sausages would cease forthwith. Philo didn't care if she never slept again: size was taking precedence over sleep. There would be no more fish and chips laden down with grease. If it took a hunger strike to shift the pounds, then a hunger strike it would be. It didn't matter if she died in the attempt, as long as she was thin at the end of it. There was going to be no oversized coffin for her. They could burn her, but there would be no last-minute catastrophe. She might even go for burial. What would they put on her headstone? *Here lies a slip of a woman, sadly missed by her children, who eat ice-cream, chocolate and biscuits.*

The day of Tommo's funeral, Philo killed two birds with the one stone and collected Sylvia's ashes. The man in the office took a great big ledger off a shelf and opened it up to check the name. *Sylvia Darcy, 102793.* He disappeared and came back with a white cardboard box. It had two handles and looked like it contained an expensive bottle of champagne. It was Sylvia, however, that nestled inside the paper walls.

Philo picked up the box and cradled it in the crook of her arm. She hadn't prepared herself for this, hadn't thought about how she would feel. It was suddenly upon her and she didn't know what to do. She had Sylvia in her arms like a baby, and it seemed the most ridiculous thing in the world. You weren't supposed to collect your mammy and take her home in a box. There should be music and men in black coats and a bit of a ceremony, at the very least.

—This is my mammy, she said to the man behind the counter.

The man in charge of urns had seen it all, from hysterical relatives to the ones who didn't care. He thought Philo was going to cry, which surprised him because she looked such a big, strong woman. He turned the ledger towards her.

—Would you like to sign for her? he said.

He made it sound like Sylvia was being released from prison.

—I can't let her go until you sign for her.

How could he stop her? Sylvia was free, without human form; she was ash, she was powder, and in a short time she'd take flight into the air as she'd requested. Why did this man think he was her gaoler?

—This is my mammy, Philo said.

—Your initials will do, that's all.

—P.D., she said, and left.

The mourning car was waiting for her at the gates. She got in the front and the driver asked her to put on her seatbelt. She pulled it across and strapped herself and Sylvia safely in.

—Is that Granny's ashes? Eileen asked from the back.

Philo nodded and opened the top of the cardboard box. A brown metal urn looked out at her, the lid held in place by two metal screws at the sides. She undid them and took the lid off. In the urn were the white ashes that had once made up Sylvia. It seemed so sad that a person could be reduced to such a small pile.

Philo gave it a shake and, to her horror, noticed black bits of grit floating in the ash. Then the thought struck her: they were the remains of the priest's coat. They'd forgotten to take it off and it had ended up mixed in with her mother.

—Can we have a look? Jack asked.

Philo's mood turned from sadness to anger. She was showing nothing to nobody until she sorted this out.

—Turn the car around, she said. I'm going back to Glasnevin.

The man in the office assumed she'd come back to initial the register. Philo lost no time making her complaint and pointing out the offending particles. The man explained that the black bits had nothing to do with the priest's coat. They were, in fact, what was left of Sylvia's teeth.

Philo felt her face was red enough to burn. She was a right eejit, but she was also glad she'd asked.

—People ask about the black bits all the time, he said. It's our number-one enquiry.

—What's the white stuff, is that her fat? she asked.

—No, that's her bones.

—Where's her fat gone?

—It vaporises. Disappears. Bones and teeth, that's all we're left with.

She was thankful for the information. Before leaving she signed her name, in full, in the appropriate space on the ledger.

They went straight from Glasnevin to Noctor's pub in Sheriff Street, where the piss-up in Tommo's honour was to be held. He might have been a bastard to Philo but that didn't mean he hadn't been popular. It seemed that every person who'd ever thrown a dart in Dublin was there, not to mention lorry drivers, dockers and pigeon-fanciers. It was great for the children to see their father remembered in such a full-blooded and spirited way. Philo, for her part, stayed out of the limelight as much as possible, hanging on to Sylvia's ashes for all she was worth.

At the end of the night, Mickser Cummins came over to her and put a bundle of money in her hand.

—Give him a nice tombstone, he said; a nice tombstone, that's all.

'Tombstone' was an old cowboy word. Tommo would have done well in the Wild West, Philo thought; it would have suited his temperament.

—Put something nice on it, Mickser went on. I'll leave it up to yourself.

They'd passed the hat around and £2,300 had been collected.

—I can't take this; it's too much, Mickser, she said.

He held an admonishing finger in the air.

—It's nice to be nice, he said, nice to be nice.

He was one of those drunks who repeated himself over and over when he was jarred and wouldn't open his mouth when he was sober.

—I don't know what to say, Mickser.

The finger of admonishment went up in the air again.

—I loved your husband, I loved that man, do you hear?

I bleedin' well loved Tommo. Why do you think I took him in?

There was just enough aggression in his voice for Philo to know the time to leave had come. She was about to get the story of how Tommo had been put out of the family home. Philo stuffed the money in her pocket and said her goodbyes.

—A nice tombstone, give him a nice tombstone.

Maybe she would, but for now her focus was on Sylvia. She sent word around the family that the ashes would be scattered off Howth Head on the following Sunday at three o'clock. It was the perfect location, high up, with the city spread out below and the picturesque Wicklow Mountains off in the distance.

On the Sunday, Philo set off with her own brood, uncertain who else would turn up. The younger ones, Philomena, Josie and Young Tommo, wanted to take the Dart train, but the station was down in the village at the bottom of Howth Hill. Instead they took the bus, which left them very close to the summit. Even so, the climb up the last part of the hill was exhausting. Philo was glad to see her da there with Sally. After all the heated words surrounding the burial, she had to acknowledge the courage it took for him to bury the hatchet and show up.

They were standing on the summit admiring the view when Andrew and Bren arrived to complete the family circle. They all walked down to a ledge and, without really meaning to, formed a line, looking out to sea. Philo offered the urn to her father, but he declined and insisted that she go first.

She poured a handful of ashes into the palm of her hand and closed her fist. She stretched her hand out and unfurled her fingers, like she was releasing a bird. A gust of wind blew across her path and lifted the ash out over the rocks, where it seemed to take on the shape of a wing, soaring into the air and flying out across the Irish Sea, beyond the Baily Lighthouse, tossing and turning in front of the Wicklow Mountains before being lost to the human eye. None of them

282

could believe what they'd seen, but they did believe, because they all saw the same thing: they saw Sylvia take flight.

They all took turns to release her, big Jack, Andrew, Bren, Sally, and then young Jack, Eileen, Young Tommo, Josie and Philomena. They let her fly back to the elements, the sea and the wind; they let her take flight the way she'd always wanted to, with total and complete abandonment.

By the time Dina was released from hospital, Philo was a fully fledged widow and had the government allowance to prove it. She was delighted with her new status. It was the one and only label she'd ever felt happy with. Battered wife, abuse survivor, overeater, she hated them all; but widow – the sight, sound and smell of it appealed to her. To think she was getting paid for having Tommo six feet under thrilled her beyond words. Had she known earlier in her life, she'd have taken out a credit union loan and employed a hit man. She thanked God that she was a young woman with years of widowhood stretching out ahead of her. The children were without a father, but they were together as a family, in a flat bequeathed to them, ironically, by Tommo.

Hers was a non-contributory pension, and, like most things in Philo's life, it had required her to fill out a form proving that she was descended from Adam and Eve. Under the heading 'Other income, from the sale or lease of lands', she made her usual declaration: 'One pound a year from the rent of my window-box.' Further down she noticed another heading – 'Other incomes, e.g. carer's allowance, dividends from stocks and shares or other pensions'. For the first time in her life she was faced with the dilemma of telling a real lie on a form.

Philo approached Cap and suggested he take over as Dina's carer. It seemed a logical step, but he knew it was a suggestion that would be met with horror. He asked Dina, under duress, and she was only short of morphing into a bat and flying out of the bed to bite him on the neck.

—I only have one home help and that's Philo, she said.

Dina wasn't home a day when there was a row over her stumps. Philo was in her flat at Liberty House when Cap arrived to inform her there was murder going on in Dowdall's Lane. The district nurse had arrived to change the dressings, only to be met by fierce resistance from Dina, who wanted Philo there to do it. It was like she reverted to being a five-year-old child on coming home. Dina was missing her legs, and Philo felt for her, but she couldn't be at her beck and call twenty-four hours a day. She had four children who needed looking after, especially in the wake of their father's death.

Philo arrived at Dowdall's Lane and knew by the face on Dina that something was wrong. The nurse was out in the kitchen boiling water on the stove.

—You're too late, Dina whispered. I had an accident in my knickers.

—Why didn't you tell the nurse? Philo said.

—I'm not telling her anything.

Philo picked Dina up and put her under her arm. She didn't feel any heavier than a six-month-old baby.

—Are you comfortable? Philo asked.

—I'm grand, Dina said, looking up at her.

—Tell me if I squeeze you too hard.

—I will.

She carried her out to the toilet under her arm. It was a technique Philo had perfected when her own were in nappies. The great advantage was that it kept one hand free at all times, making it simple to open doors and turn on taps as required. Philo filled the sink with water, pulled off Dina's knickers and cleaned her up. Every now and then she caught sight of Dina's pitiful face looking up at her.

—I'm an awful nuisance, I know I am, Dina said.

Philo could think of a dozen terms that better described her, and they all began with 'me, me, me' and 'I want, I want, I want'.

—You're going to end up hating me, I know you are.

She sprinkled Dina's bum with talcum powder and spread it all around. Philo knew Dina was looking for a pity party, but she wasn't going to get it.

—I have other plans for you, Philo said.

—What are you going to do with me? Dina asked.

—You really want to know?

—Yes.

—I'm going to buy you slippers for Christmas.

Dina thought about it for a moment before the import of it dawned on her.

—God forgive you, that's a terrible thing to say.

—It's the truth.

—How would I wear slippers?

—I could strap them onto your stumps.

—I'd look like a fool.

—That would make a change.

—A change from what?

—From me being the fool running after you. Not just me – Cap, too. And half of Sheriff Street. Not to mention the doctors and the nurses. You've hundreds looking after you.

—No one looks after me the way you do.

A stupid piece of flattery, but it took the wind out of Philo's sails. Dina felt alive when she had Philo around. She felt safe, too. She knew she wouldn't die when Philo was there, and if she did, at least she'd die laughing.

Philo carried her from the bathroom to the bedroom.

—Where do you keep your knickers? Philo asked.

—Top drawer.

Philo pulled it out and looked in. The first thing she saw was a skimpy red thong. With delicate fingers, she withdrew the lace garment.

—Where do you buy your underwear? she enquired.

—Cap bought me that.

—Not a very good choice if you're incontinent.

She put it back and pulled out a heavier pair in white cotton. She slid them over the stumps and pulled them up. The elastic was nice and springy and made a tight seal against Dina's white thigh.

—That's what you need if you're in the shits, Philo said.

—Do you think I could be incontinent?

—No, you only have the runs.

—How can you be sure?

Philo wasn't sure. She didn't want to think about Dina losing control over her bowels.

—I told you before, you're going to live to be a hundred and eight. You'll still be shitting long after I'm dead.

That put a smile back on Dina's face. They went into the sitting room and Philo sat Dina in the leatherette armchair. Nurse Collins had the tea wet and introduced herself. She'd had time to work on Cap and bring him around to the fact that the stump bandages would be changed once a week by a professional nurse from the Eastern Health Board, namely herself.

—We have to keep the wounds clean, isn't that right, Mr Coyle?

—That's right, Nurse.

Nurse Collins didn't mind if she upset Dina in the process; in the battle of wills with her, she was determined to win. Philo disliked her because she constantly deferred to 'Mr Coyle' and completely ignored Dina. She didn't make eye contact when she spoke, but gawked all around her like a curious bird. Worse than all that was the constant invocation of the Health Board, like it was the panacea to the world's ills.

—The Health Board only employs the best, believe me. Our post-op care is second to none. They send teams over from Brussels to see how we do it. We're the best-qualified nurses in Europe. You don't have to rely on any home help; you can rely on me. I'm qualified.

That did it for Philo. She didn't want the responsibility for changing the stump bandages, but she wasn't going to be denigrated.

—I'll cut these off and we'll let the nurse put on the new ones, Philo said.

—That seems fair, Cap said.

—No, I want you to put on the cream, Philo, Dina said.

—She's not properly qualified, Nurse Collins said.

—She's better than any nurse, Dina said. Tell her, Cap.

—She's better than any nurse, Cap said.

He always agreed with Dina. It was a blind, unflinching loyalty. Standing on the granite steps of the Mater Hospital after he'd given his consent for the surgery, Cap had sworn he would never cross Dina again if she lived. Every minute of every day he was living up to that promise.

—I thought you were on my side, Nurse Collins said.

Cap shook his head with annoying certainty.

—I'm with Dina on this.

—Thank you, Cap darling, Dina said, and smiled like a spoilt child.

There was a loud knock on the door. Philo went over to the window and leaned out. A man was standing on the road beside a parked van.

—Delivery for Sugrue.

—Where from? Philo asked.

—Eastern Health Board.

Philo turned back to the room.

—Your wheelchair is here, Dina.

—Begod, that was quick, Cap said.

The Health Board had done it again, and Nurse Collins said nothing, just basked in the reflected glory of the situation. Cap and Philo went downstairs to take delivery of

287

it. They stepped out onto the road and were met by a tall cardboard box.

—I'm sorry about the delay, the delivery man said.

Cap and Philo couldn't fathom what he was talking about.

—The docket should have been at the top of the pile but someone put it at the bottom of the pile, do you know what I mean?

Philo thought by the box it was the oddest-shaped wheelchair she'd ever seen. It must have been made for a very tall person. Then again, it was probably self-assembly and all the parts were adjustable.

—Do you want to try it out, Mister? the delivery man asked Cap.

—Oh no, it's not for me, it's for my lover, he said.

The delivery man thought for a second that Cap had said 'lover', before it dawned on him that he'd said 'brother'.

—How old is your brother? he asked Cap.

Cap looked at him, but before he had time to answer, Philo asked the delivery man to open the box. He took a Stanley knife from his pocket and slit it down both sides. Then he cut across the top and pulled away a rectangle of cardboard to reveal the contents – a brand new Zimmer frame.

Philo and Cap stared at it. They spent an eternity transfixed by this simple aid for walking. Cap eventually told the delivery man he had the wrong address.

He pulled the delivery docket out of his pocket and checked it.

—Dowdall's Lane, above the vegetable shop, he said.

—That's not for here, Cap said.

—What's your brother going to do? he asked.

Cap didn't have a brother. Why was this man so concerned about someone who didn't exist?

—I want you to bring it upstairs, Philo said.

It was ten weeks since she'd applied for the Zimmer frame. In that time she'd buried her husband, cremated her mother and got her children out of an orphanage. It was only by a stroke of luck (and Cap's devotion) that Dina was still on the planet. Philo was sick of the Health Board and its wonderful efficiency. On the day they were delivering a Zimmer frame for a legless person, it was time to put the case for the prosecution.

Philo climbed the stairs, and the delivery man followed with the Zimmer frame. He put it down in the centre of the living room. He acknowledged Nurse Collins and they exchanged hellos.

—You know each other, Philo observed. How strange!

—How's that strange? We both work for the Health Board, the delivery man said.

—Of course you do. It's the envy of Europe, I believe.

—That's news to me, the delivery man said.

—Did you not tell him, Nurse Collins?

Philo stared at the nurse and waited for a reply. She'd been looked down on by those in authority all her life – the faceless ones who read forms and decided people's fates, the stupid ones who lost forms and tried to cover up, the brain-dead ones who invented all the inane questions, the inquisitive ones who wanted to know what you ate for your breakfast, the mercenary ones who asked the homeless and the starving how their stocks and shares were doing. All of these were embodied by the genius from the Health Board standing before her.

It was Dina who broke the silence.

—Who's the Zimmer frame for?

—It's for you, Dina, Philo said.

—No, it's for his brother, the delivery man said.

—I don't have a brother, Cap snapped back.

—You said it was for your brother.

—I said it was for my lover. That's my lover there.

—I know what we could do, Philo said. We could hang you out of it, Dina. Like a monkey up in the zoo. You could hang on by your arms and we could spin you around. Delegations could come from Brussels to look at you. What do you think, Nurse Collins? Would that be all right with the Health Board?

Nurse Collins had been humbled into submission, a defeat so absolute that she would never take on Philo, or demean her role in looking after Dina, ever again.

18

Cap asked Dina to move in with him. It made no sense for her to go on living upstairs in Dowdall's Lane when he had the bungalow three hundred yards away in Coburg Place. Her wheelchair had eventually arrived from the Health Board, and it was no joke hauling it up and down the stairs every time she wanted to go out, which was often. There were so many compelling reasons for her to move, not least of which was her personal safety.

There had been one major scare already. It had happened on a day when Philo was late and Cap decided to move Dina on his own. First he carried the wheelchair down the stairs and assembled it. He rushed back up and put Dina on his back to carry her down. She needed to go to the bathroom, so he brought her in, waited while she peed, picked her up and headed for the stairs, forgot her cigarettes and had to go back to the living room, retrieved them and headed for the stairs again. Just as he put his foot on the first step, a light-headed feeling came over him, making him feel like he was going to fall all the way down to the bottom. He grabbed the banister and sat down.

—Are you all right? Dina asked.

Cap didn't answer. He just sat there, sick at how close he'd come to an accident.

—Imagine if I dropped you, he said.

Dina wasn't sure how to take it. Philo threatened things like that all the time, but it was different with her.

—I'll drop you, you bitch, you're annoying me, she'd say.

There was nowhere in this world Dina felt as safe as

under Philo's arm. It was strange to hear Cap say he'd drop her because he never joked about things like that; it wasn't in his nature.

—Imagine if I dropped you, he repeated.

—I don't have a good imagination, Cap.

—You'd end up breaking your arms or your neck. Imagine if you broke your arms.

—I'd look awful, wouldn't I?

Cap sat there and imagined it. Dina breaking her arms and having them amputated. Dina with just a torso. Dina with just a heart beating in the bed, nothing else.

—I don't want to lose any more of you, Cap said.

—You needn't worry, I'm going to live to be a hundred and eight.

—How do you know that?

—Someone told me, that's all. Don't ask questions.

Cap couldn't shake off the feeling of impending doom. Two days after the near-accident, he asked Dina formally to move in with him.

—I want you to move into the bungalow, he said.

—I don't want to, she replied without hesitation.

He smiled at her, thinking it might help to persuade her.

—You'd be safer in Coburg Place; there's no stairs, he said.

—I'm happy where I am.

It felt like a dead end, out of the blue. It wasn't just the refusal, either, but the manner of it. It felt like she'd been waiting to say no. He was being punished for something, but he didn't know what it was. It couldn't have been for his failure as a lover, because she never tired of telling him how wonderful he was.

He couldn't shake off the feeling that this had to do with the past. Maybe Dina still harboured resentment over the aquanaut dispute and the part he'd played in it. Despite their love affair, they'd never really talked about that. He'd never given her the opportunity to vent her anger if that was what she needed to do.

—Are you still mad at me over what happened on the docks? he said.

—No.

—You're not holding that against me, are you?

—No.

—Why won't you come and live with me, so?

—If you have to ask that, you don't know me.

Cap had taken a vow never to cross her, but they were heading for an almighty row and he couldn't stop it. He thought the solution might be in a study of psychology, because he didn't know how her mind worked. The trouble was that there were thousands of books on psychology; he didn't even know where to start. Then he thought of Philo. She might have the answer.

For a moment he felt hope, and then, just as quickly, he felt hopeless. Why was he so dependent on other people? He'd been a cripple since childhood and he was still looking for the protection and approval of others. It had cost him so much throughout his life. He'd let Dina slip through his fingers once before, and he was in danger of letting it happen all over again.

He dropped into the church to seek God's help. He sat in the back pew of Saint Laurence O'Toole's church and stared straight ahead. It was strange to be sitting there, looking up at the altar where it had all gone wrong. Dina swearing her life to Gerry Sugrue for better or worse. The drama over the ring, which Cap had mislaid and which had finally been found and put on her finger. What wouldn't he give to have those minutes back now?

If anyone has just cause why these two people should not be joined together, let him speak now or forever hold his peace....

He'd missed his chance. She was married and nothing

293

could change that fact. People did marry more than once, Cap knew that; but they were the young crowd, the new generation. He envied them. They had no problem accepting that they made mistakes. For Cap's generation, you got one chance and that was it.

These were the thoughts running through his head when a stone hit the stained-glass window at the back of the altar. It was a loud, stinging crack, shocking in its intensity. Cap was thinking about the bowsies who'd done it when there was a second crack. He was walking towards the altar to see what the damage was when something crossed his vision. It was a bird. It flew across from his left and crashed into the stained-glass window. It slid down the panes onto the floor and then started blindly scrambling around. Its head was damaged and there was blood on the top of its wing, where it joined to the body.

Cap cupped his hands and approached it. As he got to it, the bird flapped its wings and, with great difficulty, managed to fly up onto a ledge. Cap whistled and extended his hands in its direction. The bird seemed unsure what to do. If only it could trust him, he thought. If only it could do that, he'd save it. He continued to whistle and the bird stayed where it was. He offered it encouragement but without success. He stayed there a very long time, but finally he had to admit defeat and leave.

The bird was going to die, he was sure of that. It couldn't make that small leap of faith, and the consequences were sad and appalling. Cap felt he was trapped, just like the bird. The answer wasn't in books or psychology. He had to listen to his heart and trust it. Dina had been waiting all her life for him to make a move. He needed to take action, to make her feel safe; he needed to be bold. It was that simple.

He took five hundred pounds from his savings and put a deposit on a beautiful diamond sparkler in McDowell's, the Happy Ring House, of O'Connell Street. He bought the most enormous bunch of flowers from a dealer in Moore Street, and he headed for Dowdall's Lane. On his way down Sheriff Street he saw a Corporation worker standing in a crane fixing a broken street lamp. Cap thought it strangely ironic that they were attending to such matters after the flats had been levelled to the ground. He was going to say something but held his fire.

As he turned in to Dowdall's Lane, a voice whispered in his ear. It told Cap to go back and check out the cost of borrowing the crane for half an hour.

Five minutes later, Cap was standing in the bucket of the crane, being hoisted into the air. He knocked firmly on Dina's window-pane. When Philo looked out and saw him, it was the closest she ever came to being lost for words.

She put Dina in her wheelchair and brought her to the window. The look on Dina's face was priceless. Cap handed her the flowers and she thanked him. Then he dropped to one knee, opened the blue box and held it out to her. The sparkle nearly took the eyes out of her head.

—Dina Barrett, will you marry me? he said.

—Jesus, I think you're losing it, she replied.

—I'm not Jesus, I'm Cap Coyle. Now will you marry me?

She looked out at him dangling in mid-air before her.

—I thought you'd never ask, she said. Of course I'll marry you.

Philo decided to buy a new outfit for the wedding. She was delighted to have an excuse to get out of the mourning clothes. Black was her worst colour; it made her look like a very sad tent. Bright colours made her look fatter, but at least she looked as if she had female body parts. She was thinking of yellow because it was the colour of the sun. It was also the colour of ripened wheat. She remembered seeing a field of it swaying in the breeze once, back when she was a little girl staying with her mother's people in County Carlow. In her imagination, yellow was her colour. Failing yellow, she was thinking of pink. But she didn't want to fail, as she so often did where clothes were concerned.

Price was not going to be a factor. She put the cash from Tommo's farewell piss-up in her bag and headed up the town. She'd buy a nice outfit and put the rest against a headstone. Her first port of call was Evans of Henry Street, which always had a good selection in large sizes. Walking through the security barrier on the way in, she set off the alarm and brought the store detectives running.

—It's all right, Philo told them. I haven't robbed the place yet.

It was a good omen, she thought, making the alarm bells ring. It guaranteed she'd get prompt service, if nothing else.

Less than five minutes after entering the store, Philo found what she'd come out for. It was a two-piece suit in sunrise yellow, and they had it in a size twenty-six, which she'd worn before. She dashed into the changing rooms to try it on.

The jacket was all right across the shoulders but wouldn't quite button at the front. With a nice, matching blouse she'd nearly get away with that. The skirt, on the other hand, wouldn't go near her. It was four inches too small in the waist, maybe even six. It was so disappointing, because the style was perfect; it was the sort of outfit that made her look a million dollars. The skirt could always be let out, she thought, but not by four inches and certainly not by six.

The size twenty-six was the largest they had. Philo and the salesgirl discussed sewing an extra piece of material into the back of the skirt, but it was hopeless. She'd have to lose four inches, at the very least, for the skirt to fit. It seemed so cruel when the style and the colour were perfect. In her despair, she wondered if she could lose the inches with a hunger strike. Starvation and a corset might just do the trick. The salesgirl thought it was a waste of time putting a deposit on the suit because she was only going to end up disappointed. Philo didn't listen; she put fifty pounds down to secure it.

Ma, take six inches off my waist.

On the bus journey to the showrooms of McGowan and Sons, monumental sculptors, she repeated her prayer. She was shown to a waiting room and given a catalogue. It contained every type of headstone imaginable. There were Celtic crosses, large and small; slabs of black marble with white lettering and white marble with black lettering; there were polished headstones and rough ones, fat ones and skinny ones. Under each photograph was the word 'circa' (Philo had never come across it before) and beside it a price.

Mr McGowan came into the waiting room and asked her if she required more time, and Philo said she did. The truth was she hadn't a clue what she wanted. Based on how she felt, she should pick the ugliest one. But it was more for the children, so it should be something that appealed to them. She started to leak sweat under her arms with the tension of it. She decided to take the catalogue home and let the children choose.

Across the road from McGowan's, she went into a newsagent's and bought a cool bottle of water and an apple. While she was queuing up to pay she spotted a copy of *Stargazer* magazine with a celebrity wedding splashed across the front page. On the bus back into town she devoured the magazine and made herself entirely depressed. Page after page of the skinniest people in the world stared out at her. She'd never before seen such a band of smirkers and grinners with not an excess pound of weight between them.

Ma, take six inches off my waist.

On the second-last page, Philo saw a picture of a woman with a stomach just like hers. Underneath it were the words 'Lose unwanted fat!' The advertisement promised a money-back guarantee for the dissatisfied. Philo read the small print.

It was a process called liposuction; she'd never heard of it before. The procedure was carried out at the Whitestone Clinic. Philo knew of it: that was where rich people went when they were sick and needed publicity for their ailments. She figured from the address it must be somewhere near the American Embassy.

Half an hour later, armed with her copy of *Stargazer*, Philo found herself walking up the driveway towards the swanky building. She stepped inside and didn't know whether she was in a jungle or a swimming pool. There were plants standing in giant containers, hanging over balconies and jutting out of walls. Complementing the greenery was a waterfall that came down one of the walls and emptied itself into a stainless-steel trough. The reception area was an atrium with a glass ceiling. The only thing missing was Tarzan swinging from a rope.

The girl at the desk, Naomi, seemed really glad to see Philo. The name-tag on her jacket was glistening and matched her enamel smile. Philo showed her the ad and Naomi directed her to Mr Cardrew's rooms on the fourth floor. She was looking around for the stairs when Naomi came out from the desk and brought her to the lifts behind the waterfall. A person could get used to this, Philo thought. It was a long way from welfare offices and health boards and Zimmer frames.

The receptionist on the fourth floor was called Helena and looked like Naomi's sister. She took Philo's details, and after every answer she said, 'That's lovely.' After she'd done with the form-filling she asked Philo what her preferred method of payment was.

—Come again? Philo said.

—How are you going to pay?

—I'm going to give you money. How else can you pay?

—You could pay by credit card or cheque.

Philo took out the bundle of money and showed it to Helena. The girl had never seen so much cash in all her life.

—It was supposed to be for a headstone but, fuck it, life's for the living – what do you think?

Helena thought Philo was nice, in a Moore Street sort of way, but she felt intimidated by her at the same time.

—He was a right bollix, do you know what I mean?

Helena smiled at Philo and brought her straight in to Mr Cardrew.

Ma, take six inches off my waist.

He was a tall man in his mid-forties who looked like he got a lot of sun. He had a smooth tan, was impeccably turned out (a good wife there, Philo thought) and spoke with a soft south-side Dublin accent. He looked at Philo's form and then checked her heart rate and blood pressure. They chatted away, and he learned a lot about her by her answers to basic lifestyle questions.

—How many inches do you hope to lose? he asked.

—I have two thousand pounds, she said, so whatever you can do for that.

It was the first time Mr Cardrew had heard it expressed that way, and it made him laugh.

—Did I say something wrong?

—No, no, no, no, no, he jumped in, that's absolutely fine; nothing wrong with that at all, no, no, no.

By the end of the consultation he was confident that a six-inch waistline reduction was achievable.

—Would you be happy with six? he asked.

Philo felt very emotional, because it was the number she'd been throwing about in her prayers. It felt like Sylvia had been listening. She'd taken Philo into the newsagent's and drawn her eye to the magazine. She'd seen the Whitestone Clinic from her perch in heaven and put Philo on the bus to this appointment. All these years Philo had been defeated by her size, and now she was on the threshold of victory over her fat.

The feeling of euphoria lasted a day. It wasn't long before Philo's low self-esteem came battering at her door again.

Her size had been her protection, and she'd developed a personality to go along with it: she was Philo the clown and everyone got a laugh at her expense. Now that she was about to have her fat sucked out, the personality that had protected her would have to change. It was a fearful place to be, and it brought up a lot of issues around her abuse at the hands of Sam Harris. He'd come back into her life and she hadn't handled it well. Her anger towards him was palpable, but it was almost as if that anger let him off the hook, too. She was still suffering and he was walking free.

Two weeks to the day after her assessment, Philo set off with an overnight bag for the Whitestone Clinic. She'd wanted the children to stay the night with her father in East Wall, but Eileen had insisted that they'd be OK with her.

At the clinic, Philo put on her nightdress and sat by the bed. She tried to imagine losing six inches but it seemed too good to believe. Mr Cardrew came in to see her and explained where he would make the incision. He showed her a section of plastic pipe and got her to feel it.

—I'm going to suck the fat out through this fellow here, he said.

Philo couldn't believe it was happening. In the old days, when she and Tommo used to speak civilly to each other, they used to fantasise about holding up a bank together. They had it planned down to the very last detail. The thing that put them off was the risk of gaol, of course. Had she known about liposuction back then, she'd definitely have risked time for it, no doubt about it.

—Do you have any questions before we start?

—What do you do with the fat?

—We suck it out through the tube.

—No, after you suck it out – what do you do then?

—We dispose of it.

—I'd like to keep mine, if you don't mind. I'd like to take it home.

Mr Cardrew smiled at her like it was the most natural thing in the world, but it was the first time he'd had a patient make such a request.

—It's your fat, he said. You can do what you like with it.

Philo had the most wonderful dreams. She was giving birth, under water, to six babies at a time. They were sliding out of her and swimming away like fish. It was great having babies who were free and independent. She didn't mind how many came out of her, because it was a pain-free experience. As she woke up, she looked all around the room to see where her babies had gone. It took her a long time to realise she'd been dreaming, and when she did, she got upset. One of the nurses came over to her, took her hand out from under the pillow and put it on her tummy. Philo thought there was less of it there. That stopped her wanting to go back to sleep. She wanted to stay awake to make sure her reduced tummy wasn't a dream.

For the rest of that day and through the night, Philo kept pinching herself to stay in reality. She hobbled out to the bathroom and looked at her profile in the mirror. There was no doubt: she was smaller. Her tummy was sore but it couldn't keep the smile off her face. The two thousand had been money well spent. Not since she'd won sixpence in a lucky lump when she was five years old had she experienced a feeling like it.

On her discharge, Philo was given two plastic containers of her fat. It was a syrupy brown liquid that looked like melted butter. She swore she would never eat popcorn again. Her body had been a factory for the production of melted butter, and there was enough in these containers to feed Ireland. They were heavy, too, about eight pounds apiece – the equivalent of two bouncing babies. No wonder she'd had such strange dreams.

Back at home, the kids were convinced she'd lost stones.

—You definitely look smaller, Ma! they said.

Philo was wearing support shorts that acted like a corset – they'd been provided by the clinic – but she didn't tell the children. She loved their affirmation, but it was too soon to make a judgement. She would have to wait a while before she could pronounce the procedure a complete success.

Three weeks after her operation, Philo went back to Henry Street with a good deal of optimism. In Evans, she found the shop assistant who'd taken the deposit on the suit. She stood in front of the dressing-room mirror with the size twenty-six in her hand. The jacket went on first. It was comfortable across the shoulders, just like before. She stepped into the skirt and pulled it up around her waist. It was too big. There were two inches to spare between the skirt and Philo's waist. She couldn't believe it. She let it go and it slid down her legs like loose knickers. She pulled it up and let it fall again. It was sublime to watch it descend and lie limp on the floor. She repeated the action eighteen times and it never failed to look good. Finally, she grabbed up the suit and brought it to the assistant.

—The skirt's too big, Philo announced. Can you believe that? It's too fucking big!

The shop assistant was horrified.

—I'm terrible sorry, she said.

—What are you sorry about? Philo asked her.

—We'll have to get you a smaller size.

—A smaller size, Philo said. That's the best news I've heard in decades. No, it's the best news ever – the best news ever.

If it hadn't been for Philo, it is unlikely that the wedding would have gone ahead. After Dina accepted Cap's proposal, they realised they couldn't marry – not in the legal sense.

Dina and Gerry Sugrue were still husband and wife. She could have asked him for a divorce, but she didn't really want to. Any man who risked his life in a crane was good enough for her. She had the ring, he'd finally proposed, and that was all she needed. She was happy to move into the bungalow.

Cap, on the other hand, was furious. All his life he'd been bullied. He'd learned compliance at an early age and he'd been practising it ever since. Now there was something he wanted, really wanted, and he wasn't letting it go. He wanted a ceremony, something before he carried his bride across the threshold of a bungalow that had been in his family for a hundred years.

In his despair, he turned to Philo. She was horrified. There was no way they were cancelling the wedding, not after the trouble she'd endured to fit into that suit.

—It doesn't have to be a church, he said, just somewhere to tie the knot.

—Would you like the Pope's blessing? she asked.

Cap looked at her in complete disbelief.

—How are we going to get the Pope's blessing? he said.

—We might as well start at the top and work our way down.

Philo went to work on it immediately. She secured the use of the sports hall in Sheriff Street, a modern building, across from the church, that had been spared from the demolition. She approached Brother Felix and asked him to perform the marriage ceremony. He was reluctant at first, but Philo charmed the ears off him.

—You're a miracle worker, do you know that? she said.

—I'm just an ordinary Joe Soap, that's all.

—You're better than Saint bleedin' Francis.

—Stop it, now; he's a proper saint.

—He never cured bed-wetting like you did!

After an hour with Philo, Brother Felix came around to

meet Dina and Cap. He brought his old monk's habit to show them what he looked like. They couldn't believe their eyes.

—There's not many can say they were married by a monk, Philo said.

Cap and Dina were delighted with him, and there was no doubt he made them feel like they were embarking on the real thing. Dina chose her three cronies as bridesmaids; Philo suggested her daughter Eileen as a flower girl, and they instantly agreed.

—Who are you going to get as your best man? Dina asked Cap.

It was a question he'd given some thought to.

—I was thinking of asking Gerry Sugrue, he said.

—You can ask him over my dead body, Dina said.

Cap would have liked to ask him, but he suspected it was a bridge too far for Dina. The past was full of old wounds, and sometimes you got a chance to heal them; sometimes, however, you had to move on and leave them as they were. It wasn't Cap's prerogative to bring Gerry Sugrue back into Dina's life. So he chose Mucky Mannion, to avoid further conflict.

One thing he did do was close his shop for good. There was no need for two vegetable stores in the area – there never had been, really. From now on there would be the shop in Dowdall's Lane and that was all. It was a decision that brought the curtain down on the vegetable war once and for all.

19

Philo couldn't sleep, and the thought of food never crossed her mind. It was two days before the wedding and she should have been fretting about all the last-minute details, but she wasn't. She was thinking about her own marriage. She'd always looked on it as a failure. Now she wasn't so sure. Tommo was dead and she was a free woman again. It was a good feeling, but she knew it would disappear if she didn't deal with the past.

A plan of action formed in her brain. At seven o'clock she went to the bathroom and had a shower. Then she called the kids, made them breakfast and got them out to school.

She prepared herself for the day ahead. A root around in some drawers and she found the bubble wrap; she located two strong bags among her stash under the sink. She took a little more time than usual with her make-up. She wanted to look her best and feel her best. She checked her purse and made sure she had sufficient cash.

She took a taxi to Kilbarrack. At the chalets, she got out of the car, a bag in each hand, and asked the driver to wait for her. She walked up the concrete path, put the bags down and knocked as hard as she could. There was no delay; the door opened immediately and Sam Harris stood there, looking at the slimmed-down version of Philo on his doorstep.

—Can I come in? she said.

He hesitated.

—I was just about to go out, he said.

—This won't take long. I have something for you.

Philo picked up the two bags and stepped into the chalet. Sam noticed the taxi with its engine running.

—Would you like a cup of tea? he asked, hoping she'd say no.

—Sit down and relax, she said. I didn't come out here for tea.

Relaxation was the last thing on his mind. He knew there was something up; he had an instinct for these things. She'd come in and taken his ground and there wasn't a hint of deference anywhere in her manner. He sat in an armchair and tried to psych her out, but she refused to make eye contact.

Philo picked up one of the bags and placed it in his lap. Before he had time to react, she did the same with the second bag.

—They're for you, she said.

—What are they?

—A present.

Sam peered into one of the bags, but the bubble wrap made it hard to decipher what was in the plastic container. It was liquid, certainly, but beyond that he had no idea. The silence between them added to the tension. He withdrew one of the containers and tore at the bubble wrap. It made a sound like gunfire. The liquid came into view and he could tell it was no ordinary substance. It looked like melted butter, but he suspected it might be acid.

—What is this? he asked.

—That's my fat. I've been carrying it around for twenty years, thanks to you.

He stared across the room at her. She was smiling over at him. Was it conceivable that she'd put her fat into jars and brought it out to him? It wasn't possible, he thought, it had to be a joke – only it wasn't funny, and she wasn't going to have a laugh at his expense.

—What do you expect me to do with this? he said.

—I expect you to carry it, she replied.

—You're mad, do you know that?

—I've had my go. It's your turn now.

—You're crazy!

—Of course I am. That's how I survived.

—What do you want me to do?

—I want you to carry it for twenty years, like I did, and see how you get on.

Philo fixed him with a look that nailed him to the chair. He didn't know what to do with his hands. They were out of their element and he was lost. He made an attempt to get to his feet and got stuck. He started to panic.

—Help me, please, he stuttered. Please, help me.

Philo moved across to him and bent down.

—Do you remember when I was a little girl and I needed help? Do you remember that?

—No, I don't, I don't remember.

—I asked you to stop but you wouldn't stop, do you not remember?

—I don't remember anything.

Philo reached into the bags, prised the lids off the two containers and turned them over. Her fat poured out. It emptied itself into Sam's lap and he started to scream. It was a desperate cry of pain, like someone drowning in a sea of his own vomit. At the door, Philo looked back and saw her fat running down his trouser legs and onto the floor. It started to spread itself out like flood-water, engulfing the entire room.

She looked at the figure crying in the chair. He would never abuse her again. She'd stripped him of his power. She'd broken the silence. He would never lord it over her again. She would never again cross the street to avoid him. Her prison sentence was over. His was just beginning.

She stepped out onto the street and took a deep breath.

The air tasted so fresh, so sweet, so vibrant. She felt renewed. She walked over to the taxi, got in and headed for home.

Dina looked radiant in her pink three-piece suit with its matching hat. Philo pushed her with great pride all the way down Sheriff Street. They looked like two versions of the sun, bright afternoon and burnished evening, and they felt like the sun, too.

At the sports hall, Sister Rosaleen was on duty to open the doors; when they entered, the packed hall broke into spontaneous applause for the arrival of the bride, who was ten minutes late. Philo pushed her down the makeshift aisle to Cap, who was waiting nervously for her. Beside him was Brother Felix, looking like the perfect monk. With a lot of help from Cap, he'd put together a wonderful ceremony. It included an ancient Irish blessing, a Navajo Indian prayer, a Shakespeare sonnet, the Whitney Houston song 'I Will Always Love You', Patrick Kavanagh's 'Raglan Road', and, of course, 'Ave Maria', sung by a choir of nuns from the convent.

The marriage of Cap and Dina brought to an end fifty years of hostility. Who would have believed it would end that way? The flats were rubble, and no one had predicted that either. It was easy to destroy, harder to build things up. They'd pulled down Sheriff Street, but they hadn't killed its spirit. There was dust from the demolition in the sports hall, but it couldn't dampen the life within. The community was stronger than the wrecking ball.

Philo felt hope beating in her heart. She wasn't sure how much was down to Dina and Cap and how much was down to her reduction in size. She looked at Brother Felix in his habit and wondered if he'd ask her up to dance later on. Or maybe she'd ask him. The sun dancing with the monk. There was Sister Rosaleen, too; she'd brought her game of bingo, but she might prefer to dance. There were so many possibilities that Philo felt drunk with them, and she hadn't even had a drink. She was surrounded by her children and they were a family again. It was a good feeling and she wanted to hold on to it, that was all.